Friday Night Club

ALSO BY HARRY RITCHIE

Success Stories
Here We Go
The Last Pink Bits

HARRY RITCHIE

Friday Night Club

Hodder & Stoughton

First published in Great Britain in 2002 by Hodder and Stoughton
A division of Hodder Headline

2 4 6 8 10 9 7 5 3 1

A CIP catalogue record for this title is available
from the British Library

ISBN 0 340 82222 8

Typeset by Palimpsest Book Production Limited,
Polmont, Stirlingshire
Printed and bound in Great Britain by
Clays Ltd, St Ives plc

Hodder and Stoughton
A division of Hodder Headline
338 Euston Road
London NW1 3BH

Acknowledgments

With thanks to Rachel Calder, Stephan Chambers, Paul Davis, Lizzie Dipple, Phil Harmer, Nick Hornby, Sharon Maguire, Marta Roman, Toby Morison and Roland Philipps. Special thanks to Tracey MacLeod.

Part One

1

'PLEASE, PLEASE, PLEASE'

Thursday morning

'Thirty-four.'

Blimey. Come *on*.

'Thirty-five.'

Alastair squeezes his eyes shut. His arms tremble as they straighten and lock. He takes a deep breath and gradually lowers himself down again until the tip of his nose touches the rug. Then, slowly, slowly, he pushes himself back up, his arms beginning to shake now. 'Thirty-six,' gasps Alastair, and he flops to the floor. Given the chance, he'd very much like to stay collapsed on the rug but slacking is not allowed. The slow press-ups finished, Alastair clambers to his feet to do the stretching. When he has completed twelve bends to the right, twelve to the left, and twelve where his palms have to touch his toes, he straightens up and shakes himself loose.

'Righty-ho,' Alastair says to Susie, who has poked her head round the door, checking on his morning regime as per. 'A cup of tea and an orange juice.' Twisting his neck from side to side, Alastair follows Susie downstairs but takes a detour to the front door when he sees that there's post waiting for him on the mat – a Visa bill, something incomprehensible about his pension plan by the looks, and a thin brown envelope addressed to 'Eck Carr'. Alastair opens the envelope and sees, instead of a letter, two ten-pound notes. He drops the envelope into the bin that lives under the hallway's little mahogany table and stares blankly at the two tenners, holding them as if they are tickets.

Ah. They'll be from Rob. It's the twenty quid he lent Rob last Friday Night Club. When Rob was so stoned he couldn't remember his PIN number at the cashpoint on Shaftesbury Avenue. He should have known it was from Rob by the Eck.

Eck, thinks Alastair as he places the money on the table before making his way through to the kitchen. Eck. Well, it's no wonder. Alastairs, reckons Alastair, should be imposing, well-fed chaps with public-school hair, obedient, luxuriant hair, hair they can sweep back and forth in thick flicks. Alastairs aren't supposed to be wee, freckly, gingery, baldy blokes with the cheekbones of a turnip. Which goes a long way to explaining for this Alastair why he has answered to a wide variety of names throughout most of his thirty-six years – Ginger (obviously), Carrot (obviously), Jasper (as in Jasper Carrott), Algernon (briefly), Jimmy (as in Johnstone and not so briefly), Al (only more recently and only at the *Chronicle*) . . . and Eck. Short and ugly, no better than it should be. The one that's lasted since primary.

Susie's waiting for him in the kitchen. 'Bit of brekker,' announces Alastair as he fetches the carton of orange juice from the packed fridge, cheerily enough because the reminder that he's Al at the *Chronicle* has perked him up and started him thinking about the day ahead – there's a bit of the Arts section to finish off, then most of Lifestyle to knock into shape for press day tomorrow. If all goes well, he might be able to leave early tomorrow, zip over to Soho, make the most of Friday Night Club for a change.

Graham is watching Jenny as she wriggles out of her little black dress. The dress falls to the floor.

Now she is wearing only high-heeled shoes, black stockings and teensy black knickers. Jenny steps over the dress and towards a man. Who is the man? Graham can see just the man's thick, stubby fingers fondling Jenny's teensy-knickered rump. Jenny responds with a blissful moan. 'Please,' she says with a pout and a squirm. 'Please, please, please.' Jenny drops to her knees and nuzzles the man's bulbous, trousered crotch. 'Please, Alastair,' says Jenny.

Graham whimpers and twitches his head. He has been sleeping for only two hours. It will be another four hours before he is woken by the drilling of a sewage repair crew – long enough for him to have forgotten this dream, but not the one that will be abruptly halted by the first blast of the sewage repair crew's drills, the one where he'll be sprinting hopelessly along Old Street, pursued by the Chancellor of the Exchequer, the Right Honourable Gordon Brown, MP.

Sticky eyed, furry mouthed and fuzzy headed, Ian is standing in the tiny, shambolic kitchen, hoiking his long, tattered, red jumper down over the cartoon rhinoceros on the front of his boxer shorts and reflecting, as he frequently does at this time, that maybe he should invest in a dressing gown, a big, white, woolly dressing gown, the kind you probably get in expensive hotels. Ian is waiting for the kettle to boil. No, he reminds himself, he is waiting for the water inside the kettle to boil – for the kettle itself to boil would require a temperature of perhaps thousands of degrees. Ian sighs, because he has often inflicted this thought on himself since his return to the land of kettles, and he has pissed himself off each time. He stares morosely at the kettle, until the water inside begins to boil, then he pours that water on to the ground coffee pouched in a filter paper which is beigely unbleached, on account of Claire wanting to save the planet.

Claire. She'll need something to eat. How much would a big, white, woolly, five-star-hotel dressing gown cost? he wonders, while he reaches unseeingly inside the cupboard for a bowl and the storage jar of cereal. A hundred quid? Two hundred quid? Who knows. Ian opens the fridge and reaches unseeingly inside for the carton of yesterday's milk, which he pours unseeingly into the bowl full of uncooked pasta. Mind you, there'd be precious little need for a big, white, woolly, five-star-hotel dressing gown in Barcelona or Istanbul or Paris.

2

'HI HO, HI HO'

Thursday lunch-time

'Yeah, Graham, you there, yeah? No? Yeah, Chaz here. Might have a little something for you, man. Give us a bell at the mag.'

Chaz? Who the *fuck* is Chaz? Because he has yet to put the heating on and is still wearing only his dressing gown, Graham is shivering as he examines his answerphone with a bleary, truculent frown. 'Chaz, Chaz, Chaz,' he mutters to himself . . . Chaz! Youth with the goatee who hangs out at the Cantaloupe. Art director at some magazine. Yes, but which magazine? Come on, *think*. It's a commission, for fuck's sake. Money. Remember that?

Graham stumbles stiff ankled out of his study and back next door into the bedroom, where he hauls the duvet off the bed, scattering photographs of Jenny in the process, and gathers it round his shoulders. He has an idea. Quite failing to predict that the duvet's train will knock over the metal bin full of paper, crushed beer cans and pencil shavings, Graham lurches back to the study, picks up the phone and dials 1471.

After the phone's slow drum-roll of clicks, that posh robotic matron comes on. 'You were called. Today. At. Eleven. Forty. Two. Hours. We do not have the caller's number to return the call. Please hang up. Please hang . . .'

Fuck.

Ian swallows another yawn.

Meanwhile, the sales director of a prospering computer-supplies company, alumnus of the Fontainebleau Business School, proud husband and father and, by his own admission, one of the most respected members of the Nantes Rotary Club, is studying a picture in a textbook on the desk in front of him. The picture shows a woman in a shop pointing to a row of red dresses. The sales director, alumnus, husband, father and Rotarian is tapping the picture reflectively with a Mont Blanc pen. 'Zih laydee,' he says eventually.

Ian tries to sound encouraging. 'Yes, Marcel?'

There follows yet another long and puzzled silence while Marcel examines his textbook. Ian gazes out of the window, although the view is not one that can easily distract, consisting as it does of a fire escape and the back of the Krazee Kost-Kutter Klothes Kompany on the north side of Oxford Street. The location of the London Oxford School of English doesn't, in Ian's opinion, explain or excuse the school's title, but, then again, five of the English-language schools where Ian has taught have had 'Oxford' in their titles, and one of the others was the Oxbridge English Centre, which consisted of two rooms above a dry-cleaner's on the outskirts of Ankara.

'Zih laydee.'

'Yes?'

'Zih laydee bize . . . zih laydee bize zih cloazez.'

'Very good, Marcel,' says Ian. 'But remember – is buying, Marcel. She is buying clothes. And the next one?'

The Mont Blanc pen slides along the textbook and begins to tap at an image of a beshorted figure licking an ice cream. 'Zih boy,' announces this computer-sales supremo, who likes to boast to Ian about his two-million-francs-a-year-plus-bonuses salary, when he's speaking French, and who has managed to tell Ian, when he's been speaking English, that he has a big job.

'Zih boy . . . zih boy . . . eeets . . . zih boy eeets zih glass.'

Ice cream. Jesus. More to the point, twenty hours of extra-expensive one-to-one tuition and the man still doesn't understand that English has two present tenses. Is eating, Ian says to himself. Is buying and is eating, you dim twit. Should he have yet another go at pointing out the existence of the present continuous or should he have a shot at sorting out the vocabulary? Ian sneaks a check of his watch. Four minutes to one. Hell with it.

'Excellent, Marcel. Very good indeed.'

'*Vraiment?*'

'*Oui, vraiment, c'est formidable.* Remember – in English, Marcel. So, yes, very good.'

'*Bon, nous avons finis?* Um, wee . . . wee . . . feeneesh . . . wee feeneesh?'

'Yes, for today. I will see you tomorrow at eleven.'

'And mah . . . mah ack . . . mah acksentuh?'

'Excellent.'

I have made more coffee. I have eaten my bowl of serial. I have flossed my teeth. I am sitting at my desk. I turn on my Mackintosh. Nothing happens. I dial the number of the computer company. I try and explain that I must write and file my column. I think to myself that I

Alastair shakes his head and scrolls down his screen until he reaches the finale.

Having cudjilled my brians, the phone rings. It is the computer company to tell me that my modem and my Mackintosh are now okay. Hopefully, they are right. Otherwise you, dear reader, are not reading this column, because it and therefore you, dear reader, do not exist.

Alastair sighs. 'Barry?'

A bald and bespectacled head pops up over the computer facing Alastair's. 'Yip?'

'How come it's always my turn to sub Josh?'

Barry, the chief subeditor (Arts, Books and Lifestyle), pulls at an earlobe. 'That bad, eh?'

'No worse than last week. Or two weeks ago. But that's my point – I've done three Joshes in a row, Barry. It's not fair.'

'Hmm. The thing is, Al, my hands are tied, because Josh specifically asked that you sub him. He thinks you're great. In fact, Josh told Bluebottle that he doesn't want to be subbed by anyone else but you. Nobody else but you. Poo poop dee doop.'

'You're kidding me.'

'Yes, I am, actually. But look around. Everyone else is busy, hewing at the coalface of the Lifestyle section's prose.' Barry gestures expansively at the small huddle of fabulously untidy desks which comprises the Arts, Books and Lifestyle subs department, and where Derek, Yvonne and Mad Alice are all making a great performance of peering intently at their screens. 'Sorry, Al, but it looks like you're Joshing.' Barry checks his watch. 'Bloody hell. Gone one. High time we all skipped off to the canteen.' Barry stands up and flings his arms wide. 'Hi ho, hi ho,' he sings.

On cue, Alastair, Derek and Yvonne, though not Mad Alice, spring from their chairs.

'It's off to lunch we go,' Alastair sings back.

'With a bucket and spade,' trills Yvonne.

They turn and point at Derek, who chants, 'And a hand grenade.'

'Hi ho,' they sing in chorus. 'Hi ho, hi ho, hi ho.'

3

'I AM LOOKING FOR TWO FRENCH GIRLS'

Thursday evening

His last class of the day has just meandered out of the room and Ian is busy tidying up books and papers when there's a rap on his door and his employer rushes in.

'Ah, Ian, ah, might I, ah . . .'

In a display of dedicated efficiency, Ian pats a small pile of course books on his desk into a neat cuboid. Then he looks up and says, 'How can I help you, Dr Foxsmith?'

'Yes, ah, yes. I.' As he always does during any conversation with his boss, Ian notes the irony that the man runs an English-language school. Such is his employer's bumbling incompetence with his native tongue that Ian invariably finds himself becoming smoothly deferential in his presence, Jeeves to Foxsmith's Wooster.

'I was, ah, yes, in point of fact, I,' says Foxsmith.

Ian nods respectfully.

'There is, ah, a matter. Two young Frenchwomen. At present, they are but not being, as it were, stretched, so on, after, on, due to, due consideration, they will.'

'. . . Be joining my advanced class, Dr Foxsmith?'

'Quite, ah, quite. So.'

'No problem whatsoever. I'm sure they and indeed the rest of the class will benefit from their addition. Can I just say that Dieter and Stanislaw are making particularly encouraging progress.'

'Good, very. There is one other, ah, one.'

'Another pupil, Dr Foxsmith?'

'No, no, that is, ah, the same, ah, Frenchwomen. Another, ah, problem. Of an, of, that is, accommodation.'

As he offers the merest hint of a bow, Ian realises that he's also got his hands clasped in front of his groin. Maybe he's taking this Jeeves thing a bit too far. 'Perhaps I could have a talk with them, Dr Foxsmith,' Ian says, while unclasping his hands and putting them to work by picking up a stray copy of Osborne & Foster's *English Grammar*. 'Chat to them about moving up to the advanced class and see what the trouble is with their digs.'

'Excellent. Ah, kill, ah, two, ah, yes.'

'Might I ask if it's one of the school's recommended host families?'

'Indeed, ah, unfortunate as, indeed.'

'And are the students concerned still on these premises?'

Wisely forsaking words, Foxsmith grimaces then head-flicks an imaginary ball to his left.

'They're in the common room?'

A single firm nod this time. Keeping the ball down, a goalie's nightmare.

Ian sneaks a glance at the wall clock behind his employer. Six-thirty. He had planned to take advantage of Claire's early-evening visit to Briony's and pop down to Soho for a drink, with Rob if he's around. But this chat with two disgruntled French girls shouldn't delay him too much, and it'd be useful brownie points. In any case, the popping-in-on-Rob plan is probably a non-starter because Rob hasn't replied to the messages Ian left on his answerphone yesterday and today. Which is mildly annoying because he could do with a laugh and a chat with Rob – one to one, cool guy to cool guy, man of the world to man of the world, rather than the usual banter and patter of Fridays when it's Rob plus the others. Yes, these times when he's popped down to Rob's flat in Soho and it's been just the two of them shooting the breeze have turned out to be a surprising boon of London, where surprising boons have been, let's face it, thin on the ground. Ian places the stray copy of Osborne & Foster on top of his neat cuboid pile and announces, 'I'll have a word with the two students now.'

'Ah, I, I'm ah,' says Foxsmith as he backs off and away.

He has been working for twits like Foxsmith for the best part of the two decades since he gave up on university. Ian takes a deep breath to banish this thought and heads down the corridor to the common room, which would pass muster as a common room in a low-security prison. He looks around for a pair of disgruntled-looking French girls but the room's only occupant is slumped in the least rickety orange-patterned armchair by the window. Ian processes the following information and, as far as can be judged, in the following order – female, hasn't seen her before, podgy face, enormous, custard-yellow spot on her chin, mousey hair cut in a crap bob, twenty-one, twenty-two maybe, a real mistake to wear such a short skirt with those sausagey legs, no way can she be French. For the want of anything else to do, he approaches her and gives her a smile, feeling good about himself as he does so.

'Hello,' he says. 'I am looking for two French girls. Have you seen them?' That shouldn't be too difficult for her to understand, unless she's a real beginner.

'Oh. You are Mr Murray?'

The fat girl begins to lever herself out of the armchair, but gets as far as leaning forward before she notices that Ian is already perched on a neighbouring chair (the one remaining piece of furniture in the room which he trusts to hold an adult's weight) and holding out his hand ready for her to shake it. She's clearly a timid sort, for even this gesture seems to discombobulate her.

'Yes, I'm Ian Murray. Ian.'

'Oh. I am Monique.' She glances over at Ian then down at her trainers and then at the door. 'I and my friend are the two French girls who . . .'

Ian waits for a moment until he realises that she's not

searching for her friend or an elusive phrase but has finished speaking for the moment. He smiles encouragingly at the top of her bob. 'Dr Foxsmith told me that you are having trouble with your class and your accommodation. Well, the problem with the class is very easy. You and your friend are obviously far too good for the intermediate level, so you can both come to my advanced class, starting Monday at two. I'll tell Dr Foxsmith's secretary about the change. So what's the other problem?'

She risks making eye contact for a second. 'Acne.'

Ian manages not to look at her chin. 'And what's the problem with Hackney?'

She sighs. 'It is very bad. And the house is small and dirty, the landlady does not talk to us, the street is not nice and I am afraid when I walk there, and the food is . . .' She frowns and pouts. What a truly unattractive girl.

'*Dégueulasse?*' Ian suggests.

She laughs with a nervy snort and her hand flies up to cover her nose and mouth. '*Oui*,' she mutters from behind her hand. '*Dégueulasse*.'

'That is very unfortunate. But don't worry. I will sort everything out.' All he has to do is put up with her and her pal joining his advanced class, despite the fact that this one at least is almost certainly not as good as she thinks she is, and scribble a note for Moira, Foxsmith's secretary, who'll organise an immediate change of their digs. But he's hardly going to tell this fat lass that and disabuse her of the notion that he is one terrific fellow.

Which, going by the way she's beaming bashfully at her trainers, is exactly what she does think. All being well, that should be him receiving a couple of badly needed glowing assessments when she and her pal complete their course. She hauls herself up from the chair, seizes his hand and gives it an anxious shake. 'Thank you, thank you much,' she says to her trainers, before she hurries off. Ian gazes at the back of her sausage legs, a pained grin stuck on his face until she's trundled out into the corridor. Then he releases a soft groan as he opens his palm, which is indeed streaked by a slither of her snot, and wipes it down the side of the orange armchair.

I deeply reccomend the Sandy Bay Hotel to be one of the top hotels in the Carribeean. Especially it's view of the sea. A dance would be held their that very night Albert the sweet manadger told me as he giuded me round my complementery sweet with it's marbel bathroom deeply impresive bedroom and sitting room with all the things a gal could of wished for including a wellstocked miny bar where I was to spend a hole welldeserved! week of luxury. After changing into my white Versace, Albert giuded me round the Sandy Bay Hotel.

Alastair scrolls down his screen. Six-forty. Too late to start rewriting Tamara now. Two clear hours on this tomorrow morning and he'll make sure page three of the Lifestyle section carries some printable words to accompany the photographs. And that'll be one less obstacle in the way of Lifestyle going to press earlyish tomorrow evening and him making it to Friday Night Club at a reasonable time.

'Al.' Barry's bald head has popped up over the opposite computer.

'Barry?'

'Any sign of Tamara's World yet?'

'She's just filed. I've got it up on my screen.'

'I'd better message Bluebottle with the good news. So what's it like?'

'Not too bad.'

'How many deeplys?'

'I've only glanced at the intro, Barry. Just two so far.'

'What's the matter with her?'

'Don't fret. The rest is up to scratch. According to Tamara's grammar, there's going to be a dance in the sea, she's about to spend a luxurious week living in the minibar and the hotel manager is a transvestite. Barry?'

'Al?'

'Seeing that I've already been Joshed, can you not give Tamara to someone else?'

'Sure. You can swap with Derek if you like.'

Alastair leans round his computer. 'What are you doing, Derek?'

'Centre spread. Going to be the cover as well. Top-level piece.'

'You mean the fashion story?'

'Oh yes.'

'Oh God.'

'Apparently, orange is really in. Any ideas for a headline gratefully received.'

'Um . . . Something about my darling clementine?'

Derek rubs his chin. 'Not too bad. You want to take over?'

'No ta.'

'You had your chance, Al,' says Barry. 'So, as the song says . . .'

'Tamara belongs to me.'

'Exactly.' Barry's bald head ducks back down behind his computer. There follows a racket of rapid thumping as Barry hammers away at his keyboard, using his index fingers only and the violence of someone whose formative typing was done on a sit-up-and-beg Olivetti.

Moments later, MESSAGE flashes up on Alastair's screen. Alastair goes to Alt Screen then presses Receive. It's from Barry, as he thought. 'thanks, al,' the message begins, 'you're a hero. and now i have another favour to ask of you. don't worry – nothing to do with josh todd. thing is, we have a new chap joining us tomorrow and i'd like you to show him wot's wot. doubt if he'll know wot he's doing – he's just left university, so he comes to us equipped with the one vital qualification of being b/bottle's stepson.'

Alastair taps out his reply. 'well, all right, barry, but by the sounds of it he won't even know our computer system. so i'll have to spend lifestyle's press day working like a maniac and looking after the lifestyle editor's stepson at the same time. that's just about impossible.'

'correct.'

'blimey, barry. you owe me one.'

'correct once more.'

Barry's head pops up over his computer again. He gives Alastair a wink. 'Cheers, Al,' he says. 'Bloody Bluebottle, though. Right. It's a quarter to seven and it'll be a late night tomorrow.' He slaps the top of his terminal decisively. 'We should call it a day.'

'The computer?'

'What computer, Al?'

'You want us to call the computer a day?'

'Ah. Very good.' Barry slaps his forehead theatrically. 'Bloody fool that I am. Something else I meant to talk to you about but I really have to scoot. You in tonight?'

'Should be.'

'Not out carousing with your trendy Soho mates, then? I pictured you and your pal Rob in a chic nightspot. Sipping martinis. Leggy blondes nuzzling your ear.'

'I'm saving that for tomorrow, Barry.'

'Ah. The famous Friday Night Club. Of course. Well, seeing as how you're having a rare evening in, I'll call you later.'

'Anything I should worry about?'

'Yes.'

'What? What? Barry, you can't just leave it like that. You have to tell me. You have to tell me now.'

'Al, relax. I was kidding.'

'Oh. Sorry.'

'We'll talk later. And don't worry.'

'You sure?'

'Positive. Everything's fine.'

'Honestly?'

'Honestly.' Barry smiles reassuringly then stands up, claps his hands for attention and says, 'Now then, people.'

Alastair stands up. But Derek is still muttering at his screen, Yvonne is still huddled over a page proof and Mad Alice is still rummaging around in the carrier bags she's gathered around her chair.

Barry tries again. 'Come on. Look lively, staff.'

Mad Alice continues to rummage below her desk but Derek and Yvonne have taken their cue and stood to attention. Barry places his right foot on his chair. Now he extends his left hand, like a Roman senator making a speech, while his right hand appears to stroke his torso as he strums an imaginary guitar. 'It is time,' he chants with approximately rising notes.

Derek, Yvonne and Alastair sing back into fists for mikes, 'For us to stop.'

There is a brief pause before Barry chops his hand down to conduct them.

'All. Of. Our. Subbing.'

'Kicking idea, man,' enthuses Chaz. 'Godda cool vibe to it.'

'Glad you think so.' Graham checks his watch. Ten to seven. He decides to go for the bluff. 'I've just about completed the rough. I could fax it over in half an hour or so.'

'No worries, man,' says Chaz. 'Godda split. Gimme good fax tomorrow, yeah? Then I'll send over a bike for the finished artwork, yeah?'

'You sure?'

'Yeah.'

It takes several moments after the line goes dead for Graham to guess that Chaz probably considers himself too busy and basically too fucking tremendous to deliver formal farewells. Graham puts down the phone with exaggerated care, tells himself to be calm, then picks up the sheet of paper that contains all the work he has done on the illustration since

Chaz phoned back to commission it four hours ago. So far, the sheet contains one rectangle. But Graham has his idea and he knows exactly what's going to happen to that rectangle. A few hours' work and the whole thing could be done. Then post off the invoice for two hundred quid.

Two hundred quid. Ten, twelve years ago, he'd have told Chaz to roll that two hundred quid into a tight wee tube and get the Vaseline out. Well, the times they have a-fucking changed, and this two hundred much-needed quid buys another week of work on the Big One next door.

Graham scrapes back his chair and pads through to the bedroom for another check on the work-in-progress. He'll allow himself a ten-minute think about it, fucking *maximum* ten minutes, then back to the study and the rectangle. Graham stands in the bedroom doorway to appraise the installation that occupies most of the floor space not occupied by the bed but which, thanks to Nigel at CDQ, will soon be occupying a corner of the foyer of an advertising agency. Okay, so it's not exactly a top gallery, but more than useful as an advert for himself and a welcome hark back to the old days when he seemed to spend half his life dealing very profitably indeed with admen called Nigel and agencies called by initials.

Months of work he's looking at here. Months. And it could all amount to nothing but sad rubbish. Or something good. Aye, or something really good. Who's to say, though? The idea's a cracker, there's the skill of the pen-and-inks, the whole thing seems to work with the photos rainbowing over the duvet below. It's even got its own private structure (three bottles and four paint-brushes scattered on the duvet cover, the three and the four combining so that there are seven rows of photos, twelve in each row) – although why this particular structure and whether or not an installation like this needs a structure, however private, are questions which he cannot answer. How much easier it all was with those brooding oils of urban landscapes that first made his name (in a small, Edinburgh-only, just-out-of-art-college sort of a way), paintings which he knew, even as he worked on them, would be halfway decent if not actively good. But brooding oils of urban landscapes were already dodgy in 1982 and now they're just not on, unless he wants to wave the white flag, become a weekday suit and an artist every Sunday.

Those Polaroid self-portraits . . . fair enough, they complement the pen-and-inks below but . . . On the other hand . . . On the other *hand*, if he used photos of Jenny rather than himself . . . He feels the jittery excitement he used to feel quite often in the old days when he'd stroke a brush over canvas and surprise himself with the rightness of the result. Use photos of Jenny instead! Of course, of course . . .

Sod's law, by Christ. Weeks on end, his work has amounted to staring out at the window and, come five, then four, then three, then two o'clock, the day's first refreshing ale. And now the first commission and the first real progress in fucking *ages* and they come at the same time.

Well, he'd better get used to work making awkward demands if his career's to get back on track. If. Aye, if. But what about all those ifs that could have prevented him getting into this state? If his fucking agent, to name but one obvious example, hadn't paid a ridiculous sum for canalside offices and hadn't started overcharging art directors and hadn't gone bust and hadn't done a bunk owing him seven grand which he'd never, ever see . . . If he hadn't been so completely screwed by the recession which brought a sudden end to those lucrative advertising jobs . . . If he hadn't been tempted by Col's example but had stayed put in Edinburgh, where he might still be tootling along all right, doing two, three illustrations a week . . . if the newness and excitement of London hadn't given him itchy feet, if he hadn't got in with the Shoreditch crowd, if he hadn't felt disgruntled by the sight of Rob gallivanting round town, if he'd remained content with Jenny . . . Anyfuckingway, and if gallery owners weren't so fucking prejudiced against art done by artists who also happened to be illustrators rather than some Goldsmiths' bum chum of Damien fucking Hirst's . . .

Graham forces himself back to the study but he can't quite face sorting out the rectangle just yet. He picks up the phone, telling himself that he'll find out what's been arranged for this week's Friday-night bash and then he'll show that rectangle who's boss.

No luck. Rob's got his answerphones on, home and mobile. Ian's off out somewhere according to a snippy-sounding Claire. No answer even at Eck's work.

Nothing for it. Graham takes a deep breath and starts to work on the rough.

4

'HI, HONEY, I'M HOME'

Thursday night

'Susie! Susie!'

Still no sign of her. She's probably pottering around in the garden. Alastair opens the back door, pokes his head out and tries again. 'Susie!' That's a minor third, Alastair reflects – the same interval, he continues to reflect, that fans use when they chant, for example, 'Scot-land, Scot-land', or that you hear in the siren of an ambulance. And maybe even the difference created by the Doppler effect of an ambulance as it zooms past. Can that be right? Where could he look it up? Ach, it'll have to wait or the food will get cold.

'Soo-zee!' he calls again, more to enjoy the minor third than anything else. He waits for a moment before closing the door and returning to deal with their supper. He shoves on a blue mitt, reaches down to his gleaming oven and pulls out a baking tray loosely covered in a sheet of foil. 'Tah-rah,' says Alastair as he lifts off the foil to reveal three baked Marks and Sparks rainbow trout fillets. 'Poifict,' says Alastair in what he reckons is a pretty good New York accent. Waiting to accompany the trout fillets on one of the Oiseaux de Paradis plates (his favourites) are a handful of Marks and Sparks new potatoes and some Marks and Sparks spinach dressed in a good skoosh of Marks and Sparks Tuscan extra-virgin olive oil.

Alastair transfers two of the rainbow trout fillets on to his plate and sets aside the third for Susie. He tops up his glass of Marks and Sparks Chardonnay, checks that he's left the kitchen in good order, and carries plate and glass through to the front bit of the main room. 'Poifict,' says Alastair again, as he puts the glass down by his feet, perches on the edge of his red-and-white candy-striped sofa and balances the plate on his knees. That nature programme is still on. 'Beautiful,' says Alastair at a swooping aerial shot of the Highlands. He pops a new potato into his mouth, reaches for the remote and thumbs up the volume. 'In the high glens,' David Attenborough is saying, 'autumn takes hold.' Alastair swallows the potato and spears some spinach. A pine marten clambers up a tree and into its snug nest. Alastair takes a sip of his Chardonnay. 'Mmm,' he says.

The back door rattles and a moment later Susie appears.

'Hi, there, Sooz,' says Alastair. 'There's a fish waiting for you in the kitchen.'

Susie just gives Alastair one of her looks.

'I've ground some pepper on mine, but I left yours as it is. That okay?'

Susie pads over and starts rubbing her neck against Alastair's shin.

'Come on, then. Let's get your fish.' Alastair puts his plate down on the floor so that he can carry Susie through to the kitchen. 'There you go,' he says, as he picks up the spare fillet and plops it on to her saucer. ''Scuse the fingers.'

When he returns to his own meal, two pine martens are gnawing at the throat of some small woodland creature, so Alastair distracts himself by consulting the newspaper folded by his side. There's this, then *Seinfeld* and *Frasier* on Paramount, then *Newsnight*. Splendid.

The pine martens are preparing for winter and he is relishing his meal's final, special forkful – a slab of trout, a bit of squidged potato and the last of the spinach – when the phone rings. Alastair is tempted to let the machine take the call, but then he tells himself not to be so lazy, especially because it'll probably be his father asking him how to switch on the oven or what to do when the rubbish bin's full. Nearly two years his father's been coming up with queries like that so the son and heir is beginning to suspect they're really excuses to chat. Or – *or* – could be Rob. He hasn't been in touch since Friday. So Alastair still doesn't know where this week's Friday Night Club is convening. It'll probably be the Pig and Whistle, as per, but Rob had mentioned Soho House as a possibility last time. Maybe Soho House could become a regular Friday-night venue, now that Rob's got his membership. Alastair pushes himself off the sofa and over to the phone.

'Hello?'

'Hi there, Alastair. It's . . .'

'Jenny! What a nice surprise.' And it is a nice surprise, although one that still requires him to push aside the feeling that, by talking to Jenny as Jenny on her own rather than as the Jenny half of Graham and Jenny, he's somehow cheating on Graham. "How *are* you, Jenny?' Ah. That came out wrong, like a ham-fisted attempt at suave rather than friendly and interested. Oh dear. Oh well. But surely there has to be some kind of statute of limitations on talking to a pal's ex? Especially if you've known the ex since way back (ten, twelve years ago, in fact, when they were all still up in Edinburgh) and were getting to be pretty friendly with the pal's ex in her own right before she became an ex. Maybe so, but it's an awkward business nonetheless, so that he's had to dare himself to see Jenny, and only the once and only recently. And not very successfully either, with Jenny picking up on his doubtlessly desperate awkwardness, so that it seemed like they were the ones who'd split up and were trying their best to be civilised about it.

'I'm doing okay, Alastair. It's been ages, though.'

'Not since the works summer do,' Alastair says, frowning at a stab of guilt because that makes it four months he hasn't been in touch. And to think that in the good old days of Graham and Jenny he'd have had a great time with her at the summer bash. He'd been just as tongue-tied next morning, when Barry and Derek had teased him about that being his latest girlfriend and him being a sly old dog. Alastair shakes off a shiver of embarrassment at the memory.

'So I was thinking,' says Jenny in a bright and apparently unconcerned voice, 'that it's high time we caught up. And I was wondering if ... Oh, damnation. That's Megan at the door. Pie eyed, no doubt, and forgotten her keys again. I'd better go. Call you soon for a proper chat. And maybe we could meet up some time?'

'That'd be great,' says Alastair, persuading himself that it might be if he got his act together for a change and they played safe by going to see a film or something.

They exchange their see-yous and take-cares. Why does it have to be so bothersome and complicated? Alastair wonders as he puts down the phone. Which immediately starts ringing again. He's Mr Popular tonight. If that's Rob, he'll definitely ask about Soho House.

'Al.'

God. How could he have forgotten that Barry said he'd call? And what's the reason for the call? Oh God. 'Barry.'

'Well done. This an all-right time for you?'

'Fine, Barry, fine.'

'Excellent. And you're okay about nursing the new boy tomorrow?'

'Well, it's not ideal, but I'm sure it'll work out.'

'Good man.'

'Barry?'

'Al.'

'Barry, when you say "new boy", does that imply he's more than a casual or a work-experience type?'

'That's one of the reasons I wanted to call you. Too difficult to explain at the office, but basically, yes, barring some catastrophic error on his part, I think it's planned that he'll be joining us as a perm rather than a temp.'

'What's his name? And, anyway, planned by who?'

'Bluebottle's idea. Whom.'

'Is there no escape from your subbing?'

'None. A chief sub's job is his life. Which brings me to the second item on my agenda.'

Oh God. Alastair feels his palms moisten with sweat. 'Item two,' he says, for something to say.

'Just so. Now that there's probably going to be five of us, I've put it to Bluebottle that he lend his support to my campaign with the management that our rapidly expanding department acquire the new post of deputy chief sub. I'm also going to ask Bluebottle to support my proposal that said deputy chief sub be you.'

'Three subjunctives in a row.'

'I was hoping for a more conventional reply. Something along the lines of, Thanks very much, Barry, you're a great boss and a prince among men.'

'Sorry, Barry. Only this is a big surprise. And thank you. Very much. You are a prince among men.'

'Marvellous. I'll give Bluebottle the good news tomorrow. Al, I have to go. Kate's out for the evening so I've got Rachel and Dan all to myself.'

'Lucky you.'

'Yeah, lucky me. Thomas the sodding Tank Engine . . . I don't need the books any more, I just recite them.'

Alastair coughs. 'Well,' he says, 'I'd better leave you to it.'

'Annie and Clarabel were feeling exhausted. "We're dreadfully tired, we're dreadfully tired," said Annie and Clarabel.'

'The trials of fatherhood, eh?' Alastair pauses then clears his throat again. 'So – I'll see you tomorrow, Barry. And thanks again. Really. Cheers.'

He is immediately lost in a daydream about telling Rob the good news tomorrow, cracking open a bottle of bubbly maybe, in Soho House even, so that it's only after putting down the phone that he realises he didn't think to ask Barry if the promotion means a pay rise. And he still doesn't know the new chap's name. Ah well, all in good time. Now, though, he's on for a little celebration and to heck with the washing up. Alastair picks up his empty plate and strides into the kitchen. He puts the plate in the basin of warm water to soak with the saucepans and the baking tray, rubs his hands and takes out the wooden box from its hiding place behind the coffee jar.

Several painstaking minutes later, Alastair replaces the packet of King Size Rizlas, the pouch of Honeyrose Special herbal tobacco and the bulging bag of home-grown back in the box and appraises this first joint of the night.

There are times, he thinks, when things are all right. One of the secrets is in getting on with it and doing good work. Graham drains the can of McEwan's and inspects the nearly finished artwork on his desk. What was a rectangle has become a dancing photocopier, which has come along nicely. Perhaps a little reminiscent of Saul Steinberg, he might grant you that, but only a little, and would Steinberg have come up with that magenta background? He appraises the artwork once more. Yes. This definitely will be the best thing he's done for weeks. Young Chaz at *Business Matters* will love it. One evening's inspired toil and he's already earned a good part of that two hundred quid.

Graham lobs the can towards the metal bin. The can hits the bin's lip and clatters to the floor. Graham leans back in his chair and clasps his hands behind his head. He'll have one more can. That'll make it four for the night. Four and no more. Then bed by twelve, a gentle, relaxing flick through an art book and definitely no staring at photos of Jenny. Then a good night's sleep and up at a normal time, fax the rough, finish the artwork, get it biked over to Chaz in Camden, and he'll be all set for a proper Friday night out with the boys tomorrow. Easy. Easy fucking peasy.

Here's Ian, walking – a little unsteadily, if truth be told – down the ammoniac tunnel which leads out of Vauxhall station and up to the six-lane racetrack that is South Lambeth Road. Usually, Ian has a free spirit's disdain for such things as pedestrian crossings, but at this junction the alternative to waiting for the permission of the green man is a sprint that might be a bit risky – in the sense, he notes to himself, as he always notes to himself at this junction, that eating an unpinned grenade might be a bit risky. So he has to linger until the first three lanes of traffic come to a halt and he can move on to the traffic island, where he has to linger again while a second set of cars charges straight at him before deciding at the last minute that it's not worth the court case and veering sharply to the left and round the corner.

Now that he's reached the precarious safety of the island, Ian turns his back on the oncoming traffic and watches a trashed train clatter along over the arches and on to the bridge which has been decorated with a twee silhouette of a choo-choo, presumably a prettifying measure and every bit as effective as slapping a smiley sticker on the Oval's gasometer.

There are times when London's resolute ugliness depresses the crap out of him, not least because the six months he's lived here have offered him far too many opportunities to appreciate that, quite unlike anywhere else he's laid his hat, the only way you can avoid horribleness in this city is by spending hilarious sums of money, and if you don't have the cash, then you end up doing things like standing in a traffic island in the middle of an inner-city M6 on your way home to a run-down, one-bedroom sublet with sheets for curtains.

Of course, there is the obvious factor as well as the extraordinary fact that his next birthday will be his thirty-seventh, but it is London which he blames most for making him question, for the first time really, the wisdom of dodging around Europe teaching English. Instead of sticking at some godawful career that would have given him a salary and a mortgage and stuff. Because it is London which mocks his two hundred and forty quid a week with its contemptuous extortion, its sneering prices and smirking bills, its airily dismissive manner of shoving a series of noughts on to the cost of anything that might just offer the faintest glimpse of a decent quality of life. 'An edible meal out with okay wine? That'll be a squillion pounds. Sir.' Not only has he begun to see the point of what Rob has done – slaving away in the unthinkably terrible world of investment banking but for an inevitably huge pay packet – he's even found himself envying Rob's lot. Until he arrived in London, he would still have scoffed at the very notion that he might feel jealous of Rob's club-class trips to luxury hotels, Rob's MG, Rob's tailor-made suits, Rob's credit cards, and Rob's Soho pad. But now that he has an inkling of just how much any kind of life here costs in this Weimar-priced city, and just how little of a life anyone can buy for two hundred and forty quid a week, he has sometimes felt not only a grudging admiration for Rob and Rob's ability to assume that money is just there to be used and enjoyed, but also the curious suspicion that not choosing a normal career could have been one very big and ghastly mistake.

No. Hell with it. He's in no mood to give in to self-doubt. Ian presses the back of his hand against his nose, has a rattling good sniff and senses the petrolly aftertaste of cocaine. Yeah, think of all those people who are too afraid to do anything but daydream about what he's done for real. He has lived and worked in Paris, Athens, Berlin, Paris again, Madrid, Ankara, Istanbul, Barcelona, then Paris for a third time – an impressive CV, for sure. Yeah, pretty impressive, and there's no way he should start beating himself up.

The second set of traffic jolts to a halt and Ian finally makes it to the other side of the road. He walks alongside the kind of new office building that has puzzled him since he returned to Britain. When did they all spring up, those supermarkets and schools and health centres and offices, with their brightly coloured brickwork and their Legolandy bits and bobs? Now, if he'd only played it safe, he could be spending every weekday, nine to five, in an office just like this, with nothing to look forward to except holidays and the prospect of a farewell carriage clock in forty years' time. Make that twenty-nine years.

Maybe he really would have ended up in an office like this, if he hadn't decided, on the spur of the moment when he was twenty-one and driving a van for a wine merchant and forty-eight quid a week, to take up that TEFL course in Edinburgh. No, that's crap, because the start of it was the year before, when he'd gone abroad for the first time, inter-railing with Graham for a couple of months before they returned to a wet and windy Edinburgh August, Graham to begin his last year at art college and Ian to chuck in his history degree and muck about on the dole. Yeah, it was the interrailing that did it. Made him realise that there were countries in this world where the sky didn't usually look like old washing-up liquid, where there were cafés and boulevards, and where raven-haired temptresses were two a centime.

Of course, Ian concedes in what strikes him as a mature, considered, generous-spirited sort of a way, there have been occasions in the fifteen years he's spent wandering from foreign city to foreign city when the going's got tough and he's felt lost and adrift. But the bad spell in Berlin belongs to the past, as does Madrid and the strange, brief glitch that was his marriage to Cristina.

Ian wipes a liquefying nostril. Well, he muses, nobody can get to this age unscathed and his scathings have been few and light. And if Cristina was a mistake, then it's one he's learned from, isn't it? Lesson number one – don't settle for somebody who isn't attractive enough to stop him hankering after other women. Lesson two – find someone who doesn't devote all her energy to telling him off. Lesson three – if a woman wakes him up, the morning after the third date, by playfully running a fingernail round his nipple and asking if she's special, that third date will be the last. Schoolboy errors, schoolboy errors, schoolboy errors. But he's eliminated them from his game. Hence Claire. Who has made him immune to hankering. Who is not only sweet natured but twenty-four years old, and therefore impressed even by his first-hand memories of punk. And who'd never in a million years give him any nipple-circling nonsense. Although she has been getting a bit tricky recently, seeming very young at times . . . and doing a pretty good job of making him feel that he's not pulling his weight. Which is to ignore some fairly important shit. Look, for example, at the way he handled her news last month. And before that as well – she wanted to quit Paris and what happened? They left Paris. She wanted to return to her home-town, and where are they living? Correct. When she told him her news, did he go mental? No, he did not go mental. He handled it with cool maturity . . .

Claire. Even in Paris, she turned heads. Sometimes they'd be walking along a street and he'd hang back a step or two, to notice any signs of hunger or pained yearning on the faces of men who'd checked out this passing gamine with her astonished eyes, her cropped blonde hair, her long legs, her tight bum and startling breasts. Unlike every other beautiful person Ian has ever known, Claire seems quite unaware of her own beauty and the effects it has (just as well, in his opinion, otherwise she'd probably be every bit as dull and self-centred as most beautiful people, who've never had to work at being liked), but Ian's radar has kept up a vigilant scanning for beeps of male lust. And of envy, because there've been a fair few times he's caught men checking him out as well, doubtless wondering what kind of a bloke could get a girl like this, and discovering that the answer is a tall, slim, handsome man of the world with a male model's bone structure and a full head of thick, ink-black curls. Times he'd be lying in bed, his hands stroking her honeyed thighs, Claire arching forward to dip a remarkable breast into his gaping mouth, and he'd think of those men and how they'd never know such erotic ecstasy, doomed as they'd be to the joyless humping of some roly-poly missus. While he knows exactly what it's like to watch Claire lowering her impeccable, creamy bottom on to his face or feel her running her hard little tongue round and round his ear and whispering, 'You can do anything. Anything you want.' If those men only knew . . . Christ, they'd lynch him.

Yeah, things are going to be just fine. Look at the way the job's improved since the bad start (though why that Polish student had to register a complaint still beats him). Helped in no small measure by this renewed hobby with the coke – an excellent teaching aid. And it keeps him on his toes, ready and waiting. For what he couldn't say exactly, but *something*, as if, round the next corner or after the next drink, he'll find himself invited to a party in a chic apartment where there'll be champagne in a bucket and a couple of girls with bodies so firm he could chop out top-ups on their tummies . . . Yeah, take coke and say goodbye to banality, regain that buzz of excitement he used to get as a teenager, for no reason, when he'd be just walking down the road or staring into space, and as an adult when he'd just moved to a new city or started a new affair. *Also*, there's something so beguiling, so secretly naughty, something so undefinably glamorous about the whole procedure, from unfolding the wrap, trying to guess which bit of which glossy magazine the wrap has been made from, then tipping out a tiny heap of powder, chopping into the little lumpy bits, pushing and patting it all into a couple of fuzzily thick lines . . . And no side effects to speak of, although the first toot of the day can have him scooting off, rectum twitching, to the shunkie, and there are times, like now, when his nose suddenly runs like a two-year-old's, a few others when his chest aches like his tubes are sore, and some mornings he could do with a sculptor's hammer to clear an airway through his nostrils. But he's got it under control, stuck to his rules, resisted the temptation to start on the ciggies again (no small achievement) and he can stop it any time he wants, just as he did in Barcelona when he was mucking about with that bunch of well-heeled drop-outs who were tonked off their tits half or indeed most of the time, and marvelling at the way they could each neck a bottle of brandy and stay alert with a couple of grams.

Another good thing – strange at times though it feels to be mucking about again with Rob and Graham, and Eck (and there are times when Ian has to gag the little voice in his head that tells him this is a sad regression), the regular Friday-night shindigs mean that he's found a ready-made social life here – and one that features guys he's known for ages rather than people he's just met and whose friendship won't, despite everyone's protestations, survive his next departure. Weird, though, especially now that he looks like a retired drummer, all paunch and flabby face, to be able to remember Graham at primary, spruce, Brylcreemed, shy and his bestest friend. Or first year at the high school, Graham shuffling up one breaktime and not so much introducing as explaining the gangly but curiously confident boy by his side: 'This is Rob. He's at the same dinner table as me. He's kissed Kirsty Barclay.' Despite his jealousy (Kirsty Barclay being an object of hopeless desire for every male in the year – except, of course, for Derek Paterson, who, last Ian heard, had opened his own salon in Sydney), he'd taken an instant liking to Rob. But then that's what people have always done to Rob, with his jauntiness and his affability, his air of being permanently on for a good time. Like in the mushroom gag – a fun guy to be with. Which would explain, come to think of it, why Rob was accepted by the school's various adolescent tribes – the sporty lot, the arty mavericks who hung around the music department, the ones who'd soon become mild punks, the posher decadents of the tennis club, even the hard men who sucked on their fags and joints behind the school library – and why Rob could then recruit people from different groups for what was to become the first Friday Night Club. Daft name, Ian's always thought – even at the time it struck him as the sort of thing a swinging vicar might call his Bible studies group – but an excellent institution, as he and Graham realised after Rob plucked them from the fringes of the hard smokers' crowd and invited them to a party, where the dozen or so core members of the FNC turned out to include Kirsty Barclay's successor, Fiona Macgregor, the babe of the fifth year. Never mind that it was Steve who got to Fiona first, because there were other girls and those were good times – alfresco sessions with cider and Pomagne, the trip to Aviemore, parties at Steve's and at Keith's when he'd be dressed up in his best army surplus to dance to Bowie and swig lager from cans with bikinied dolly birds, the eager if inept romps with Joanna. Yeah – happy days. When the world was brand new and waiting to be played with. And he was, ludicrously, half the age he is now.

And now here the four of them are, twenty years later, brought together by London and marriageless freedom, unlike the rest who all disappeared long ago into their own lives, their spouses and their kiddywinkles and their pension plans. In contrast to him and Graham and Rob, even Eck, because they can still muck about, just like in the old days, except this time round without the likes of Fiona and Steve and Bill and Keith and Joanna, and in Covent Garden and Soho instead of Kirkcaldy High Street or the Beveridge Park.

Ian boots aside a still-full carton of takeaway curry. Okay, so London's a toilet, but he won't stay here long – he enjoys a flash of his current fantasy where he and Claire are swinging a sunhatted toddler between them as they stroll down a hot and deserted stretch of Greek beach – and there are compensations, like British telly . . . and easier access to the Rovers' results . . .

These final concessions are a real tribute to an unexpectedly fine evening on the charlie. After the chat with the fat French girl, Ian had sauntered down to Soho and Rob's flat in Bateman Street, even though Rob hated people dropping in on him unannounced. In any case, Rob had been out, or quite possibly in and too busy seducing to answer. The prospect of an early and defeated return to Vauxhall had threatened to get Ian down, until he reminded himself that he was but twenty yards from the Pig and Whistle, and that the Pig and Whistle boasted a clean, refurbished shunkie. A pint of lager and a line had bucked him up no end. So he'd been in great form when he'd seen Paolo from the advanced class mooching about outside Ronnie Scott's. Turned out that Paolo had been dissed by some other student he was after. Also turned out that Paolo was generous with his cash, liked a drink, and was quite a boy for the coke as well – amazing, really, because, in Ian's experience, young Italian blokes tried their very best to live up to their reputation as a bunch of spoilt, preening mummy's boys who would never touch cocaine, on the grounds that (a) it was illegal and (b), and far more pertinently, it might fuck with their skin-care regimes. Not so young Paolo. Into his football, too.

Between them they'd had, by his uncertain reckoning, one packet of salted peanuts, ten pints, four brandies and six huge lines (him supplying the charlie, Paolo most of the cash), then next thing it was quarter past nine and Paolo had to get back to his landlady in Wood Green. No problem – another trip down to the Pig and Whistle's bogs had set them both up for the journey home. In fact, he had seriously considered walking back, the scenic route over the Mall, down Horse Guards Road and through Westminster, but by Piccadilly Circus he'd thought fuck it, and got the Tube.

So here he is, back in Vauxhall betimes, feeling no pain and wondering if he might do a uey and slip into the Royal Oak for a swift one before facing up to Claire.

Nup. Needs must, there's a bottle of Sainsbury's brandy in the kitchen, but it won't come to that because, by luck rather than cunning, he has achieved that so-often-elusive goal of balancing drink and drugs. All he has to do is not screw up and be cool with herself. No problem there.

As Ian turns left into Vauxhall Grove, it occurs to him that when he and Claire first lived together, he used to bound up the steps of the Métro and quick-march down the rue de la Réunion, resenting every second it took him to reach their sweet little flat. That was only two years ago . . . The road twists round into the hippie enclave of Bonnington Square, where vast plants and dustbins jostle for space on the pavement. A slight stumble makes him think it might be an idea to step behind the enormous fern on the left and take a last, invigorating pinch of coke. Just a little dab . . . He takes out his wrap, licks his finger, places the finger on the powder, pushes the finger up his nose and sniffs . . . Excellent.

He's at the corner of the street. Now he's at the front door. Shit, the wrong key. No. The right key after all. Now he's climbing the dishevelled flight of stairs, and now he's outside the door of the flat. He pauses for a moment, puts a smile on his dial and opens the door.

'Hi, honey, I'm home.' That came out nice and normal. He's fine.

'Through here,' comes her voice from the main room, but when he walks in, it's to find the main room empty.

'Behind you.'

He swivels round too quickly and has to throw out a hand against the armchair to steady himself as he looks down on Claire, who is lying behind the sofa and on the rug Omar gave him in Istanbul. 'There you are,' he says.

'Here I am.'

'You all right?'

'A bit yucky.' Claire winces as she pulls her head up and struggles to support her back with her hands.

'Can I get you anything?'

'No, it'll pass.' Claire closes her eyes and seems to swallow bile. 'How was work?' she asks after a while. 'Hard day at the office?'

When has he ever had a hard day at the office? He has

devoted his entire adult life to avoiding anything like a hard day at the office. 'It was a bit,' he says. 'A hard evening as well. I had to calm down a fat French girl about her digs and then Foxsmith asked me to take Paolo and a few others from the advanced class out for a tour of historic Soho.' Almost faultless delivery.

Claire raises her eyebrows. 'In other words, a tour of historic Soho's historic pubs.'

It seems to be just a tease so he gives an appreciative snort of laughter and blows out a white speck of coke on to the back of the armchair. 'Yeah,' he says quickly in case she notices, 'but at least I got a couple of free pints out of it.'

Claire smiles. 'And how many paid-for pints?'

He returns the smile, using this brief pause to consider the best number to select. 'None. How was your day?'

'Oh. All right. Well, not really. And I didn't make it to Briony's.'

'Ah.' Ian's mouth twitches because he's remembered one of Paolo's punch lines. 'This guy tonight, Paolo, I don't know if I've told you about him, he had this cracking Carabinieri joke, you know how the Italians have the police like the French have the Belgians or we have the Irish, anyway, there's this young policeman from Naples, right, and . . .'

'Ian.'

'What?'

'Aren't you going to ask me why I didn't go to Briony's?'

'Oh. Okay. Why didn't you go to Briony's?'

'Because I've been feeling terrible all day and I . . .'

'Sick?'

'Sick, dog tired, dizzy. And in a bit of a state, really.'

She certainly looks all four. Aren't women supposed to bloom and blossom with pregnancy? Look great, feel fulfilled, carry their neat, round bumps with pride and panache? Not Claire, though. Just three months gone and the fit, lithe, stunning girl he once ran home to and who turned Parisian heads is looking more and more like a victim. If she washed her hair, which, as usual these days, is coated with an oily, jaundicey sheen, wouldn't that help? Surely to Christ it would at least cheer her up.

'I left a message for you at the school this afternoon.'

Ian shakes his head, although he does now recall Moira popping in during the advanced class and handing him a note which he put on his desk and immediately forgot about because Paolo and Dieter were giggling at some mistake of Stanislaw's.

'So I tried Briony instead and she came round.'

I must to study more. That's what Stanislaw had said to set Paolo and Dieter off. 'And how's Briony?' Wrong tone. He tried for a neutral sound but has struck a note of polite sarcasm. Small wonder, though, given that the question had to feature that name.

'Oh, Briony's fine. After all, she isn't the one who's pregnant.'

'Come on, Claire. It's not an illness.'

'Well, it felt like one today.' She grunts as she makes, he thinks, an ostentatiously brave effort to sit up straight. 'It's not that, though, Ian. It's . . . Look, Ian, I'd really like to have a talk. I'm getting a bit scared by this.'

'Ah, don't worry, Claire. Who wouldn't be? I mean, it'll be like trying to shit a basketball, but if it frightens you too much maybe you can get a thingummy.' She seems to swallow bile again as he searches for the word. 'Yeah, a Caesarian.'

'That's not why I'm scared.'

'Okay, well, this sickness thing is just a phase. Another couple of . . .'

'Ian. Please just listen to me, will you? I know you're off your face and everything but please, can you not just let me say something?'

'Come on, a couple of beers.'

'Ian, I'm not your mum. I'm not going to give you a row, but I do want us to have a talk.'

'Fair enough. Let's talk, then. But first things first. I am not off my face, okay?'

'If you say so.' She looks steadily at the back of the sofa. 'Okay, well, this has to do with one of the things I want to say.' She frowns at him. 'I don't think you can keep on doing this.'

'What? What can I keep on not doing? Not keep doing.'

'Acting as if nothing's happening. I'm pregnant, for God's sake, and you're still going out all the time, getting hammered, getting wired . . .'

'I told you, I'm not.'

'Spending money we don't have.'

'Aw, okay, I see, so it's all my fault for not having a fucking trust fund.'

'No, Ian. I mean, I'm not saying we don't need the money because we do. And the translating might not bring in much, but I won't be able to do even that in six months' time. But what I'm really . . .'

'This is Briony, isn't it?'

'I haven't said anything to Briony. This has nothing to do with Briony. This is about me and you.'

'Or about me not being a fucking millionaire.'

'Can't you just listen to me, Ian?'

'Listen to me. Now listen to me.'

'What?'

'*The Ipcress File*. It's what the guy says when he's trying to washbrain Michael Caine.'

Claire examines the sofa. 'This is hopeless,' she decides. 'I'm going to take a bath.' She gets to her feet and heads for the door.

'Make it a red real letter day for the diary and get the shampoo out,' says Ian to her back. He holds his breath until she's left the room and shut the bathroom door behind her.

Then he sighs, with as much frustration as a sigh can manage. What's he done to deserve all this crap? He falls on to the sofa and glares at the pile of newspapers and the two poly bags of empty bottles beside the telly . . . Ah. He forgot to take them round to the recycling. Is *that* what's bugging her? Ian forces his gaze away from the recycling pile and round the rest of the room – his Jacques Tati poster listing on the wall and revealing a blob of Blu-tac which should be attached to the poster's top-right corner, the cushions he picked up in Clignancourt scattered on the floor, the unironed washing heaped on the card table. Christ, couldn't she have tidied up a bit? . . .

Right. She's deliberately left everything in a tip to make a point. Well, two can play at that game, and he could have the room looking spick and span by the time she gets out of her bath.

Hell with it. He has a much better idea. He tiptoes up to the bathroom door and listens for the telltale sound of Claire immersed in what is bound to be one of her longer soaks. She's stopped running the hot water. He hears a soft splash, then a little grunt. He tiptoes back down the hall and into the kitchen, where he treats himself to a slash in the sink before settling down at the Formica picnic table with a tall glass of tap water, a half-full bottle of brandy and, resting on the back of a small, rectangular mirror, a nice little line of cocaine.

5

'IT! IT! IT!'

Friday morning

Dearie me. Talk about feeling the burn. The thirty-six slow sit-ups were bad enough but by slow press-up number twenty-five he'd felt like going back to bed. However. That's the regime completed for the day.

Alastair carries his cup of Earl Grey out into the garden. He squints up at the cloudless sky. Either it's unnaturally bright or he might have a bit of a headache. He bends down, takes a pinch from the lavender bush and sniffs it. Together with the scent he registers a dull twinge where his hairline used to be. He does have a bit of a headache. 'Damn,' Alastair tells the lavender bush. 'And it's a Friday.' He sips his tea and thinks of the day ahead, which promises to be a typical Friday nightmare. There's Josh and Tamara to finish off, the new boy to nurse, his promotion to discuss, and then the whole fraught fandangle of getting Lifestyle off to press. Be lucky if he gets out of Canary Wharf by ten.

Alastair frees a crisp packet from the bed of heather, twists it into a long, thin, scrunched-up strip, folds one end over the other and pulls until it looks like a psychedelic bow tie. Then he drops it on to his instep and sends it flying with an ambitious volley. At the end of its high parabola, ten feet away, it plummets straight into the empty plant-pot by the kitchen door. 'Goal,' says Alastair, just as Susie appears, on the off-chance that the crisp packet might be tormentable. 'I should still make Friday Night Club, even if it's later on,' Alastair tells Susie as if passing on gossip. 'At Rob's flat maybe. Or Soho House. He's a member now. And I've never been.' Alastair takes another sip of tea and wanders back inside, having first picked up the squidged crisp packet from inside the plant-pot and dropped it in the bin. 'Yes,' he says thoughtfully to the bin, 'Soho House.'

Graham's right leg twitches under the duvet, which is spattered with photographs of Jenny topless in France. He is playing for the school team but he is twenty years older than everyone else on the pitch. And he's forgotten his school strip, so there he is, standing in the centre circle in jersey and jeans, surrounded by seventeen-year-old team-mates who are trying to ignore him because they are all the right age and wearing the proper kit. But then he sees Rob, wearing the school strip, looking happy and confident and running into the box. Rob is yelling for a pass. Who has the ball? Graham looks around, perplexed, then realises that the ball is at his feet. Two of the schoolboys approach him, shaking their heads in disgust. 'We didn't want to pick you,' says one. 'You're thirty-six.' 'Where's your sports kit?' asks the other. 'Pass it,' Rob shouts. 'Over here.' But Graham has forgotten how to kick. He swings a stiff right leg and manages to toe-poke the ball with his Timberland boot. The ball starts off travelling towards Rob but it soon veers away in a wild slice to the touchline, where Jenny is looking on, hunched into her long raincoat. She traps the ball and flicks it disdainfully to Rob. Rob laughs and the school bell rings to mark the end of the games period. It keeps on ringing. And ringing. And ringing.

Graham awakes. It's the dodgy alarm at number twenty-three. He groans into the pillow and keeps his eyes clamped shut as the alarm clatters on and on. 'Please,' he mumbles into the pillow. 'Please, please, please.'

'How many lines did you have after I went to bed?'

'Jesus, Claire. What time is it?'

'Ten to eight. So. Tell me. How many lines?'

'None. Honest . . . Is there coffee?'

'So you just decided to stay up till half past three pottering about in the kitchen. Sure. And no there isn't any bloody coffee because there was hardly any left because you said you'd do some shopping yesterday and didn't do any and because I've drunk what little we had because I woke up so early because I was feeling sick and because you were bloody snoring like a . . .'

'Walrus? Elephant seal?'

'Like a bastard.'

'Ah, Christ, Claire, give me a break, will you?'

'No, Ian, you give me a break. As if it's not bad enough trying to get to sleep when I'm worried sick and I'm turning into a . . .'

'Walrus? Elephant seal? Come on, Claire, you're not putting on any weight. And I can't help it if I snore.'

'. . . a bloody Michelin Man, I have to lie there listening to you. And you can help it, because you only snore like that when you've been doing a lot of coke.'

'So because maybe I snored a bit, this is you getting your revenge by waking me at the crack of dawn to give me this fucking shit. And no coffee.'

'Fuck the coffee. Fuck you.'

'Ah, fuck off.'

'No, you fuck off.'

'Fucksake, Claire, this is what you're like when you miss out on half an hour's sleep, what kind of state are you going to be in once you've had it?'

'It! It! It!'

'Okay, what the fuck are you going to be like once you've had him stroke her? Christ. And how come there's no fucking coffee?'

'Shut up. Oh no, not again.'

Claire throws off the duvet, puts a hand over her mouth, and lurches off towards the bathroom.

6

'YOU ALL RIGHT?'

Friday lunch-time

Look on the bright side, Graham tries to persuade himself. He's hung over, he's had four hours' sleep, thanks to number twenty fucking three's alarm, and he feels like he's recovering from minor surgery, but check out all the work he's done. Faxed through the rough, finished the artwork (including lots of fiddly balloons and streamers to decorate the dancing photocopier), phoned Chaz to arrange a bike, washed his brushes, cleaned up most of the workbench, and it's still only twenty to one.

Graham leans back in his chair and yawns. Why oh why did he move on to the whisky last night? He was fine after those four cans. Aye, but that was the problem. It's impossible to imagine now but it had also been impossible to imagine feeling sleepy come midnight, so he'd decided to have a little nightcap and before he knew it the nightcap had turned into tumbler after tumbler of Johnnie Walker Black Label. And, to be perfectly honest about it, those tumblers had all been pretty fucking full. Fuck. Ah well. There's always the chance, the usual ambient racket of the usual road-repair team permitting, of a nap after the bike arrives. Aye, but then he'd be back in the old routine of being wide awake and wandering round the flat at four in the morning, thinking about Jenny, nursing yet another hefty tumbler, trying to fend off yet more images of Jenny naked and lying on a stranger's bed, or Jenny naked and kneeling on a stranger's carpet, or Jenny naked and . . .

Stop that. Only one thing for it and that's to keep going. And maybe make a couple of calls to tout for more work. Nobody's saying it's going to be easy, though, because somehow he seems to be feeling worse than he did when he woke up, and he felt fairly fucking mince then.

Okay. First things first. Get rid of the rest of this litter on the workbench. He sifts through a pile of magazines, fly-sheets, delivery menus, sheaves of doodles and empty envelopes. Nothing there to keep unless he wants to try ordering one of Pizza Planet's Euro 96 specials – the Gazza, maybe (large, thick-crust, double pepperoni) – a year late. His attention is drawn to another component of the litter – three sheets of paper stapled together. What in the name? . . . It's one of those round-robin happy-family letters. Graham frowns as he recalls that he received several such letters (addressed to him and Jenny, which proved that the senders were either very distant acquaintances or sadists) at Christmas, and solemnly set each alight in the kitchen sink. This one must have fled the flames.

1996 was of course the Year of the Conservatory!!?! More of that saga later!! When he's not been chasing the builders, Keith has enjoyed his new responsibilities as head of the department at Fife College but the workload means that the bad news is that his handicap has rocketed to six. Keith has cut down some clubs for Cameron and Jasper and Cameron already boasts a fluent swing and some pinpoint accuracy with his long irons although we also have high hopes of Cameron as the new Gavin Hastings! He captained his side to triumph in the mini-sevens this year and celebrated by scoring two tries in the final!!! We're still a wee bit concerned about Jasper but at least his eczema has got much better with the steroid cream and who knows it might help him build up those muscles before he goes to school next year!!!! But we're all very proud as well of Cameron's success at the 16th Fife – where I can forget all about the dratted builders and the new conservatory's underfloor heating as Akela and where Cameron's badge count has

'Cunts,' says Graham. 'Fucking cunts.'

When he reaches the bottom of the first page and Cameron's scout badges, Graham scrunches the three sheets of paper into a tight ball and shoves them into the overflowing bin. Just how much of a fucking *arsehole* do you have to be to write such a document? And haven't these people any notion of tempting fate? Or that some of their readers could be unemployed or grieving over a stillborn baby . . . or struggling away in a one-person family after their partner has gone? Anyway, who the fuck *are* these cunts? Who is Keith? Who is I? Fife College? . . . The Tech, in other words. This Keith is probably one of those who has taught plumbing to morons for a decade and now calls himself a lecturer in sanitation studies at the University of South Kirkcaldy. Obvious that they're a right pushy pair, and it's safe to say that Jasper is suffering under the stress, and with a name like that the wee guy doesn't have his troubles to seek. Mind you, even in Kirkcaldy, Jasper's future colleagues in Primary One will probably be called things like Swithin or Starchild.

What's so wrong with normal names? Elizabeth. If he and Jenny'd had a kid, Elizabeth would have been a great name for a daughter. Tea's ready, Lizzie! Fancy a trip with Daddy to Legoland, Beth? John for a boy. Jack, even.

Maybe he should do his own round-robin letter this Christmas. Graham and Jenny are still split up!! And Graham's 'friend' Col did mention recently that Jenny might be seeing someone else these days!!?! Graham is finally getting it together again workwise, which is just as well because he still owes the taxman £12,000. But he's also finding time for his favourite hobby, so business is booming in Finchley's Thresher's!!!

Enough. Graham forces himself up and out of the chair but immediately has to grip the workbench for support . . . He really does feel mince. Graham shuts his eyes and gulps in air as though he's preparing to swim a length underwater. After a moment, the wave of nastiness recedes. Having risked opening his eyes to the extent that he can peer at the dancing photocopier, Graham pushes himself away from the bench and, slowly and unsurely, makes his way out of the study and next door to the kitchen.

The kitchen is Graham's favourite room – or least unfavourite room – in the whole benighted flat, since it is the room least haunted by the ghost of Jenny, who was never a one for the cooking. The sitting room at the front, that's a terrible place, full of memories of the times they'd eat the dinner he'd made, plates on their laps and *Brookside* on the telly, and of course of that one time in particular when she stumbled in, squiffy after a work do, kneeled in front of him as he sat on the sofa, peeled down his zip, hoiked out his flummoxed cock and, demonstrating unexpected skill, applied her mouth to it until he cried out and came as he'd never come before, with helpless, juddering anguish. No, the sitting room is a dangerous place. Not as bad as the bedroom, obviously, although that has improved a bit since he painted the walls a very unJennyesque, Colman's-mustard yellow, sold their bed, made do with a mattress on the floor, bought a new duvet cover and recycled their old one in the installation. But more dangerous than the bathroom, even with the significant gaps on the shelves where she used to keep her Body Shop stuff, and where the vanilla whiff of her skin cream seems to linger still. In fact, at the minimal cost of not watching television, Graham has rather given up on the sitting room, which now functions like the front room of a pre-war working-class family, as a place to receive guests, and that's something Graham does rarely, or never, these days, even if he counted Rob, Ian and Eck as guests, which he wouldn't.

So here he is, back in the kitchen, slumped at the long wooden table, gazing out through the French windows at the tiny patch of overgrown garden, and trying to remember just what he thought he was doing at exactly this spot last night, slurping at tumbler after tumbler of Johnnie Walker Black

Label. Hadn't he come up with some scheme? Ah yes. His whisky-inspired brainwave – to stop his occasional night-time trips to Jenny's street in Notting Hill (when he's in the area and like as not drunk and can't resist), quit scanning her windows, put an end to wandering and wondering and driving himself crazy with the thought that she might be in there with another man . . . to stop all that and do it properly, rent a room opposite and use it as a surveillance HQ, so that he can find out once and for all if the rumour Col passed on really could be true and she really is being fucked by some bastard.

The thought of Jenny being fucked, of Jenny opening her legs and inviting, actually inviting, another man's veinous, purple-helmeted erection to pierce her most precious, most secret . . . Last night, by the time of the third or fourth tumbler, he'd convinced himself that if he could only see it happening, perhaps through binoculars trained on her conveniently but improbably uncurtained bedroom window, he'd be able, somehow, to cope with the terrible reality instead of not coping with the many and various appalling images his brain creates to cause its owner such sharp pain.

Now, for example. God alone knows where this scenario originally came from and why it should be quite so vivid and convincing, but here he is picturing the one with Jenny in a hotel room in Leeds – why Leeds? – wearing only a pair of black stockings, lying face down on a floral valance, a pillow under her groin, offering herself to the businessman who has just finished chatting her up in the dead hotel bar.

'Oh no,' Graham moans into his hands. 'Please, please no.' He reminds himself that he's got his health and his friends and that he'll be seeing Audrey on Saturday night, but, as usual with such reminders, each one seems as effective a morale-booster as remembering that there are people starving in Africa. Weakened by exhaustion and the hangover and now the thought that even Cameron and Jasper's shitey parents have got it together to build normal lives for themselves, he can't stop the moan building into a pulse of dry, racking sobs, and then into a fully blown greet.

He's halfway through a long and uncathartic wail when the doorbell rings. Graham jolts upright. In fact, he comes as near as he'll ever come to jumping out of his chair. He gives his eyes a quick rub and yells, 'Just a moment' in the vague direction of the front door.

Composure, he reminds himself. Composure. Having blown his nose into a wodge of kitchen towel and thrown some cold water over his face, he judges that he's just about fit to be seen in public. He paces steadily to the door, like he's measuring the distance, and opens it. 'Courier from *Business Matters*?' Graham says brightly.

It's only now that he registers the curious figure standing in front of him, a person kitted out in a dark, visored helmet and perv's black – zip-covered jacket, leathers, boots, the lot. Unfortunately, the figure is so tall and thin that he looks less like a biker than someone attending a fancy-dress party as a biker. Or, now that he's standing to attention, a thoroughly burnt match. The figure flicks up the visor and exposes a pair of cheap-looking, rectangular, black-framed spectacles whose lenses are so thick they make the eyes behind them obscenely large and watery.

'Pick-up from Anderson,' says the courier. Then he peers down at Graham. 'Here. Are you all right?'

One of those London accents that are all vowels. Eeah. Ah ewe awe wigh. There is a pause while he tells himself to get a grip. He has always felt weepily vulnerable at moments like these, ever since he was of an age to scrape his knees or be stung by wasps and his mother would ruin his resolution not to burst into tears by telling him he was her poor wee thing and her brave little soldier. The temptation to cry into this long streak of misery's leather shoulder is there now, but he resists. He will not lose it in front of anyone. Especially a specky wimp who's too soft to use consonants. Graham glares up at those marmoset's eyes and, reminding himself to broaden his own accent so that he'll sound hard, says, defiantly, 'Ah am abso fucking lootly splendid. Pal.' He turns and heads back to his study, where he waits for a moment, rubs his face again, and picks up the artwork.

Back at the door, the courier tucks the dancing photocopier under his arm and proffers a clipboard in return. 'Just sign there, mate.'

Theh mye. Maybe the face-rub hasn't worked, or perhaps there's a catch in his voice when he says, 'There you go,' as he scribbles his jagged signature on the pad and hands it back. Whatever the cause, the courier wrestles off his helmet, leans farther down towards him, like an adult quizzing an infant, and says, 'Sure you're okay? Anything I can do?'

Shaw. Anyfink. And just what the *fuck* is going on here? 'Oh, aye,' Graham says, as he senses with real gratitude the anger swelling inside. 'That's just what the fucking doctor fucking *ordered*. A hand-job from an eight-foot, eight-stone twat wearing welder's fucking goggles. Soo fucking *perb*. That'll be fucking *right*.'

It's the accent. Works every time. The biker takes a step back. 'I was only . . . Tell you what, mate, you should see someone, bit of professional help, that's what you need.'

'Is that fucking right? Well, I tell you what, pal.' (The courier has put his helmet back on and casually flicked down his visor.) 'You don't fuck off out of it pronto, you're going to need.' (The courier has turned his back and is ambling calmly away and towards a vast bike gleaming beside Graham's rotting Golf.) 'Professional fucking help from a.' (The courier has mounted the bike. Now the courier kicks the bike into roaring life. Just as well, because Graham was running out of steam and would probably have fucked up the final bit about a casualty ward or a surgeon.)

After he has closed the door, Graham leans back against the wall. Fucking hell, he thinks. Things can't go *on* like this. Things have to fucking *change*.

* * *

'You on for the usual?'

'I'm up for that.' Ian feels something stab him in the small of his back. He swivels round to see a grinning Paolo walking backwards down the corridor and giving him the finger. 'You okay, Graham? Sounds like you've got a cold.'

'Nah. I'm fine. Just went a bit overboard with the sauce last night. Out with a couple of people.'

'Snap. I've got a fair-sized hangover on the go after a sesh at the Pig and Whistle. Then getting all sorts of grief from herself. Here. What's the best thing about fellatio?'

'Go on, then.'

'Ten minutes' silence.'

'Very good. So what do you reckon – Soho?'

'Oooh, sir. Suits me, sir.'

'What's that?'

'Come on, Graham. *The Fast Show*. You must have seen it.'

''Fraid not . . . Where will we go?' A rising note of what could be petulance or anxiety in that question, which Ian puts down to the fact that Graham's taken it on himself to make the arrangements for once – and probably also resents not having the chance to moan about whatever time and place Rob has sorted out. 'You were at the Pig last night.'

'Doesn't mean we have to kick the habit.' Ian swallows a yawn. 'Pig's fine by me. Eight?'

'Done deal . . . I'll give Rob a bell, by the way. You heard from him?'

'Nup . . . But he'll be around. Friday night, for Christ's sake. He gives you any crap, tell him he can always shag supermodels some other time.'

'Too fucking right. Oh, and I suppose I'd better call Eck as well.'

'Oh yeah. Eck as well. Here. Why are Italian men small?'

'I don't know, Ian. Why are Italian men small?'

'Because when they're young their mums tell them that once they're big they'll have to leave home and get a job.'

'I don't get it.'

'Oh, come on, Graham. It's a cracker.'

'Sorry.'

'It's referring to the way Italian guys always live with . . . Oh, stop me. Nothing worse than explaining a joke. Which reminds me. I've got a class of Germans in ten minutes. I'd better go and fish out my list of gerunds for them to memorise. Christ knows where I've put them but the hunt'll be worth it, because, believe you me, a class of Germans with a long list to learn by heart is a happy class.'

'Give the buggers hell. See you at eight.'

'*Au revoir*, my man.'

Ian yanks out his phonecard, turns round and collides with the sausage-legged French girl. 'Hello, there. All yours,' he says, and points to the booth.

'No,' says the girl . . . Monique, that's it. 'I do not want the telephone. I want to speak with you.'

'Oh. Right. Well, that would be nice, Monique, but I have to prepare for a class.'

She does her shoe-inspecting act. Hang on a minute. Is she blushing? Oh yes – definite beamer there. 'I want to say,' she tells her trainers, 'thank you for the help. We had a conversation with the secretary of Dr Foxsmith and it is okay, today we move to a new place.'

'Good news. Where's the new digs . . . I mean your new place?'

'Bow.'

'Good. And where is it? Sorry, Monique,' he adds, when he sees that she hasn't got his translingual quip. 'That was supposed to be a joke. So.' Ian beams down at this dumpy little creature while he tries to think of something else to say. 'So. You will join my advanced class at two o'clock on Monday?'

'Jaw in?' Dearie me. She really is crap. She'll be completely out of her depth with the likes of Paolo and Dieter in the advanced lot. Ah well, the customer's always right. She looks up at him with a face so scrunched up by bafflement she could win a girning contest. 'Ah. Join. Yes.'

Ian takes a step back. 'So, Monique, I am glad you feel better. But if you will excuse me, I have a lesson to prepare . . .' He is about to head off to the shunkie before scouring his desk for gerunds when he notices that the top of her bob is gently vibrating. She can't be . . . yes, she's crying. Ian bends down in an attempt to make eye contact but she turns away to wipe her tears on a chubby forearm. What on earth is the matter with her now? Ian inches forward and gives her a couple of awkward pats on a hefty shoulder. 'Shoosh, shoosh,' he murmurs. 'Shoosh, shoosh.' He's remembered. The gerund list is in his teacher's copy of the *Advanced English Primer*. Still. He can't hang around here for ever waiting for this one to calm down. 'Now then, Monique, what's wrong? Is there anything I can do?'

She gives her bob a brief shoogle. 'No,' she whispers. 'You are very kind. It is just . . .'

'Yes?'

'Everything.'

'Everything?'

'Everything. I am here a week and I am so . . . nostalgic?'

'*Je crois que tu veux dire* homesick.'

'*Oui, c'est ça.* Ohm seek.'

'But now that you have a new landlady, perhaps you will feel better.'

She yanks out a crumpled tissue from under the sleeve of her blouse, blows her nose with unexpected vigour and returns to watching her trainers. 'Yes, that is better I hope but also I think it is because I do not like . . . I am sorry. It is not important.'

'No, tell me,' says Ian, although he already has a good idea of how the rest of her sentence will go.

'I am sorry but it is here. Not the school, I mean, but this city, this country. It is so different than Toulouse. Dirty and cold and . . .'

'*Dégueulasse?*'

'*Oui.*' The hint of a smile.

Ian gives the hefty shoulder another couple of pats. 'Don't you worry, Monique. But there are good things here too. The . . . well, lots of things. Pubs . . .'

She glances up from beneath her fringe. 'Pubs? I have not visited pubs.'

Is that a come-on look she's just given him or just her being coy and shy? Surely to God it's shyness, because she can't genuinely think that he . . . Mean to say . . . Got to be shyness. Even so, best to play it safe. 'Okay. Well, I usually take the advanced class on a tour of a few pubs so you can come along. Next week some time. And you can bring your friend too.'

'Chantal?' Monique performs a Gallic pout-and-shrug.

What's he said now to put her in a huff? Ah, maybe it was mentioning the friend that did it. She must have been after a hot date after all. Steady on. Why, then, does he give her his crinkly-eyed sexy smile and her shoulder a little squeeze when he says 'See you at two' before heading off to the bog?

'Force of habit, my man,' Ian tells the empty gents'. 'Talking of which.' Ian sidles into the cubicle, where he whisks out his little mirror and assembles a quick line.

'Okeydokey,' he says a moment later. Yeah, life is fine and it's all going to work out. 'Now then,' he mutters, 'time for the Jerries' gerunds. Yes, yes, yes, indeedydoody.'

Alastair is stumped. This being the third week in a row that Josh Todd has devoted his column to the difficulties he has experienced in filing his column, Alastair cannot come up with a third consecutive punning headline about Josh's Macintosh and modem after last week's 'Not OK Computer' and 'Only connect' the week before that. 'E-mail chauvinism' is Alastair's least bad effort so far, but that's only because the one other phrase that he has scribbled on his notepad is 'The art of modemism' – lame and only works visually, if at all. He is busily scoring heavy black lines through both phrases when his phone rings.

'Subs.'

'Eck.'

'Oh, hi, Graham. How are you?'

'I feel like shite warmed up but don't let that worry you. Nothing a drink tonight won't solve. You on for it?'

'Yes. Absolutely. Looks like I'll be turning up late again, though.'

'Oh, aye, right. Giving the Arts bit its jammies and putting it to bed.'

'Lifestyle, actually.'

'Is that the bit with that Josh Todd in it?'

'Alas, yes.'

'Now he is a cunt and no error. How much does that cunt get for that shite?'

'Eighty grand a year, I heard.'

'Jesus fucking *Christ*. Eighty fucking thousand fucking notes . . . Fucking *hell* . . . He must be knobbing that bloke, the Fly.'

'Bluebottle. Yes, that was one theory we had as well. Anyway, Graham, sorry to be a bit abrupt but I'd better get on. Where tonight?'

'Pig. If there's a problem, try my mobile or Rob's.'

'Great! You've got hold of him.'

'No such fucking luck. Left a message on his machine, though.'

'Here's hoping,' says Alastair with a casualness that is feigned because a meeting of the Friday Night Club without Rob isn't what he had in mind. What he did have in mind is the residually embarrassing image of the four of them propping up a chic bar in Soho House (one that might even have a black marble counter and gantries that jutt out from a long mirrored wall) and bantering away in a lively yet sophisticated manner, like chaps in a Gillette ad. Then they'd adjourn at, say, one to Rob's flat where they would, as per, continue the crack with the help of Rob's mightily strong grass and Rob's drinks table and stereo. Ideally, a bit more civilised than usual, to be honest. Though they've been jolly, sometimes, in their way, these new FNCs. Different, of course they are, from the old FNCs. And from more recent days when it was just him and Rob, and Rob always on such good form, with his stories about some caper in the City or his latest romantic imbroglio, so that Alastair had often found himself wondering what on earth he'd unwittingly done to deserve such entertainment. But a Robless FNC would be . . . well, it wouldn't be the FNC at all. Just him inexplicably out on the town with Ian and Graham. He is wondering whether or not to mention the possibility of Rob getting them into Soho House when he sees Barry striding towards him, a pale and small youth in his wake. 'Er, Graham, sorry about this but I really had better get back to work. See you all later. Maybe tennish.'

'Whatever. 'Bye, Eck.'

''Bye, Graham,' Alastair says to his phone, and 'Hi, Barry' to his boss. Assuming that the pale and small youth in tow is the new sub, Alastair gives him what he hopes is a warm and welcoming smile, but the youth fails to respond, being too busy examining the surrounding jumble of computers and desks and litter with the fearful suspicion of an American tourist hopelessly lost in Cairo. His edginess is apparently infectious, because Barry looks quite ill at ease and fails to perform any introductions.

Instead, he says, 'Al, my pal,' and tugs an earlobe. 'Got a minute?'

Much as he would like to correct Barry's social oversight, Alastair can't catch the youth's eye and Barry is already on the move. Puzzled, Alastair follows him over to the table strewn with proofed pages. Barry surveys the mess of paper and gives his earlobe another pull. 'Maybe this'll be the historic night when we won't manage to get Lifestyle off to press. How's Josh?'

'Tosh. Never mind that, though, Barry. What's going on with the new chap?'

'Him? Bloody hell.' Barry looks at a proof of the cookery column as though he's been libelled in one of the recipes. 'I should have bloody known that Bluebottle would land us in it.'

'What?'

'You'll see, Al. And while I'm on the subject, we'd better all remember to ditch our *nom de guerre* for the Lifestyle editor while his stepson's around.'

'Ah. Of course. Richard it is.'

'One more hint. We'd better go easy on taking the piss out of the new boy as well.'

'Come on, Barry. Subs' solidarity. Why would we be nasty to him?'

For a moment, Alastair wonders if Barry is about to spit. 'How long have you got? But one obvious reason is his name.'

'What's he called? Ivor Bigun?'

'Very amusing, Al. And not so far off the mark. His name is Bond. James Bond.'

'No, really, Barry.'

'Yes, really. He is James Bond. Thatsh hish name. Oh oh sheven.'

Alastair can't help a snort. 'Blimey. Sho heesh a shub.'

'Eggshackly. Well, except he's not.' Barry picks up a proof of the cookery page and makes a show of scanning it. 'A sub, I mean. Nor does he have any desire to sub. Bloody Bluebottle. So keep an eye on him, Al, and make sure he doesn't screw up.'

'Righty ho. But why is he starting at the end of the week and on our busiest day? Why not wait until Monday?'

'God alone knows. My guess is that Bluebottle wants to impress him with the wonderful excitement of a press night.'

'Really?'

'Either that or Bluebottle has even less of a clue than we dared suspect. Yes. That's got the horrible ring of truth about it. Anyway, see what you can do with the youngster. And remember, hard though it might be, go easy on the Connery stuff.'

'Of course, Barry. Poor chap. He must have been persecuted his whole life. What were his parents thinking about? Surely, if your surname is Bond, James has got to be the last thing you'd call your son.'

'You're right. Definitely worse than Brooke or Basildon.'

'But what about him?' muses Alastair. 'I mean, I know your name can be just one of those things you're stuck with, like having a big nose or sticky-out ears. But if it's that bad, then why not go for the equivalent of plastic surgery? If your name was James Bond, wouldn't you change it by deed poll, or even just call yourself Jim, or by your middle name, or anything for that matter?'

'Well, you know, Al, I think it might be a bit like you and me being up front about being bald, rather than opting for a sad pretend hairstyle like the Bobby Cha . . . Oh, bugger. That's Derek arrived and he's already nobbled young James. Remember what he was like with the work-experience guy from Oxford?'

'Did James go to Oxford?'

'No.'

'Then he should be all right.'

'Cambridge.'

'Oh dear.'

Alastair looks over at the subs' desks, where the new boy is looking even paler and smaller as he is loomed over by Derek, who seems to be ominously jovial. And now he's slapping little James on the back and laughing.

'Bloody hell,' mutters Barry. 'What is that big lump saying?' Barry and Alastair hurry back in time to hear a delighted Derek telling a distinctly crestfallen James Bond, 'because he sounds like the character in the Goons, he buzzes around to no effect and he loves shit'.

'Now then, Derek,' Barry announces. 'Isn't it your turn to get the tea?'

'*Jawohl.*' Derek clicks his heels together. 'And what can I get *you*, James?'

'Coffee, please.'

'Milk, sugar?'

'Just black, please.'

'Shaken but not stirred?'

'Just black, please.'

Derek narrows his eyes, nods sagely and whispers, 'An excellent choice, Mr Bond.'

Oh dear, thinks Alastair. Oh dear, oh dear, oh dear. 'I'm Alastair,' he says abruptly to James, and busily shakes his hand. 'While Derek's doing the tea run, perhaps I could show you what we do here.'

James shuffles reluctantly towards Alastair's desk, while Alastair calls up his partly subbed version of Josh. Barry gives Alastair a wink and makes his way to Bluebottle's office, to talk about the new arrival or even, it occurs to Alastair, the frantic day ahead.

'How *strange*,' says James in a voice even higher and squeakier than his stepfather's, and Alastair marvels yet again at how his social betters really seem to have no idea how grating their voices can be.

'What do you mean, James?'

'It's all squiggly down the right-hand side.'

'Ah, yes. Well, that's just the way text appears on the screen. The computer will do the justifying when it's printed.'

'Justifying?'

'Um, where the words all line up straight at the sides. So, James, have you done any editorial work before?'

'I have done quite a bit of journalism for the college mag, actually. Theatre reviews, mainly.'

'Good, good. And any subbing? Subediting? Copy-editing?'

Alastair looks over his shoulder to give James another encouraging smile. James replies with the wary grimace of a schoolboy who's being told about felching.

'Okay,' says Alastair. 'Good. And has, ah, Richard told you much about what you'll be doing here?'

'Actually, he said I'd be learning the ropes . . .'

'Excellent.'

'. . . before I start to write things. I mean, that's why I'm here, actually. Not . . . *this*.'

While he tries to outstare his screen, where the cursor is blinking beside the word 'cudjilled', it occurs to Alastair that he may have got it slightly wrong about James being nervous and overawed.

'Excuse me, Alan, but shouldn't that be brains? It says brians.'

'At the moment,' says Alastair, pleasantly. 'I haven't finished this piece yet. You see, it's our job to make sure these errors don't creep into print. There's another one just after the comma of brians. Can you spot it? "Having cudjilled my brians, the phone rings." '

James gives his shoulders a token shrug. 'Seems fine to me, actually.'

'Okay. Good. Well, what we have here is a dangler.'

'Got Al to show you his dangler?' The returning Derek wiggles his eyebrows and plonks the cardboard tray of polystyrene cups precariously on top of Alastair's terminal. 'I thought you'd be a ladies' man, Mr Bond.'

'In fact,' Alastair continues hurriedly, 'quite a classic dangler. You have to watch out for them with Josh Todd. Oh, and Tamara as well. All of them, really. You see, James, what he's got at . . .'

'Your coffee, Mr Bond. Black. With the merest twist of vermouth.'

'. . . the moment is a subject in the second clause that relates erroneously to the verb in the first clause, that's to say a dangler. "Having cudjilled my brians, the phone rings." You see, at the moment, this means that the phone was attacking Josh's head with a cudgel.'

'If only,' says Derek. 'Wotcha, girls. What time do you call this?'

Mad Alice scurries towards her workstation, places her lucky crystal on the desk and switches on her computer. Yvonne, by contrast, flings her handbag on to her chair and stands over it, pursing her lips and noisily blowing air out of her nose. Evidently too preoccupied to acknowledge the fact that she is in the company of a pale and small youth she hasn't seen before, Yvonne shakes her head and growls. 'That fucking *wanker* Bluebottle,' she says.

'Yvonne,' says Alastair.

'Bluebottle only comments on us coming in late.'

'Yvonne.'

'Today of all days. When Bluebottle's usual fucking incompetence . . .'

'Yvonne.'

'. . . will no doubt mean we'll all have to stay here till tomorrow morning.'

'Yvonne.'

'Honestly, Bluebottle is such a fucking *arsehole*.'

'Yvonne.'

'*Fucking* Bluebottle. Hello,' she says to the new and open-mouthed person who is staring at her.

'Yvonne James James Yvonne,' says Alastair, before directing a dry cough into his fist. 'Yvonne, perhaps you should know that James is . . .'

'A shpeshull agent,' says Derek.

'Richard Marshall's stepson,' says Alastair.

'With a lieshensh to kill,' says Derek.

Yvonne's eyes dart around, as if she's a burglar outflanked by the cops.

'Yes,' declaims Derek. 'This is the new bug. Who has joined us directly from the University of Cambridge. And his name is Bond.'

'James,' says Alastair.

'James Bond,' says Derek.

'Right, then,' says Alastair briskly. 'If you'll excuse us, I was talking to James here about subbing Josh.'

Alastair does not have a very good feeling about any of this.

7

'WHERE THE BLOODY HELL IS THE BLOODY THING?'

Friday evening

Here's Ian, drinking lager and feeling completely cream-crackered, despite the after-hours nap in his classroom and the two slices of takeaway pizza from Caffé Nero. Or maybe because of. Anyway, if the Pig and Whistle wasn't so crammed and noisy and sulphurous with smoke, he could quite easily have another little snooze.

'Excuse me, is this seat taken?'

Ian looks up to see a bulky bloke in a stupidly hooped rugby shirt pointing to the adjacent chair.

As if. Would Ian Murray really be sitting in a pub, on his own, on a Friday night? 'I'm keeping it for someone,' Ian says blankly. 'He's late.' As usual with Graham, who'd turn up late for a free dinner with a young and bare Sophia Loren. On account, Ian suspects, of Graham's urge to come across as a head-in-the-clouds artist and bohemian, although, as far as Ian can see, it's just Graham being crap. Mind you, the man's reliable unpunctuality does have its advantages . . . Ian turns to the young couple to his left and asks them to watch his two seats, then he gets up to begin insinuating himself through the throng and down to the basement shunkie.

Thank you, Jesus, that there's a travelcard, a straw and a good wrap in his back pocket to sort him out, and that the cubicle is free. And that the cubicle has a door which locks. Damn. He must have left his little mirror in his desk drawer.

Ian pulls down the seat lid, gives the (wooden – not ideal but okay) surface a cursory wipe with a fist of loo paper, hunkers down, fetches out the wrap and prepares a long, thick line.

Now that is a sight for sore, red, knackered eyes. He takes a good blast up each nostril. Woah. Oh yes, yes, yes, indeedydoody. He licks a fingertip and passes it over the wooden seat, picking up a few stray flecks of coke and (Ian always thinks this and always battles to dismiss the thought) countless millions of molecules of unpleasantness. He rubs the fingertip over his gums. Now then. Time for a drink.

'By fuck, do I need this pint. Fucking Northern Line, by the way. Know what it said when I got to the platform? Morden fifteen mins. On a fucking Friday bastard evening. They're all there at Tube HQ, wondering how can we fuck over the punters tonight? Tell you fucking what, we'll put on a skeleton fucking service using the oldest fucking carriages. Fucksake, the one I squeezed into should have had gas lamps. Adverts for the new Charles Dickens. Having a good fucking laugh down at Tube HQ, I tell you. Fucking fifteen mins. You wired?'

'Nup.'

'Come on, Ian. Look at the fucking state of that.' Graham points to the ashtray, which is brimming with the remains of a beer-mat Ian has shredded into stamp-sized pieces.

'It was something to do while I was sitting here for' – Ian checks his watch with a hammy flourish – 'oh, going on half an hour. And I'm not the person who has just gone off on one, ranting and raving about the Northern Line. Anyway, it's not exactly news that the Tube's rubbish, is it? I mean, if you compare it to . . .'

'The fucking Paris fucking Métro, fucking don't fucking tell me.'

'Well, yeah, but it's true. Hey, have I told you the one about the guy trapped on a desert island with Claudia Schiffer?'

'And he makes her dress up as a man and he says, "Hi, Frank, you'll never guess who I'm shagging." Aye, Ian, you told that one last Friday. Not that I'm surprised you've forgotten.'

'When last Friday?'

'Back at Rob's . . . Any word from him?'

'Nup. Maybe he's gone on a trip. Or it's some new babe.'

'Aye.' Graham purses his lips into the silence. Would Ian's absence be as disappointing? he wonders. Probably not. It's a thought which leads Graham to asking himself why it took a good few years of him being down in London before he got round to seeing Rob on a regular basis, which leads immediately to the pangful answer – Jenny. Jenny and him ensconced in their own world out in Finchley.

Ian flicks at a shred of beer-mat. 'Rob told you who he's bedding these days?'

'No. Who?'

'Nup, this is me asking.'

Graham shrugs.

'I suppose,' says Ian, 'it'll just be the next one in the queue of oiled bimbettes. Way Rob goes on, it's like he's got one of those things outside his flat going up to his bedroom window, filled with girlies. You know, one of those old kind of lifts like conveyor belts where you get on it while it's moving. A paternoster. Yeah, a paternoster, filled with oiled bimbettes and the queue to get on it stretched along Bateman Street. Maybe he has a . . .'

'Ian.'

'Graham.'

'Shut the fuck up.'

'Sorry, was I . . . ?'

'Yes. Back to the real world.' High time for a change of subject, thinks Graham, but then he's stumped when he tries to think of a subject to change to. Football, he decides, if only because that should stop Ian blethering about Rob. 'So who've the Rovers got tomorrow?'

'Hamilton away.'

'. . . What're Hamilton like these days?'

'Search me. The usual west-coast mix. Psychopaths with tattoos on their teeth in defence. Up front a pair of wee ginger blokes with scurvy. Hey – Eck could have got a game with that lot.'

'Fair dos, Ian, he was a good wee player was Alastair.'

'What was it? Two seasons for the university and a couple of games for Lochgelly Albert? Come on.'

'More than you or me could have done.'

'Yeah, but Lochgelly Albert? Christ, it doesn't even sound like a team. A notorious local sex offender, yes, but not a football club.' Ian sniffs. 'Eck coming along?'

'Aye. Said he'd be late, though.'

'Got a date, has he?'

'Settle.'

'Maybe there's a convention of Swedish porn stars in town and Eck's on call to pleasure them with his expertise.'

'Just how much of the marching powder have you had, Ian? You are blethering shite.'

'None. Mind you, I'm more than a wee bit fatigued. A trip downstairs would be just the thing. Excellent suggestion, Graham. You want to accompany me?'

'That'll be right.'

'Maybe I can persuade Rob to partake of a wee line later.'

'Doubt it. And I couldnae get hold of him.'

'Ah. Damned shame. Rob is around, isn't he?'

'The fuck am I? His fucking secretary?'

'Just asking.'

'Where is it? Where is it? Where the bloody hell is the bloody thing?'

'Found it, Barry.' Alastair waves a photograph of a young blonde woman naked but for a tiny bikini, arm in arm with an improbably muscled black man who is wearing no more than a gold posing-pouch and a smile.

'Thank God for that. Where was it, Al?'

'In among the proofs.'

'No information on the back, I suppose?'

Alastair flips the snap over. 'Sorry, Barry. That's definitely Tamara, though.'

'Well, yes, but who the bloody hell is her Caribbean consort?'

'Doesn't say.'

'Oh God. So we don't know if he's a passing fisherman or some famous cricketer or the local prime minister's son. Oh, bloody hell. Bloody hell. Bloody *hell*.'

'Doesn't matter, Barry. We can wing the caption.'

'Looks like we'll bloody have to. Why the bloody hell we have to run that dim Sloane's holiday snaps as well as the drivel she supplies as copy I do not bloody know. Yes I bloody do. Because Blue . . . Okay. Al. And James. James? Hello, James? Good. Two minutes to think of a caption. A pun. Something witty. Across three columns. And James? Could you maybe sprint over to Design with the photo so they can get it through the system?'

James shrugs, picks up the photograph, then slopes off.

Barry tugs at an earlobe. 'Then,' he mutters, 'we might just have a chance of getting this bloody section off to press. No thanks to that little . . .'

'Barry?'

'Prick. Al.'

'What about something like "On the beach" or "Life's a beach", colon, then just some vague stuff about Tamara gets to grips with the locals?'

'In run-of-the-mill circumstances, Al, I'd say it was bollocks, but at this time of night . . . Will it fit across three columns?'

'Should do, with a bit of tweaking.'

'Then it's sheer bloody genius. What headline did you get for Josh?'

'Still blank.'

'Sorry, Al, I don't get it.'

'No, Barry, I'm saying we haven't got a headline yet.'

'Bloody hell. Bloody *hell*. That page should have gone bloody *ages* ago. What are the contenders?'

'Um . . . E-mail chauvinism?'

'Yuck. Shove it in.'

8

'YOU KNOW WHAT I HATE ABOUT CEEFAX?'

Friday night

First thing he does when he gets back is slam his mobile down on the table. If the mobile had some self-repairing device, he'd smash it against the wall. The fuck is Rob playing at? 'Called him up but got the answerphone, even broke the golden rule and went over to buzz on his door. Fucking zilch,' he says.

'Damned shame,' says Ian. 'Tell you what. If he's not turned up by eleven, we'll try him again, maybe do a tour of the drinking clubs, see if he's around, and even if he isn't we'll have made a night of it.'

Graham takes a deep breath. Composure. 'Possible,' he says. 'See how I feel. Maybe I shouldn't have a late one.'

'What's this, what's this, what's this? A health drive?'

'That'll be fucking right. Nah. Just that what with Rob not turning up . . . And I've got this thing in Shoreditch tomorrow night and I want to be on good form for it.' Graham glugs down a good half of his pint. 'Especially as,' he says. 'I may be. On for. A spot of. Shagging.'

'Really? You're joking. Or are you? Are you joking?'

'Yes, really. And no I'm not.' Graham fiddles with his mobile. 'Fucksake, though, the last time I had sex was . . .'

'During the Cold War.'

'Last October. Fucking last October.'

'And that was on your own.'

'Remember Audrey?'

'Audrey, Audrey, Audrey. Nup.'

'Aye. Audrey. You met her at the Cantaloupe. The time when you and me went on to a do at Marty's place.'

'Hee hee. One of Marty's parties.'

'Fucksake, Ian. Those trips to the basement are really doing your brain in, by the way.'

'What did we eat? Smarties?'

'Christ. Anyway. Audrey. Dyes her hair a kind of red. Almost vermilion. Nice. Knows the people I shared the studio with in Curtain Road. No? Col, Tim, Amanda, Jason, all that lot. Three, four years back.'

'Before my time. I'd be, let's see, yeah, yeah, yeah, I'd be in Barcelona. Or maybe, just maybe, Paris. That would have been about the period when . . .'

'You fucking did meet Audrey. Definitely. Fucksake. The point is that Col reckons she might be on for a wee spot of hochmagandy with yours truly. There'll be a whole crowd of us at the Cantaloupe. Kind of an old studio reunion. Col'll be there, a few others you've met. Come along if you want.'

'No can do, my man, no can do. Claire's having a little soirée with a couple of her pals. At ours, so I've got to be there. So that's my Saturday night well and truly down the pan.'

'So that's my Saturday night well and truly down the pan.'

'Suit yourself, Ian. By Christ, a man could die of thirst waiting for you to get a round in.'

'Okay, okay, hud yer wheesht.' What am I saying? Ian asks himself. Hud yer wheesht? How is it that he occasionally can't resist being infected by Graham's dialect schtick? And how is it that each time it happens, he sounds like he's auditioning for *The Broons*? Odd when you think about it, thinks Ian, given that he's the one who was brought up in a grey box on a windswept council estate and Graham's the one whose daddy's a doctor and whose accent has been slaloming down the social scale ever since he used to get beaten up at primary for sounding English, i.e., not brought up on a windswept council estate. Maybe not so odd after all.

In case Graham decides to take the piss out of the wheesht, Ian gets up in a hurry and starts to make his way through the crowd to the bar. As he takes up a position behind a bloke in a suit who is either coming to the end of a massive order or is in the middle of buying drinks for the entire pub, he tries to recall an Audrey. Dyed red hair. Nup. The trouble with Graham's trendy-wendy Shoreditch crowd of artists and photographers and designers is that they all look the same, all of them with daft hair and all dressed for a guerrilla mission or a shift at a construction site. 'Glamourflage', Claire calls it. Ian catches the barman's eye and orders two pints. Mind you, a night out with a bunch of urban warriors he barely knows strikes him as much better than a night in, on best behaviour, with Briony and Co.

Ian squeezes back to the table, the two pints clutched to his chest and surviving a jolt as some oaf nudges him in the back just when he's about to place the drinks on the table. 'You watching Ceefax tomorrow?' asks Ian.

'Maybe.'

'You know what I hate about Ceefax?'

'Believe me, Ian, I haven't a fucking clue what you hate about Ceefax.'

'Page 311,' says Ian eagerly, ignoring both the faint recognition that this urge to say something has little to do with the importance of the content and the never-to-be-mentioned suspicion that Graham's not into his football as much as he should be. 'Now that we're not in the Premier we have to share a page that's divided into three kind of sub-pages. Last season all we had to do was keep it on page 310, and there it was, no problem, all the Premier results on the screen together. Unless there were millions of goals and people being sent off, so that they ran out of space and had to continue on a second page. But now with 311 there's the First Division on the first page, the Second Division on the second page, and the Third . . .'

'Ian. I get your drift.'

'Okay. So you know what I'm saying.'

'Fucksake, it's no exactly one of life's big traumas, is it? And all you do is keep the First Division bit on hold on page 311. End of problem.'

'But I keep thinking if you put it on hold it won't show the latest scores. Just the scores as they were when you put it on hold. It's not that, though. It's a sign.'

'Of?'

'Our decline.'

'Yes. They got relegated.'

'Much more than that, though, Graham. Just think. We're back to sharing page 311 with Brechin and Stenhousemuir, and it was only two years ago, almost to the day, we were going mental at half-time in the Olympic Stadium and that massive scoreboard above us saying Bayern Munchen 0 Raith Rovers 1.' As he says this, Ian indulges in a memory of the screaming pandemonium after that goal. A great trip that was, two years ago, when the Rovers' improbable success had inspired a militantly genial binge in Munich by several thousand supporters, including him, Rob, Graham and Eck. A prototype of the FNC Mark II, as it turned out – the four of them converging for the occasion at Rob's urging, Ian from Paris, Eck and Graham from London, Rob himself cutting short a business trip in Japan, and Ian gaining ample opportunity throughout those three days to marvel anew at the thickness of Rob's wallet and the reliability of Graham's disdain.

'Trust you to think that the very best thing was the Rovers playing abroad.'

'Come on, Graham, second round of the UEFA Cup, that scoreboard at half-time, you're not going to argue that wasn't the highest point ever.'

'I suppose. But we knew it wouldn't last. We even knew they'd lose that match.'

'Remember when we hit the side netting just after the break? Could have made it two.'

'Aye, right, and Bayern had no fucking chance, by the way, only two–nil up from the first leg and with numpties like Klinsmann.'

'Okay, but that's not my point.'

'So what is your point?'

'My point, my point is that, yeah, you're right . . .'

'Way hay.'

'. . . we knew at the time we were going to get knocked out and that would be it. I mean, Bayern Munich, we had no chance. But it's one thing knowing at the time that this would be as good as it ever gets, and another thing having to live through the bit afterwards knowing that that really was as good as it gets and from now on in it'll be page 311.'

'Fucksake. So you would have been a whole lot fucking happier if they'd never got into Europe and never played Bayern Munich?'

''Course not. But you know what I'm saying.'

'I do. And it's shite.'

'Terrific news,' says Derek dolefully, after he's wandered back to his desk. 'Bluebottle's having trouble with the editor.'

Barry narrows his eyes. 'What kind of trouble?'

'Oh, nothing much. Just the Lifestyle cover.'

'What! The Kate Moss!'

'That's the one.'

'Mother of Jesus. If the bloody editor changes the cover, Bluebottle will probably have to ditch the fashion centre spread. Bloody hell.'

Alastair coughs. 'It might be all right, Barry. You never know with the editor.' While Barry slumps in his chair and groans, Alastair looks up at the clock. Five to ten. Just when he thought they were about to send Lifestyle off to press. And Yvonne's already gone home in a pointed protest at Bluebottle, Mad Alice left early for a session with her homoeopath, young James has long since sloped off . . . Judging by the way he's gathering together his bag and coat, Derek isn't too keen to stay either. Just be him and Barry, then. Unless this turns out to be a false alarm, he's going to miss out on Friday Night Club and have most of his Saturday scuppered too, since he'll have to spend the best part of the weekend recovering from being here until three or four in the morning.

'Bad time and all that, Barry, but I really have to shoot,' says Derek, shrugging on his raincoat. 'I promised Edith I'd be . . .'

'Sure, Derek, don't worry. It won't take three of us. See you Monday.' Barry slides farther down his chair. 'Suppose I should call Kate and tell her I won't be home till the kids are up. Oh, bloody hell.'

'Cheer up, Barry. At least we might have something to add to the editor's list.' Even as he's speaking, Alastair realises this is a fairly silly thing to say, but he felt he had to make some kind of chirpy contribution, to cheer up Barry, who looks like somebody's stolen his scone. Plus he just couldn't pass up a chance to refer to the editor as 'the editor'. Ritual use of the title rather than the person's name, save when addressing a newspaper's editor face to face, is one of the few Fleet Street traditions which have survived in Canary Wharf, so 'the editor' is a phrase that he finds almost as evocative as 'Hold the front page', which, he knows full well, he will never, ever have the chance to say. Mind you, gauche though his remark undoubtedly is, it seems to work. Barry grants him a rueful smile and reaches out in mid-slump to the top drawer in his desk. A rummage later, he pulls out two photocopied sheets of paper.

'So. We can add Kate Moss to the editor's list.'

'Barry, we don't know that for sure.'

'Yes, we do. Kate. Moss,' says Barry while he turns a page then scribbles down the name. 'There you go,' he says, and sits up straight to hand the document over. 'That's three more today. Ballet Rambert, kiwi fruit and now Miss Moss.' Barry resumes his slump.

Alastair scans the list – compiled by Barry, Bluebottle, Nicholas the Arts editor and Davina in Books, the subs, in fact just about everyone at the paper's shallow end – of all the subjects on which the editor has poured scorn, as hilariously arcane or as the implausible figments of his underlings' diseased imaginations, in the four months since he was briskly and unforeseeably transformed from 'Jonathan in News' to 'the editor', thereby filling the vacancy caused when his predecessor took a risk and filled the front page with that unsourced story about Peter Mandelson. The list's first fifty-odd entries, down to the middle of page two, Alastair could just about recite by heart, but he hasn't seen it for a week and now page two is nearly full. Glastonbury, Mr Bean, Ruud Gullit – no, these are old. But Marco Pierre White's a new one. Philip Glass, the Superbowl, Ted Hughes. Yes, these he hasn't seen. Anthea Turner, Our Price, salmon farming, continues the list. E.M. Forster, Real Madrid, Pizza Express, *Blind Date*, skunk, Francis Ford Coppola, aromatherapy, the Mercury Music Awards, Kim Basinger, CenterParcs, Ballet Rambert, kiwi fruit, and now Kate Moss.

'Well,' says Barry, 'no point just sitting here and waiting for the bad news to hit us. Fancy a trip to Design?'

'Why? Because the editor will be there?'

'No, Al, because I want to play Nintendo on the Apple Macs. Because I want to drop my trousers and sit on the light-box. Because I'm going to mount a daring raid on their bloody biscuit supply. Of course it's because Bluebottle and the editor will be there. Where else would they be looking at the Lifestyle cover?'

It's not much of an outburst and by the standards of the

rest of the office would almost qualify as a pleasantry, but this is Barry and the subs desk and they're all supposed to stick together and . . . Alastair clears his throat as if that will somehow also clear his head, but his only thought is that he's cowed and hurt, just like all those years ago when he was picked on at primary.

'Apologies, Al. It's late and I'm pissed off and you must admit you can be . . . No, look, I'm sorry.'

'Don't worry, Barry. Honestly.' Pull your socks up, Alastair orders himself. He taps the Save button on his keyboard and raises his head over his terminal to show Barry that he's smiling. 'All righty. Let's hit Design.'

'I'd rather hit the editor. So,' says Barry as he re-extricates himself from his slump and beckons Alastair to accompany him down the office, 'how did you get on with the charming oh oh sheven?'

What Alastair wants to say is that James Bond and Derek's incessant baiting of James Bond have helped make this one of the worst working days of his career, and that everything, just *everything*, about this dismal nepotism has demeaned a skilled and demanding profession. However. 'Not bad. He knew a few of the basics and he picked up on the computer really quickly.'

'That's something, especially given the steam-driven system we've got here. But you would have thought with a name like that he'd be . . . Never mind. Good work, Al. I'll tell his stepdaddy. Why,' he adds under his breath, as they near the Design department, 'speak of the devil.' They move slowly towards the desk where Bluebottle and the editor are standing to inspect the screen of a large Apple Mac. 'We can hang about over at the light-box,' Barry whispers. 'Try to look busy.'

Alastair picks up a fawn folder and flicks through the photographs inside. 'Why have the Picture Desk sent down the file for Carrie Fisher?' he whispers.

'Filler pic for the satellite TV pages,' mutters Barry. 'Apparently, the editor said he wanted more glamour in the listings. Said he was fed up with all those pictures of American films and series none of our readers had heard of.'

'Like what?'

'Like *Cheers*. Oh, and *Baywatch*.'

'Two more for the list. And isn't Carrie Fisher an . . .'

'Shush, Al. I want to hear what's going on.'

Keeping their heads lowered, they both cast furtive glances over at the small group gathered round the computer screen. What is going on isn't very much. Young Tania – lovely, sweet, beautiful Tania – is hunched in her seat and busy pushing the mouse around its mat. Bluebottle is now gazing out of the window, possibly in an attempt to convey the air of a man at peace with himself and the dark, twinkling world outside and twenty-four storeys below, but succeeding only in looking like a man about to travel down those twenty-four storeys by the quickest route. The editor, a fleshily overweight man in his mid forties, is standing behind Tania, his pink paws resting on her shoulders.

'Try it in black and white,' he barks. 'At least give it a bit of class.'

By leaning to his left, Alastair can just see Tania whizzing the mouse around the mat. The image on the computer screen changes, the strikingly bright image of Kate Moss bedecked in a tangerine-coloured gown and shimmying down a catwalk giving way to a grey, grainy picture of Kate Moss walking down a catwalk.

'Christ,' mutters Barry. 'The whole point of the piece is that orange is the new black. And now he's . . . oh, bloody hell.'

The editor swivels round to turn to Bluebottle. 'You see, Richard. It's just not working. Even in black and white. What happened to the cover you promised me at conference? The one with the glamorous girl?'

'Well, I . . .'

Despite his anxiety level – because he is nervous whenever he is near the editor, because of the editor's size and sudden authority and already notorious bad temper, and because this impending cover crisis is clearly going from bad to worse – Alastair is entranced. So this is why Bluebottle and Nicholas and Davina return to the shallow end each Tuesday morning from conference, spluttering that they can't defend themselves against the editor's attacks because their only option is to offer explanations so basic and insulting that their next move would be to collect their P45s.

Credit to Bluebottle, though, for he's giving it his best shot. 'But don't you think that this being a big fashion story and this being a, well, a fairly celebrated model and that the original, as it were, colour version has . . .'

'No. No. No. A thousand times no.' The editor lifts his right paw from Tania's shoulder and holds it up, palm outward, in a stop sign. 'Richard, I have spoken on this matter.' The editor performs another ungainly swivel which brings him round to face Alastair. 'Now then,' he proclaims at Alastair, 'let's see what we can rustle up by way of a proper Lifestyle cover. A cover our readers will want to see.' Alastair is under the uncomfortable impression that he should be a large audience. 'A cover our readers will like. A cover our readers will *understand*. What have you got there?'

Before Alastair knows what's happening, the editor has loped over to him and snatched the fawn folder from his grasp.

'Ahah! *This* is more like it. *This* is our cover. *This* is the stuff.' The editor has thrust a paw into the folder and hauled out a large monochrome photograph of Carrie Fisher, with her headphone hair, as Princess Leah. 'Marvellous,' bawls the editor. 'There you are, Richard. *Star Trek* Style. Even given you a cover line.'

Alastair is aghast but he reckons he must be the picture of mental health compared to Bluebottle, who looks like he has been paralysed in mid-shout. There is a short but eerie silence which is broken by the soft chirruping of Tania's phone. She clamps a hand over the mouthpiece and looks uncertainly behind her. 'It's your secretary, um, Jonathan.'

The editor slaps the folder down on the light-box and marches over to grab the phone. '*Yell*o . . . I see . . . Uhuh . . . When? . . . Fantastic.' He hands the receiver back to Tania and surveys the middle distance for a moment. 'Look, Richard, I have to dash. TV crew in my office. Completely slipped my mind.' He stretches his neck as he fiddles with the knot in his tie. 'Being interviewed for Channel Five News.'

'So . . . the cover?' asks Bluebottle.

'Cover? What? Yes. The cover.' The editor rubs a paw over his forehead. 'The thing is, Richard,' he explains with the heroic patience of a remedial teacher, 'I can't do fifteen things at once. Okay, okay, *okay*. We'll go with your one but I want to see *this*' (he brandishes the Carrie Fisher photograph) 'on the Lifestyle front next week.'

As the editor marches off, Bluebottle manages the merest hint of a nod. 'Tania,' he says, when the editor has gone, 'do me a favour and put Kate Moss back in colour, for God's sake.'

'Richard?'

'Barry.'

'Does that mean we're done?'

'By the skin of our teeth.'

Alastair looks at the clock. Twenty past ten. He might still make it.

9

'LIKE ANKLES'

Friday night

'No. Farther along the bar.'

'The one with the blue top?'

'No. The one next to her. Grey jumper.'

'Got you. What about her?'

'Superb tits.'

'Fucksake, Ian.'

'Serious, man. Just superb. Wait till she turns round a bit and she's in profile. An amazing shape to her jumper. You just know they're going to be perfect.'

'Or that she's got scaffolding for her bra.'

'No way, my man, no way.'

'Get the bra off and you could be looking at a pair of spaniel's lugs.'

'No way, Graham. That shape is tight. You can always tell.'

'Like ankles.'

'How do you mean?'

'Ankles. You can always tell what a woman's legs are going to be like by her ankles. You've got to have a really defined tendon at the back, and that hollow either side. Fucking convex.'

'Concave. And you're wrong about the ankles. I mean, it's one of the things people say, although in fact, and I've spent some considerable time thinking about this, as you can imagine, the ankle is an important but not foolproof indicator of a good leg. For instance, you could have a . . .'

'Aye, but see if the ankles are fat or don't have that delicate shape, you know the legs are rubbish.'

'What a little cracker she is. Young girls now? The number of them with big tits? It's extraordinary.'

'Aye, but that's because they're eating Big Macs all the time. Fat, that's all.'

'No way. Telling you, we should have been born in the seventies. You should see some of the talent at the school. And remember I went to that party with Claire couple of months back?'

'The one that turned out to be some sort of rave?'

'Kind of. In a warehouse. Yeah. It was Claire's pals who were giving the party, right, so they're all early twenties, twenty-six tops, and I couldn't believe it, man. The number of beautiful women there. All with shiny hair, great teeth, tall, thin, with big tits, it was extraordinary.'

'That's just you turning into a dirty old man, by the way. You want to start wearing a greasy mac.'

'No chance. Telling you, Graham, women are just getting more beautiful. Fact. There's statistics to prove it. Like the average bra size is getting larger, more people with fewer fillings. That party, they were all dancing away to that house music – what a racket, man, it was like being in the middle of a steelworks – and I just stood there not believing my eyes.'

'And wanking under your mac. Fuck knows how Claire puts up with you.'

'Tall, dark, handsome, superbly hung, brilliant in bed – yeah, fuck knows.'

'Give me fucking strength. You want another one?'

'Struggling with this.'

'Have a short.'

'Go on, then. Calvados.'

'They got that?'

'Brandy if they haven't.'

* * *

'There you go.'

'Cheers.'

'I did ask for Calvados. Boy looked at me like I'd ordered a Babycham. I mean, this is a pub in London, not some fucking bistro in Normandy.'

'Calm down, calm down.'

'What's with the accent and the wiggling hands?'

'Come on, Graham. Harry Enfield's Liverpudlians.'

'Never seen it. By the way. Talking of parties.'

'Were we?'

'A minute ago, aye. Fucksake. Anyway, Marty, right? Did I tell you what happened at his last bash?'

'When the cops arrived and everyone thought they were in fancy dress?'

'Nah, that was months ago, Ian. This was a week or so back. Col was telling me. So Marty was out of it. Six in the morning, something like that. He'd been doing E or maybe acid. Anyway. The boy was lying out on the window ledge, and mind, this is two storeys up. He falls asleep, right? And . . .'

'Don't tell me.'

'Topples off. Maybe thought he was in his bed, who knows. So, he topples off . . .'

'Jesus. Was he okay?'

'On to the top of a parked car. And he's lying there flat on his back for about three hours before anyone spots him.'

'Nobody see him fall?'

'Obviously not. Eck!'

'Eck. You're here.'

'Ian. Graham. Hi, there. Sorry I'm so late. No sign of Rob?'

'Nah. I tried him on the fucking mobile but no luck. Last orders, by the way. You want a pint?'

'The bar's closed, I'm afraid.'

'Have the rest of this lager if you want.'

'I wouldn't mind a sip, Ian, ta muchly.'

'Sorry, Eck, I'm just finishing this story. You met Marty? No? Anyway, Ian, the thing is, he was fine. No bones broken, absolutely okay, didn't even wake up.'

'Kidding.'

'Straight up. He was so fucking out of it he just fell on to the car roof, no problem. They think that was what saved his life, him being so relaxed.'

One sip of lager, that's what his Friday Night Club is going to amount to. One sip of somebody else's tepid lager. However. You never know. Rob might be in or they might even catch up with him if they go on to Soho House. And at least he's not stuck in Canary Wharf, with nothing to look forward to but manically subbing some cobbled-together piece on Carrie Fisher. Graham and Ian are still talking about this bloke he's never heard of. Something about the chap not killing himself. Which drugs he may or may not have taken. Ian's fine but Graham seems pretty pissed. Not that he's slurring his words or anything but he's got the heavy eyes, drooping jaw and booming voice of Graham when he's had a few. Right, then – that's both of them finished their drinks at last.

'Shall we try Rob's mobile again?' asks Alastair.

10

'ONE–NIL DOWN'

Saturday afternoon

'Come on. Answer.' Ian rubs a finger down each side of the telephone's 3, 6, 9 and # buttons. His fingertip is grey with dust. He remembers not to rub his gums.

'Hello?'

'Oh, you *are* there.'

'Ian. Fucksake . . . What's up?'

'What's up? What's *up*? You haven't been watching it, then.'

'No. No, I've been working. So, what's happening?'

'One–nil down.'

'Still. Plenty time left.'

'You kidding, Graham? It's gone half past four. I've been watching that zero by our name since three o'clock and it's still going to be there at quarter to five, believe you me.'

'No need to shout, by the way. It's a phone, Ian, no a fucking loudhailer.'

'You'd be worked up too if you'd been staring at page 311 all afternoon.'

'And if I'd been hoovering up a couple of lines in the meantime.'

'Not at all,' says Ian, feeling genuinely aggrieved.

'Aye. That'll be right.'

'*Shit.*'

'Oh, pardon me, Ian, I mean, what on earth would have made me think that . . .'

'No, I said shit because it is shit because Hamilton have got a second.'

'Oh.'

'*Fucking* Ceefax. *Fucking* Rovers. Why wasn't I born in Milan?'

'. . . You heard from Rob, by the way?'

'Shit. What? No.'

'Maybe give the boy a call, find out what happened to him. Phone me back at full time.'

'Yes, Master. *Toute à l'heure*.'

'What are you like? Okay. Oh fucking rivwar.'

The line goes dead. Ian decides that he will try Rob – something to do as well as staring at Ceefax. He stabs the seven numbers, shakes his head at the television, then tucks the phone under his ear just in time to hear Rob saying 'at the moment, but please leave . . .'

'Shit,' Ian tells the phone, and bangs it down. Still two–nil. And Ruth and Briony coming round later. This has all the makings of one crap Saturday.

At least, and despite the usual Saturday-afternoon hangover, mind you, he's done something with his day, even if that something amounted to no more than the couple of hours he's just spent tinkering with the installation – still, he's got more to show for his Saturday than an afternoon watching Raith Rovers lose on Ceefax . . . Only typical, mind you, of that waster.

Odd. Ian's return, seeing Ian once a week instead of once a year, you'd have thought that he would have made more of an impact. As it is, this new Friday Night Club caper has turned out to be, well, usually a good piss-up, in its defence, and it is something to do on Friday nights . . . But really it's Rob rather than Ian who has been proving the easier to get along with – Rob not quite so full of himself as he used to be, plus he's acquired that air of metropolitan chic as well as of glitzy bachelordom. Rob's done stuff. Like gone to a Damien Hirst launch, met Jay Jopling at a party . . . So he can chat to Rob about the Shoreditch scene, all that, even the installation a bit. And, to be fair to the boy, he's been gratifyingly interested.

Anyway, another date in the diary for tonight, and not only a date but maybe a date date into the bargain. Aye, *this* is more like it.

Weeds in his left hand, trowel in his right, Alastair ambles back to the kitchen, leaving Susie to sun herself beside the forsythia. He stops at the back door because he's begun to fret again about the promised promotion. If 007 isn't going to be a sub after all, will there still be a need for a deputy? And if there isn't, what should he do? Stamp his foot, call up one of the subs he knows at the *Telegraph* or the *Observer*? Why, though? Where else is he going to find a subs desk as jolly and friendly? It's the kind of problem he should know how to tackle by now. Ach, but even if he did know what to do, would it be worth all the worry and bother? He'll deal with it on Monday. Somehow. And forget about it in the meantime. Alastair chucks the weeds in the dustbin, slips off his garden shoes, tugs off his garden gloves, and replaces the trowel in the garden cupboard.

Now he appraises the kitchen. Nothing much to be done here. Actually, it's looking pretty good – everything neat, clean and tidy, without being sterile like a show house. The vase of white freesias on the table, the triangle of softening Brie and the small cylinder of *chèvre* under the cheeseboard's clear dome, the gathering of pans gleaming on their hooks above him . . . yes, it's all just about as it should be.

Alastair walks up the three steps and into what used to be a poky little dining room and is now the back bit of a main room whose varnished wooden floor extends all the way to the bay window at the front. The only drawback with the main room is that Alastair can never quite decide where he should stand to gain the best view of it. Probably here, at the entrance from the kitchen, because he can survey the room's entire length and admire the back bit's mahogany Victorian dining table and its four mahogany Victorian chairs (reupholstered in cream), as well as the red-candy-striped sofa (and the coffee table, carefully strewn with the current editions of *Time Out*, *Men's Health* and *World of Interiors*) which dominates the front bit. But even this vantage point, his favourite, fails to afford a decent view of the front bit's side walls – the three framed Doisneau prints partly hidden to his right and then the marvellous left-hand wall, whose pair of alcoves each holds five shelves of his best-looking, mainly hardback books and whose centre boasts, thanks to Alastair's redecoration, a tiled fireplace, marble mantelpiece and a large, gilt-framed mirror.

Fair enough, so it's not flash like Rob's flat, and N4 is three digits off the ideal postcode, and he doesn't have a huge basement kitchen with white fitted units, discreet spotlighting, beech-wood floor and kids' paintings on the fridge, but this main room in his two-up-two-down in Finsbury Park is as near as Alastair reckons he'll get to living in one of the perfect town houses he used to peek at during his entranced night-time walks around Islington – from Noel Road and St Peter's Street over to Theberton Street and then Barnsbury – after he swapped the subs' desk of the *Scotsman* for the subs' desk of the *Evening Standard* and arrived in London all of (blimey!) nine years ago.

Twenty-five to five. Ten minutes to go. Maybe it's sunny and they're two up. Or it's cold and rainy, three down, and people are shouting abuse as yet another simple pass goes astray. Or maybe Keith Wright has a hat-trick and they're all singing 'Take My Hand' . . .

Righty ho. He has ten minutes to do something, anything, to keep busy and not give in to lazing on the sofa and watching the latest scores. He'll take the duster upstairs, do the study and the guest room, Jif the bathroom if there's time.

11

'OUR MAN IN MARBELLA'

Saturday night

'Skeeble dibble dee. Skip dibble doodle. Skibble dabble doo . . .'

He's singing under his breath but Graham still cuts short his version of 'Strangers In The Night' as he turns into Rivington Street and sees a girl carrying a portfolio case coming towards him. The night ahead, not to mention the pair of big tequilas he had back at the flat, may have put him in a strangely jaunty mood, but it'll take more than a few tequilas and the prospect of a shag for him to risk making an exhibition of himself.

Especially in front of a, yes, a very pretty girl. As she trudges past, her eyes flicker at him for a fair fraction of a second. Here. Did she fancy him? Or was she checking him for a weirdo? Maybe she did fancy him. Now why's a pretty girl like that lugging a portfolio case around Shoreditch at nine on a Saturday night? She should be out with her mates. Having a well-earned rest after the weekly grind. She should take a tip from him. Under the pretence of being about to cross the empty street in strict adherence to the Green Cross Code, he looks over his shoulder to clock her arse. Fucking hell. Aye. He could definitely teach her a thing or two.

Now he's reached the building where Hermann used to have that fucking disgrace of a studio with a bit of wall missing and which Marty has been tarting up to house the offices of his company, D:Zine. Another sign that Shoreditch might be coming up in the world. Not something Graham could have predicted when he first rented his space in the Curtain Road studio seven years ago and found himself dodging around a dark district of clothing wholesalers, obscure printing works, and run-down studios for artists and illustrators who'd yet to make it big.

Maybe Marty's about to make it big. He and D:Zine are obviously doing pretty well for themselves at the very least. Last time Graham was down Rivington Street – three weeks ago, a month? – the ground floor was filled with rubble. And now look at this. Big, swish reception area, complete with vast plants, a wrought-iron spiral staircase, aerodynamically efficient, sunshine-yellow chairs and a grandly curving reception desk. Knowing Marty, weekdays that desk'll be manned by some teenager who looks like he should be pouting sulkily for a *GQ* fashion spread rather than telling folk he's putting them through. Marty, eh?

Graham moves on, skirting the racket of some indie shite from the juke-box in the Bricklayers – a pub that used to function as the Shoreditch crowd's staff canteen until they all decamped farther down Charlotte Street when the Cantaloupe opened a couple of years back. Odds on that they're going to have to find another place soon, because the Cantaloupe has begun to attract hordes of suits from the City, out for an evening in Bohemia. Looks okay tonight, though, the suits all necking their Budweisers back home in Essex.

Taking a sly keek through the window, he spots Col, Tim, Amanda, Hermann, Jason and Sue sitting at a table back left. No sign of Audrey. Then he notices a flash of purply red hair. She's sitting behind Hermann. As Graham looks on at the old studio crowd sitting at the table, it dawns on him that the half-hour he spent dithering at his wardrobe was a thirty-minute countdown to disaster. White T-shirt, dark blue blazer and faded blue 501s? What was he thinking about? Look at the others. *Black* T-shirts for Tim and Jason, and, doubtless, black Dockers for breeks. Col looks as if he bought his rubbery-looking jacket, with its insignia and its red, white and black stripes down the sleeves, from Halfords. And as for Hermann's outfit – fantoosh raspberry shirt with vast, flappy collar, sleeveless jersey with a yellow-and-blue golfer's-style diamond check, mainly red and green tartan trews – well, the boy would raise eyebrows at a clown school. Not counting a business suit, or perhaps tennis whites, it would seem impossible to commit a sartorial faux pas in such company, but strict rules, which he has never learned, govern this apparently wild, devil-may-care spurning of convention. And now he fears that, with what he suddenly realises is his wincingly orthodox, smart-but-casual get-up, he might just as well walk in with a placard announcing that AIDS is the work of God's justice. But he's never got the arty thing right. You'd think it was enough to be able to draw and paint, but, as he found out at art college, that was only part of the whole shebang. And since he's come down here, he's begun to suspect that an ability to draw and paint is completely irrelevant. A drawback even. Put up a tent filled with names of folk you've shagged, make shapes out of elephant shite, call it art. Long as you're in with the Goldsmiths' in-crowd and folk think you're cool. Not much danger of that for him. Graham takes a deep breath, keeps his stomach sucked in, tells himself to stay calm, and walks in. Judging that there's enough people to offer him cover, he then heads straight to the bar – no messing and, besides, no risk of a crippling round.

A minx of a barmaid with a stud in her navel gets him a pint of Guinness and a big, straight tequila. He pays the minx, downs the tequila and steels himself to carry his Guinness over to the table. Don't worry, he thinks. I worry too much, I always worry too much.

There's a spare seat by Audrey but that would be too obvious. Wouldn't it? Or would it? He decides to play safe and stand. 'Hi, guys,' he says.

'At last,' says Col. 'Our man in Marbella. Where's your Rolex?'

'Left it in the Bentley outside,' says Graham, mustering a smile. 'What have I missed?'

'The usual,' says Jason. 'Tim and Hermann had a fist fight. Some lesbian action with Aud and Sue.'

'Heard Jason's news?' Tim asks Graham.

'What, he feels he's trapped in a man's body?'

'Funny guy,' says Jason. 'Very funny guy. But if I was, at least now I could afford the surgery.'

'What's this?'

Jason leans back in his chair expansively. 'Do the words "British" and "Telecom" mean anything to you?'

'Oh no,' says Audrey, without looking round. 'Don't get him started on the blah blah blah.'

Jason reaches over to pat her thigh. 'I shall cover you with rubies, my princess. Anoint you in oriental potions.'

Graham tries not to think about Jason anointing Audrey, who's gone back to chatting with Sue, in oriental potions.

'Oh yes,' says Jason. 'Commission from BT. Big campaign. *Big* campaign.'

Graham puts down his Guinness. 'How big?'

'Big. Newspaper ads, posters, maybe telly. Twelve grand minimum.'

'Fucking hell. Confirmed?'

'Absolutely. Twelve big ones.'

'Drinks are on Jason,' says Hermann. 'In fact, they will be on Jason if he does not belt up. Can we please talk about something else?'

'What could be more interesting than me?'

'Tim's exhibition,' replies Hermann. 'The do at Marty's place later. Niall in LA. Marty and Niall splitting up. The weather. Graham's jacket. Anything.'

'Seat free over there,' Col says to Graham. 'Haul up a pew.'

Graham nods. He drags a wooden chair across to the table and nudges himself into a space between Tim and Col. He tells himself that it's only because of Jason's news or them taking the piss out of his jacket, but he knows, definitely, resolutely, with an unshakable certainty, that this sinking feeling in his gut is nature's way of warning him that, whatever happens tonight, he's going to find it difficult to chat to, far less up, Audrey, who's still ensconced with Sue. By this time, a swordsman like Rob or Ian would be sitting beside her and making her wide eyed and wet with some spiel. But how is it done? What do you say? Can I get you a . . . What's a lovely lady like you . . . What do you want for breakfast? Will the keys to my Porsche fit in your handbag? Graham finishes his Guinness. Twenty years on, and he still doesn't have a fucking clue. He gives the table a couple of slaps. 'Come on, then, Jason,' he announces. 'Tequilas all round.'

'I mean, how can they need a second runway?' says Ruth.

'Bizarre,' says Ben.

'I mean.' Ruth screws up her face. 'Manchester.'

'Bizarre,' says Ben.

'I didn't even know they *had* an airport in Manchester,' says Ruth.

Ben studies his wire-thin roll-up. 'It's bizarre,' he says.

Briony, who's been getting a bit twitchy, on account of not having said anything for nearly a minute, gives her jowls a quick shake of outrage. 'Just typical,' she mutters.

Of what? Ian thinks. The military-industrial complex? A cement-addicted patriarchy? Manchester? He pushes his chair back. ''Scuse me,' he mutters. 'Loo.' Ian smiles to show that this isn't an obvious pretext to escape. Which, of course, it is. Similarly, as he passes Claire, he gives her shoulder a gentle squeeze to show that he's not at all pissed off.

When he reaches the bathroom and closes the door, Ian shuts his eyes and expels a sigh. Not for the first time tonight, he thinks about the wrap in his wallet. He mustn't and he won't. One, it would be against his rule of charlie-free weekends (or at least Saturdays and Sundays, though not including Sunday evenings, obviously); two, he's vowed to be extra nice to Claire tonight; and three, if he had a line now, there's every chance he'd pick an argument with Ruth or ask Ben why he is such a tosser or tell Briony to do everyone a favour and get herself laid.

Ian has a dribbly piss, for form's sake, then gives his hands and face a long and thorough wash. His performance this evening has been, though he says it himself, nothing short of heroic. Two and a half hours of looking concerned and amused and *interested*, as Claire, Ruth and fucking Briony exchanged news and views about their contemporaries at Sussex, before Ruth and Ben, Ruth's new boyfriend, took charge to lament the pollution levels in eastern Europe, then to provide a day-by-day report on their recent holiday (presumably after a journey by eco-friendly clipper or canoe) in Bali, and now to debate the destruction of the Lancashire rainforest.

But it's not just the sheer, screaming boredom, Ian reflects, as he applies the towel to the skin between each finger, of listening to those three twerps congratulate themselves for being the first people, in the entire history of Western civilisation, to be truly enlightened and caring. It's not just the boredom, is it? Or even the background anxiety about Claire being pally with them. No. It's not. It's also that this evening, he, who has never felt intimidated by or estranged from youth, for he is just about the coolest person he knows (with the possible exception of Rob, but Rob's cool in a designer-suity sort of way), has been made to feel like a backbench Tory. Even when the conversation turned, briefly, to music there was no respite. He'd ventured a liking for the Prodigy – cool enough, you'd think, but no, there had been an uncomfortable silence and Briony had looked at him as if he'd just sung the praises of capital punishment or the M25.

Truth to tell, another hour of this lot and he'll be all set to campaign for the return of National Service. He already wants to tell Ruth (allegedly an actress/singer), Ben (who describes himself as a film-maker, if you please) and Briony (who has an undefined and part-time involvement in a holistic bakery) to get off their arses and find proper fucking jobs, in a building society or a shoe shop. Yeah, but why should they do that when there are mummies and daddies to fund Ruth's workshops, Ben's supply of beanie hats, Briony's eating disorder?

It's almost time to leave the sanctuary. He folds the towel into a neat rectangle and carefully adjusts it so that it hangs over the rail in equal lengths. And, come on, admit it – there's another thing below and beyond all that. Yes. There is. And it's the inescapable fact that when Briony, Ruth and Ben – and Claire, let's not forget Claire – uttered their first cries of dismay at being ejected into a wicked, Sunblest-eating, tree-felling, tarmac-loving world, he could already recite the verbs that take *être* and all the words on *Transformer*. So it is within the realms of biological possibility, perfectly conceivable in fact, that all four of those people crammed around the card-table could be his children.

Time to go back.

'Which is what I'm saying,' Ben is saying. 'If you think about it, it's really bizarre.'

Ian smiles broadly and sits down. 'What're we talking about?'

'*Friends*,' says Claire.

'The people who were at Sussex with you?'

'No,' says Ben patiently. 'It's a series on television.'

Be cool, he thinks, because this is a chance to show willing. He's seen *Friends*. He knows *Friends*. He likes *Friends*. 'Great,' he says. 'The sharpness of the script in *Friends*, you just don't get that in . . .' He's spotted Briony rolling her eyes at Ruth.

'Ah,' says Ruth.

When Briony speaks, it is with some show of doing so more in sorrow than in anger. 'Ben was just saying how *Friends* is actually really racist.'

Ian tries to catch Claire's eye but she's studying the remains of her *salade niçoise*. 'There aren't any black characters in *Friends*,' says Ian, bamboozled.

'Bizarre,' says Ben, who is being ironic.

Excellent, thinks Alastair, who is lying on the sofa and still savouring the memory of his main course – half a Marks and Sparks broccoli quiche, Marks and Sparks new potatoes, Marks and Sparks rocket salad with shavings of Marks and Sparks Parmesan. And the Fleurie turned out to be a really good choice. Went well with the quiche, and it'll be downright splendid with a few slithers of the Brie and the *chèvre*. Alastair pours himself a second glass which will last him the hour before *Match of the Day* at half-ten.

With his tummy full and his current favourite (*Northern Exposure 2*, mixed by Sasha and John Digweed) on the CD player, Alastair could quite happily spend the next hour stretched out on the sofa. Then again, a wee wander out to the garden might be just the thing. Ooh, yes. A wee wander.

Alastair swings his legs round and on to the floor. He picks up his glass of wine and the ashtray with its one spent joint. Now he walks slowly, and with heartfelt appreciation of the back bit's table and chairs, through and down into the kitchen. The pans are glistening on their hooks. The freesias look and smell terrific. And the garden . . . well, he considers as he steps outside, the garden is in fine form. He has another sip of the Fleurie and gives his shoulders a little squirm of pleasure. Mind you, it's not warm, is it? However, that could promise a clear, starlit night. He looks up at the sky, hoping that he might be stoned enough to get that feeling of staring into the endless black space of this little part of the universe. But there's only one dot of light, low to the south. Must be a planet. No sign of the moon yet. Nights like this must have been really scary before electricity.

As it is . . . Alastair looks back at the spotlit kitchen, which provides a sight so cosy that, just for a moment, he can't resist imagining the picture being completed by a woman, a sweet and beautiful woman, standing at the window and beckoning him in . . . But such moments are dangerous, so Alastair reminds himself to count his blessings. Health, home, some sort of peace of mind . . . And if his emotional life might sound a bit threadbare to some – no wife, no partner, no girlfriend of any description, no children, no siblings, one parent four hundred miles away – then at least it's not the tangled mess some chaps his age have blithely created. And he does have his friends. Rob. Barry. Keith and Joanna back home. Bill (another Friday Night Clubber, though long since emigrated to York, so very much a phone and now e-mail friend). Gary, even since he swapped the subs desk at the *Chronicle* for a snazzy office in Soho as chief sub of a travel glossy. A few others. Ian and Graham now, in their way. Mainly Rob, though. Who's always been a talented entertainments officer and anecdote-teller, but who has, in more recent years, also acquired the abilities – rare in men, Alastair reckons – to ask and listen. Which no doubt helps explain Rob's ever-burgeoning popularity, probably his salary hikes too, and definitely the swoonings of his women. Rob's just one of those people who have a gift for friendship, and that he has bestowed that gift on him, Alastair, has always seemed an enormous stroke of good luck. And this London part of their friendship, with Rob letting him in on his life of snazzy bachelordom, has almost let him not notice the lack of a close female friend, like Fiona was at school or Cathy. (Yes, and who's he got to blame for that lack? Nobody but himself.)

Maybe it's him getting so accustomed to this life, but it's got to the point where it's no longer a girlfriend but a girl (new word) friend he's after. Although, granted, there are those times when he aches with frustration or worries what to do for holidays, or daft things even, like having to go to parties on his own and walking in and fearing that people will look at him and think, Which is it? Little boys? Rubber frocks? Farmyard accident? But at least he's safe now, safe from harm, and November 1988 is nearly a nine-year-old memory, old enough for him to remember the split-up with Rhona and the Incident with Cathy, and not spend the next hour rocking back and forward and moaning to himself. No. It's all right. It's okay.

Alastair gives himself a shake, does a couple of stretches and lets the joint kick in again. Sure enough, the pang soon gives way to a rush of happiness so full that it almost aches. Last night might have been disappointing, even by the standards of the new FNC – five minutes in the Pig and Whistle, five minutes watching Graham fail to get Rob on the mobile, five minutes hanging shiftily around the reception area of Soho House before they had to accept that Rob wasn't there, that his membership couldn't have been processed yet and that there was no way past the girl in reception, and forty minutes on a grim Tube filled with young, loud drunks – but this more than makes up for it.

Maybe he should have another joint and get really stoned before *Match of the Day*. Ach, but then he won't remember half of it. No, a top-up of Fleurie, that's the ticket. And go back inside to the warmth.

He reaches the sofa in time for the CD to have reached 'Reeferendum' by someone or some people called Fluke, a track which can, if he's not in quite the right mood, sound a bit samey, even to him, but which can often, as now, inspire complete joy. Those drums, that bass line, and now those high arpeggios . . . just as well the curtains are closed, for he's up off the sofa again and dancing.

Who would have thought it, thinks Alastair, as he sets the CD-player for a second go of 'Reeferendum' and puts the volume up another notch. Him at thirty-six and a fan of house, dancing like a maddie around the sofa. A fan from the moment he first heard the thudding bass, when Rob persuaded him along to a club in Clerkenwell, his first year down here that must have been, early '89 maybe, and, despite feeling like a vicar at an orgy, he found himself quick-marching on the spot and nodding as if in eager agreement with the sternum-shaking beat.

Now what would the Alastair of fifteen or even ten years ago have thought about the 1997 Alastair's devotion to this music? It's a question that brings 1997 Alastair to a halt and back on to the sofa. 'This is the sound of the future,' he explains to 1987 Alastair. 'Machine made. And you see,' Alastair expounds to his former self, 'the beauty of house music is that it's simple and formulaic but in a way that allows for complexity. Basic hammering beat but lots of beats within that, basic chords but layers of stuff all kept in place by the simple patterns. Like baroque. Except baroque doesn't make you want to dance.'

But then, 1997 Alastair reflects, snuggling deeper into the sofa as the daydream conversation promises to develop as it usually does, that's what life is like now. Modern life is brilliant, isn't it? He settles into an even comfier position, for this is his favourite theme, one he can warm to at the most mundane moments, let alone a blissed-out Saturday night with *Northern Exposure 2* on the CD and *Match of the Day* coming up. There's a rattle at the back door and a moment later Susie pads into the room.

What it is, he reckons, is that we're all so used to thinking that things are getting worse and worse, and will only continue faster and faster down the slippy slope to global cataclysm, that nobody's noticed that things are actually getting better and better and better. And if anybody has paid attention to the development of democracy or anaesthetic or the near-doubling of the average lifespan this century, then nobody gets fully enthusiastic about it because optimism sounds foolish or, at the very least, like it's asking for trouble. Susie settles down by the telly, shoves a hindleg in the air like a gymnast and embarks on some energetic grooming.

'It's all a matter of social evolution,' Alastair tells Susie. 'Despite everything that everybody assumes, life is gentler and nicer than in the old days, because we're not desperate for food or shelter, so instead of stealing each other's livestock or walking around with our sword arms free, we get on with each other because we've got more to lose by being nasty.' Yes, and more to gain by taking part in the great venture of a civilisation that has given even someone like him, Alastair, the opportunity to live in complete comfort, earn an annual salary of thirty-six thousand of your Earth pounds, eat great food, drink wonderful wine, smoke quality spliff, watch brilliant TV, and listen to great music courtesy of an eminently affordable piece of technology which reproduces that music perfectly. Key question: is there any other time in the history of humankind when he, Alastair, would rather have lived? Only possible answer: absolutely not. Of course, he wouldn't mind having a go at living in the future, because now that we've reached the stage of peaceful, co-operative, scientifically advanced social democracy, things could really take off from here. Yes, everything's on schedule for the millennium. This really could be the dawning of a new era.

'So ask me,' Alastair demands of the room and 1987 Alastair, 'about what things are like now.'

'All right,' he replies. 'What about politics?'

'Thatcher's long gone and out of her box, Reagan likewise, Labour's in on a landslide, it's looking good for peace in Northern Ireland and devolution back home.'

'Foreign affairs?' he asks himself.

'The Lebanon's fine so it just disappeared from the news one day, the hostages were all freed, Arafat's for peace, Nelson Mandela was released and now he's President.'

Impressive enough, but now it's time for the big one. 'The USSR?' he asks.

'No such thing,' he replies. 'The Soviet Union collapsed, so now there's Russia and a million separate republics, no more Iron Curtain, there were people's revolutions all over eastern Europe when democracy triumphed and hardly anyone died apart from the Ceausescus, the Berlin Wall came down, Germany's been reunified, there's no more Warsaw Pact and in fact they all want to join NATO.'

'Goodness,' he says as Stunned of 1987. 'So there hasn't been a nuclear war?'

'No,' he says. 'And there's no longer any threat of one. Okay, granted,' he concedes, 'there could well be a local disaster or a loon like Saddam Hussein might explode a nuclear device, but the end of the world isn't nigh.'

He stops to consider this point. No, the end of the world isn't nigh and the nightmares he used to have – of sleek, black bombers overhead and four minutes to find his way home – are a thing of the past.

'You know what people are really worried about now?' he asks.

'Tell me,' he says. 'The ozone layer?'

'A bit,' he says, 'but even that's not as worrying as it used to be.'

'So what's the anxiety now?' he prompts.

'You wouldn't believe it,' he says.

'Try me,' he says.

'I mean, it's so ridiculous it proves my point.'

'Okay,' he says, 'what's the big threat?'

'Asteroids. Hiya, Sooz.' Alastair dangles a hand for her to rub her cheek against. 'Oh, yes,' he says, for the CD is segueing into 'Purple' by Gus Gus and that fantastic vocal line which he has to sing along to. 'Ooooh oooh ah hah wah ha ha.' And *Match of the Day* in half an hour.

12

'SO YOU HAD HALF A BOTTLE'

Sunday morning

'Yeah, right.'

'Honestly, Claire, I wasn't anywhere near drunk. What were the empties? One bottle of claret, two bottles of white.'

'Yeah, like I was really knocking it back.'

'That still leaves four of us. That Ben guy had his fair share, and Briony isn't one to hold . . .'

'Don't you start about Briony.'

'I'm not starting about Briony. All I'm saying is . . .'

'You've said quite enough in the past about Briony.'

Not true, Ian thinks. Not true by a damned sight. 'Hey,' he says brightly, 'do we need any washing-up liquid?'

''Course we need washing-up liquid.' No sign of the vile mood she's been in for the past few days disappearing. He might as well have asked her if they need to breathe air.

'I think it's back a few aisles. You stay here, I'll go and fetch it.' Times like this, Ian thinks, a cigarette would help – and he'd be able to scoot outside and leave her to do the Sainsbury's thing on her own.

He walks back, past walls of bread and bog rolls and biscuits. When he returns, Claire is holding up a large bottle of extra-virgin olive oil and scrutinising it from every conceivable angle.

'Can't afford it,' she decides, and bangs the bottle back on the shelf. Next thing, she'll be over at the pyramid of baked beans on special offer, yanking out a couple of cans from the bottom row.

'There you go,' Ian says, placing a tube of Fairy into the trolley.

'Okay, so you had half a bottle. But you certainly made the most of it.'

'Claire, what does that mean?'

'It means, Ian, it means that there has got to be a song and dance about the wine, hasn't there?' She holds a hand in front of her mouth, four fingers circling to her thumb. 'Noat as gid as the eighty-tooo,' she squeaks, 'but ah think yeel bee amyooosed by the noaz.'

He retains enough self-control to wonder if an accurate piss-take would make him feel crushed rather than enraged. As it is . . . He spends a few moments surveying the contents of their trolley. Pasta, coffee, apples, bananas, a bag of spinach, four pink bricks of salmon, a cellophaned box of potatoes, the tube of Fairy . . . 'Claire, it's not often we get the chance to drink nice wine, and I haven't had a good Bordeaux for . . .'

She puts her head to one side. 'Aye, aye, fur a gid fyoo yeerz.'

'Please, Claire. Don't do this.'

She must judge that she's gone far enough because she begins to pay particular attention to a nearby jar of mustard. Although she does make sure that he can overhear her muttering 'eighty-two' with a smirk of contempt.

He has to be big about this. 'I'm sorry, Claire. I did try my best. I know they're your friends and I . . .'

'Hah! That reminds me.'

'What?'

'Nothing.'

Neil Hamilton has no chance of a new career on telly. Dublin is urging the IRA to keep to the ceasefire. Kirkcaldy's great man in number eleven plans a surprise bonus for the elderly. American economists are talking about a golden age of low inflation and high growth.

Alastair is eating toast and scanning the Sunday papers spread out in front of him on the sitting-room floor – his weekly concession to chaos, but it's a jumble that he can easily tolerate because he'll have cleared it all up by four. By which time he will also have done the vacuuming, had a look-see round the garden and phoned his father. Because by four o'clock, according to Alastair's traditional Sunday plan, he'll be back lying on this sofa, a glass and a bottle of Highland Spring on the coffee table, an ashtray on his tummy and a joint in his hand, ready to watch Liverpool–Newcastle live on Sky.

Now he takes another bite of toast and has a quick look at the *Sunday Mirror*. Ginger Spice has been wearing a partly see-through dress. Alastair discards the *Mirror* and picks up the *Observer*. 'Aitken to face trial,' says a headline. Alastair sips his Earl Grey. This is the life.

'Is this Graham?'

'Eh . . . yeah.' Christ, where did that growl come from?

'Friend of Bobby's, right?'

Graham yawns, rubs his eyes and tries to force his brain into action. It's some woman, she's got one of those Londonish accents that vaguely posh English folk acquire in an effort not to sound vaguely posh, and he hasn't a fucking clue who she is or what the fuck she is on about. 'Aw-way,' he says through another ear-popping yawn. 'Christ,' he says when the yawn is finally over. 'Bobby. Who's Bobby?'

'Oh, *damn* it.' Whoever this woman is seems to take a deep breath. 'Is this oh one eight one, three four two five eight nine one?'

'Eh, yes. Aye, it is.' Graham scoops gunk out of the corner of each eye, but he still can't focus. He shuts his right eye and peers at the can of Spray-Mount beside the phone. Okay. Now he closes his left eyelid. The lettering on the can of Spray-Mount and everything else in the world blurs. Someone's smeared Vaseline over his right eyeball. Then shat in his mouth. He shies away from the phone to avoid the reflection of his own halitosis when he says, 'What do you want?' He immediately regrets the rather brusque tone, because he's just had a startling thought. 'Wait. I'm sorry. Is that you, Audrey?'

'Audrey? No, no, my name's Louise. Louise Turner. You might have heard about me from Bobby.'

Count to ten, Graham urges himself. He reaches four and gives up. Losing his rag won't help him get back to sleep, but there's no other option. 'Look,' he says. 'I haven't heard of you, I don't know any Bobby, you've got the wrong number *and* you've woken me up *and* I've got a fucking terrible fucking hangover. So, please, please, *please*, whoever the *fuck* you are, fucking fuck *off*.'

'Don't hang up, don't hang up. All right, Graham, you don't know me, but I've got your telephone number here and you do know Bobby. Bobby Mackenzie. Scottish, lives in Soho, good chum of yours, *that* Bobby Mackenzie.'

Until this moment, Graham had thought that the act of holding the telephone away to examine it when being told surprising news was one of those things people did only in films, like leaving a car unlocked or falling in love with a suspect. He returns the phone to the side of his face. 'You mean Rob. Rob Mackenzie.'

'Whatever. Jeez. Yes.'

'What about Rob? Oh, fuck, wait a minute, is he all right?'

'That's the thing. I really don't know.'

Part Two

1

'VERY ODD INDEED'

Sunday lunch-time

It's a joke.

It's because of him being the fretful sort. And Bateman Street looking unusually empty. And Friday Night Club, or three-quarters of it, meeting up on a Sunday afternoon. That's why he feels that someone has blow-dried his mouth and scooped out his stomach with a spoon. Certainly not because he's suddenly acquired a paranormal ability to detect impending doom. No, this definitely has to be a practical joke.

Alastair crosses the narrow street yet again to look up yet again at the three windows of Rob's flat. He can still see only a tiny corner of the sitting room's ceiling.

However. This is some sort of a prank, no more than that. Like the time when Rob spiked Jimbo's tea.

Still only twenty to. Perhaps he could kill some more time by getting himself another coffee at Bar Italia. No. He'll wait for the others in the pub, order a rare lunch-time pint, and grab a table at the back where they'll be able to talk in peace.

It's definitely a joke.

This makes absolutely no sense whatsoever. *Nada. Rien.* Were he a betting man, Ian would lay a couple of quid on this being the result of Graham being crap, as usual. Some woman phones up and Graham gets the wrong end of the stick, grabs the stick and starts whacking people round the head with it. 'Fucking Rob's done a fucking bunk. Meet me at the Pig at one' – what kind of a message is that to leave on an answerphone? A normal message, Ian supposes, if your brain has been addled by alcohol and self-abuse. Or maybe Graham actually got a ride off that girl he was seeing last night and his synapses exploded with the shock.

Ian turns into a strangely underpopulated and carless Old Compton Street. He overtakes a Japanese couple dawdling without a clue about how to occupy the long hours of a tourist's London Sunday and dodges past a group of bleary young ravers wearing jumpers with zips and hoods. Whatever they've been on to keep them swigging from their little bottles of Evian until ten to one the next afternoon, he could fair go a shot of it. And not a care in the world, the lucky little bastards.

He's early and Graham is bound to be late and an espresso would hit the spot, so Ian loiters for a moment outside the Bar Italia but then he picks up the pace again. He's edgy enough after this morning's performance by Claire. Plus he has the feeling that simply by being in the Pig and Whistle he'll somehow get this daft business over and done with all the sooner. Ian hurries up Frith Street and into the pub.

'Ian.'

'Oh, hi, Eck. Get you a drink?' Ian says from the bar.

'Grassy arse, but I'm fine with this.'

'Sure? Pint of lager, please . . . So. Any sign of Graham?'

'Not yet.'

'Big surprise.'

'It's a wind-up. Like when Rob spiked Jimbo's tea. A wind-up.'

'Ah. Got you. So Rob hasn't turned up yet and this is your theory, that it's a practical joke.'

'Has to be.'

'Some joke. This mystery woman, is she coming?'

'According to Graham. He said she'd be a bit late, though.'

'Probably beat Graham to it by a good day or two. Rob ever say anything to you about her?'

Alastair shakes his head. This wordless reply seems to set a precedent. Ian settles into refining his fantasy monologue wherein he puts Claire to rights ('You want us to spend a Saturday evening with your pals so I spend a Saturday evening with your pals. You want me to go to Sainsbury's with you, so what happens? Correct.') so the silence is ended only by one of Alastair's coughs. 'It's all very odd,' Alastair says.

Ian replies with a nod. '*Then*,' continues the monologue inside his head, 'you spring the news on me that we're to be trekking up to Stanmore for Sunday lunch with your parents, and for once I say no, because (a) it's the first *I've* heard of it, (b) how am I supposed get from Stanmore to St John's Wood in time for my freelance class and (c) there's this Rob business to deal with.'

'Very odd indeed,' says Alastair eventually.

'Yes,' says Ian. He flips a beer-mat. Maybe it's just the pregnancy. Weird hormones or something. Well, whatever's up with Claire, he could really do without it.

Just what the fuck is Rob playing at? And just who the fuck is the bird on the phone? And how the fuck is he supposed to get through the day feeling like microwaved shite? As if his life isn't full enough of questions – what's he going to do without Jenny? Is she being screwed? Who by? – that make him feel like he's been hoiked in off the pavement, the crook of some bastard's umbayfuckingrella round his neck, and forced to sit an algebra exam. But you never know – maybe a pint and a chat is all it'll take to sort out his hangover and this Rob thing. If only the big ones had such straightforward answers. Graham pushes open the door and sees Ian and Eck staring glumly into space at the back of the pub.

'Graham, you're only five minutes late. This must be serious.'

'Hi, Graham. Any news?'

'Eck, what am I? The magic man? We'll have to wait on this bird to turn up.'

'It's a wind-up. Like Jimbo's tea.'

'The fuck you talking about, Eck?'

'The time when Rob put a tab of acid in Jimbo's tea.'

'Uh-huh.'

'And Jimbo started tripping when he was refereeing a rugby match. Remember? He tried to swim down the pitch because he thought the second fifteen were sharks.'

There are times, and this is one of them, when Graham wonders if anything has happened to the wee man since 1978. 'Aye, Eck, I do mind that, oddly enough, but I don't see that there's much fucking comparison between spiking a gym teacher's tea and doing a fucking runner. If that's what Rob has done. Fuck knows. Only thing I know for certain is that I'm off to the bar. Anyone? No? Suit yourselves.'

While he waits for his pint, Graham tells himself to stop being het up because there's got to be a simple explanation for all of this. That bird has to have something to do with it . . . He'll look back on this moment and wonder at how daft he was not to realise what was going on. This part of the proceedings is just like whenever he lost something as a kid and could only assume that the object had been stolen with a top-secret ray gun.

Graham carries his pint back to the table with a relatively steady hand. Ian's flipping a beer-mat. Eck looks like he's trying to add up several six-figure numbers in his head.

'Right, then,' says Graham, because somebody's got to take charge here. 'Time to compare notes. I haven't seen Rob since last Friday. Or heard from him. Anyone improve on that?'

'Nup,' says Ian. 'I've left a few messages on his answerphone, but I haven't heard from him since we left his flat and took him to the cashpoint.'

'I'm surprised you remember that much, fucking state you were in.'

'Same with me, Graham. I haven't had any contact with him since last FNC. Well, not Friday's Friday Night Club but the Friday before that, the last proper one. I mean . . . And he was fine then, wasn't he? In fact, he was on pretty good form, as I recall. Before he lost it. He was going on about the football on Eurosport, remember?' Eck lets out a nasal laugh. 'And a man jumping,' he quotes, in a poor approximation of a commentator's expectant tone. 'In the air.'

Graham samples his pint and suppresses a shudder. 'So none of us have seen or heard from him for over a week. Nine days if you include today. And none of us had a scooby that anything was amiss, right?'

'Right,' says Ian.

'Let's suppose,' says Eck, 'that Rob has gone away somewhere. Where would he go? And why?'

'Christ knows where,' says Ian. 'But if he really has gone away some place for longer than a fortnight, and that's a very big if, the why part would be pretty obvious.'

'Is that so? And what obvious fucking reason is that, oh sudden expert on missing persons?'

Ian shrugs. 'The reason most people do a bunk. They're pissed off with the life they have so they decide to have a shot at another one. Guy has enough of doing the same thing day in day out, tells the wife he's popping out for a packet of fags, comes back twenty years later to say he's been shacked up with a series of nymphets in the Seychelles. Happens all the time. Thousands every year.'

'Aye,' says Graham, 'but why should Rob be one of them?'

'*If*,' says Eck with unEckian emphasis, '*if* he's done this for real, then he must be in some serious trouble. Why else would he just give up all the things he's got? His flat, his friends, his . . . his *life* . . .'

Graham has another go at his pint. That's better. 'What I think is this,' he says. 'It's got to be woman trouble. Specially with a champion shagger like Rob. He'll turn up in a day or two with a story about being chased by some husband with a shotgun. Tell you one thing. I bet this female knows a lot more than she let on to me.'

Ian nods his head. 'Here's my theory, right? Rob's written her a letter to give her the push and she's got it completely wrong. Wouldn't be the first time a woman has mistaken being chucked for the end of the world. Won't be the last.'

'Well,' says Graham, 'this looks like our chance to find out.'

Ian leans forward. 'The girl that's just come in? How do you know it's her?'

'Male intuition,' says Graham. 'That and the fact that she's the only bird in the place. Aye. Must be her. Either that, or Eck's just pulled.'

'Excuse me, are you three Bobby's friends?'

Bobby again, notes Graham. Bobby. Yeuch. Mind you, Rob was a fairly noncey name for the man to pick for himself as well. Why not be like the other Roberts from back home who were Rabs or Rabbies or . . . Roberts? Eck's stood up and offered a hand for her to shake, registering too late that she is holding a little bag in one hand and a bottle of Becks in the other. Graham looks on benevolently as the wee man tries to adapt the gesture by gallantly beckoning her towards the spare seat. That's the great thing about Eck – he can make every bloke in his vicinity feel like Omar Sharif.

His footering around has also given Graham the chance to size this one up. Only five two, five three, something like that, and a bit of a skinnymalink, so she's much smaller than he assumed that, for no reason other than that she's one of Rob's, she would be, but she's got a nice enough face framed by dark, wavy hair, biggish brown eyes, slim nose, and, unless she's sooking a secretive sweetie, good cheekbones. Not a stunner, by any means, but she wouldn't frighten any horses. Black, high-lapelled jacket, white T-shirt, black clingy trousers with a touch of the flare about them. How old is she? Time was when he could confidently pinpoint someone's age, particularly a female's, but that's a knack that seems to have disappeared as he's got older, together with an ability to run more than fifty yards and first-thing-in-the-morning hard-ons, to name but two, and he has to settle for mid to late twenties. She sits down beside him and raises her bottle in an ironic toast.

'Hello. My name is Louise,' she says. 'And I'm an alcoholic.'

Lassie's obviously joking but the Eckster's all over the shop. 'Oh,' he says. 'I'm. That's.' Fucksake.

She gives Eck a quick smile. 'Not really.'

'Oh. Right. Ha. Well, it's very good to meet you. Though not under such . . . I'm Alastair. And this is Ian. And this . . .'

'Is Graham,' says Graham.

'Charmed, I'm sure. Well.' She puts her bottle down. 'This is a to-do.'

Eck coughs. 'Graham mentioned a note,' he says. 'I don't want to be rude but do you think that you might, that we could . . . have a look at it? I mean, if you haven't got it, that's fine, but . . .'

'Don't worry. Sorry, Alexander, is it?'

'Alastair.'

'Alastair. Dizzy little thing that I am, by some miracle I did remember to bring it.'

'Sorry. I didn't mean.'

'Chill. It's in here.' She pulls her bag up on to her lap. It's a little leather backpack, of the kind that's obligatory in Shoreditch and which Graham always thinks would do just fine for a hiker who is three years old. She fiddles around in the miniature rucksack. 'There you go,' she says. 'For what it's worth.' She flourishes a scrap of paper with little ripped ribbons still clinging to the perforated edges and waggles it with a grimace. 'All the charm of a square of loo roll. Then again, I don't suppose I was ever going to have it framed. Here.' She hands the scrap to Graham. Ian and Alastair move in from either side so that they can read with him.

Louise – I can't go on. By the time you read this I will have started a new life with a new name in a new place. Don't waste your time trying to find me. Any queries, ask my lawyer – he's called Maddox. 826 3436.

Ian is first to look up. 'That's it?'

'Yip.'

'Where did you find it?'

'Shoved under my door. First thing I saw when I got back this morning. I'll say this for Bobby, his timing's pretty good, because this has cured my jet-lag. I'm just in from New York,' she explains in reply to Ian's unspoken question.

'Wait a minute,' says Graham. 'Can you talk us through exactly what happened?'

'I might skip the bit about waiting in a long queue for a taxi, if you don't mind, but here goes. I get back from the States, okay? Must have been about nine by the time I opened my front door. This note was lying on my hallway carpet, no envelope, no nothing. I figured it must be some kind of pissy joke so I went up to Bobby's flat to, I don't know, give him a fright back or . . .'

Ian's shaking his head. 'Let's put the brakes on. You say you went up to Bobby's, Rob's flat?'

'Spot on, Sherlock. That'll be because his flat's the one above mine.'

'Oh,' say Ian and Graham. Eck's too busy looking at her blankly to say anything.

'Oh,' she says in return. 'I see. Not only have you never heard of me, you didn't know that his girlfriend has the flat downstairs?'

It's as Graham suspected. She does think that she's Rob's girlfriend.

'You went up to his flat,' Ian prompts quickly, presumably in case Eck says something obvious and devastating.

'Yeah, up to his flat, and everything was normal except there was no sign of Bobby. At first I assumed I wasn't thinking straight, with the jet-lag and all, so I went back to my place, made myself a cup of tea and read the note about a thousand times. Then I phoned Barbara.'

Ian raises his eyebrows. 'And Barbara is . . . ?'

'My mother.'

'Right.'

'And she said if I was so bothered, why didn't I phone the police. So I did. There's a copper coming round to see me later. More of an exercise in being seen to be nice than anything else, I imagine. The man I talked to, he must have been the desk sergeant or something, he told me not to worry, happens all the time, give Bobby a couple of days and he'll be back with his tail between his legs. But he would say that, wouldn't he? . . . Then I went back up to Bobby's to have a look around.'

Ian swirls lager round his glass. 'And what did you find? I mean, is there anything unusual or odd about the place?'

'No. That's just it.'

'What's just it?'

'I didn't find anything unusual or odd or, weirder still, missing.'

'But that has to be a good sign,' Eck says eagerly. 'Maybe he's just popped out. Or gone away for a couple of days.'

She takes a deep breath. 'A tremendously good point. If you ignore the existence of this shitty little note. And if you were popping out or going away for a couple of days, what would you take with you? I'll tell you what you would take, Alastair. You would take your wallet, yes? A change of clothes. Your passport if you were popping out to a foreign clime. Maybe your shaving stuff and things to clean your teeth. But his wardrobe's full and all his stuff is still there. Keys, wallet, credit cards, passport, cheque book, razor, the lot. 'Course, he could have packed a suitcase with a couple of shirts and a book or two and I might not be any the wiser, but it would have to be a new suitcase since the three I know about are still under the bed. Far as I can make out, everything of Bobby's is still there. Intact. It's as if he's just vanished. Or been abducted by those aliens with big heads and slanty eyes.' She takes a sip of her Becks. 'Being a great one for looking on the bright side, I like to think that the note at least proves that he isn't having a medical on an intergalactic spacecraft. So next thing, I spotted his address book. I decided to go through it, see if there were any names I recognised or at least of people I could call, and there under A was an entry for someone just called Graham in capital letters, so I guessed that person had to be a fairly good friend. Then I phoned. And here we all are.'

Aye, well. One thing, she's certainly keen on the sound of her own voice. 'What about this Maddox?' Graham asks. 'Has he told you anything?'

'No, be . . .'

'Fucksake. I bet he gave you some confidentiality shit. Could you not have asked him questions that were kind of indirect? Or maybe waited till he went out the room and had a peek at his files?'

'Not possible, I'm afraid.'

'How come?'

'This is Sunday.'

'Ah.'

'I thought that the event fell into the long-queue-for-a-taxi category, but first thing I did when I got this . . . note was dial that number, but of course there was only an answerphone saying the office was closed. I'll give him a call first thing tomorrow morning. Now, can I take my turn and ask you chaps a question?'

'Hey. Sure.'

'Fucking bash on.'

'Fine, of course, we'd be glad to be of . . .'

'Do any of you have any idea what the hell is going on?'

'Well,' says Graham, 'us three really are completely in the fucking dark.'

'Really? Bobby never said anything? Didn't give any of you the teensiest hint that something was wrong?'

'Nup,' says Ian. 'Like we were just saying, he was fine when we saw him last Friday. There's been no sign that he was about to do a Reggie Perrin. I mean, we're not hiding anything from you if that's what you think.'

She gives Ian a bemused look. 'Reggie who?'

'Thing is,' says Graham quickly to prevent Eck launching into what would probably be a comprehensive summary of Leonard Rossiter's career, 'thing is, we don't know anything about what Rob's done or why. We've never even known anything about you. And until this morning, you didn't know that us three existed. Or that your Bobby is actually called Rob. Far as I can see, none of us know anything about anything.'

She delves into her toddler's backpack again and brings out a packet of Marlboro, removes the last cigarette and crumples the packet slowly in her fist. 'Then again,' she says, 'that's just our starting point, isn't it? From here on in, all we can do is learn. And not only what's happened to Bobby but, perhaps, valuable lessons about ourselves. From this experience, we will grow. As friends and as human beings.' She drops the packet in the ashtray and lights her cigarette.

They all study the mangled packet. 'You're joking, right?' asks Ian.

'Duh.' She blows out a thread of smoke which whorls into a shaft of sunlight. 'Now, I don't want to come on too strong to you boys, but what do you say we all finish our drinks and go on somewhere else? I know a little place just along the road. A flat belonging to our mutual and absent friend.'

2

'WAS IT SOMETHING I SAID?'

Sunday afternoon

Over two hours now they've been pottering around Rob's flat and all for nothing, as far as Ian can see. The place is exactly as it always is – tidy, clean, tasteful in a clutter-is-so-uncool, minimalisty way. And the only thing missing is Rob. Being in Rob's flat without Rob there definitely got to everyone at first – the four of them moving slowly and together from room to room, surveying the few items of furniture with an inhibition that reminded Ian of a Romanian tour group he once saw shuffling through Versailles. But then, to his astonishment, the other three got into their stride, and before you knew it were ransacking cupboards like they were detectives with a warrant. Well over the top, if you ask him, and when Rob turns up in a couple of days' time, he's going to be really thrilled about having his flat turned over by a search party. Ten minutes it took them to transform Rob's two spruce bedrooms into sites for a jumble sale.

As if chucking shirts and jerseys and shoes all over the place would help solve a problem that doesn't exist. Because Rob's going to call up from Barbados or Sri Lanka and tell them about the wobbly he threw or the bender he's gone on. Or the grief he's been getting from this Louise. Because that's what's happened, he'd bet on that – Rob's had enough, just as he had enough when Cristina launched into a screaming fit of hyperneurotic violence spectacular even by Cristina's high standards, and he couldn't be arsed to reply but quietly and calmly packed his bags, shut the door gently behind him, and left Cristina to it.

Horse walks into a pub, orders a pint. Barman goes, 'Why the long face?' Fair enough, what Rob's done, if he really has done it, will take a bit of getting used to, but it's not as if the man is dead. And he'll probably be in touch soon when the dust has cleared. Or when he gets bored. But to look at Graham, Eck and that Louise, you'd think they'd found Rob in the shunkie, a bottle of whisky and a service revolver by his side, half his head staining the shower curtain. If you ask him, the others are maybe even getting off on this glum, fretful atmosphere, in the self-important way that people do get off on misery.

Behaviour that is all the more obviously ridiculous in a place where it's always been party time. Presumably there has been the odd occasion when Rob's had a quiet night in watching the telly but that's as easy to imagine as – he tries to think of something really unthinkable – okay, Eck pole-dancing.

Ian flumps down on the couch. By the sounds of it, the in-depth investigation has moved through to the kitchen. How much more of this is there going to be? And what should he do to keep himself occupied? Ian gazes at the room's only other item of furniture, not counting the TV or the sound system or the empty vase on the floor – the glass-topped coffee table in front of him. Granted, it's a Sunday afternoon and therefore, strictly speaking, against his rule, but this is kind of a special occasion. And this glass table might as well have come with a free razor blade and a rolled-up twenty. Not that Rob has ever been a great one for the cocaine, but he's certainly got the table for it.

Ian fetches out his wrap and tips a tiny pile of powder on to the table. There really is nothing quite like cutting out a line or two on a fuck-off, posh glass table. The man was into his grass, though. Jamaican weed, Thai stuff, skunk . . . God, yes, the skunk. Ian pauses, the straw held in his fingers like a pen as he remembers his first Friday night out in London with Rob and Graham. Eck popping in later. The first meeting of the new version of FNC, come to think of it. The night he also got chatting to that Spanish girl in the Pig and Whistle. Mih something? No. Meh, moh, mah, mah . . . Ian starts to sift the tiny pile into a pair of lines. Margarita? Maria? Nup . . . Marta – that was it. Marta. Very tidy little number. Marta. Anyway, the skunk. Just a couple of pencil-sized joints back here and they were all giggling like schoolgirls. Five minutes it had taken him to get up from the floor and stagger through to the shunkie (for what turned out to be a record-breaking piss), so he'd really had no option but to accept Rob's offer and stay the night in the spare bedroom. Sheets so clean and smooth that, according to his rather hazy memory of the event, he spent his few remaining minutes of consciousness gently writhing with the pleasure of their touch. Claire, of course, had gone ballistic the next evening when he finally made it back to Bonnington Square. Fair enough, so maybe he should have phoned, but the way she'd gone on he might as well have spent the night with his head clamped between that Marta's thighs. Now that, thinks Ian, is a thought.

Now that, thinks Graham, is a pretty fucking good view.

She's looking through one of the drawers in the sparse and spotless kitchen. Fortunately, the drawer is the second-lowest of the three in the unit beside the stainless-steel Tardis that is Rob's fridge, so she is bending down, allowing Graham to appraise her legs and arse. She is too thin, he decides, but at least the legs are straight and the arse has got a wee bit of a curve to it. Not enough shapeliness going on, though. Unlike, say, Jenny, who had excellent legs and a proper bum, one that could really fill a skirt . . . It got so that it became one of their bits of patter, her going all wide eyed and mock coquettish, twiddling an index finger against a cheekbone then bending from her waist to pick up a pretend something from the floor . . . Somehow, this thought soon evolves into a picture of Jenny doing her bending-over routine with someone else, which is such a fucking terrible image that he has to clutch hold of the shiny kitchen top for support.

With a triumphant 'ah-ha!', she pulls herself gracefully upright and turns round to show him her trove – a packet of ten cigarettes. She bends from her waist again, but only slightly this time and in profile as she lights one of the cigarettes on the shining black hob. She takes a puff, examines the packet, then looks enquiringly at him. 'Maybe you can tell me,' she says.

'Bash on.'

She shakes the packet. 'What exactly is the point of these?'

'Don't ask me, hen, I don't smoke. There is no point. Unless you really want to get cancer.'

'Fat chance of that. Silk Cut Ultra. I'd get a bigger hit from a pot of yoghurt.' She takes another long, scandalised suck on the cigarette.

'You're lucky to find any fags at all, I'd have thought.'

'Ah, no. This is the emergency supply, from the days when Mr Smooth always had a packet in the flat lest his latest victim smoked.' She gives him a sarky, cheesy smile. 'Or didn't smoke but might whimsically fancy a post-coital gasper. Not a source of comfort to me, I have to say, when I was in New York and trying to believe his declarations of undying fidelity. Silk Cut Ultra, though, I ask you . . . Was it something I said?'

'Er, no. No. It's, well . . .' Graham purses his lips and nods reflectively, hoping she'll assume that he's been afflicted by the strangeness of this Robless gathering, whereas what he's really struggling to cope with is the thought that Silk Cut Ultra was the brand Jenny used to smoke. Isn't there anything that won't remind him of her? Can't there be any escape from her ghost? Because here he is now seeing a naked Jenny puffing away in bed, grinning contentedly beside some big, hairy Bluto who's got one arm clasped round her shoulder and another reaching down to . . .

Graham mumbles that he's going through to the living room. Where he finds a handy distraction in the form of Ian crouched over the glass table.

'Fuck me, what a surprise. Would that big line of powder consist, by any chance, of a cocaine–Ajax mix?'

Ian surveys his handiwork with approval. 'It's a fair cop, guv. Got me bang to rights. Hey – you fancy one, Graham? Come on, it's a special occasion.'

The latest, Silk Cut-inspired ache leads Graham to toy with the notion, but then he reminds himself that, on the handful of occasions when he's taken cocaine, he has felt only anxious and agitated, at the cost of instant diarrhoea, sweaty palms, a cardboard tongue, an itchy scalp, and a nose so blocked up the next morning that he had to breathe through his mouth, like someone from Birmingham. A bargain at ten pence a molecule. 'I'll pass,' says Graham, though he does join Ian on the sofa.

While Ian pushes a straw over both lines, Graham picks through the small pile of magazines that have been left fanning the coffee table's shelf. Mostly *Economists*, but three issues of *Art Monthly* which come as a mildly intriguing surprise, a couple of *Vizes* which come as no surprise at all, a glossy magazine called *European Traveller* which last year had the fucking nerve to make him redo his illustration of a sun wearing sun-specs, and, sandwiched between a year-old *New Yorker* and an inexplicable *Elle*, Rob's curiously cheap-looking and skinny week-to-a-page diary.

'Heyheyheyhey,' says Ian. 'Rob's diary.'

Graham is too busy looking through the little black booklet to say anything sarcastic in return. Ian peers over Graham's shoulder for a very short while then, suddenly fed up with that game, gives up and breenges over to the other side of the room, to have a look through Rob's CDs and to sniff a lot.

Graham flicks through to this week's page. Only one entry and it's for today – 'L returns'. That Louisa, presumably. Next week's page? Blank. The week after? Blank. All the pages that follow – blank. Graham starts to flick back. Not counting today's, the diary's final entry is for the previous Friday – '8: FNC, Pig'. He turns back another page. Wednesday he met a J at 4. Friday there's the same – '8: FNC, Pig' (the night when they had the argument about Tony Blair and Eck did his usual Friday-night act, turning up after last orders). Graham flicks back another week. Sure enough, there they are again – '8.30: FNC, Pig' – and nothing else bar J for lunch at the Coach and Horses on the Tuesday. He tries to recall that Friday night – of course, the one here when Ian droned on about Barcelona's nightlife and Rob rolled those joints that made Graham feel he was being watched by a malevolent, supernatural power.

Graham riffles though another dozen or so pages. Not much in them, which is a bit surprising but also reassuring, because it's good to see that Rob's just about as unconscientious about that kind of thing as him, not that there's been too many top-level meetings and glamorous nights out for him to be not putting in his diary recently. Rob, though, he'd have put down as the meticulous type, but there's only a couple of entries a page. And the past few weeks, the ones that aren't the Friday Night Club are mostly afternoon or early-evening appointments with this J character.

Graham stares at the diary. Keep calm, he reminds himself. Keep calm. Then he forces himself to take another look, from the start. Quite a few Js earlier in the year, then a gap, then they appear every month or so, until the end of August. Then they start: '5.30: J's office', '6: J, Coach', '1: J, Dell'Ugo' . . .

Graham's throat produces a brief, low, constipated groan. J. Silk Cut Ultra. Her office handily placed a few hundred yards from this very flat.

J.

'That's me shooting the craw.'

'Graham. Are you okay?'

'Oh, aye, comm fucking pleetly tip fucking top. See you later, uh, Louisa.'

''Bye.'

''Bye, Graham. I hope you'll be all . . .' Alastair's farewell fades away, for Graham has already gone. The bedroom walls vibrate briefly as the flat's front door bangs shut.

Louise raises her eyebrows. 'I'm just guessing here but I think your friend might have left. Where's the other one?'

'Yo, guys, what's up, what's happening, what is occuring?' Ian marches in and bounces down on the end of the bed. He skims a hand over the duvet absent-mindedly then rubs his nose. He's clearly on edge. Well, no wonder. This is a strange and upsetting business.

'Incidentally, incidentally,' Ian announces. 'Found Rob's diary through there. Bugger all in it.' He glances at his watch. 'Shit. I'm late.' He jumps off the bed and gives them a thumbs-up. 'Talk to you soon Eck nice to meet you it'll be all right Christsake though 'bye.' Ian strides out of the bedroom. Two seconds later, the bedroom walls vibrate.

'Goodness,' says Louise. 'Is he always like that?'

'Well, he's obviously worried,' says Alastair.

'And wired.'

'Really? But it's only three o'clock.'

'Oh, well, goodness, I must be wrong, then.' Louise rests her hands on the duvet behind her and leans back. A little to his surprise, Alastair notices that he's noticed that this position emphasises the pertness of her breasts. 'Why did they both call you Eck?'

'Ahem. Well. It's just a nickname.' One of those things you're stuck with, he wants to say. Like being a bald ginge. 'Quite a common one in Scotland, although usually for Alexanders. Sometimes Alastairs as well, because the name Alastair is related to Alexander. Mind you, Alexanders are often Sandys. Or Alexes . . . Alecs . . .'

'Should I call you Eck as well?'

Alastair tilts his head in what he hopes is a take-it-or-leave-it way.

Louise smiles. 'Okay, Alastair. Now what would you say to a drink? Not including "Hello, drink". I think we could both do with a large, stiff one.'

Alastair, who was indeed about to say 'Hello, drink', nods feebly.

Louise slaps her thighs and pulls herself up with embarrassing grace. 'Come on, then. I really need to get out of this room.'

Alastair follows her to the kitchen where she heads for the fridge. 'This is weird,' she murmurs. 'Look at all this stuff. Fancy a pesto, raspberry jam and old broccoli omelette? Nice of him to leave a bottle of tonic, though.' Alastair is busy remembering all the times that he's stood in this kitchen, chatting away while Rob fetched bottles of beer or a bottle of cold white, when Louise offers him a tall glass clinking with ice. 'Flange,' she says.

'Flange?'

'Isn't that what Scots say?'

'Oh. Got you. *Slàinte*.' Alastair takes a sip of what is clearly not-quite-neat gin and coughs.

'Yeah, slange. So. What's the story?'

'Sorry, Louise. What's what story?'

'You three musketeers. Who are you?'

'Oh. Yes. Of course. Well, we're all friends of Rob from back home, basically. The Friday Night Club. Rob must have mentioned it. Kind of a joke thing really . . .' Alastair was going to explain how this is the second version of Friday Night Club, the title a knowing but fond acknowledgment of their shared past and one that this time round was christened by Rob, and maybe adding something if he possibly could about it being him, Alastair, who came up with the Friday Night Club title originally, when there were about a dozen of them one underage jamboree in the Harbour Bar and he dared himself to propose the name, ostensibly as a joke, but something in the way Louise is looking at him, as if he's just claimed that Paris is the capital of Germany, stops him short.

'Friday Night Club?' she asks.

'Yes. Oh . . . So he didn't . . .' You are an *idiot*, Alastair tells himself. For some reason, it's only now that it has dawned on him how strange and, to be honest, hurtful it is that she really doesn't know anything about the FNC or, to be more honest, him. 'It comes from schooldays,' says Alastair, soldiering on. 'It started in fifth year, I suppose. Not just us four, there was a whole crowd of us. All because of Rob, really, I mean he was at the centre of it. And it was called Friday Night Club because we'd . . .'

'Meet up on Friday nights, yes, I *think* I see. And you three and Bobby kept on doing it.'

'Not kept on doing it, not really. It, I mean this new version of the FNC, has only been on the go for five, six months, really since Ian returned from abroad, though we'd seen Graham occasionally after he came down here then split up with his girlfriend. And as it happens, the four of us did meet up in Munich a couple of years ago to . . .' Alastair lets the explanation tail off, because he's beginning to witter. Then it occurs to him that he'd have to witter a lot, lot more to explain the intricacies, the complexities of the various degrees of friendship at work here. Also, there is the fact that anything he wants to say at this point – about him and Rob being best pals since primary, despite the odd years when he and Rob didn't see so much of each other, about Graham and Ian being their own best pals rather than Rob's, about this Friday Night Club being quite different from the first Friday Night Club, because that had girls in it for one thing, and about the new Friday Night Club being something he often feels he has to put up with and not resent for having replaced nights out which had been just him and Rob – would sound distinctly ungrown up.

Louise seems too lost in her own thoughts to have noticed his lapse into silence. She purses her lips. 'Friday Night Club. Every Friday night?'

'Just about.'

'Goodness . . . Well, you bosom buddies must be wondering who the hell is the piece of work who appears out of nowhere and takes over the whole show.'

'No, no. Not at all.'

'You're a sweet man, Alastair, and a truly untalented liar.' Louise takes a good swig of gin and gives her head a shake. 'Boy, that hits the spot.' Then she strolls over to the coffee table, licks the tip of her index finger, dabs it on the glass and rubs the fingertip over her gums. 'So how bad's his habit, the energetic one?'

'Ian? I don't think he's got one, not really. He can't have, not on what he earns.'

'I'm right, though, aren't I?'

'About Ian?'

'No, silly. About me. More specifically, what you lot think about me.'

'Not at all. I mean, you musn't assume, that's to say I think we're all a bit taken aback because we didn't know about you, but I'm sure none of us resents . . .'

'Chill. Go on, then. Ask me who I am.'

'Sorry?'

'You heard me, Alastair.'

'Oh. Yes. All right, then. Well, um . . . who are you?'

'I'm the person who came back from the States because she thought she was, one, going out with someone, two, that the someone was called Bobby, and three, that the someone called Bobby was going to be someone she was going to be living with when they both sold their flats and moved in together.'

'He was going to sell this place?'

'Yip.'

'Move somewhere else?'

'Yip.'

'With you?'

'Don't sound too shocked. It's not like I've got a prison record or a secret penis or something.'

'But, but . . . but why haven't any of us heard about this? Or about you? Surely Rob would have said something.'

'One would have thought so, wouldn't one? One would also have thought that this note is not what one was expecting to find when one made one's triumphant return from exile. No.' She takes another slug of gin. 'That is definitely not what one expected. At least not this one.'

3

'ANY PARTICULAR REASON WHY YOU MIGHT BE HERE, SIR?'

Sunday evening

Here's Ian, walking down St John's Wood High Street and lugging a Sainsbury's carrier bag filled with textbooks. Collecting these books is always a real pain – he has to stop by the empty school and let himself in with the keys he copied off a set he nicked from Moira's desk. But it's worth it because these course books are essential accessories for his weekly freelance assignment.

The woman in front has great legs and Ian bets himself that she's wearing stockings. Sheer, black material, with that shortish black skirt and on the legs of someone who looks like she spends a lot of money and a good part of each day at the beautician's. The kind of woman, come to think of it, that he expected Louise to be . . . Yeah, got to be stockings. The woman scissors into a shop, so Ian decides to dawdle for a moment just in case she reappears. He pretends to examine the nearest window, an estate agent's. Nice little town house on offer – three bed, two recep, his for £720,000. With a twinge of pride at his worldly acumen, Ian starts to divide by three and a half to work out the salary needed to raise the necessary mortgage, but gives up as soon as he faces dividing £1,440,000 by seven. 'Course, he could always do it on his present income, as long as he could raise a deposit of . . .

£680,000.

Until very recently, he would have postponed further thought about this arithmetic to some notional era in the future when he'd have an insider's knowledge of normal, adult life. But now that he is, ludicrously, forty months short of forty and six months away from becoming a parent, he's beginning to accept that the orthodox, adult world of mortgages, lawnmowers and insurance policies is destined to remain as distant and incomprehensible as baseball. This reflection soon gives way to a vivid image of him, Claire and some sulky, bulky schoolboy dodgemming around the flat in Vauxhall, but he manages to replace that with a vision of himself in about an hour's time, when he'll be ordering a celebratory double brandy in that pub across the road and then taking himself off to the pub's reliably quiet, clean gents'.

Still no sign of the stockingy woman. Ah, well. Assuming the air of a man with a mission, Ian crosses the road, takes a left and quickens his pace as he nears the mansion block where he will be giving his weekly private tutorial.

The building's main door has been propped open by a bucket of soapy water, so Ian saunters into the plush hallway, which boasts dark, panelled walls, an enormous and slightly worrying chandelier and a small, antique lift protected by wrought-iron gates. Ian wonders if he could afford the mortgage for the lift . . . Or the chandelier . . . Probably not even the bucket of soapy water. He hauls open the gates with needless force, steps inside, clunks them shut, presses an ivory button marked six and remembers, as he always remembers at exactly this moment each week, the even smaller lift that used to take him up to the apartment on the Boulevard des Invalides where he flat-sat for six months. Best thing about that Parisian lift was the manufacturer's plaque – *'Schindler: proche de vous partout dans le monde'*. 'Schindler's lift,' he'd joked, though nobody seemed to think it was funny, until that first date with Claire, when they'd gone to a screening of *Toy Story* on the Boulevard St Germain and she'd come back with him. 'Schindler's lift,' he'd pointed out, and she'd replied with a smile that shone and then with such a fit of the giggles that, by the time they stopped at the fifth floor, she'd had tears of laughter running down her wonderful face and he had realised, with something between joy and panic, that he was falling in love. This lift, though, is a British lift and therefore an ignoble, clanky object which seems too exhausted to do anything but give up halfway through its task and plummet to the ground. Powered, according to his fancy, by a rooftop team of well-whipped workhouse urchins cranking a colliery-sized wheel, the lift begins a slow and juddery ascent, until it comes to an abrupt, sickening stop at the sixth floor. As Ian wrenches the gates open and steps out on to the lushly carpeted landing, he reflects that anyone looking in on this bit of his life might predict that he's about to teach English to a diplomat or a sheikh. Definitely not the small, thin, young Spaniard suffering from rampant paranoia and rampant acne who awaits him behind the door of Flat 12.

Today, though, the door is opened by a teenage girl who is wearing only a pair of greying knickers that reach up to her navel. He notes her sallow skin and the blue-black sheen of her hair which tumbles down to her bony shoulders – as well, of course, as the disappointing breasts – and decides that this must be the man's girlfriend from back home and that he should therefore be ultra-smooth.

'*Hola*,' says Ian with his crinkly-eyed smile.

She glares at him as if his words taste of celery. 'Fook off,' she says in broad Yorkshire, and disappears into the nearest room, closing the door behind her with an authentically adolescent slam.

'Ah, Johnny?' Ian calls out in a singsong that reminds him of his mother when she used to announce teatime. Suddenly, the door next to the one slammed by the adolescent is flung open to reveal a scrawny youth with a pair of sunglasses slithering around on hair apparently rinsed in cooking oil and above a face as red and cratered as Mars.

'Johnny', for it is he, nods his head solemnly while signalling, with an O formed by his thumb and index finger, that he is pleased to see Ian and that he himself is, as ever, in control. Yeah, right. Mr Big. The man who thinks that wearing Ray-Bans on his head or calling himself Johnny (instead of Ramón, his real name, or at least the name on the passport that Ian once spotted lying beside the dusty bread bin), mark him out as a king of the streets, rather than, as Ian suspects Johnny/Ramón actually is, a daft middle-class twat who's using his stay in Britain to play at being a coke dealer. Still, he thinks as he follows Johnny down the flat's long and murky corridor, an upbringing, however privileged, in Vigo seems to have given the little twat a taste for one of the more lucrative Galician traditions.

'Hoakay, my frenn, we make the class here.' Johnny beckons him through to the rancid kitchen. 'Today we work hard, hoakay?'

'Yes indeed, Johnny.' Ian makes a great show of pulling books out from his carrier bag. Johnny nods in serious approval of this scholarly display, although Osborne & Foster, the *Let's Speak English!* workbooks and the *Advanced English Primer* are completely useless for his unique linguistic needs. Which is why Johnny turned up for three of the sixty-four lessons he paid for at the London Oxford School of English, before he treated Ian to a drink and a testing-the-water line in All Bar One and invited him to be his private tutor, one who could instruct him in the terminology of his profession and prevent his colleagues and customers taking the piss out of him behind his back. An impossible task, because even if Johnny spoke like Mad Frankie Fraser rather than Manuel in *Fawlty Towers*, he'd still be a twat, but Ian has been more than happy to address his charge's fear of ridicule by teaching him terms like 'deal', 'charlie', 'sorted', 'wrap' and 'gear'. After the second lesson, Ian had exhausted his own knowledge of Dealerese so he has taken to eavesdropping on

Vauxhall's teenagers. He's not quite sure about the subtle connotations, or basic meaning, of words like 'mong', 'dark' and 'yard', but it doesn't really matter because Johnny won't remember anything he's taught and, belying all the books Ian is piling up on the kitchen table, their lessons together will resemble lessons for, at most, five minutes.

Ian adopts a pensive expression and begins to pace up and down the kitchen because Johnny appreciates a pedagogical performance, no matter how absurd. 'Right,' says Ian. 'Today, we are going to revise words for the police.'

'Feelth,' says Johnny.

'Good, yes, excellent. And as we have already learned, there are many other words for the filth, so for this revision I have prepared a list.'

With some ceremony, Ian produces from his carrier bag an A4 sheet of paper. Johnny grabs it and scans what is a very short list with the grim dedication of a general assessing a decoded report. 'Rozzers, plods, old beel . . .'

'Bill.'

'Beel. Feds, peegs . . .'

'Pigs.'

'Peegs.'

'Pigs.'

'Peegs.'

'Excellent.'

'*Muy bien, muy bien.* Rozzers, feds, plods, old beel, peegs. Ah.' Johnny gives the sheet of paper a triumphant slap with the back of his hand. 'And feelth.'

'Excellent. Now. Let's return to the words we studied last week. How many pounds in a pony?'

'Ees ten.'

'Very close. It's twenty, remember?'

'Twenny.'

'Correct. And a monkey?'

'*Mono, sí?*'

'Exactly, *mono*. How many pounds in a *mono*?'

'Ten.'

'Almost. Good try. In fact it's five hun . . .'

'Good.' Johnny springs up from his seat. 'Ees good. Now conversation.'

'Yes. Conversation.'

Johnny prepares for this part of the lesson by taking a kitchen knife to a lump of cocaine he's conjured from a drawer and arranging it into two thick lines. Stretching out his arms like an umpire signalling a wide, he lets it be known that his is a generous spirit. 'My house your house, my frenn. Then we talk, hoakay?'

Two minutes later, the conversation segment of the tutorial is well under way, with Johnny talking animatedly. About what Ian isn't quite sure because Johnny is blethering in a heavily accented Galician dialect. There'll be another half an hour of this, then both parties will have deemed the lesson a great success. Johnny will rest content that Ian has increased his linguistic armoury. Ian will hand over £25 and Johnny will hand over two massively discounted grams. High and buzzing, Ian will clasp Johnny's hand in farewell, they will maintain the meaningful, manly eye contact which Mr Big seems to think confirms their comradeship and his own status as Mr Big, and Ian will relish the lift back down, perhaps imagining that a young and distraught Billie Whitelaw is pleading at him to return to her love-nest or that he's dodging the bullets of the Soviet agents who tried to ambush him in his glamorous bachelor pad. Then he'll take himself off for that double brandy at the pub with the nice gents.

Sorted.

Alastair grins wanly and shakes his head. The chances of him saying the right thing are, he estimates, slim. 'I couldn't say,' he says.

'Thirty-one.'

'Really?'

'You thought I was older?'

'No, the opposite.'

'So I look like a little girl, is that it?'

'Not at all,' says Alastair. He allows himself a silent sigh of exasperation. Why does she have to turn everything into an argument? Apart from anything else, it's just so exhausting. He puts on what he hopes looks like a polite smile.

'I'm sorry, Alastair,' says Louise. 'I'm all over the place about this, but God knows I shouldn't be taking it out on you. After all, he's dumped you as well, hasn't he?'

'Rob, you mean?'

'No, I was referring to . . . There I go again. Yes, Bobby, Rob, whatever he called himself. No, anyway, what I meant was he's left you in the lurch. Not that he split up from you or anything, but he was your friend.'

'Is. Is my friend.'

'Hmm. As you like. Far as I'm concerned, after this little stunt, it's was. *Was* my boyfriend. *Was* the man I *was* supposed to be coming back to.' She purses her lips and looks off into the distance. 'I can't tell you how stupid I feel. I mean, I really did think that this time it was going to work out. And chucking in my job, really, what brand of fool am I?'

Alastair nods sympathetically.

'Actually, I'm exaggerating a bit about the job. All I've done really is move from the New York office back here.'

Alastair is busy doing more sympathetic nodding when he is struck by an obvious thought. 'Sorry, Louise,' he says, 'but I don't even know what it is you do.'

'Advertising.' She scrunches her face. 'How exciting.'

'I don't know,' says Alastair, who is now desperately trying to think of anything positive to say about a job in advertising. Perhaps he could say something instead about his idea that advertising has changed from exploitative brainwashing into entertainment, thus reflecting the shift in capitalism itself whereby exploited workers have become consumers who have to be courted with things they might want rather than . . . Maybe this isn't the time. 'It must be fun.'

'Sometimes. Not recently. Tell the truth, I wasn't too unhappy to leave the States. I mean, most of it was great but the work . . . Jeez.'

'I suppose it must have been difficult. Trying to adjust to another culture and so forth.'

'The opposite. The accounts I was working on, they were all the same. Say what you like about the Yanks, but they're into their bowels.'

'. . . Really?'

'Laxatives, high-bran cereals, high-fibre breads, my whole working life was devoted to keeping Yanks regular. With the same ad, no matter what the product. Shot of young businessman dancing round office to soundtrack of James Brown singing "I feel good". Cut to young easy-shitting businessman's secretary looking surprised then delighted as her boss whisks her round in a whirly waltz. Cut to close-up of product. Deep, earnest voice-over – "Eezee-Crap Chocograins. Because you're full of shit." Collect salary at end of month.'

Alastair coughs. 'Was it in America that you met Rob, then?'

It's an obvious question to ask, given that Rob spent so much time in New York when he had his affair with the CNN reporter, but it seems to have stymied Louise. 'No,' she says after a moment. 'We met because I live in the flat below his. Funny. I had him down as just a City smoothie when I first moved here. But then one night he knocked on my door and it wasn't to barge in, smoke a joint and tell me all about his salary. This time he was quiet, thoughtful, got talking about his parents, how much he still missed his mother, all that, and it was like he was a different person.'

Alastair responds with an understanding nod, although

what he's thinking is that Rob's sudden double bereavement, what must be a dozen years ago now, is one of the few topics Rob doesn't like to talk about, him being the kind of chap who prefers to keep things light. Or so he had assumed. And to think that Rob had been so good about listening to him bang on and on when his own mother died. Why hasn't he, Alastair, returned that favour? It happened twelve years ago – can that really be a reason or even any kind of excuse?

I failed him, Alastair tells himself. There's a lump growing in his throat. I failed my friend.

This is fucking *useless*.

Over two hours now he's spent monitoring Jenny's flat and what has he found out? Fuck all, that's what.

Times he's peeked in on her flat before, that's all he's done – been in the area, taken a wee detour, sidled up and down her street a few times, had a keek in at her window, then sloped off, heart pounding, guts churning, brain very depressed. But this proper surveillance business is a completely different kettle of pish.

Over two hours of lingering and dodging about, of trying to look casual and normal as he has walked up and down her street, pausing briefly each time to check out the two front windows of her first-floor flat. And all that he's got to show for it is one terrifying glimpse of Jenny with her hair tied back, wearing a jersey and jeans, carrying a vase or something through to the kitchen maybe, and a couple of sightings of Megan, her fat flatmate, who seems bent on spending the entire day wafting around in a pink fucking kimono.

No sign of Rob – but he could already be inside, couldn't he? Rob could easily have spent the last two hours in the kitchen at the back, or in the bathroom, or – let's be fucking candid about this – in Jenny's bedroom, where even now he could be pawing her, slobbering all over her, shagging her, for fucksake . . . This is such a heinous idea, it seems ridiculous to

Graham that he can't just report his strong suspicions of this outrage to the police and that the police wouldn't respond by immediately surrounding Jenny's flat, breaking down the door, catching the culprits in the act and bundling them into a van with blankets over their heads.

That snooty-looking woman at number one has come to her window again. She's looking straight at him. Typical Notting Hill bitch, with her trendy wee glasses and her trendy big house. West eleven – hate it or loathe it, you can't help despising the whole fucking area and its stuccoed pillars and pastel-coloured houses and shitey new bars and nosey fucking bitches wearing trendy wee glasses. Why Jenny chose to move here after they split up he'll never fucking know. And now she's turned her flat into a love-nest with Rob. Rob, of all people . . .

Graham pushes himself off the wall because he's got to do something to halt that train of thought and because he's had enough of casting theatrical glances at his watch and taking discreet peeks at Jenny's place thirty yards up the road. He'll take another wander up her street, maybe find a new place to park his arse. Possibly even risk hiding out in that apparently derelict basement opposite Jenny's. Then again, he could . . .

'Can I *help* you, sir?'

Graham turns to reply to the voice behind him and comes face to chest with a dark blue uniform. As he looks up, his recent train of thought makes Graham wonder for a moment if this very large and obviously world-weary policeman has arrived to help him on his stake-out. Then it clicks that someone – probably the snooty bitch at number fucking one – has been on neighbourhood watch duty and alerted the authorities to the fact that there's a man in the area not wearing this season's colours.

'Any particular reason why you might be here, sir?'

'No. Well, yes, I'm . . .'

'Waiting for someone, is it, sir?'

'Ah . . . yes.'

'Only we've received several reports of a gentleman answering your description, sir, acting in a manner that could be seen as worrying to local residents, sir. Residents who are naturally worried, sir, about the remnants in this and nearby streets of, among other activities, the sale and purchase of illegal substances. Now, would it be one of the area's younger entrepreneurs that you were waiting for, sir?'

'Fucksake, all I was doing was standing here, minding my own . . .'

'Do I *look* like a cunt, sir?'

'. . . Sorry?'

'Do I look like a *cunt*, sir?'

'No. No, you don't.'

'Then there's no reason to fuck me around, is there, sir?'

'. . . No.'

'And possibly every reason why you, sir, might be best advised to move on.' The policeman's hands flutter by his side, as though he's shooing pigeons. 'At least to the end of Ladbroke Grove, sir, since that's where my beat ends, sir. Oh, and sir?'

'Yes?'

'Have a pleasant evening.'

When he's walked five yards away from the corner of Jenny's street, Graham looks back to see the policeman still standing where he was, giving him an encouraging smile and another shooing flutter. And behind the policeman that snooty bitch is at her window again. Fucking Notting Hill *cow*.

His heart's going like the clappers. His hands are damp with sweat. Keep calm, he tells himself. Keep calm. But it's in a daze of nervy panic that Graham walks through street after street of lavish houses until he reaches a junction and a row of shops. And, thank fuck, a pub.

The place is almost empty, and no wonder. It smells of stale beer, stale tobacco and stale air. And the carpet feels like it's been skooshed with Spray-Mount. Graham gets himself a pint and a big whisky (Teacher's, which goes to show the shiteyness of the gantry), gulps down both as quickly as he can, then heads for the door, steadfastly refusing eye contact with the pooch on the floor or the several old fucks gawping at their drinks. How many years until I'm one of them? he thinks, as the door clunks behind him and a cool breeze soothes his hot face. Ten? Five? One? That's what Rob and Jenny are doing to him. Giving him a big push down the chute towards the social garbage heap where he can spend the rest of his fucking life being a morose old fuck with nothing to show for his existence but a pint and a fucking leash. He has to do something about this, but what? Welcome to Shit Creek, here's your barbed-wire canoe and bon fucking voyage.

Graham digs out his mobile and pokes out Ian's number.

'Ian.'

'Hello?'

'Ian.'

'Eh?'

'Ian, for fucksake, it's Graham.'

'Sorry, you'll have to . . . Graham? Is that you, Graham?'

'Aye. Can you hear me now?'

'Where you phoning from? A wind tunnel? This is a terrible . . .'

'Notting Hill someplace.'

'On your mobile, right?'

'What? I said Notting Hill somewhere.'

'Man, I can hardly . . .'

'I'll call you back.'

'You'll what?'

'I said. Never mind. Fucksake.' Graham slaps his mobile shut and heads for the nearest phone box which, as sheer chance would have it, is actually working. And which, this being central-ish London, is decorated with dozens of hookers' postcards – 'Fully equipped Dungeon', 'Watersports nr Baker

Street', 'TV Transformation' . . . By Christ, does nobody want a normal shag in this town? Graham unearths a phonecard from his wallet, taps out Ian's number again and is trying to calm himself down by examining a card's line drawing of an Edwardian lady contentedly sitting on a prone gentleman's face when Ian answers.

'Yo, Graham.'

'Is this any fucking better?'

'Loud and clear, my man, loud and clear as a bell on a bright wintry morn.'

'Aw naw, you're wired.'

'No way, José.'

'You're off your face.'

'No way, no way, no way.'

'Fucksake. Okay. Look, Ian, have you got a minute?'

'Sure sure sure. So what is occurring in the vicinity of your area of occurrence?'

'Fuck*sake*, Ian.'

'Graham, you may think I spend all day every day charlied out of my head, but that's where you are very very very very wrong. I'm just in the door, right, and I'm about to start preparing for tomorrow's advanced class, if you must know. Verbs that take both gerunds and infinitives.'

'Eh?'

'I like to get up at eight.'

'What's that got to . . .'

'But I don't like getting up at eight.'

'Ian.'

'See the difference? Like plus infinitive – I like to go to the dentist – for something you think is good for you. Like plus gerund, the -ing – I like eating chocolate – for something you enjoy doing.'

'You really have just done a huge line, haven't you?'

'There's another example. I like taking cocaine, but I also like to be sensible about it.'

'Is Claire in?'

'Out with a couple of pals discussing placentas.'

'So you've definitely been at the marching powder. Look, Ian, can you keep a straight head for this? I need to talk. I'm going fucking insane here.'

'Talk away, talk away, talk away. I am all ears. I like talking with my friends and I also like to talk with them. Hey, are you okay?'

'No, I am not okay. Look, Ian, this is about Rob, all right?'

'With you so far, my man. Shoot.'

'This is fucking awkward, by the way. Did Rob say anything to you, I mean, there's every reason why he wouldn't have, but did Rob mention anything to you about . . . him and Jenny? Like, him seeing, being with, fucksake, shagging Jenny?'

'You mean Jenny? Jenny? Jenny Newman?'

'Aye. Jenny. Rob and Jenny. Jesus.'

'Rob's been shagging Jenny.'

'Fucking *hell*! You fucking *knew* about it!'

'Hey hey hey. I was only repeating what you said. Rob's been shagging Jenny.'

'Stop *saying* that, for fucksake. But you fucking *knew*.'

'Hey, let's just put the brakes on. This is the first I've heard of it, Graham, okay? Honest. Anyway, what makes you think Rob's been shagging Jenny? Sorry, I mean, that the two of them have been . . .'

'Ian.'

'Shagging.'

'Ian. Stop *saying* that. I just know, all right?'

'How, though?'

'It just adds up. There's the Silk Cut in his kitchen, the diary is full of Rob meeting J, he was always flirty with her . . .'

'Graham, you're making as much sense as one of my beginner classes.'

'That fucking diary, Ian, it was full of times he was seeing

Jenny. J at her office, J for lunch, J after work, J this, J that.'

'But J could stand for anything. Julia, Julian, June, Jane, Joan, John, Jonathan, Jonty, Jason, Jerome, Jeremiah . . .'

'Aye, but . . .'

'. . . somebody else called Jenny, or Jennifer, or Jack, Jackie, Jacqueline . . .'

'But how do you explain . . .'

'. . . Jessica, Jemima, James, Jim, Jimmy, Jimothy . . .'

'Jimothy?'

'That one I screwed up, but you get the idea.'

'Then how do you explain the Silk Cut?'

'I don't because I don't know what the hell you're going on about Silk Cut for. Look, Graham, you're taking two and two and making four.'

'Two and two do make four.'

'You know what I mean.'

4

'HELLO'

Monday lunch-time

'And there are four young girls. Giving me water from a vine leaf. Just dropping it on to my tongue.'

The bass is going to kick in after a few more bars of ethereal, plinky-plonky stuff. Normally, the sudden reappearance of the beat (BOOM cha, boom boom cha) – in Alastair's opinion, the greatest reappearance of a beat in the whole history of house stroke trance stroke ambient stroke dance music – would have him struggling not to skip through the carriage, arms waving in the air, hips shimmying. Today, though, even the first track of William Orbit's *Strange Cargo III* – usually a favourite for the soundtrack of his journey in – has lost all of its joyful, haunting energy. Actually, he can't be bothered with any of it. He presses the Stop button on his Discman during the plinky-plonky bit as the train slows down.

He looks out of the window at a Bangladeshi woman hanging sheets out on a brick-walled balcony of a horrible-looking council block. The train draws into Shadwell. Normally, the opening of the doors would have him primed to spot grown-ups stealthily muscling their way to the front seats, because this is the Docklands Light Railway and a driverless train, and front seats in the first carriage are much prized by a surprising variety of human beings, many of them over the age of ten, who like to play, surreptitiously, at being the driver. Today, though, even the sight of a banker type in his fifties and a young chap in paint-spattered overalls discreetly racing each other to the front scarcely registers.

It makes less and less sense. His trip this morning with Louise to Moorgate and Rob's lawyer wasn't at all what he expected. That chap, Jeremy Maddox, for a start. A sleazy individual, he thought, or maybe that's just his prejudice against any man wearing a double-breasted suit *and* one of those stripey shirts with a white collar. Pleased with himself too – sitting behind that old desk in his poky little office, claiming that he's a good friend of Rob's from the Coach and Horses, a pub that he has never even heard Rob mention before, and then telling them that Rob's instructions, imparted over the course of several lunches and appointments in the weeks before Rob left, were simple and clear – to arrange the sale of his MG and furniture and stuff, everything really, and then to put the Bateman Street flat on the market. And despite his alleged friendship, despite all those chummy meetings, despite those on-going financial arrangements, Jeremy Maddox maintained that he had no forwarding address for Rob, no knowledge of what Rob's up to or why he's up to whatever it is he's up to, and absolutely no idea where Rob has gone.

Their appointment had been for eleven. By 11.20, he and Louise were back outside on City Road and wondering what on earth to do for the rest of the morning they'd both taken off. They'd idled down Moorgate, then Louise had pointed out that they were only ten minutes away from the NatWest Tower. She hadn't known Rob's work number either, but she'd got going on her mobile, only to be bounced around by the switchboard. They'd decided they'd go to the Tower anyway – and hadn't made it past the security guy on the front desk. No Robert Mackenzie listed. Eventually, Louise had charmed the security guy into putting them through to Personnel, but Personnel could only divulge that they had no record of any employee called Robert, Rob or Bobby Mackenzie.

The train decelerates into Limehouse. At least Barry was nice about him taking the half-day. Mind you, Mondays are always quiet. A bit of Books to do, some mucking about on Arts . . . Blimey, he hasn't begun to think about the promotion business, or about trying to teach the subbing basics to 007. No, all he can think about is the same few questions which have been whizzing round his head. Why didn't Rob ever mention Louise to them? Or Jeremy blimming Maddox? Where has Rob gone? What *is* he up to?

The doors close again and the train glides off. Normally, he feels a twinge of excitement as the train nears Gotham City. Today, though, Alastair looks out at a ghastly array of grim, grimy houses and the huge, shiny tower ahead of him, and he sees only a mess of deprivation and poverty surrounding an oversized monument to stupidity and greed. He feels . . . what? It's a peculiarly dismal, empty feeling. One that reminds him too strongly of several very bad episodes in his past – the worst being the combined Rhona split-up and Cathy cataclysm of '88, the first being the time when the Friday Night Club, the original Friday Night Club, ended up back at Steve's house and he and Fiona were getting on brilliantly and he was busy summoning up the courage to tell her that what he most wanted to do right now was hold her and kiss her and she abruptly confided that she'd just lost her virginity to Steve and she knew she could tell him because she could trust him and he and she were such good friends. Yes. This is like then. So it's not only confusion or anxiety he's feeling. Nor even loneliness, although that is part of it. No, more than anything, what Alastair feels is . . . sort of chucked.

'So I thought I'd give you a bell, say I liked the phodocopier vibe, see if you're into doing a liddle something for the next issue.'

'Sure, Chaz. Fire ahead.'

'Sabout doing business in the EU. I'll, like, fax you the thing, yeah?'

'Okay.'

'Only thing, keep it priddy straight, man. I mean, me personally I loved the dancing phodocopier, the vibe was cool, but *Business Madders* is, like, a priddy straight mag, yeah?'

'So no fancy stuff?'

'For real.'

'And the fee?'

'Same. Two hundred, yeah?'

'Okay. Just how straight do you want this, though, Chaz?'

'Priddy straight.'

'So if I did an illustration of, I don't know, two businessmen shaking hands across a dotted line for a border, would that be pretty straight or far too straight?'

'That'd be priddy much the vibe.'

Jesus Christ on a fucking bike. 'Okay. So I'll bring this one into the office?'

'Cool.'

'By Wednesday?' asks Graham, but the phone has gone dead. Fuck *off*. So this is what it's come to. Ten years ago he thought he'd done the last of those clichéd pieces of shite for business magazines. Fucksake, he was one of the people who helped make those clichés clichés – churning out all those drawings of risk-taking businessmen teetering on tightropes, of suddenly inspired businessmen standing under gigantic light bulbs (with optional dollar sign for the filament), of optimistic businessmen pointing to mountainous pound signs on the horizon, of fit, lean businessmen poised for a sprint. No. Drawing two fucking businessmen shaking hands across a dotted line for a border is *not* what he thought he'd be doing or what he fucking should be doing at this fucking age. This should be his fucking *prime*, and what is he doing? He's drawing two businessmen shaking hands across a dotted line for a border is what he's fucking doing.

The phone rings again.

'Graham, Jason.'

Oh, *just* what he needs. 'Mr Megabucks. How's tricks, Jason?'

'Tricks is great. Listen, I'm getting another little night out together here.'

'Where's here? Shoreditch?'

'Is there anywhere else in the world? 'Course Shoreditch. Cantaloupe or the Brickies, who knows? Friday night. You up for that?'

'I don't know, Jason. Fridays I'm usually booked up. And I've got a lot on at the moment.' A bare-faced lie, but the last thing he wants is a night out listening to Jason crow about his BT commission.

'You should try and make it. Audrey'll be there.'

Now why is Jason saying that? Maybe, just maybe, it's because Audrey really is keen and she's told him so. 'I'll see, Jason. I'll call you later in the week, all right?'

'Good man. Listen, I've got to run. This meeting to go to.'

Aye, right. The boy has this big, fucking important meeting. 'Good luck with it, Jason. Give them hell.'

'Oh, yes. See ya.'

Graham puts down the phone and tells it to fuck off.

Ian has his head halfway into his desk drawer when he hears a rap on his door.

'Ah, Ian, ah, I was ah.'

Never one to panic under pressure, Ian simply drops his straw on to the mirror, has a little sniff, lifts his head, and casually pushes the drawer shut. The act of a man who was just peeking inside his drawer. No problem, then, except he'll have to get through an hour of verbs that take gerunds and infinitives with a tantalising three-quarters of a line untouched and a metre away from his nose. 'Dr Foxsmith,' says Ian, as he gets to his feet. 'How can I be of assistance?'

'I believe you are, this, about to, this is, will be.'

'My advanced class, Dr Foxsmith?'

'Ah.'

'Yes, it's due to start in a couple of minutes.'

'In, that is, indeed. And with, I have, here is, are the two, ah, new.'

'Of course.' Ian inclines his head. 'The two French students who will be joining the advanced class today.'

Monique has turned up to occupy a substantial amount of the doorway. Foxsmith places an avuncular hand on her chunky shoulder and smiles at Ian. 'This is, ah, is, ah, Chantal,' declares Foxsmith. Monique is too busy blushing and simpering at her trainers to notice the error. 'And I gather, you already have, ah, have already met Monique.' Foxsmith shifts into profile to allow Monique's sidekick to appear. She steps forward and offers her hand. Ian retains just enough presence of mind to hold the hand, this cool, dry, slender, elegant hand, in his. She shouldn't be here, is his first thought. She should be busy appearing in adverts for cars or perfume. Or, come to think of it, for women. Twenty-one, twenty-two maybe, round about five eight, jackpot body since she's slim and 34C at an educated guess, excellent, long legs in soft blue jeans, rich, auburny hair that tumbles to her shoulders, and the kind of perfect face – oval shaped and containing a pair of large brown eyes beneath angular black eyebrows, a thin, straight nose, and a full, wide mouth – that makes any usual kind of face look like an inexplicable aberration.

'I'll ah, that is, leave you to, leave you, ah.' Foxsmith backs off and away.

'Chantal,' says Ian to Chantal with his crinkly-eyed smile. He remembers to release her hand. 'Hel*lo*.'

5

'THIS LION WALKS INTO A PUB'

Thursday evening

He can even remember what they were listening to on Rob's new hi-fi – Big Audio Dynamite. And there's Rob, nine years ago but still vivid, sitting cross-legged on the floor in his flat in Clapham, rolling what was to be Alastair's first-ever joint. He'd felt a bit strange to start with, then heavy limbed, as if it was the second half of extra time on a muddy pitch, and then he'd laughed until it hurt at the stories Rob told him about having sex with his secretary in the stationery cupboard then going to a meeting and a sheaf of Post-It notes falling out of his trousers. Alastair's first week in London, so he'd felt like a hopeless bumpkin as he marvelled at this racy new world Rob was showing him of illegal drugs and sex in the office. And they'd just picked up where they'd left off. As if that gap of three, nearly four years, when Rob had migrated south and proved so hopeless at returning postcards and phone calls, had never happened.

Alastair shifts his focus from the middle distance to the page proof on his desk. '. . . pinch sea salt,' he reads, character by character. '2 handfuls flat-leaf parsley, 1 tsp lemon juice, 66 tbsp extra-virgin olive oil.' Alastair is scoring a red line through the second 6 on his proof of Hugo's cookery column when he becomes aware of a commotion behind him. He glances over his shoulder and sees the editor, who must have loped past while he was concentrating on Hugo's recipe for chickpeas with Swiss chard, looming over Davina in Books. Davina is looking perplexed and the editor is looking very angry indeed.

The editor slaps the top of Davina's terminal.

The room goes quiet.

Alastair exchanges a worried look with Yvonne. Only James Bond seems oblivious to the on-going drama, for he rises from his seat and ambles towards his stepfather's partitioned office.

'But Jonathan,' Davina says, shakily, into the hush, 'this is an excellent piece by a leading . . .'

Now the editor is holding his right hand in the air, palm outward. 'Davina,' he barks. 'I have already spoken on this matter. When you wanted to commission David Allcock.'

'Derek Walcott. Who won the Nobe . . .'

'And what words did I speak when I spoke?'

'Jonathan, I really must . . .'

'I said that I wanted names. Big names. Not your obscure chums from literary parties.'

Alastair taps the Alt Screen key and sends a message to Barry: 'wot going on?' That done, he risks another glance behind him. Davina puts her elbows on the desk and starts to massage her forehead. The editor is leaning towards her, as if anxious about her health.

'This is the *Sunday Chronicle*, Davina. Not *The Times Literary Review*.'

MESSAGE is flashing on Alastair's screen. He gives the Receive key a gentle pat. 'big trauma re book review,' says Barry's reply.

'pls explain trauma,' Alastair messages back.

'So spike this piece of commie propaganda and get me an article by someone our readers will have *heard* of.'

'davina commissioned book review by prof called stuart hall.'

'Someone our readers will *like*.'

'stuart hall famous academic man? wot problem?'

'Someone our readers will . . . *read*.'

With a final slap on the top of Davina's terminal, the editor turns on his heel and strides past Alastair's desk, dislodging a set of proofed pages as he does so.

By the time Alastair has gathered the pages together again, MESSAGE is flashing on his screen. 'acc/ding b/bottle, ed thght d had got s hall broadcaster.'

'wot?' Alastair types back. 'it's a knockout s hall?' As he taps the Send key, he hears a series of dull thumps behind him. He looks round to see Davina banging her head on her desk.

'Spot on,' says Barry, forsaking messages now that the editor's gone.

'Blimey.'

'Now then, Al.' Barry scrapes back his chair and comes round to stand by Alastair's side. 'Let's leave poor Davina to her grief and turn the oil-tanker of our attention gradually round to Lifestyle and the special treat I have for you.'

'All righty. As long as it's nothing to do with Josh Todd.'

'Uncanny.'

'Oh, no, Barry. That'll be four Joshes running. That really isn't fair.'

'Al, my pal, be of good cheer. Derek's turn to do the actual subbing, as he's about to find out when he comes back from the tea run. But I thought you might want a look at a column of historic importance.'

'Historic how?'

'Because Josh Todd has found something to write about.'

'You're joshing.'

'I'm not but Derek soon will be. And he will be joshing with a Josh Todd column wherein our hero writes about . . . no, you're going to have to guess.'

Alastair ponders various unlikely answers. 'An issue?'

'There's no need to go over the top.'

'Sorry, Barry. Oh, blimey, I don't know.' Alastair tries to think of a slightly less unlikely answer. 'Somebody other than himself?' he suggests tentatively.

'Warm.'

'Then it has to be somebody important to him.'

'Warmer still.'

'Parent? Sibling?'

'Cooling very quickly.'

'Friend?'

'Getting warm again.'

'A close friend?'

'Hot, hot, hot. And how.'

Alastair reminds himself to close his mouth so he can start his next unfeasible question. 'Josh has a girlfriend?'

'Congratulations. You have won the chance to be the first person after Bluebottle, me and the editor, who, by the by, was anxious to look at a Lifestyle piece for the first time in his career, to read the touching account of Josh's romance. And, boy, do I mean touching.'

As Barry returns to his workstation, Alastair calls up the latest Josh Todd and begins to read the copy that has appeared on his screen.

I am waiting for the lady in my life to come back to my bedroom. She walks into my bedroom smiling and nude. 'Hi, Tiger,' she says to me and smiles. I smile back. Then I pull the lady in my life down towards me and soon I am kissing her. I am kissing her neck. I am kissing her breasts. I am carressing the insides of her thihgs. I am kissing her belly button. I am kissing the brilo pad of her pubic hair. I am kissing her labbia. I am probing with my tongue. I am tasting the inside of

Alastair looks over at Barry. 'We can't print this.'

'That's just what we're going to do. Bluebottle loves it. The editor loves it. They say they're looking forward to a huge mailbag from our readers.'

'Yes, from even more readers saying that they are cancelling lifelong subscriptions because of Josh Todd.'

'That's as maybe. But isn't it nice to think that Josh is no longer on his tod?'

'One thing, I suppose that can be our headline.'

'Tragically, no. Josh has already supplied his own and both Bluebottle and the editor love that as well.'

Alastair sighs. 'Just tell me.'

'"I used to think cunnilingus was an Irish airline."'

'No, really, Barry, what's the headline?' Alastair waits for Barry to crack but his expression remains steadfast. 'Oh no,' says Alastair. 'No, no, no, no, no.'

Barry nods his head. 'I'm really not joking.'

'Joshing.'

'My mistake.'

Absent-mindedly, Alastair scrolls down to the end of the copy. 'I can wait no longer,' says his screen. 'I am bursting into orgasm. I am feeling the spurting of my seed. I am COMING.'

'Blimey,' says Alastair.

'That is a very big one,' remarks Paolo. 'Very, very big.'

If he weren't sharing a toilet cubicle with an eighteen-year-old boy, Ian might have a little private smirk at Paolo's Carry On comments. Because he is, and even though he's fairly confident that there's nobody outside, Ian puts a finger to his lips.

To no effect.

'Possibly too big for me,' Paolo declaims. 'Because it is very thick and long.'

As Ian pushes the coke into two substantial lines on the cistern's top, he ponders the thought that, were someone to come in and push open the uncertainly bolted cubicle door, copping a blowjob off an eighteen-year-old boy would have to be his alibi.

Despite his alleged misgivings, Paolo takes first go and snorts his line with disarming gusto. He proffers his rolled-up note but Ian has his straw at the ready . . .

No more than a minute later, Ian and Paolo have side-shuffled out of the bog and casually rejoined the group upstairs in the Pig and Whistle. 'Right, then,' says Ian, rubbing his hands and suppressing a sneeze, 'who's for another drink? Paolo? Dieter? Stanislaw? Monique? Chantal, anything for you? No? Chantal? Positive? Just me, then.'

Since everyone else, with the exception of Paolo, is back on fruit juice or mineral water after their experimental halves of bitter, Ian orders a tonic, then relents and asks for a double brandy on the side. He necks the brandy at the bar and returns to the group with his nose twitching and his oesophagus on fire.

'No, no,' Dieter is saying. 'The present perfect tense is bad, naturally, but worse are the phrasal verbs.'

'Ah, come on, Dieter, come on, come on, come *on*,' says Ian. 'Verbs plus prepositions. Simple, simple, simple. You learn them through use.'

'Naturally, yes, but . . .'

'Put and up, for example. You can remember them by remembering examples. I put up with him, I put him up for the job, I put up the thing on the wall.'

Dieter holds his hands aloft in mock surrender.

'Come along, Dieter,' Ian says heartily. 'I put to you that you shouldn't put off using phrasal verbs. Don't put them down.'

'You see,' Dieter says. 'Put up, put on, put in, put down, and so many meanings. Impossible.'

Paolo stops twitching about in his chair, leans forward and says, 'Put out. A cigarette, yes? And girls.' He grins and raises his glass towards Monique and Chantal, who are both frowning at him with concentration.

Ian realises that he's wearing a similar expression. 'What do you mean, Paolo, put out girls? Oh, got you,' he adds, but too late.

'Yes, girls. She puts out. Also, she puts it about. Means

sex,' he explains to Monique and Chantal, who are both now frowning at each other. 'Or,' Paolo adds with a sarcastic-looking smile, 'she is lesbian and she puts off you.'

'Puts you off,' says Ian, who is busily wondering whether or not to explain the several meanings of putting someone off when he sees Chantal gathering her books together and Monique following suit. Damn damn damn damn *damn*.

'We are obliged to leave,' Chantal murmurs as she stands up and shrugs on her coat. 'We must to return to the landlady.'

'Who is putting you up,' Dieter says, much to his own delight and the consternation of the French girls.

There follows an awkward silence which is finally broken when Monique says 'Thank you, Ian' with her unfortunate simper. 'We enjoy the pub. We see you tomorrow.'

'Yes,' murmurs Chantal, 'tomorrow. Goodbye, Ian. And thank you very much,' she adds with a heart-breaking, groin-tingling, stomach-lurching stretch of those glorious full lips. It's too much to think about the body that must exist beneath the clothes, so Ian concentrates on that naked mouth. What he wants, more than anything else in the world at the moment, is to cover that mouth with his. But now she's going, and with her any point to staying here. He forces away a stare as Chantal leaves with a farewell wiggle of her fingers and Monique clomping along behind.

'Okay, chaps,' says Ian, drumming his fingers on the table-top. 'I'm sorry but I'd better go too.'

'Can't you put it off?' asks Paolo, who then lets out a coked-up yelp of laughter at this terrific joke.

Ian finishes his drum-roll and takes a last sip of tonic. ''Fraid not. See you all tomorrow.' He winks smoothly at Paolo. 'Enjoy yourselves.'

It's only as Ian marches out into Bateman Street that he realises he doesn't have anywhere to march to. Normally, his first move would be to get to a phone and see if Rob's in . . . But hey, that Louise might be around and, you never know, she might even be into partaking of a line or two . . . Funny how she's not what he expected and how that has made him realise that what he did expect was based on nothing more than a notion of Rob's type, some glossy kind of babe who'd fit into Rob's life of clubs and restaurants and in-crowd shenanigans. Someone not unlike, for example, Chantal, who really is a babe and no mistake. One of the great things about language schools – the way they offer up a regular supply of babes, and babes, moreover, who have to spend an hour or two a day lost in helpless admiration of their tall, dark and very handsome teacher.

Ian presses the bell below Rob's. The intercom crackles into life. 'Yes?'

'Hi, Louise? It's Ian. Rob's, Bobby's, Robert's pal. Can I come up?'

The door buzzes by way of a reply. Ian climbs the familiar stairs and stops unfamiliarly short at the first landing, where he sees Louise waiting for him just inside her open door. She's leaning back against the wall, her hands on her hips, her black Lycra skirt not quite reaching her raised knee, her right foot propped behind her in classic hooker's pose. 'Hello, sailor,' she says. 'You likee jiggyjig? Nice girls, clean girls.' She beckons him in. 'Love you longtime.' Ian follows her through a hallway decorated with old film posters and into a sitting room furnished with only a battered leather settee, a boom-box and a scattering of CDs on the wood floor.

'Is there some rule in this building that says you can't have a lot of stuff?'

'Feng shui,' she says. 'The room faces south and I'm an Aries, so any more clutter and I'd be looking at a very heavy, negative aura.'

'That right?' says Ian, mimicking mild interest.

'Well, it's always possible, I suppose, but I was kind of kidding.' She sits down, cross-legged, on the floor. 'I just haven't bought any furniture yet.'

'Right . . . When did you move in?'

'Getting on for three years ago. But I've been in New York for most of that time, remember?'

'Right.'

'But enough of this merry banter. Do you want to go up to Bobby's or what?'

'What, really. I was in the area, I thought I'd call in. To see how you were doing.'

'Ah, village London. Well, I'm doing excellently, given that the man I thought I was going to be with has apparently packed a few supplies into a red, spotted hankie, shoved the hankie on to the end of a stick and run away from home.'

'Right, right,' Ian says softly, in the hope that this sounds earnest and caring enough, as he lowers himself, a bit too creakily for his liking, on to the floor. 'So what I was wondering,' he says, 'was maybe you might want cheering up.'

She raises one eyebrow. 'And this proposed cheering up, what's it involve? You removing all my clothes and impaling me on your lance of manhood?'

'No. No. Absolutely not. No. No way. No.'

'That's a no, then?'

'Definitely.' But now that she's said it, the image of her slender legs astride him and her pushing slowly down is stuck in Ian's head. 'What I have in mind is Dr Murray's Medicinal Compound. Most efficacious. In every cay-ay-ase.'

'Let me guess,' she says. 'Would this be a curative that comes in powdered form?'

'Correct first time.' Ian produces his wallet and then a wrap from his wallet. 'How's about a toot?'

'Lawks a mercy. You really are quite the cokehead, aren't you?'

'Me?' She's only saying that because now he's brought out his little mirror, and just as well he had it, the only other available surface to chop a couple out on being the floorboards. 'Nup.'

'How much a week?'

'Dunno. A gram? Maximum.' He's placed the mirror on the floor and is cutting out a pair of, what, three-inch lines. Almost as long as the mirror, at any rate, so they should do the trick. He thinks about letting her go first, then thinks, hell with it, kneels down, whisks out his straw and gives his right nostril a blast. He pushes the straw and the mirror carefully over.

'Thank you.' She hunkers down by the mirror, tidy little bottom in the air. 'At the risk of sounding ungrateful,' she says, still hunkered down, her line still untouched. 'Liar, liar, pants on fire.'

'No way. My pants are made of asbestos.'

'Is that so?' She snorts up most of her line, then sniffs. 'I suppose I'm just wary of it, what with Bobby's days on the charlie. And me working with a bunch of powdered-up wankers. I mean, excellent treat but dangerous.'

'Sure,' says Ian, still lost in his idle assessment of her bottom.

'Just saying. Change of subject. You ever do anything like what Bobby's done?'

'. . . How do you mean?'

'When you were a kid.'

'Yeah. Not with a spotted hankie, though. One time I set off with my cowboy hat and holster. Silver revolver as well, like. Made it to the end of the street, then remembered I hadn't had my tea. You?'

Louise pinches her nose and shakes her head.

'Come on. Every kid tried to run away.'

'Disagree. Every *boy* tried to run away. Girls didn't do that.'

'Now look whose pants are ablaze.'

'True. Well, *I* didn't and none of my friends did.'

'You mean you never did the big bid for freedom thing?'

'No. Whenever things were really bad, I used to hide out with Mr Buggles. My rabbit,' she explains. 'I'd run to the bottom of the garden, get in the hutch with him for a cuddle and tell him all about it. A significant difference, if you think about it. Running away versus taking time out and being emotionally articulate.'

'Yeah, with a rabbit. How the hell did you squeeze in?'

'Oh, there was plenty of room. Until I filled out a bit when I was nineteen or twenty . . . Jeez, it's ages since I did this stuff. You forget how twitchy it makes you. And chatty. Oh my.'

'Just say the word if you want any more. There's the best part of a gram here.'

'God, no. I feel like I'm on intravenous espresso as it is. So,' she says, tapping her knees with her fingertips. 'Let's get down to business. What's your explanation for Bobby's disappearing act?'

Just for a moment, he feels tempted to say what he really does think – that some shit's gone down between Rob and this one, with the result that Rob's had no option but to get the hell out of it – but he'd prefer to avoid any kind of conversational heaviness and kick-start something a bit more frivolous and enjoyable. 'He's probably just stomped off with his cowboy hat and his holster. The man'll do the equivalent of remembering he hasn't had his tea and dawdle back in a day or two.'

'Well, it's a notion that does have the advantage of conforming to Turner's First Law.'

'What's that? Who's Turner?'

'Me, silly. And my law which is mine states that all men are effectively five years old.'

'Uh-oh. Feminism alert. Feminism alert. This is not an exercise. We are at Defcon three. We have a feminism alert.'

'Unfortunately, it really works. It's like science. When you know the basic secret – electrons, molecules, all that – then you can explain just about everything. No need for voodoo or witch doctors, just take the sample to the lab.' She holds a finger in the air. 'Similarly, the apparently impenetrable enigma that is male behaviour can be solved if you bear in mind the crucial fact that, to all intents and purposes, men are children. Everything falls into place. The football thing or really getting off on cars and gadgets – toys and games. Or the wonderful way you lot cope with illness. The fondness for farting. Crap attempts at deception. Sulks. Absolutely normal behaviour if you're four and or a chap.'

'Oh, how fair is that?'

'Then there's Turner's Second Law.'

'Turner's Second Law.'

'Which states that when analysing the actions of allegedly adult males, take the most cynical explanation possible, double it, and you might be in sight of the really awful truth.'

'Okay, Louise. So what's your cynical explanation about Rob's disappearing act?'

'That Bobby could have a relationship with me as long as I was safely tucked away on the other side of the Atlantic, but when I called his bluff and came back he couldn't handle the reality instead of his little fantasy so he took the easiest and daftest way out by buggering off.'

'A bit cynical, isn't it?'

'But strangely convincing, wouldn't you say?'

'Dunno. Hey – you got anything to drink? Needn't be alcoholic. Water, juice, anything.'

'Your whim is my command.' She jumps to her feet. A minute later she returns with two glasses and a bottle of Evian as large as her torso. Dry though his mouth is, the request was mainly intended to act as a diversion. Unsuccessfully, if the expression on her dial is anything to go by. She places the glasses and the bottle on the floor and sits down beside them. 'You know, I've thought about nothing else since I read that pissy little note. Obviously. And the only definite conclusion I've come to is that I really, really wish I was gay.'

Oh, super. Maybe if they have another line, she'll lighten up a bit. He gets out the gubbins again. 'Don't be daft. Just 'cause Rob's thrown a wobbly doesn't mean . . . well, anything much. Hey – what do you think . . . ?'

'Look at it this way. If I had a nice, warm, soft, loving girlfriend, there's no way I'd be having to put up with Bobby or whatever his fucking name is and whatever it is he's playing at. Incidentally, if one of those is for me, I'll pass. Where was I? Yes. Men. No offence, but Jesus. This is a Terry-Thomas impersonation coming up, by the by – you lot are an ebb-soh-loot shah.'

'You feel like that, *go* gay. Nobody's stopping you.' He snorts one of the lines. And then – hell with it – the other. Yes indeed, yes indeed, yes indeedydoody. 'Then you'd see what we have to put up with.'

'Oh, right. I'd be forced to have a relationship with someone I'd have to see more than once a month, someone who didn't snore and didn't go off in huffs or bang on and on and *on* about whether or not they should really be going out with you or, God, I don't know, all the usual *rubbish*. And then solving everything quite brilliantly by buggering off.'

'I think you might be doing what's known as generalising from the particular.'

'Uh-huh? Have you ever thought about how truly crap it is being a heterosexual female? All the things that nobody thinks to teach you when you're in first year at middle school and beginning to get all tingly about your Duran Duran posters. If only some wise woman had taken me aside and said, Okay, Louise, get interested in boys if you must, but remember that they won't have grown up since you last had any contact with them. And they will continue not growing up until the day they selfishly expire before you. The wise woman could also have pointed out the neat little catch that there are indeed men who are not only incredibly handsome and muscly and well dressed but sensitive and enlightened as well, but they're all only interested in other men. Thanks, God. Like, you want to buy a car, madam, well, certainly, madam, although I regret that madam isn't permitted to buy anything from the top range, but perhaps madam might consider this clapped-out Trabant.'

'Same for us.'

'Is *that* so?'

'Sure. You don't get to shag George Michael, we have to put up with all sorts of crap.'

'Like?'

'Okay. Periods.'

'I'll see your periods and raise you with shallowness.'

'Never being able to find your keys.'

'Complete and utter selfishness.'

'Not finding your keys because they're in your handbag and the handbag's got enough stuff in it, it's like you're going on your holidays.'

'Emotional dimness.'

'The whole palaver about *diets*.'

'Mindless violence.'

'Changing down a gear *after* you turn a corner.'

'Every crime against humanity.'

'Not being able to read a map, not having a clue which way's north.'

'Be serious. That's north.'

'Isn't.'

'Is.'

Louise gives her nose a quick, vigorous rub. 'I think you might be doing what's known as talking out of your arse.'

'*And*. How could I forget?'

'What?'

'No sense of humour.'

'Oh, don't be ridiculous.'

'True. Blokes get together and have a laugh. Fair enough, we might not always be having in-depth discussions about *relationships* or *love* or just *exactly* what our partner does in bed, but at least blokes are funny.'

'Ah. Of course. Women have no sense of humour. How right you are.'

'Think about it. 'Course women have a sense of humour but it is a bit dodgy at best and one thing you lot can't do is tell a decent joke.'

'Point one, I'm not entirely sure that makes up for millennia of oppression and evil. Point two, you're just plain wrong.'

'Yeah?'

'Yeah.'

'Okay, then, Louise. Tell me a joke.'

'Oh, this is ridiculous.'

'You see?'

'Utterly ridiculous.'

'I rest my case.'

'Right, then. A joke. Let me think . . . Okay. This lion walks into a pub. Barman says, "What'll it be, Mr Lion?" The lion looks at all the taps at the bar and says, "I'll have a pint of . . ."' She frowns.

Ian keeps a straight face. There's a beat. Two. Three. Four.

'. . ."a pint of Theakston's, please."'

Despite himself, Ian gives her a nod of patient encouragement.

Louise replies, with a sweet smile, 'And the barman says, "Why the big paws?"'

'. . . Right. Not bad. Kind of like the one about the panda who goes into the bar, you heard it?' And Ian starts to tell her the one about the panda who eats, shoots and leaves.

The back of seven, so that's a good half-hour since Ian went in. Either the boy has keys to Rob's flat or he's gone to see that Louisa. Why? Fuck knows. The only fucking certainty is that there's been no sign of Jenny, or of Rob, in the two hours so far that he has spent skulking around Bateman Street, loitering first of all with a couple of pints and a group of afternoon drinkers outside the Pig and Whistle and then the Carlisle, then hanging out beside the minicab office on the corner, and now sipping coffee in this daft wee café-bar-type joint whose studenty customers seem completely content to loaf around on the armchairs and sofas, playing Jenga and talking shite, apparently oblivious to the fact that the place does not possess a fucking *licence*.

Well, that's quite enough of that particular anthropological fucking experience. Time to wander back to Broadwick Street and the pub next to Jenny's office, though knowing her she'll be chained to her desk until it's long gone eight. Graham finishes his glass of now-cold caffe latte, hands over his six quid – six quid! For a few cups of coffee? They're taking the pish – and pulls his jacket collar up (just in case Ian has chosen this particular moment to stand at the window and look down on the street) before moving off and away to start the second part of today's surveillance programme – the tailing.

All goes to plan, here's what'll happen. He'll hang around outside her office, wait for her to appear, then follow her, in all probability to her rendezvous with the Judas who used to be his friend. And who, it's now horribly clear, has used that friendship to get at Jenny. To think that Rob was there, every Friday night, pally as you like and, the moment his back was turned, having a right good laugh. The Friday Night Club. What a joke. What a big fucking joke . . . Got to hand it to him, though, the boy knew what he was doing – using the Friday fucking Night Club to keep tabs on him then Saturday to Thursday screwing Jenny. The Judas. The fucking Judas.

Graham tacks through a series of side streets filled with puddles and beggars until he reaches the corner of Wardour Street and Broadwick Street. What he'll do, he'll keep on Jenny's office's side of the road so that he's less likely to be spotted if she glances out from her desk, which is – or at any rate used to be – right by a window on the fourth floor. And he already knows that she should be at the office rather than at a conference in some Moat House because he phoned the switchboard, asked if she was in today, got put through and immediately hung up. You cunning fox, Anderson, Graham says to himself, more as reassurance than anything else, because his heart's thumping like a bastard and there's a pre-runs buzziness in his guts.

Graham turns into Broadwick Street. He is thirty yards from the pub that will be his lookout base, twenty yards from the atrium of Jenny's office block, and just getting into stealth mode, when Jenny walks out into the street.

He stops dead in his tracks. In fact, his entire body seems to shut down for a moment. She seems both anonymous – thirtysomething woman in dark suit, carrying briefcase – and uniquely Jenny. His Jenny.

She's stopped too, her back to him, her briefcase between her feet, her hands on her hips. Her hips . . .

He forces himself into action. He scurries across the street and finds some sort of sanctuary in the doorway of an art shop. So there's his excuse if she does catch sight of him – okay, the shop's closed but he's just checking out the wares. He pretends to be pricing easels while he takes peeks round his shoulder. Jenny's still on the other side of the street. And now she's being joined by another woman in a suit who's just been slung out by the atrium's revolving doors.

Okay. This is the new plan. He waits here while Jenny has her chat, then he follows her. Simple. Graham takes a few deep breaths but he still feels nervous like he hasn't felt nervous since his Grade One violin, when he so very nearly wet himself. Now Jenny's picking up her briefcase. Are they about to move off or . . . ?

Oh, *shite*. Jenny and her pal are turning round. Shite, shite, *shite*. They look like they're about to cross the road. He is beginning to rehearse his lines about window-shopping for easels when a taxi draws up abruptly beside Jenny and her pal and between them and him. Well, thank *fuck* for that. Right. This is his chance to get out of the art-shop doorway.

Soon as he sets off, he realises that he should just have gone back the way he came. As it is, he's hurrying along on the other side of the road from Jenny and the taxi, hunched into his jacket and beginning to affect a slight limp. He decides against taking the first right into Poland Street because that's the way their taxi will probably go and continues scuttling along the interminable length of Broadwick Street to the corner of Marshall Street, where he ducks behind some kind of pottery shop. Only now does he risk a look back through the shop's right-angled plate-glass windows.

And sees Jenny. Still there. On her own. Why didn't she get in the taxi? *Shite.* She's crossing the road and she's aiming straight for him. Perhaps, he thinks, as he breaks into a trot, this is what your pulse is like at the start of a heart attack. He forces himself to keep up the jog, turning left and then right before slowing to a walk as he nears a pub on the corner. Panting as quietly as he can, Graham lingers for a moment among the office workers drinking outside, then checks behind him. And there's Jenny – still coming towards him. Fucking hell. Fucking *hell.*

Graham breaks into a jog again, down a little cobbled street. What is it with this fucking warren? He had no idea this bit of London existed. More to the point, he has no idea where he's going. Even more to the point, there's every chance that Jenny's about to round the corner behind him. Fuck*sake.* Graham takes the next left and finds himself in a narrow passageway. He slows to a fast walk until he reaches – aha! – Carnaby Street, then panics at the sight of so many people wandering around, for who's to say one of them might not be Jenny if she's taken some short cut he doesn't know about? He dodges past a slumped wreck of a tramp who's holding up a single copy of the *Big Issue* and turns into the first open shop he sees.

'Can I help you, sir?'

Graham looks round. A wee serving girl is looking up at him with a gummy smile. Time to resort to his polite fuck-off tactic, the one he uses for market-research birds with clipboards. He puts on a puzzled expression and unleashes his one German sentence: '*Ich verstehe nicht.*'

'*Kein Problem. Moechten Sie sich unsere Sonderangebote anschauen?*' She gestures towards a shelf of miniature Big Bens and toy police helmets. Only now does he register that this shop is packed to the rafters with leather jackets, unfunnily logoed T-shirts, football scarves, general shite for tourists and, beside the cash till, a sign whose second-top line carries a German flag and the declaration '*Man spricht Deutsch*'.

'Nine,' he says.

She's not going away and she's still smiling. '*Schauen Sie sich nur um. Gefällt es Ihnen bei uns in den Ferien?*' she says.

Keep it simple, stupid, he tells himself. He shakes his head decisively. 'Nine,' he says.

For some reason, the wee serving girl looks a bit worried by this, so Graham nods reassuringly and gets the fuck out of there, having momentarily forgotten why he went into the shop in the first place but instantly remembering when he sees Jenny ten yards to his left and leaning down to give the *Big Issue* boy a coin. The sensible thing would have been to have gone back into the tourist shop, but he thinks of that only after he's beetled away in a panic along Carnaby Street, through a well-timed throng of possibly Italian youngsters. When he reaches Liberty's on the corner of Great Marlborough Street, he risks another glance behind him.

She's still coming this way.

Maybe, he wonders, she's taking the pish. Nah – how would she have known? . . . Fuck*sake*, though. He takes advantage of a pedestrian crossing and a gap in the traffic to cross over towards a crowd of people gathering outside the Palladium.

And looks behind him again. She's *still* following him. Where the fuck is she going?

The Tube. Of course. The Tube. Central line from Oxford Circus. If he can only get to the top of this street and turn right into Oxford Street, he'll be safe. Unless she's going shopping . . . He'll have to take that chance. He weaves in and out of theatregoers, then some drinkers outside a pub, and then a clutch of dithering schoolgirls, until he can finally hang a right.

Ten, twelve paces into Oxford Street, Graham stops at a kiosk and pretends to examine the rack, like he's a connoisseur of chewing gum.

There's Jenny now. Turning left and away from him, thank *fuck*, and heading towards the Underground entrance. He looks on, his panic replaced by a horrible yearning, until Jenny disappears into the crowd.

6

'JUST BE COOL AND IT'LL GO AWAY'

Saturday afternoon

Here's Ian, flat out on the bed and staring at the cracks which trail across the ceiling like rivers seen from orbit. Next door, the television is on with the sound turned down and page 311 on Ceefax relaying the news to an empty room that, four hundred miles to the north, Raith Rovers have just drawn 0–0 at St Mirren. It'll be another hour before Ian knows this, because he has another hour to go of this all-afternoon stint, not of painting the kitchen as he promised and intended, but of staring at the cracks which trail across the ceiling like rivers seen from orbit. And of trying to evade the Fear.

It's only because he had four hours' sleep last night. And his system is probably run down. Plus he's feeling a bit crap about not painting the kitchen.

But no matter how hard he tries to persuade himself otherwise, he knows the Fear is still there, skulking in the undergrowth, waiting for the right moment when his guard is down and it can pounce.

As long as he keeps his cool, he'll be all right. And one thing he's learned from past experience is that the Fear can be thought off.

So think.

Right. He'll think about the view from the flat on the Boulevard des Invalides . . . The view fades quickly away . . . He'll concentrate instead on his real, specific worries. First – money. He has none. Okay. Second – Claire. Who is still treating him as if he's suddenly acquired BO, but that's a phase, probably hormonal mood swings, and it'll pass, and soon they'll be having a laugh and a good time just like they used to. Maybe . . . Anyway, third. Well, third is Chantal. So why is he bugged by Chantal? Because . . . because she's started to occupy a place in his life, not only as yet another girl to fancy and flirt with but as an upsettingly beautiful reminder of all the upsettingly beautiful girls who are going to turn up in the future when he'll be stuck in a world of buggies and Huggies and crying. Which leads to worry number four – that the party that has been his adult life to date is winding up, with even the hardcore drinkers in the kitchen beginning to drift off into the night, and soon the music will stop and the lights will come on and he'll have no option but to stumble away . . .

Ian turns on his side and hugs himself tight. It's only a coke comedown, he tells himself, and four hours' sleep, and not painting the kitchen, and Claire being off with him . . .

But it's no use. He could be losing it here, for the thinking hasn't prodded the Fear away – just encouraged it to edge closer and closer. Because the Fear can sense his weakness.

He has to show it he's strong. Otherwise the undergrowth will rustle and next thing he'll know the Fear will have pounced.

'Just be cool,' Ian pleads into a pillow. 'Just be cool and it'll go away.' Claire. He'll think about Claire. Beautiful, beautiful Claire. He'll remember the way she looked at that party on the rue Monge when she wore a turquoise dress that showed off her tan. Or her fit of the giggles in Schindler's lift . . . So why is he not doing the right thing by her now? A beautiful, funny, adorable woman and he's not doing the right thing with her because he's scared, scared that this time he's made a mistake he can't ignore or leave behind. He feels a sharp stab of envy of Rob. The others still seem bamboozled by it all but what's happened is glaringly obvious. Louise put him under pressure to settle down, Rob's thought, hell with it, and made his great escape. Why? Because Rob could. Whereas he . . .

'Oh, Jesus,' Ian moans into the pillow. 'Jesus Christ almighty.' A mistake he's going to be stuck with for the rest of his life. A mistake which is going to deprive him of money, sleep and freedom. A mistake which will do the opposite of disappear. A mistake which will grow and grow.

The undergrowth rustles.

Nil-nil. Well, at least they kept a clean sheet. He'll get a match report when he phones his father tomorrow. By which time both his pow-wow with Louise and his night out with Ian and Graham will be in the past and all the better for it.

Alastair shoots the TV with the remote and returns to the back bit's Victorian table, where he has set out his photograph albums – twelve identical volumes covered in black, velvety material and each containing thirty stiff pages with clingfilmy covers. It had taken the best part of three consecutive weekends a couple of years back to fill these with the snaps that had been lying in an appalling jumble in a kitchen drawer until he applied chronological method to this ungoverned madness and out of chaos created order.

Perhaps, Alastair considers, the next step should be to construct some sort of index and reference system. Ah, but that would discourage browsing, and browsing through these twelve albums, as he has rediscovered this afternoon, can be really fulfilling. Flicking through album after album for photos of Rob, he's dallied over countless other images from throughout his life, recalling a host of Sunday car rides to the Lomonds or the coast, family holidays in Morecambe and Llandudno, teenage parties with the FNC, the trip in '82 to watch Scotland in Spain, weddings, dinner parties, more weddings, holidays in France and Italy and Morocco – a festive miscellany populated by friends and family (and, very occasionally, Alastair himself), squinting into the sun or carousing with devilish, red eyes.

Rob makes his first appearance in volume three, as a happy,

blond boy wearing school blazer and shorts and standing beside a forlorn, ginger-haired runt who is, fortunately, mostly hidden by the football he's clutching as though it is a lifesaver. Which, Alastair reflects, is exactly what it turned out to be, for it was the discovery that he could pass and dribble and shoot that propelled him up the primary-school social scale, from bullied geek to rarely tormented star winger. That and, of course, the friendship of Rob, after Rob moved in six doors up the road. There's no photo to commemorate the occasion, of course, but he still has a clear memory of how it began – Rob sidling up to him in the street while he was concentrating on his keepie-uppie with a ruined, grey tennis ball and Rob asking, in the exotic Lancashire accent which he was soon to discard, if he, Alastair, wanted to go hunting (oonting, he said it like) for Jerry soldiers in the woods. And that was it, the start of the era when he and Rob were inseparable, building gang huts, stalking spies, playing football, going to the football . . . and finding in each other the companion neither of them had had. For, like him, Rob was an only child, although, unlike him, confident, extrovert, with even a touch of wildness in that willingness of his to take a risk, put on a show.

Volumes four to seven and ten to twelve feature Rob so often that a casual peruser would assume these albums are his. Alastair opens number five at random – and finds Rob in Aviemore and a pair of tartan bondage trousers, so that'll be from the Friday Night Club's summer trip of '78. He turns a handful of pages and sees Rob starring in four pointlessly similar group shots of another FNC, each snap showing everyone making faces at the camera, Rob and Steve in the front, lying on their sides and propped rakishly on their elbows, like Edwardian footballers. Alastair's heart sinks as it dawns on him where and when he'd taken those group shots – Steve's party, towards the end. So even while he was taking those photos, he must have been summoning up the courage to importune Fiona, and very soon after he took those photos he was going to be rewarded for his ridiculous presumption by her devastating him with her news about her and Steve.

With some haste, Alastair slams volume five shut and puts it down. He picks up volume six and lets it fall open. To reveal Rob in the kitchen of the flat they shared in that first year at uni, pointing to the beer-mats that covered one wall. Over the page and there's Rob and a nameless girl at a party, above Rob in Seville, the '82 World Cup, wearing a Scotland flag like a shawl. And opposite, Rob at Steve and Fiona's wedding, the one photo Alastair could bring himself to take of that day. Rob's kilted up and doing a joke sword-dance, arms aloft and mouth forming a silent hooch, socked legs poised on tiptoe around the X formed by two large, silver, inexplicable fish.

Alastair looks at the ceiling while he picks a page earlyish in volume seven – where a grinning Rob has his arm around Rhona, carbon-dating that snap to the first half of '85, before Rob's parents died and Rob moved to London. Eight and nine are Robless, of course, but he starts to turn up again in ten, and here he is, at the wheel of his MG, somewhere south of the Pyrenees, the summer of '90 when the pair of them drove down to visit Ian and that woman he was with – Caroline? Christine? It's bad he can't remember, and that could well be the marijuana to blame – in Madrid. Then it's Rob, Rob and yet more Rob until the most recent entry in volume twelve – Rob in the garden, a couple of months ago, toasting the camera with a can of Stella and a ginormous spliff.

But where is Rob now?

When will Rob come back?

. . . Will Rob ever come back?

She's a hundred yards in front and still heading towards Ladbroke Grove. Maybe she's going to the florist's on the corner. No. She's reached the corner but she's ignoring the flowers. She's waving to someone up the street. No. *Shite* –

she's hailing a taxi. Graham ups the pace and gets to the corner of Ladbroke Grove just in time to see the back of Jenny's head getting smaller and smaller as her cab trundles south.

There's a taxi with its light on coming down towards him. But now it's stuck behind a bus. It's overtaking the bus. Anyone hails this fucker before him, there's going to be fucking trouble. Graham sticks out a hand, the taxi pulls up, and he hurries to the opening window.

'Yes, mate?' The driver is a large individual aged between twenty-five and fifty.

Graham points down the road, where Jenny's taxi has – thank fuck – drawn up at the lights. 'Follow that cab,' says Graham.

'Ewe tine a piss?'

'Seriously,' says Graham, pulling the door open and getting inside before the driver can refuse. 'Just follow that cab. At a safe distance, by the way.'

'So which is it?'

'Which is what?'

'MI5 or jealous asbund?'

'MI5.'

The cabbie switches on his radio. Graham hears a few seconds of a programme where the presenter is trying to interrupt someone who has phoned in to say that he's sorry but she deserves a proper monument, before the cabbie reaches behind him to slide his window shut. Graham sits back and tries to calm down but he's too full of adrenalin and anxiety.

Could Jenny have seen him get in? Fuck off. Who looks behind them when they're in a taxi? Will he manage to keep track of her cab? Fuck knows, but so far, so good – they're almost at Holland Park Road and up to now there's been enough traffic to provide cover, not enough to make tailing too difficult. Things get only slightly trickier as Jenny's cab nudges along towards Notting Hill Gate, shifts into the right-hand lane and then swings down Kensington Church Street. Where in the name is she going? He's not going to find out at this rate, because his cab's still stuck at the junction, waiting for a filter right.

Is this worth it? He can recite the answer by now. Yes, because this way, and unlike Ian and Eck, he's actually doing something about tracking Rob down. If he keeps following Jenny, Jenny will eventually lead him to Rob, who's gone into hiding to avoid confronting the wronged parties in this affair, i.e. Louisa and good self. And yes, that's not the only reason he's doing this because yes, it's the Jenny bit of the Jenny and Rob thing that bugs him, and yes, this is a way of regaining some sort of control over a situation that clearly threatens to get completely out of fucking order.

Finally, the lights change and his taxi bounces down an abnormally clear road. They pick up Jenny's cab again down at the junction with Kensington High Street. It's heading a short queue to turn left. With some astute lane-dodging and racing of amber lights, his cab keeps Jenny's in sight all the way along, past the Albert Hall and Kensington Gardens, to Knightsbridge, where Jenny's taxi pulls over and Jenny gets out.

Fifty yards behind, Graham raps on the window, hands over the fare plus a twenty-pence tip and manages to sneak out in the middle of a handy three-lane jam. He reaches the pavement just as Jenny starts to cross the road. Graham watches as she weaves through the throng of cars and people.

Oh, fucking great. That's him drawn another blank. Because that's her going into Harvey fucking Nichols. Well, shopping was something he refused to do when they were together, so he's fucked if he's going to start now.

Jenny goes inside. Graham crosses the street, has vague second thoughts about following her into the shop, dismisses them and heads off to the Tube.

7

'YOU TAKING THE PISH?'

Saturday night

He's the first to arrive. Ian thinks about getting himself a drink but then he has a far better idea. Okay, so it'll be breaking his rule, this being a Saturday, but there's a little bit left in his second wrap and the second wrap is in his wallet and he'll be stocking up when he goes to Johnny's tomorrow and a toot will dramatically improve what has been a horrible, terrible, dreadful day. Took a heroic performance just to keep going after the Fear episode. But did Claire see it like that? Woah no. You'd have thought that he'd spent the afternoon in bed with her mother the way she went on. Or, to be more accurate, didn't go on, because not painting the kitchen seems to have been yet another terrible crime which must be punished by pained selflessness ('Really. That's fine. As you please.') and, well, pregnant silences.

Ian takes the stairs down to the shunkie. Mere moments later, the world seems a much more encouraging place. He catches his reflection in the mirror and narrows his eyes. Looking good. Feeling good. Yes, oh yes, indeed. Anyway, what's the big deal? He's having a night out with his pals, she with hers, and could he really be expected to remember that this is the day when Briony celebrates her twenty-fifth with a 'dinner' 'party'? No way, especially with Rob's disappearance still unsolved, as he pointed out to Claire, who seemed mutely content to accept his point that he just had to cry off the Briony thing and attend this high-powered meeting with Graham and

Eck instead, although he reckons it won't be a high-powered meeting at all but simply another meeting of the FNC – with only a seventy-five per cent attendance, mind you, and on a Saturday and in a subdued atmosphere, the three of them coming to terms with the obvious reality that one of their mates has had to take drastic steps to escape from a relationship he didn't want.

Ian sniffs, rubs his nose and takes the stairs back up to the bar, where Graham has appeared. Bang on time for once, so either the man is taking the Rob business seriously or he's gagging for a pint. What are the odds?

'Here, I'm just ordering. Pint of lager?'

'Yip, yip, yip, yip, yip.'

So that's Ian useless. Graham drums his fingers on the bar. There are times, and this is one of them, when Graham wonders if there's any way to split up from your friends, find a new and better set. (It's just that I need some space, Ian . . .) Mean to say, how is it possible to have anything like a conversation when Ian's ripped and his eyes glow with daft, chemical enthusiasm? Fucking student. Come to think of it, that's just what Rob has done – betray one of his best mates and fuck off. Arm in arm with Jenny. The image brings on a rush of horror which leaves Graham trying very hard not to gasp. Or sink to his knees and lie curled up on the enormous ashtray that is the floor, sleeping tight until he can wake up to find Jenny beside him and the world normal again.

They carry their drinks over to the wall covered by old brewery mirrors. Graham makes sure he's facing back towards the bar. 'By Christ,' he murmurs, as he examines his Guinness, the brown foam churning. This feels exactly like anticipating the first pint of the day, which only goes to show the effects of his hour-long ramble through Mayfair after he treated himself to three badly needed nips and two troubled pints in a small, snotty, braying pub in Knightsbridge. 'Am I gagging for this.' He takes a long, two-gulp pull on this pint, turns to Ian and does a swift double-take. 'What are you grinning at?'

'Nothing,' says Ian with an innocent look. Then he has another smile at his lager.

Graham's face suddenly quivers into a mask of wide-eyed fury. 'You taking the pish?' he says between gritted teeth.

'Nup. No way. Fucksake, calm down, man.'

'Oh, blimey, I'm really, *really* sorry. I called in on Louise, you see, and didn't realise the time until . . . actually, until I happened to look at my watch, completely by chance, and I had no idea, I mean, it seemed I'd only been there for five minutes but it had already gone half eight and I couldn't believe it. Anyway, I am really sorry.'

'Cool, my man.'

'Nae problem, Eck.'

Alastair finds an excellent spot at the bar, right by the till, but that makes no difference to the three young chaps behind the bar, who ignore him and his twenty. Eventually, when the three chaps have served every other customer, washed every spare glass and conducted a surprisingly heated debate about the wonkiness of the till's buttons, Alastair catches the eye of one of the barmen, who seems quite nonplussed by this turn of events, and orders a round.

While Alastair waits for the barman to pour the drinks, and to take a well-earned break from this toil by adding a lengthy footnote to the wonky-till discussion, he mulls over the information he and Louise have collated. There's hardly a lot, but even so his thoughts are in such a jumble that he tries to simplify matters by itemising the key points with blobs, like they do in the Comment section.

- Rob has been going out with Louise for nearly two years, without telling her about them or them about her. Or telling anyone about his allegedly great drinking buddy, Jeremy Maddox.

- Whatever he's done, Rob has been planning this for some time, what with getting Maddox to sell his flat and stuff.
- Judging by the note and Jeremy Schmeremy's evasiveness on the issue, Rob has concocted a new identity for himself, maybe like in *Day of the Jackal*, taking on the name of a little boy his age who died, or something.

Stick to the facts.

- Rob seems to have been deleted from the NatWest's personnel records.
- The police aren't concerned or even vaguely interested, mainly because Rob doesn't appear to have committed, or been the victim of, any crime.
- Louise is probably right, and the only way they're going to discover anything about what's happened is by buying professional help – i.e., hiring a private detective.

Which seems such a drastic step, and not only drastic but desperate, intrusive and, yes, seedy, that it makes Alastair feel just hopeless that he can't find stuff out on his own. If this was a film, with, say, Sandra Bullock as Louise and him played by . . . God, it'd probably be the one who's George on *Seinfeld*, then Sandra and George would progress from being stumped to gradually unearthing clues by hacking into computer networks or stumbling across an intriguing 555 phone number hastily scrawled on a book of matches advertising a strange club or bar where they'd go and they'd meet an acquaintance of Rob's they didn't know about who'd give them another lead and they'd follow that up and . . . But this isn't a film, and he and Louise do not possess a single clue or the slightest idea of how to go about finding one. So Louise's idea does make sense, and she does know of someone who could help, an investigator type hired by a chap at her work whose dippy daughter was embroiled with a crack dealer. Well, even though the detective won't be a glamorous, wisecracking dude in a hat but some fat bloke who probably spends most of his working life looking into adulteries and dubious insurance claims, at least the fat bloke might come up with an explanation to better and kill off all the thriller-inspired explanations that have been flying around in his mind – Rob has unearthed some financial scandal and has had to go on the run, Rob belongs to a covert security force and has had to go on the run from terrorists, Rob is not Rob but a sleeper agent run by a covert security force, who has been under deep cover disguised as a normal citizen, since the age of eight.

His stubby fingers straining around the three glasses, Alastair joins the others, who are both oddly quiet. Hardly surprising. He doesn't feel much like it's party-time himself. Well, maybe so, but he knows from experience – specifically, the one, protracted experience of coping with his mum's decline into a fearful imbecility which ended only when she took her rattling last gasp – that all you can do when bad things happen is keep going and hang on in the hope that the bad thing will, in time, get less bad. Hope, mind you, not expectation, because, for all the wonderfulness of modern life, the benefits of having a washing machine or a vote don't matter when it comes down to grief and sorrow – or they do matter, to the extent that given the choice of being distraught and watching colour TV or being distraught and having so little to do that the visit of a pedlar is the highlight of the year, then he'd opt for being distraught with the colour TV. But, far as it goes, that only goes so far, and even with all the advantages of living in an enlightened, prosperous, peaceable democracy which is part of a Western world whose technology, infrastructure, knowledge, expertise and sheer prosperity are such that it dwarfs every preceding civilisation, like in *Independence Day*, where the city-sized flying saucers are but tiny adjuncts of a mother ship so vast it could cause an eclipse, life comes with no guarantee of anything but its own extinction.

'Hey,' says Ian into the silence. 'Knock, knock.'

'Fucksake,' says Graham, who shakes his head and swigs his beer.

'Who's there?' says Alastair.

'Diana,' says Ian.

'Diana who?' says Alastair, with some misgivings because it's only been a couple of months and he's never seen the appeal of topical bad-taste jokes.

'Ah, how quickly you forget,' says Ian.

There's a pause before Alastair realises that this is the punch line. 'Hah,' he says politely.

8

'SHOOSH, SHOOSH'

Monday morning

A stone's throw ahead, Jenny turns left, her long raincoat billowing in a gust of wind. He flies up to the corner of the street, in time to see her opening her front door. As soon as she shuts the door behind her, he scoots up the street and starts to hover outside her flat. No sign of her, so he wheechs round to the back garden and looks in on her bedroom. There she is. Lying on the bed and already naked. And now she's holding out her arms to a man standing out of sight in the doorway. It has to be Rob. He peeks in her bedroom window. He watches as Rob moves forward from the doorway, takes off his jacket, kicks off his shoes, leans down to remove his socks, unbuttons his shirt, unzips his trousers, pushes down his boxer shorts, and stands there, admiring the knobbled weapon that is his vast erection, clutching it in both hands, like he's a flag-bearer heading a march. Graham screams and pummels the window with his fists. Neither Jenny nor Rob pays him the blindest bit of notice. Only now does he realise why he can fly through the air and hover twenty feet above the ground. He's dead. He's a ghost. And this is how he's going to spend eternity, hovering in midair, pummelling Jenny's bedroom window, and watching her beg to be skewered. 'Please,' she begs Rob. 'Please, please, *please*.'

'Thirty-three.'

Alastair focuses on the bit of floorboard directly below him. His arms straighten and lock. He takes a deep breath.

And then he thinks, Why? What on earth is the point? Alastair flops down on to his stomach. The floor is squashing his left cheek. He is gaping at a grey smudge of dust on the corner of the skirting board. Give it up, he thinks. Give up this ludicrous regime. Hire a cleaner. Phone in sick. Quit geeing himself on to keep things going, keep up the whole pathetic pretence that it's somehow worth it. This is as much as he'll ever have. For all his wittering to himself about this part of his life being a period of quiet recovery after trauma, it's actually been nearly a decade when he's done nothing while everyone else has been playing and winning at the mating game, getting together, getting married, having children, finding some purpose to their lives. Not him, though. The first half of his life has already been and gone, and what has he got to show for it? Nothing. No soul mate. Nobody to share his life with. He couldn't even hang on to Rob. And no wonder. He's small, he's bald, he looks like a cartoon of Jimmy Johnstone, and he's pathetic. So just what *is* the point?

There is no point. But that's not the point. And it will not be an excuse.

Alastair places himself back in position, then slowly, so slowly that his arms shake with the strain, he lowers himself down, until the tip of his nose almost touches the rug, then up until his arms straighten and lock.

'Thirty-four.'

Two more. Come *on*.

Sticky eyed, furry mouthed and fuzzy headed, Ian is standing in his tiny, shambolic kitchen and staring morosely at the kettle as he waits for . . . the water inside the kettle to boil.

'Oh dear.' It's Claire, still in her nightie. She's holding on to the door and looking decidedly groggy.

'Hey,' says Ian. 'Are you all right?'

She shuts her eyes and shakes her head.

Ian goes to her, strokes her shoulders, then holds her in a

gentle hug. 'Ah, Claire,' he says. 'Don't you worry. It'll pass in a moment.'

'Mm,' she says into his chest.

He nuzzles her blonde crop with his chin. 'Shoosh, shoosh,' he mumbles sleepily. 'Shoosh, shoosh.' Behind him, the kettle clicks off as the water inside comes to the boil. He can feel the strange little thickening of her tummy now for she's relaxing into a proper cuddle. 'Better?' he says.

'Mm. Much better.' She gives his chest a peck, and another, and another, then she rises on tiptoe and her mouth moves towards his. There's a moment when her lips stay an inch away from his and he feels a rush of exquisite longing. And then they kiss. He savours it all, the softness of her lips, the tender flickering of her tongue. He cups her bottom in his hands, pulls her towards him. They should have enough time, if they skip breakfast, and when did they last do it? Nineteen hundred and . . . Okay, fair enough, two weeks ago, but it seems a distant memory.

'Claire,' he whispers into her ear. 'Claire. Let me take you back to bed.'

She groans. He can feel her pubic bone grinding against the base of his dick, which he's sure is going to burst very soon, like an ineptly cooked sausage.

'That'd be nice,' she says.

'Oh yes,' he says.

'Just for a cuddle, though,' she says. 'I do feel a bit queasy still, and I've got to meet Briony in half an hour.'

'Eh? Why?' is what Ian says, although what he's thinking is that the way he's feeling this deadline would still give her twenty-eight minutes to get herself ready.

'Oh, she's got some baby stuff from her brother that she wants to give us. Clothes mainly. Maybe a cot as well.'

'Right. A cot.'

'But there's always this evening,' she says, nuzzling his chest again. 'After the AFP.'

'AFP?' Ian says to the top of her head.

'The tests. At the hospital. Five-thirty. We're going together, remember?'

'Ah.'

'Oh, Ian, you haven't forgotten, have you?'

'No. 'Course not. I just didn't realise it was today.'

'But you can make it?'

'That's the thing. I've got an extramural trip with the advanced lot this evening.'

'Oh, Ian.'

'I'm sorry, Claire, I've got my days muddled up. And I've already told Foxsmith that I'm doing it.'

'Oh, Ian.' She's pulled away from him. She's crossed her hands in front of her breasts. Her eyes are squeezed shut and her mouth is stretched into a taut, thin line.

9

'HE COULD HAVE MADE AN ACCIDENT'

Tuesday afternoon

'Graham, my boy, hi, it's Nige at CDQ.'

'Ah, Ni . . .'

'How are you, good, excellent, top man, thing is, Gray, my main man, the thing is, this is a bit awkward, but what it is, we have a bit of a problem here at Calder Davies Quinby with the exhibition.'

'What kind of problem?'

'Basically, in essence, a timing problem. Nothing to do with you, logistics that's all, no reflection on you, your work or anything. What it is, Saul Quinby was over in Prague last week, bumped into Brian Eno, and Saul was sold on this scheme of Eno's, so what it is, the period CDQ allocated for your thing has been reallocated.'

'What do you mean, Nigel?'

'Again, don't get me wrong, this is not a cancellation and it's certainly not in any shape or form a rethink about you. As I said, Eno's got this installation.'

'Uh-huh?'

'It's a kind of interactive Internet thing, very cutting edge, very multimedia, very now, very exciting.'

'Sounds, ah, exciting.'

'Yes, we're all very excited about it, everyone at CDQ's very up for it, very excited about it, and since we've got the chance to host an Eno event, we can't pass it up and of course, as I said, Saul and Eno go way back, so there you are.'

'But where is that?'

'Say what, Gray?'

'Where does that leave my exhibition?'

'As I said, we're going to host the Eno event for a non-defined period, a timeframe which means that we can't host your exhibition at the same time. What it is, we're going to have to rethink the parameters.'

'You're postponing it?'

'Exactamundo.'

'Till when?'

'That's out of my hands, Gray, I mean, that's a real fifth-floor job, and as I said, we'll be re-examining the situation after the Eno thing, reassessing the schedule, with a view to letting you know the outcome at that point in time.'

'. . . Well, Nigel, I realise the problem, and I quite see, with Brian Eno and everything . . .'

'Yes, well, we are all very excited about it. Top man, Gray, top man. Okay, so we'll be in touch, okay? As I said, we'll be hosting the Eno thing for at least a year, so we'll be in touch in the fullness, okay? You take care, Gray, my main man. Laters.'

'Goodbye, Nigel.'

There's a clattering noise as Graham replaces the phone while he gazes at the wall, and then there's only the background mayhem of the drills and thumps of the Thames Water crew out in the street.

This is bad. This is very, very bad. Very, very, very fucking *bad*. Unless he's misunderstood and Nigel was only talking about a postponement. Ahah. Of a year. At least. And then what? Nah – he's definitely being shat on here.

How long can things go on like this? When is he going to get a break? Just one fucking break. Is that too much to ask? A break. That's all. Not world peace or a win on the lottery or a shag off Liz Hurley. Just a break.

What's he doing that's so wrong?

And what the *fuck* is it with Brian fucking Eno? And Damien fucking Hirst and Tracey fucking Emin and all the rest of that fucking bunch of *fucks*. With their commissions and their exhibitions and their TV appearances and their tents and dung sculptures and fucking fish in fucking formaldehyde. Who the *fuck* are they? What makes them so good? And him so cancellable? Eh? Come on. What's the fucking difference? What's the fucking magical quality that they've got and he hasn't?

By Christ, he's had better ideas than that Sensation lot. He had better ideas than them when he started on this six months ago, and he jettisoned them all, because the idea he has is so much fucking better than the other ideas and especially their trite shite which is only the kind of fucking garbage that you'd expect from a bunch of fucking *students* . . .

Graham pushes back his chair and stumbles through to the bedroom, where he stares at the nearly completed installation in a dwam of disbelief. He has an impulse to wreck the whole thing, tear down everything, tear it into shreds, sweep everything on to the floor, rip it all up, stamp on it and keep on stamping and ripping and shredding until it's all no more than litter.

No. He's not going to do that, and he's not going to do that for the very good reason that this time there's a real chance that he has hit on something. His every instinct tells him that this work just *has* to be good. Not because the alternative would be such a calamity – although it definitely would be, no two doubts about that – but because he's put in so much effort and time and emotional fucking energy into this, and it's such an excellent concept, so bold and, basically, brilliant, there's no way this should fail. No *fucking* way . . .

And what about that thing about good art being born of torment? *My Struggle* by Damien Hirst? Fucking *settle*. But him? His career's hit an iceberg, his overdraft's a joke, and the woman he loves is getting screwed by his best friend. Okay, second-best friend, but who's fucking counting. Aye, he's struggling and no fucking mistake, and this work comes straight from the fucking heart. Fuck the lot of them. Fuck Eno. Fuck Calder Davies Quinby. Fuck Rob. Fuck fucking Jenny.

Fuck them all.

'He should have used a knife.'

'Oh, yes indeed. Stanislaw?'

'They ought to have driven slowly.'

'*Good*. Dieter?'

'They should not have swam so far.'

'Swum, Dieter. Swum swum swum swum swum.'

'Swum.'

'Paolo?'

'She needs to lose weight and go to the Versace shop.'

Ian glances down at the row of cartoons in his teacher's copy of *Let's Speak English! Volume Four*. These cartoons depict, from left to right, a man hacking at bread with a spoon, a car upside down in a ditch, two children waving forlornly amid a storm-tossed sea, and a matronly figure wearing a triangular frock and a top hat. 'Very funny, Paolo.'

'Thank you.'

'But remember we're using modal verbs. Should have, would have, could have. What *should* she have done?'

'Okay. She should have eaten less food and she should have bought a hat by an Italian designer.'

This brings a cheer from the rest of the class, apart from Chantal and Monique, who continue to stare anxiously at their textbooks. Paolo leans back in his chair to exchange a high five with Dieter.

'Very good, Paolo. Let's move on to the second set. Could have. What *could* these people have done? So we're making a guess about them. Chantal. What could this person have done?'

Ian spends the puzzled silence that follows by examining Chantal's tumbling, shining, auburn hair as she leans over her book and the cartoon of a man lying in bed, mummified by bandages, all four limbs hauled into the air by pulleys, a pair of skis improbably propped against a wall.

'He . . . could have . . . made an accident.'

'That's excellent, Chantal. Excellent. Really really really good.' Lesson 36, the modal verbs, the constructions of second guesses and second thoughts, of regret and recrimination – he should have done this, he could have done that, he would have done the other thing, given another chance – has never been one of his favourites. Today, though, he's in a fine mood and on sparkling form, and even the modal verbs seem dedicated to benevolent advice and benign reflection. No doubt about it, this sunny ebullience has been inspired by the sight of Chantal but two metres away. Plus, to be fair, a pre-class pick-me-up. Ian swallows a sneeze and checks out the next drawing, where a footballer is holding his arms aloft and being hugged by his team-mates. 'Who's next? Monique?'

'The man could have . . . could have . . .' Monique shakes her head.

'Okay, Monique, good try. Anyone? Yes, Paolo.'

'Obviously,' says Paolo. 'This guy is celebrating his transfer to Juventus.'

'Could have, Paolo.'

'Where he could have the chance to play good football.'

I could have had an even bigger line, thinks Ian. And I should never have got pally with that little wanker.

Alastair shuts his eyes and gives in to an enormous yawn. He arrived at work so late that he was just in time for the lunch break, but it's been a busy old morning nonetheless. And a long one, what with him forgetting to shut the bedroom door last night, allowing Susie to nudge her way in and wake him early, at 6.24 to be precise, by clambering all over his face. However. Sweet. And he'd been able to have a good go at the garden before making it down to Holborn for the eleven o'clock with Louise and the detective she knew about.

A grander office than Alastair had expected – all thick carpet, glammed-up receptionist and pastelly abstracts, and nothing like the Portakabin-style cubicle he'd so confidently pictured. The detective, Mr Hilton, was another surprise – neither a wisecracking dude in a hat nor a fat, sweaty bloke but an imposing, suited man in his late fifties with the studiedly formal manner of an old-school ex-cop who has had to train himself how to be polite to the public. That, at any rate, was how Alastair interpreted his fondness for sirring, mistering and mizzing. And Mr Hilton was so ready to reminisce about his days on the Flying Squad that the three of them managed to exchange a mere sentence or two about other, minor issues, such as Rob's disappearance. Well, Alastair had thought, perhaps that was as much info as Mr Hilton needed at this stage, as he'd tried to tell a rather downcast Louise over coffee afterwards. A quick hug outside the coffee place and a tortuous journey east on account of a suspect package at Liverpool Street, and that had been the morning gone.

And now it's one of those post-lunch-time lulls. Despite his late arrival, Alastair can think of only three things that he has to do – wait for James Bond to return from the tea run, digest the canteen meal which is sitting in his stomach like a brick, and regret his decision to bypass the salad bar for once in favour of a plate of what looked like deep-fried sock and chips. Alastair has another yawn. He's worked in offices for . . . it must be fourteen years now, but he's never got used to the fact that working in an office invariably means being forbidden to have a little lie-down after lunch. He'll have to rest content with this moment when the phones aren't going and the other subs have yet to return.

Alastair takes a deep breath and tries to summon one of his daydreams – about the ramshackle gîte he could do up, or the mansion in Fife he could swap for his two-up, two-down in

Finsbury Park. Instead, he finds himself remembering the time in Primary Three when Rob told his new classmates that his family had just moved up from Lancaster so that his father could continue developing his hovercraft design, and Alastair was so proud to be best pal and desk-sharer of this assured, awe-inspiring newcomer. 'Hovercrafts, is it?' his own father had said with a smile when he told his dad all about Rob's revelation that evening. 'And there was me thinking Nairn's made lino.'

Come on, now, Alastair tells himself. This won't buy the baby a new bonnet. He gives his head a quick shake, turns to his screen, and scrolls down the Lifestyle files. Ah, Tamara's copy has arrived. Well, that'll certainly keep him busy for a while. He calls up the file and skims the intro.

Was I deeply pissed of or what. Imadgine my horror when for the first time in my life I had to turn right when entering the airoplane. Fare enough, it was a 12-seater island-hoping byplane but still you would of thought there would of been a first class but no and nor was there any room for my lugage

Alastair taps on the Alt Screen key and types out a message to Barry, who is returning with Derek, the pair of them holding their stomachs and groaning theatrically, James Bond following sullenly behind and brandishing a grey cardboard tray of drinks. 'strordinary news. tamara just filed on time. and the first par has only one deeply. shall I do her or'

His phone rings. Alastair tucks the handset between his ear and his shoulder, like a maestro with his violin. 'Subs,' he says, while he adds 'do you want' to the message to Barry.

'Hi, Alastair.'

'Hello, Louise.'

'Here's your tea, Alan.'

Clamping a kidnapper's hand over the phone, Alastair looks up to thank James, then ungags the phone to add, 'How are you doing, Louise?' Then he types 'to have a go 1st?' and presses Send.

'A bit better. I still don't know about that Hilton, though.'

James Bond shoves the Styrofoam cup down on top of a very precarious pile of marked proofs. 'We could always try someone else,' says Alastair as he reaches out to rescue his tea and approximately ten hours of collective work.

'Shimply shooper,' Derek says to James, who's handing him his tea.

'We-ell, yes, Alastair, I suppose we could.'

'Shooperb.'

'But, thing is, I've already made another appointment.'

'Mmmm. Moasht shatishfying.'

'I know it's a bit rash but I felt I had to do something and if we had another time fixed I thought that might gee him along.'

'A taisht shenshaishun.'

'Friday at two. Can you make it?'

Friday. Lifestyle's press day. 'Difficult, Louise. It's our busiest day, you see.'

'Let me gesh. PG Tipsh?'

'And Canary Wharf is so far out it's technically part of Amsterdam. Shit. I really wanted you to be there with me.'

'Or Lapshang Shooshong?'

'Bloody hell, Derek. Give it a bloody rest.'

'Shorry.'

'I'm bloody serious, Derek.'

'I don't think I'll be able to make it, Louise.'

'Damn.'

'Well, I'll be with you in spirit and you can call me as soon as it's over.'

'I'll do that. You're a good man, Alastair Carr.'

'Don't be daft, Louise. Talk to you later.'

'You will indeed. Oh. I almost forgot. Remember you mentioned that Bobby had been in New York?'

'Yes?'

'When was this?'

'A couple of days ago.'

'You what?'

'When I mentioned it. No, sorry, Louise, that was a stupid joke to make. Let's see. Ninety-four, ninety-five, something like that. When he was seeing . . . staying at the Paramount, as I recall. Why do you ask?'

'Because that *shit* told me that he couldn't come out to see me in the States because he was on some Yank blacklist.'

'A blacklist? You mean he said he was banned from the States?'

'More or less.'

'Did he tell you why?'

'. . . Yes.'

'Louise?'

'. . . He said it was because he'd once been arrested when he was on a demo about Nicaragua outside the American embassy.'

'Are you joking?'

'Nope.'

'Only that Rob would be as likely to, I don't know, join the Salvation Army or something as go on anything like a demonstration. Far less get arrested for it.'

'I don't know about that. He threw an egg at Mrs Thatcher, didn't he?'

'Not that I know of, Louise. To be honest, Rob's never been into politics.'

'Don't be silly. What about the SNP thing?'

'What SNP thing?'

'Him being a party member thing. Him working in the SNP campaign office thing.'

'. . . Blimey.'

'I see. Maybe you and I should have another session comparing notes about Robert Mackenzie. Don't you think?'

'It does seem that way, yes.'

'Next you'll be telling me you didn't know about Bobby being a scoutmaster.'

'What?'

'That really was a joke. Not the rest, though. Damn, the other phone's going. I'd better dash, Alastair. Talk to you later.'

'Okay, Louise.'

'Pip pip.'

'Pip pip.'

Frowning to himself and moving in slo-mo, Alastair replaces the phone. He turns to his computer and sees MESSAGE flashing on his screen. It's from Barry. 'gd news abt tamara. you have a go 1st if you want. also s/thing to report re 007. and wot you smiling abt? hot date? lucky swine.'

'yes. she won't leave me alone, that cindy crawford. wot to report re 007?'

Barry starts thumping away at his keyboard. A moment after the thumping stops, Alastair's screen flashes MESSAGE. 'gd news and bad news, al. gd news is that b/bottle has decided 007 won't be with us for long but will go to Arts to write bits n bobs. so we won't have to put up with derek and his bloody connery act for much longer. bad news is that dep chief sub plan is no more. aplgies.'

That's it? aplgies? To his own surprise, Alastair realises that what he is feeling is very pissed off. 'Barry,' he types, using a capital letter because this is not going to be a friendly message. 'Not only do I resent the fact that the offer of my promotion has been withdrawn, I also object to the way that you have informed me of this withdrawal. I deserve better and you know it.' He gives the Send key a biff before he can think twice.

After a few moments of silence, Barry pops his head up over his terminal. 'Bloody hell, Al,' he whispers. 'What's got into you?'

Alastair's not quite sure what the answer to that question

is himself. Refusing to meet Barry's eye, he stares steadfastly at his keyboard. 'I am sorry, barry,' he types, but then he tells himself not to be such a wimp. 'Actually, that's not true,' continues the message, partly to Alastair's own surprise. 'Messaging me like that, it isn't good enough.' Alastair presses the Send key.

Barry starts thumping.

'bloody hell. i know, al, and i really made a balls up. I hate doing things like that so I tried to do it chummily and it was wrong. I am sorry. Truly.'

'thanks, barry.'

Barry pops his head up again. 'Al,' he says. 'How can I make it up to you?'

'Actually, Barry, there is something.'

'Fire ahead.'

'I'm going to take a long lunch break on Friday.'

'Friday? *Fri*day? Don't be absurd.'

'I'm not being absurd. You're always saying you owe me one. Well, now you definitely do owe me one, and that one is a long lunch break on Friday.'

Barry holds up his hands in mock surrender. 'All right, all right. Take the long lunch. I trust it's with a pretty damsel?'

Alastair smiles. 'As a matter of fact, it is.'

'Should have said so in the first place. Can't stand between a man and the eternal mystery that is lurve. Now, as a further peace offering, I can give you a real treat.'

'Which is?'

'Josh Todd.'

'Oh, no, Barry, not . . .'

'Don't you fret. It's Derek who's earned another Joshing. But I thought you might like a sneak preview.'

'His copy isn't in, though. I just checked the Lifestyle files.'

'When?'

'About ten minutes ago.'

'Aha. That's your problem right there. The new Josh arrived

about nine minutes ago. I've got it on-screen, so call it up on Read. Should put you in the mood for your Friday lunch.'

'I doubt it.' Alastair quits Tamara's latest and replaces it with a copy of the file labelled JToddnew.

I see the lady in my life waiting for me at the bar. I walk over. I say 'hello' and then I order myself a drink. I decide that I want a gin and tonic with ice and lemon and I tell the barman that this is what I want. The drink arrives. I hand over my money. I take a sip of the drink.

Josh seems to have rediscovered the gift of tedium, thank goodness. There's room on the screen for only one more paragraph, so Alastair orders himself not to scroll down, otherwise he'll just get annoyed and want to edit the worst of the rubbish and, before he knows it, he'll be subbing Josh again.

I take another sip, and another, then another, and soon I have finished the drink. 'Lets go,' I say to the lady in my life and she agrees. Soon I am leading her out of the bar on the fifth floor of Harvey Nichols and out to the street. I hail a taxi. We go back to Notting Hill where she lives where I immediately grasp her from behind and pull her back towards me. She twists round to face me so I unbutton her coat and I kneel down in front of her and then I am burying my face in her lap. Then I am lifting up her skirt and taking down her pants because she is wearing stockings. Then I put my mouth on to her groin and soon I am tasting her vagina as I lick it with my tongue.

Oh dear, thinks Alastair. Oh dear, oh dear, oh dear. Dearie, dearie me.

'Derek?' says Barry.

'Yesh? Sorry, yes?'

'Have I got a treat for you.'

10

'HAPPY NOW?'

Wednesday evening

Here's Ian, swerving through the crowd of post-work drinkers and heading towards the back of the pub and the door marked 'Fir'. He pushes the door open with a creak. The place is empty, apart from the person occupying the one cubicle. Oh, super. Ian marks time by taking a piss, directing his stream round and round the blue puck of disinfectant, then blasting the sucker with a final burst that lasers down, slap bang on its centre.

Still no sound from behind the locked door. Ian zips up, wanders over to the basin, starts washing his hands. A faint rustling noise from the cubicle but no more than that, so he adopts Plan B. Taking quick, small steps, he moves back to the door, pulls it towards him with a creak, shuts it again, and returns with a heavy, clomping tread to the urinal. He waits there while he counts to twenty, then he clomps over to the basin where he ekes out some more time by running the hot water and examining his reflection in the small, mottled mirror.

Looking good. Ian tweaks and pats a couple of his less ruly black curls. Yip. Damned good.

The luck of it. Think how different his life would have been if he didn't look like this. One thing, he'd probably have settled down a lot earlier, it being one of his theories that what gets and keeps many or most relationships going is not desire but need and fear. How else do you explain the pairing of, for instance, his employer and his employer's spouse? Desire couldn't enter into such an arrangement, what with Foxsmith being a ferret-faced arsehole and the good Mrs Foxsmith, who made the mistake of once visiting the school, turning out to have, surprise, surprise, the body of a weeble and the face of someone who, as an infant, must have run headlong into a sturdy wall. Don't try to tell him that they actually wanted each other. They were just delighted at finding another person ugly enough to be flattered by another ugly person's interest in them. Reason for marriage, and cue two lives of unimaginably hopeless masturbation.

Whereas he . . . well, he's been able to go for women he's fancied, hasn't he? Granted, this gadding about has had drawbacks, and his sexual CV (which is, let's be frank, long) includes more than its fair share of tears and trauma (though not for him, obviously, his energies having had to be spent on a variety of elaborate pretences, all of them constructed to spare the soon-to-be-ex partners a basic truth – 'I have been / I will be sleeping with someone else. She is prettier / sexier / newer than you. So that's me off and you dumped') and he has no doubt that his name is Ian Mud in selected circles in a clutch of European cities.

Yeah, but all that goes to prove is another of his theories, which states that men like him get a bad rep only because, one, they have the wherewithal and the gumption to follow their restless, roving instincts, and, two, because the instincts of females – for stable relationships, nest-building, kids, all that – are seen as moral only because they're convenient for society. Patriarchy? Don't talk to him about a patriarchy. If this were a patriarchy, if men got to do what they really wanted to do, there'd be an anarchy of mindless rutting – no candlelit dinners, no foreplay, no cuddly stuff afterwards, just grab, grope, ride, then on with the trousers and shut the door behind you. So although he has acquired a score of eighty-four shagees (though down to seventy-eight if the criterion is actual penetration), even that impressive score is but a tiny fraction of his unrequited lusts. And any self-respecting gay guy would think a score of eighty-odd not just crap but completely sad. Like when he compared tallies with that gay guy who taught at the Oxford School in Barcelona – little chap, not good looking or anything, camp, but funny, palled about with that porker from Dublin (the pair of them corroborating that joke – Why do poofs exist? So fat girls won't feel lonely), Rih, Rah, Roh, yes, Roger, appropriately enough, tried it on with him when they first met, gave him that gay guy's pouty, big-eyed stare a couple of times, before he put him straight – and it turned out that, in the course of that year alone, and it was only September or October, Roger had nearly bested his lifetime score, which must have then stood somewhere in the mid-seventies. Gay guys, what are they like? Well, that's just it – they're like what straight blokes would be like if straight blokes didn't have to obey rules made by and suited to women. Compare and contrast gay guys to gay women. No bathhouses or cottaging for lesbians, oh no, none of that rampaging for them, just support groups and couply-douply trips to furniture shops.

There's a flush, then the cubicle door opens and a suited youth emerges, rubbing his nose. Aye, aye. Ian takes his place. Ten seconds later, he is hunkered down by the toilet bowl, head bent over the lidded toilet seat, left index finger pressed against his left nostril, right hand angling a straw over a thick, three-inch line. Ian snorts half the line up his right nostril, switches to his left, discovers this passage is so blocked that he might as well try sniffing through his feet, switches back to his right and sucks up the rest of the powder.

Ian pulls the flush, for protocol's sake. He packs the wrap and the straw into his wallet and steps out of the cubicle, remembering as he does so that, according to the story he told Claire, he should be rejoining Graham to talk about Rob. Well, it's not really a lie, since he would be about to rejoin Graham and maybe talk about Rob, had Graham not cried off.

Still nobody else around, so he treats himself to a rattling good sniff. See, that was the thing about Claire, because she offered a way out of what appeared to be the cul-de-sac that his thinking had led him into. There's a moment when he struggles to remember just what that thinking was. Yes. If straight men had the same licence as gay ones, then he would have spent his entire life sleeping around – flingettes, two-night stands, or, more likely, encounters that would last the time it took to chat a girl up and give her one before sloping off for the night bus. And, let's face it, he would be happy to oblige, say, one in five of the women he meets. Push came to shove, like in that game fuck-or-die, then the proportion would have to go up to a third or even a half, even more, since he doesn't come up against too many Brionys, women he would simply refuse to have, unless for an enormous fee or under the threat of expertly applied torture. So that's one problem which, he came to acknowledge, would face him in any relationship – that a good part of the time he'd be checking out other women, wondering how they might compare to the present incumbent, what they'd be like under their clothes. Factor in the threat from the élite – your Isabelle Adjanis, your Sophie Marceaus – and your everyday extras, like the piece of work with the ridiculous breasts he's spotted working in the Krazee Kost-Kutter Klothes Kompany, and he really did have a problem, because even with a good-looking woman like Cristina there were always those subversive, taunting reminders – on billboards, on telly, on the covers of women's magazines (now what is *that* about?), or merely passing him in the street – that there were women out there who were much sexier than the one he was with, so how could you do the equivalent of settling for an all-right house in Kirkcaldy when you could have the equivalent of a stonking great big apartment in Paris?

He'd thought he'd solved the problem with Cristina, when the initial falling-in-love bit of the relationship had been amazing, like having a bright light shone in your face, so that he just didn't notice anything in the background, just as he didn't pay any heed to her nipple-circling, am-I-special? routine. For weeks he'd wandered around Madrid, oblivious to that city's miniskirted, sloe-eyed minxes, entirely unbothered by the vamps on billboards. Then those weeks passed, the odd row started appearing, and he learned the occasional eyebrow-raising fact about Cristina, notably when she confessed that she really couldn't be doing with oral sex. And, slowly at first, the bright light had waned and the figures in the background had re-emerged into focus.

Old enough by then to do a post-mortem on the bashed mess that was the Cristina relationship – shit, marriage – he had concluded that the only reasonable thing he could do would be to concentrate on the élite, casual stuff apart. Cue several years of casual stuff. Then along came Claire, bringing with her a light so massive and powerful she could have staged evening fixtures. A light that shone at him so brightly that everything else would stay in the background for ever and ever.

Well, that was the theory. He checks the mirror and gives a stray curl a tweak. Then he's out back into the body of the kirk, swerving through the crowd of post-work drinkers until he reaches his companions for the evening.

'Can I get you girls another drink?' Ian asks. 'Monique? Chantal?'

'What can I get you?'

Pint of Guinness and a quadruple tequila, is what he badly wants to tell the barman, but he has to keep a clear head, so he says, 'Mineral water, please,' and, trying to ignore a twinge of desperation at this denial, tells himself that it's just very dull to spend an evening without alcohol. Or anything else, by the way – no distractions, no chatting, just mineral water and fuck all.

Three hours he's been waiting in this pub. Three fucking hours. Three hours of sitting on his own, reading the *Evening Standard* (never a sign of a happy, busy time), doing the *Standard* crossword (ditto, and some), pretending to be waiting for someone, then giving up on that pretence and becoming what he was – the sad bastard on his own in the corner – while he toyed with glass after glass of mineral water. Man of steel, though. Man of fucking steel.

This all started when he phoned the switchboard at Jenny's work and, by cunningly claiming to be a client, secured the information that she was away for two days at the conference she was organising in Hampshire. Which was all he fucking needed, by the way – to be immediately assailed by images of Rob waiting for Jenny in her hotel room, wheeching off her knickers then impaling her. Also, it put the kibosh on his half-formed plan to have another, better go at following Jenny after she left her office.

Then he had his brainwave. Megan. The fat flatmate. He'd follow Megan instead – and bump into her, accidentally, as you do, make polite chitchat and ask her politely, with an air of kind concern, as though enquiring about the health of a distant, elderly relative, about how Jenny was doing these days. Was she okay? Was she seeing someone? That's great. Good for her. Anyone he knows? . . .

Simple, yet brilliant.

But things had not quite gone to plan. Not a fucking tall to plan, in fact. Although everything had gone fine to start with. He'd had to hang around for only ten minutes outside the twee little office where Megan did whatever the fuck Megan did in the exciting world of restaurant PR, before Megan had appeared. Looking like the kind of person who'd describe herself in lonely hearts ads as a bubbly, vivacious blonde – i.e., a dumpy wee fat bird who likes her drink. Easy enough to follow her, though, as she waddled her way towards the Tube, despite her lack of height, because her frizz of yellow hair made for an excellent marker, even in Covent Garden's usual milling gaggle – tourists, fire-eaters, jugglers, some cunt dressed as an android, a couple of women holding babies and placards that announced in scrawled capitals that they were hungry and from Bosnia. Uh-huh. Bosnia. Tinkers, more like. So the idea at this stage was to bump into Megan casually in the Tube – perfectly natural, folk meeting at a Tube platform, going the same way, having a wee chat, easy fucking peasy.

Aye, but Megan being Megan, she had swung away from the Tube station, hoiked a right and headed down Long Acre, towards Great Queen Street and all those shops selling masons' shite, then trundled into a pub, one of those new-fangled Oirish joints where you can have all the time you like to admire the buckets of nails on the gantry and the antique road signs to Tipperary because you're being served by a moron who's just off the plane from Auckland and is pouring his first-ever pint. Packed to the rafters, like, but he'd still heard Megan's shrieks and managed to catch a glimpse, as he ambled past, of the commotion as Megan met up with Megan's pals, a yelpy squad of Megan look-alikes. On for a session, it seemed, so he'd dodged across the road to a normal pub – or as near to normal as you can find in London – on the corner and settled down to keep watch and stay sober. Three and a bit fucking hours ago.

He's about to crack and order a Guinness and a whisky chaser when he spots Megan coming out of Mickey O'Fenian's or whatever the fuck it's called. On her own and clearly pissed. He waits for her to pass his pub on her way back to Covent Garden Tube station, but instead Megan suddenly veers east, swerving a bit as she walks by the weird row of masons' shops. The fuck is she going now?

Ah, Holborn Tube station, just down the road, Central Line direct to Snotting Hill. Fuck. And she's got a good hundred yards' start.

Graham hurries out, crosses the road, narrowly avoiding death by taxi, and trots along behind her. When a side street appears on his left, he decides to take a gamble – run up the side street, hang a right if there is one, hang another right if there is one and not a dead-end, and stroll down Kingsway where he'll bump into Megan coming towards him. That doesn't work, he'll double back and get her in the Tube.

Graham jogs along his detour, which, rather to his own surprise, does indeed lead him into Kingsway. He stops on the corner for a moment to recover his breath, then starts to mosey south. And that's her now.

'Megan!'

It takes her a few bleary seconds to get him into focus. 'Oh, hello. Where you going?'

Way ewe gown. Christ. 'Just . . . down the road here. So. How's Megan?'

'Good, good. Bit squiffy, to be honest.' Wee flicker of a smile there.

'Excellent. Girls' night out, eh?'

His heart sinks as soon as the words are out of his mouth but she doesn't seem to notice his blunder. 'Asswipe,' she says cheerily enough, though he still needs a moment's thought before he realises that she's agreeing with him.

He nods encouragingly and remembers to keep smiling. 'Still living with Jenny?'

He couldn't have been more casual or chummy, but the very mention of Jenny seems to remind Megan that she should be frosty with him. 'Yes,' she declares. ''Bye, then.'

'Hold on, Megan. I'll walk you to the Tube.'

'That's the opposite direction for you.'

'Nah, not really. And I'm a gentleman.'

'Hmm,' says Megan as pointedly as it's possible to make a hmm. She makes a move to go past him. Graham responds by turning side-on to accompany her.

'And how is Jenny? She doing all right?'

'Fine.'

'I hear she's seeing someone.'

No reply.

'That's great, I think. Really good. I mean, I'm really pleased if she is. Seeing someone, like.'

No reply.

'I just hope she's happy, that's all.'

Megan keeps on walking.

'Always difficult, isn't it, to start up another relationship. If that's what it is . . . No, really, I'd be happy. For her. If she's seeing someone.'

'I'm going to cross the road now. Goodbye.'

That's it. He's had enough of this shite. He grabs her by a flabby arm and hauls her back. 'Just tell me, all right? Jenny. Jenny and Rob. What the *fuck* is going on? When did it start?'

Megan studies the hand that's gripping her flesh. 'If you don't let go,' she says softly and pleasantly, all trace of squiffiness gone, 'I am going to scream for help. Then I'm going to start crying. And those two big blokes coming up behind you look very gallant.'

Graham lets go of her arm.

Megan nods once. 'That's better. Now. For the second time, goodbye. Or, should I say, fuck off.'

'But you've got to tell me. I know you know. Jenny is seeing someone, isn't she?'

Megan puts her hands on where her hips might be and sighs. 'Yes. She is. And well done her, is what I say.'

'It's Rob, isn't it?'

She tuts and looks to the orange night sky.

'Fucksake, all you have to do is . . .'

'I tell you what. If you get down on your knees, clasp your hands like a good little boy saying his prayers, ask me nicely, I'll tell you everything I know.'

Out of the corner of his eye, he can see two burly young men in suits looking at him as they pass by. He lowers himself down until he's kneeling on the pavement. He puts his hands together and says, 'I'm begging you to tell me, Megan.'

'Please.'

'Please.'

'Pretty please.'

'. . . Pretty please.'

'You have no idea how much I'm enjoying this. Okay, so all I know is this. Jenny is seeing someone. He's very keen on her, you'll be pleased to hear, and he is called Jay.'

Graham frowns at Megan's podgy knees. 'Jay?' he says.

'Yes, Jay. I don't know his full name. That's his initial.'

'J?'

'J.'

'J?'

'J.'

'But that's what Rob calls her in his diary.'

'Who *is* this Rob?'

'And she can't call him J because he'd be R. Or B, I suppose.'

'I haven't the foggiest what you're talking about. Oh, I can tell you one other thing.'

'What? What?'

'The one other thing I know about this guy, and I just know this will cheer you up, is that Jenny met him through one of your ickle chums. And that's your lot. Happy now? You can get up if you want.'

Graham lurches to his feet, feeling woozy as he does so, whether from the change in altitude or the befuddled state of his brain he's not quite sure. He takes a deep breath and stares uncomprehendingly at a blob of chewing gum fixed to his right knee. 'So it's someone called J something who's screwing her, not Rob. You sure it's not Rob?'

Megan rolls her eyes.

Graham's stomach lurches at the terrible thought which has just filled his brain. 'Jason! Fucking hell, it's Jason! Jason . . . She must have met him through Col. It fits. Col's the friend. She knows Col. Jason . . . It's Jason . . .'

'Well, there you go. Goodbye.' As Megan steps round him, she shows him a fist, then steadily raises her middle finger.

'Jason,' says Graham.

'Blimey,' says Alastair. He stubs out the roach and flops back into the comfiness of the candy-striped sofa. Susie seizes the chance to jump up and lie on his stomach. 'Good grass,' says Alastair. This strikes him as a very cool thing to say. Then it strikes him that, right now, anything would strike him as a cool thing to say.

'Where would I be without grass?' Alastair whispers to Susie. 'In an even bigger neurotic mess, I suppose,' he whispers back. As it is, he's mustering a smile as he remembers the incident on the DLR this evening, when he was astounded to see, farther along the carriage, standing with his back to him and reading the *FT*, Rob. Before he'd had time to think, Alastair had rushed over and, just as he began to reach out, realised that he was about to hug a stranger. Nice chap, fortunately. Financier from Stockholm. Lars. And he didn't seem at all bothered. Quite the opposite, in fact, and by the time they got to Bank, Lars was asking him if he knew of any good bars in the Earl's Court area . . .

Blimey, thinks Alastair, for it has just occurred to him that maybe Lars was gay, and maybe even chatting, him, Alastair, up. Oh well. Oh dear. Oh well. He tries to banish his embarrassment by concentrating on the Discovery Channel documentary he's been half watching about the CIA.

Not too bad, reckons Alastair after a minute or two, but he still switches it off, because it's going to be a whole programme of American-sponsored ghastliness and that will only depress him in the end. It was bad enough even half watching the carpet-bombing in Vietnam, the coup in Chile, the Bay of Pigs fiasco there in black and white, the poor old Guatemalan banana-growers, and then the Contras and Reagan pretending they were freedom fighters. 'As if Cuba was a threat,' he scoffs at Susie. Or even the Soviet Union – a country where folk had to queue for bread and drank shoe polish. But maybe people'll think the same kind of thing in twenty years' time, when they look back on the great baddies of this decade and wonder why the big fuss about Libya or Iraq or whatshisface in Belgrade. Anyway, what are they compared to the old days, when watching the news was like supporting Scotland and the best to be hoped for was the avoidance of catastrophe? That's why he can now be such a smiley optimist about democracy and world peace and so forth – because he grew up in the seventies and the firm expectation that civilisation was about to end in a mushroom cloud as big as the planet.

Same syndrome, come to think of it, as supporting Scotland, at least since the '78 World Cup, when he, along with an entire nation, learned to aim low and avoid disappointment. Keeping your hopes down – it's an approach that has come naturally to him and has usually worked quite well. Even with sex. So he's always, or almost always, managed, fairly instinctively it seems, not to think about girls who were out of his reach, from Kirsty Barclay onwards. And, over the past nine years of singledom, he's definitely found that it's easier to cope with not having sex if he doesn't have any expectations of having any sex. And that's not difficult. After all, when did he last get a glimmer of having sex? Okay, fair enough, this summer, at the *Chronicle* party, when Antonia, the rather attractive (he thought) temp on the picture desk, seemed to be chatting him up. But how could anything happen when Antonia was supposed to be living with a website designer? Anyway, not to forget that it was also bad form leaving Jenny to fend for herself for a noticeably ungallant half an hour . . .

That kind of rare incident apart, he's become so accustomed to the lack of sex that he can go for days at a time now, and almost not think about sex. And it's certainly become odd to think that he has had sex in the past, that there are four women in this world who have had sex with him.

Now, is he stoned enough to go through his short list of

exes? 'I'll give it a shot,' Alastair whispers to Susie, although she seems to have fallen asleep on his lap.

- Carol, 1982. Final year at uni, when he was swotting like crazy, never going out, hardly ever seeing Rob, who in any case had begun to hang out with a hippie crowd, but a rare night out had somehow ended up with him back at Carol's and Carol encouraging him to lose his virginity.
- Angela, 1982. Two months after the one-night stand with Carol and, on a roll now, he got off with Angela at a post-exam party. Sweet, nice-looking Angela, who turned out to be a real demon in bed. Only four months they went out together, before they graduated and went their separate ways, but long enough for him to learn a variety of surprising moves.
- Pat, 1985. A *Scotsman* leaving do, he got off with Pat, a fellow sub, and, amazingly, got away with having an office affair for three weeks, until Pat cut it short because it was in danger of becoming serious. Well, that's what she said, but at least it was good of her to do it gently.
- Rhona, 1986–8, the nearly three years which in hindsight have to be seen as a golden era, one to rival that of the first FNC. Nearly three years when he was blessed with his longest-ever relationship *and* a vigorous social life (even though Rob had disappeared down south by that time, taking with him those great nights out in the Café Royal) – what with his *Scotsman* pals, Rhona's lot, Jenny a bit, before Graham and Jenny also decamped for London . . . and Cathy.

Cathy, whom he'd got to know through Rob but who stayed on as a friend after Rob left. Yes, as a friend, he'd reassured Rhona, and himself, every time he arranged to meet Cathy for a drink or a curry. But he could make those reassurances only because he hadn't got past acknowledging that Cathy was way out of his league, Rangers to his Cowdenbeath. Even so, that supposedly innocuous friendship definitely contributed to the real reason he and Rhona split up – that he wasn't actually in love with Rhona. Whereas he could easily have fallen in love with Cathy. With her eventually unavoidable loveliness. Not that there was any chance of Cathy reciprocating. As he soon found out. Less than a month Rhona had been gone, and Cathy had taken so much trouble to make sure he was all right, checking up on him, treating him to an evening at the Kalpna, and how had he repaid her kindness? By getting drunk back at her flat and asking if he could go to bed with her. Appalling. Appalling, appalling, appalling . . . Cathy, of course, had turned down the bumbling, crass proposal, which broke the rules of their friendship and, effectively, ended it. Over ten years on and he'd repeated the Fiona catastrophe – starting off by being grateful just to be in a beautiful woman's oxygen space, then becoming friends, then making a disastrous pass, thus destroying a friendship and himself in the process. Brilliant.

'Nine years ago,' Alastair whispers. 'Nine years.' Nine years of celibacy – it sounds a horrifyingly long period of time, though lately he has begun to wonder if maybe he's not that abnormal, if maybe lots of people aren't having sex, if maybe most people he knows don't have much or any sex. Gadabouts like Rob excepted, of course . . .

Not that Rob's ever gone on too much about his gallivanting – no names, no pack-drill, and no indiscreet details. Rob's innate tact would be the reason for that, Rob just lapsing occasionally into mentions of a pick-up at a club or another affair with another bored secretary or besotted housewife.

Alastair sits bolt upright and Susie springs off his lap. 'Louise,' he says, for only now has it dawned on him that every time Rob has had one of his escapades, he must have been two-timing Louise . . . Well, there's another good reason for Rob not to brag too much.

11

'YOU SEE MY PROBLEM?'

Friday lunch-time

'Hi!'

'Hello?'

'Graham!'

'Speaking.'

'. . . It's Audrey.'

'Oh, hi there, Audrey. How are you?'

'Oh, you know. Same old, same old. There I was, thinking haven't seen you, you haven't been around, dah dah dah dah dah, and yes, there was the Cantaloupe thing but we didn't get a chance to, like, and all the rest of it, so on and so forth, blah-di-blah-di-blah, so I thought I'd whatever. So. How's the exhibition coming along?'

'Aye, well, not so good.'

'But that's the way it happens, isn't it, the ups and the downs of the creative process, the this and the that, the blah blah blah, and you've just got to keep at it, keep going, dahdahdahdahdah.'

'Aye, I know what you mean, Audrey, but it's more than that. They've been bum-licking Eno at CDQ so they've got some installation by him instead.'

'Oh, *no*. Oh, but Graham, that's just, those *swine* . . . What about Marty?'

'What about Marty?'

'Col, or maybe it was Hermann, whatever, was like, Marty's got this big space on D:Zine's ground floor and he's on for turning it into a kind of gallery thing, exhibitions, installations, dahdahdahdahdah.'

'And you reckon he might be on for hosting mine?'

'Sure. He knows you, he's on the lookout for whatever, he needs art in there, blah blah blah. Why not?'

'That is brilliant news.'

'Glad to be of, you know, whatever. You can buy me a free drink at Jason's studio thing tonight.'

'Studio?'

'See, that's you in Finchley, out of the Shoreditch thing. Party, celebration, launch kind of thing for the BT campaign thing Jason's been doing. At his studio. Jason was like, it's open house, party-time, let's all celebrate my fantastic success, blah-di-blah-di-blah, so why don't you come along?'

'Oh, aye. He never told me it was in the studio. What time?'

'Well, seven or eight, whatever, but I've got another thing I've got to go to rehrehrehrehreh*reh*, but later, yeah, and it'd be great to see you, talk about the Marty thing, catch up, whatever.'

'I'll be there. And thanks, Audrey. Really.'

'Oh, blah-di-blah-di-blah.'

'See you tonight.'

'Ciao.'

'Honestly. Don't worry . . . I'll remember. Honest . . . Okay. See you later.' Jesus. Ian places the phone back on its cradle and wonders if his life is ever going to be the same again, or whether this really can be the start of decades of chores, tasks, responsibilities, things to do, things to remember to do. Don't panic, Mr Mainwaring, he tells himself. It's only a trip to Superdrug. Still, though, but. Ian wanders along the corridor to the common room, which is empty, so he is mulling over whether or not he could risk chopping one out when somebody appears in the doorway. Chantal. Smiling uncertainly and looking good enough to eat.

'*Bonjour*,' Ian says, and follows this up with a crinkly-eyed smile. '*Fais comme chez toi*.'

'*T'es trop gentil*.' Chantal props her dinky bottom on the edge of the orange-coloured armchair.

Oh, most fortunate edge of the orange-coloured armchair. 'How are you, Chantal? *Tout va bien?*'

'*Oui, assez bien*. Well enough.'

'Excellent,' Ian says, while racking his brains to find something to talk about. The weather? The landlady? Monique? Toulouse? . . .

'I want to ask a question about the class today.'

'Great! I mean, good. Ask away.'

'Like. I do not like like.' She makes a face, as though like were sour. 'It is so difficult. I like to do this but I do not like doing it, I detest the dentist but I like to go . . . Bof. Terrible.'

She's wearing a skirt that shows off the inch above her knees and her skin is the colour of caramel. Ian has another go with the crinkly-eyed smile. 'Yeah, it's a difficult one, Chantal. Okay, gerund first. Ing for enjoying. What do you really like doing?'

'I like . . . eating good food?'

'That's it. What else do you like doing?'

Little bait being dangled there but she doesn't bite. 'I like seeing my friends. I like . . . holidays. No, a moment. I like going on holidays.'

'There you are. Now, like to. You like to do something that is good for you. But you might not enjoy it. For example, I like to, oh, I don't know, I like to get up at eight, but I don't like getting up at eight. So what do you like to do?'

'I like to . . . I like to study English.'

'Oh, Chantal.' Here's another chance to flirt and he isn't going to pass it up. 'Don't you like studying English?'

She crosses her legs to reveal a perfect triangle of slim,

caramelly thigh. 'I like studying English with you.' She puts on a face of mock seriousness. 'Mr Murray.'

Ian laughs. 'Excellent attitude. You may call me sir.'

Chantal uncrosses her legs, places her hands on her knees in good-girl pose, then treats him to a glance of playful coyness with those big, almondy eyes. When she speaks it is with the hint of another pout and at a level just above a whisper. 'Sir,' she says. Then the pout disappears and that wide mouth slowly widens farther.

'Subs.'

'Alastair?'

'Jenny! What can I do you for?'

'Oh, Alastair, I know I said I'd call you and it's not as if I haven't wanted to. Only . . . well, I . . . it's . . . I'm sorry, Alastair, but do you have a moment?'

''Course, though I have to leave at one to see a detect . . . Blimey, you won't know about Rob, will you?'

'Rob from Kirkcaldy? What about him?'

'It must sound crazy but Rob seems to have gone AWOL. That's where I'm off to, a private detective who's trying to trace him.'

'God. And Rob's disappeared? But then he's always been a bit odd, hasn't he?'

'Has he?'

'Kind of. That suave, sophisticated act of his . . . I'm sorry, I know he's your friend. I only knew him a bit, because of Graham. Although that didn't stop him trying it on soon as Graham and I split up.'

'. . . Blimey.'

'Not that he got anywhere, I assure you.'

'Blimey.'

'Anyway, Alastair, why I'm phoning, I was wondering if you could do me a favour.'

'Blimey . . . Yes, Jenny, of course.'

'And tell me something about this Sunday's Lifestyle.'

'I thought as much.'

'What?'

'You're a spy from the *Telegraph*, aren't you?'

'Oh. I see. Yes. Foiled again. The thing is, Alastair, I am spying but for myself. What I want to know is . . . It's about . . . Oh, this is just appalling. I can't believe . . .'

'Jenny, are you all right?'

'Not really, Alastair, to be honest. The thing is, I need to find out what's in Josh Todd's column for Sunday.'

'Josh Todd? Don't tell me you're a fan.'

'Not exactly. I just want to know if his column on Sunday is going to be anything like last week's.'

'Oh, yes. It's the usual drivel about nothing, really. Josh blethering on about him and his new girlfriend.'

'And is there anything about him and this woman having sex?'

'Blimey, yes. Cringe-making stuff. Maybe even worse than last week's. Apart from anything else, I feel really sorry for the girlfriend. Oh, no, wait a minute. That's why you're phoning, isn't it?'

'I'm afraid so.'

'You know her, don't you?'

'Well, that's a matter for debate.'

'Is it anyone I know? No, no, don't tell me. It'd be unfair on her. And if I ever met her, I just wouldn't be able to look her in the eye.'

'Alastair, I do hope that isn't the case, otherwise you and I will never see each other again.'

'Sorry?'

'Please don't make me say it.'

'What? Oh . . . Oh, God.'

'You see my problem?'

'Oh God. Yes, I . . . Oh. Ahem. I see. Ahem . . . So . . . how did you meet him, Jenny?'

'At the *Chronicle* party.'

'Oh, no. Oh, God. But then this is all my fault. Oh, Jenny, I am so sorry.'

'Don't be daft, Alastair.'

'But it's my fault. If I hadn't taken you to the party, you wouldn't be . . . you wouldn't have met Josh.'

'Alastair, you are not to blame for this. And I did have a great time with you at the party.'

'Oh, blimey.'

'There was a bit towards the end when I lost track of you. He came over, we got chatting, and he seemed quite nice at first. And I suppose I was kind of flattered. I mean, I've got to the stage when I walk past a building site and hope to hear wolf whistles.'

'I cannot believe that for a second.'

'True. So there I was being chatted to if not up, and it was a bit of a morale-booster, that was all. I mean, I didn't flash my knickers or give him my number or anything. But then I bumped into him a month or so back. I was having lunch at the Ivy . . .'

'Very posh.'

'Work, I needn't add. He was there waiting for me when I went to get my coat. He asked me out for a drink and it seemed too much bother at the time to say no, so I said yes, so we went for a drink and that was okay, so we had another date. And the rest you know. As do millions of *Chronicle* readers. Thanks to that incredibly stupid, selfish, ghastly *wanker*.'

'Circulation's down to six hundred thousand, if that's any comfort.'

'None whatsoever, Alastair, I assure you. When I read his column on Sunday . . . I simply couldn't . . . I had to . . . Of all the . . . Basically, I've never been so angry with any man in my life, and for an ex of Graham Anderson's that's saying something, believe you *me*. Apart from anything else, he's making most of it up so that he sounds like some kind of demon lover, although he's one of those clueless types. Clitoris, oh yes, the capital of Lithuania. But I can't even put the record straight because that would mean . . .'

'. . . Is that what you wanted to tell me when you called before?'

'No. No, I was trying to keep it quiet. And now look.'

'He doesn't name you. There is that.'

'And you won't tell anyone, will you?'

''Course not, Jenny.'

'Promise?'

'I promise. Blimey, though, it must be awful for you.'

'Thanks, Alastair. And, yes, it is. Beyond awful. As I told Josh when I also told him that if I ever saw him again, it would be through the cross-sights of a machinegun.'

'If you want a hit-man, any of us on the subs desk would do it for free.'

'I'm keeping that job for myself, if you don't mind. So how bad is this week's?'

'Ummmmm . . . Bad.'

'Oh God . . . Could you maybe fax, no, bike round a print-out?'

'Not according to the rule book. But this is different, and it's not as if you're going to be showing it around.'

'You're right about that.'

'Well, if you've split up with him, the silver lining is that this'll be the last column he writes about . . . about you.'

'I really hope so. After all, we only had two proper, you know, fully fledged dates. The second and last was on Saturday, because the next day I read his shitty little column.'

'Yes, this one's about Saturday. I can tell you the thrust, I mean the gist, of it now, if you want. All that happens is that he meets his unnamed girlfriend at Harvey Nichols, and then they both go back to her flat.'

'What about the party?'

'Nothing about any party, thank goodness. This is all about Saturday afternoon.'

'Not Saturday night?'

'No.'

'Oh shit.'

12

'WHICH WAS REALLY BIZARRE'

Friday night

Pine tables, leather chesterfields, an exhibition of not bad black-and-white photographs of rural pylons on the wall, menus folded around little glass vases all holding a single small iris in full bloom, a blackboard detailing the day's specials in faultless italic, a list of specials that includes the words crostini, seared and teriyaki . . . No way is this pub a pub. An art gallery with tables, maybe. A restaurant that sells beer, possibly. But a pub? No way.

Ian dips his crusty bread into the saucer of olive oil. So when did this all happen? When did British pubs start being so cool and civilised they could almost be Dutch? What happened to fizzy beer and flock wallpaper, a menu that stretched to one cellophaned roll filled with a rectangle of processed cheese and a large, violent ring of onion? Young guy over in the corner, he's sipping from a stemmed bowl of Leffe and reading a book on post-structuralism, if you please. Had Ian tried that when he was a student back in late-seventies Edinburgh, when you were considered a poof in bars like the Diggers and Drummonds if you didn't smoke or still had two ears, he'd have been able to finish the book at his leisure and in the peace and quiet of the Royal Infirmary.

'Which was really bizarre,' Ben is saying as Ian turns his attention back to what has to be, please, the end of Ben and Ruth's account of their experiences at this summer's Womad festival – a heady day out which featured, Ian now knows, Ben and Ruth particularly approving of a Malinese dance troup and a Hasidic rap artist, Ben and Ruth finding themselves gratifyingly adept at the tabla workshop, Ben and Ruth joining in the mass jeering as Concorde flew overhead, and Ben and Ruth returning to the carpark to find that the windscreen of their Peugeot 206 was one of several which had shattered on contact with Concorde's sonic pollution.

'And then we had the most amazing journey back from Reading,' says Ruth. 'Didn't we, Ben?'

'Yeah, it was bizarre, actually, because . . .'

Oh, for goodness' sake. Ian nudges the saucer of olive oil over to Claire. She replies with a tiny shake of her head and a slightly less tiny smile, which could be anything from cool politeness to naughty complicity. Who knows? Not him. Not any more. This pregnancy business is turning a transparent, happy-go-lucky girl into an inscrutable woman of mystery.

'. . . decided to avoid the motorway because of the windscreen and go by the B-roads instead, so we . . .'

When's she going to turn back to being nice, loving Claire again? How much more of this . . . apartness does he have to take?

'. . . on the radio that the M4 was jammed solid. So our route was much quicker, wasn't it, Ruth?'

'Definitely quicker. I mean, why they have motorways ruining the countryside when they just get clogged up . . .'

'Yeah. It was really . . .' Ben furrows his brow as he searches for *le mot juste*.

Please, God, thinks Ian. Strange. Unusual. He realises that he's digging his fingernails into his palms. Surprising. Disconcerting.

'. . . bizarre,' says Ben.

'Ah, young James,' Barry announces heartily. 'Did you manage to find out what was happening in Design?'

'Yes.'

'And what was that?'

James Bond twitches his left shoulder. 'Not much.'

'Did you ask about the cover?'

'Yes.'

'And what did you find out about the cover, James?'

'Doesn't like it.'

'Oh, bloody hell. Bloody *hell*. The editor doesn't like it?'

'Yes.'

'What doesn't he like?'

'Hasn't heard of him.'

'David Beckham? He hasn't heard of David Beckham?'

'Says he's too obscure for the Lifestyle cover.'

'Oh, *bloody* hell. But what the bloody hell could Blue, Richard find as an alternative? Al, any ideas?'

'Well, there is the piece about Vivienne Westwood. The editor might have heard of her.'

'Possible. Unlikely, but possible. Sorry, James, what were you going to say?'

'Says he likes the Josh Todd article.'

'That's good, but I'm more worried about the cover, James.'

'Says he might want Josh Todd on the cover.'

'Do what?'

'Says he might want Josh Todd on the cover.'

'Bloody, bloody, bastarding, fucking hell. I'd better have a word with B . . . Richard about this. He can't put Josh on the cover. He can't, he can't, he just can't.'

'Says he'll make a decision on it when he gets back.'

'Gets back from where, James?'

'Oswestry.'

'Eh? What?'

'Gone to do a thing for Sky News.'

'Right. Osterley, you mean. Even so, the editor might as well be popping up to Shropshire, the state of the traffic, and it's right out by Heathrow. Gone ten now, so it could be midnight before he gets back. Unless he phones in. Or . . . Oh, bloody hell, this is going to be a late one. A very, very late one.'

A week ago, in a previous lifetime, Alastair would have tried to reassure Barry at this point, at least offer to stay with him until the bitter end. But as it is, Alastair says nothing and resigns himself to the inevitable.

In fact, Alastair doesn't mind at all the prospect of endless hours waiting for Lifestyle to go to press. With Friday Night Club suspended and little to do in the way of work, except come up with the occasional remaining caption or headline, he can take this chance to have a good think about the second meeting with Mr Hilton – and the aftermath, when he was saying goodbye to Louise and she suddenly stepped forward, put her hands around his back, and began to sob into his chest.

Graham licks the salt scattered on the back of his hand, downs another tequila, sucks a slice of lemon, shudders, coughs. 'Fucking get in,' says Graham, then he looks around the studio for a buckshee beer chaser.

There's an unopened bottle of Budvar on Col's workbench. In fact, the first thing he noticed when he arrived several hours ago was two dozen unopened bottles of Budvar chilling in a bucket beneath Col's workbench, but by now Graham is far too drunk to recall their existence. Invigorated by the tequila, he lurches over and grabs the Budvar before any other bastard can get to it. Hah! He opens the bottle, takes a swig and surveys the scene.

Col is chatting with Tim over by the high window that looks out on to Curtain Road. Sue's with a group of half a dozen children Graham's never seen before who are solemnly smoking a joint. Hermann's at the back of the room, sitting on what was, once upon a time, Graham's desk and chatting up an improbably tall, thin girl who may or may not be some kind of model. A quartet of Jason's pals are beginning to dance around the boom-box. Jason's nowhere to be seen. The bastard.

Audrey hasn't turned up yet. Aye, well, fuck it.

Time for a slash.

Graham pushes himself off towards the studio door, then down the corridor to the bogs. Just think, he thinks – four years back, I used to do exactly this walk every time I wanted a dump. Until I had to sack myself. How low can you get? Losing your job as a freelance illustrator, that's got to come pretty fucking close.

Graham shoulders the door and stumbles into the toilet. Where he sees that Jason is scrubbing his hands in a basin full of soapy water. Fucking *poof*. Wanker probably puts a towel over the fucking bedsheet before he shags her. Big pack of fucking Kleenex on the bedside table.

'Well, well. If it isn't Jason,' announces Graham before lining himself up in front of the urinal.

'Graham. All right?'

Awe wigh? His pish batters at the urinal. 'So, then,' Graham shouts over his shoulder. 'That's you washing yourself nice and *clean*, eh, Jason?' Graham tucks himself back in, failing to notice as he does so that his conspicuously laundered chinos are acquiring what will soon be a New Zealand-shaped stain.

Graham makes his way over to the row of basins and stops a foot behind Jason. Graham leans forward so that his reflection appears alongside Jason's in the small, cracked mirror. He feels quite pleased with himself at having inadvertently created this cinematic moment. But now he has to say something else.

'Having a good wash, eh? Ya *bastard*.'

Jason peers at Graham's reflection. 'What's this?' he asks.

'What's this?' says Graham. 'What's this? *This* is what this fucking is.'

The idea was to clout him across the ear. But by the time Graham has drawn back his fist and taken a swipe, Jason has swerved out of harm's way. Jason turns and grabs him by the shoulders.

'Graham. What the fuck are you playing at?'

'Oh, aye. Playing, is it?' Although he's never tried it before, Graham feels a surge of confidence as he tenses his neck then delivers his head-butt.

A small fraction of a second before he makes contact, it occurs to him that the proper target for a head-butt might be somewhere about the top of an opponent's nose, not the brickwork of an opponent's forehead. As it turns out, Jason ducks to the left so that Graham catches him a glancing blow on the side of his temple.

'Ow!' says Jason.

Graham says nothing, for it would have needed many, many more tequilas to block out the confusion of pain in his skull. And now a sickening dizziness which has him clutching his head and reeling from side to side.

Jason, by contrast, seems to have suffered damage that can be cured with a little light rubbing. 'What the hell was that all about?' he says. 'Jesus Christ, Anderson, you drunken *idiot.*' For further emphasis, Jason pushes Graham in the chest. It's not a big push but Graham's on his heels and off balance and the push propels him backwards towards a cubicle.

'Jason. The fuck you doing to Graham?'

It's Col, standing in the entrance and staring in astonishment as Graham staggers into the jamb of the open cubicle door. Graham's first reaction is heartfelt gratitude, because there was a moment there when he feared that he was going to keep on staggering into the cubicle and down on to the lidless and seatless toilet, coming to rest as though he's in a cartoon about dysentery, the back of his head against the cistern, his arse slumped from view and his legs dangling over the side of the bowl. His second reaction is to notice the pain.

'Graham, Jesus, are you all right?' says Col from somewhere far away.

Part Three

1

'TALKING IN MY MIND'

Saturday morning

'Thirty-four.'

Blimey.

'Thirty-five.'

Alastair closes his eyes, takes a deep breath and lowers himself down again. Then he pushes himself back up, his arms trembling as they straighten and lock. 'Thirty-six,' he gasps, then he staggers to his feet to do the stretching. He does twelve bends to the right, twelve to the left and twelve where his palms have to touch his toes. Then he straightens up and shakes himself loose.

Twisting his neck from side to side, Alastair makes his way to the bathroom, where he steps on the scales. Ten stone two. Say what you like about upsets, but they're pretty good for the waistline. Alastair squeezes Colgate out on to his toothbrush and starts to scrub his teeth. Rob, he thinks, now that he doesn't have anything else to think about. Rob . . .

Alastair spits, rinses and waggles the toothbrush at his mirror image. 'Come on, now,' he tells himself. 'This won't buy the baby a new bonnet.' So. Here's what he's got to do. One, not obsess about what Rob's been up to. 'Two,' he says, as he puts the toothbrush back in its beaker, 'make the most of the Saturday.' Which means ignoring the fact that he was subbing Lifestyle until 2.30 in the morning. And that means having a plan of action. Which will also help him not think about Rob . . . So. Bit of brekker, shower, shave, all the rest of it. Then off to Marks for the weekly shop, maybe pop into the garden centre for a look-see, back here to clean the place up. And, no getting out of it, give the windows a going over with hot soapy water and last week's Comment section. Then the results, then off to the Pig and Whistle for the summit meeting with Ian and Graham, tell them his news. About Rob. Why? Why on earth would Rob . . . ?

'Soo-zee,' Alastair calls out in a minor third to distract himself. He lets the minor third elide into a couple of bars from one his current favourites, 'Everytime' by Lustral. Whoever she, he or they are. 'Can you hear me? Talking in my mind,' sings Alastair to cheer himself up as he makes his way down to the kitchen, his cup of Earl Grey and his orange juice.

Graham is following Jenny as she hurries down St Martin's Lane towards Trafalgar Square, her long raincoat billowing in her wake. Just before she reaches the end of the street, she turns abruptly left and into a very narrow and very dark alley. He breaks into a trot. But by the time he has reached the alley's entrance, Jenny's nowhere to be seen.

He can hear her, though. She's somewhere near by and she's moaning. 'Oh, please,' she says. 'Please, please, *please*.' He takes a few steps into the alley and immediately realises that he's been lured into a trap. There's a faint light at the other end of the alley, but he knows he won't reach it in time. He spins round to see a figure standing in silhouette. The face remains in darkness but he recognises only too well the swot's side parting, the hunched stance, the looming rectitude.

'Got you,' says Gordon Brown.

Sticky eyed, furry mouthed and fuzzy headed, Ian is standing in his tiny, shambolic kitchen, blowing his nose into a wad of toilet roll while he waits for, oh Christ almighty, the water inside the kettle to come to the boil.

When it does, Ian chucks the damp wad of loo roll into the bin, pours water over the ground coffee pouched in a beigely unbleached filter paper, rescues the two slices of bread which are starting to blacken under the grill, then smears them with butter and marmalade. Balancing the plate of toast on two mugs of coffee, Ian picks his way back to the bedroom, where Claire is sitting on the edge of the bed, elbows on her knees, head in her hands and her T-shirt riding up to reveal a patch of her smooth, taut back.

'You okay?' asks Ian as he hands Claire her mug and her toast.

'Oh, God. I don't know if I can face it.'

Now, a lot of men at this point would make the mistake of thinking that she's talking about the toast, but Ian is too well versed in the ways of women, plus he's seen far too many crap French comedies (Comic hero to gendarme: 'I've lost my dog.' Gendarme: 'Name?' Comic hero: 'Fifi.' Gendarme: 'Okay, Monsieur Fifi') to make that schoolboy error.

Ian places his mug on the floor, sits down beside her and rubs the exposed small of her back. 'Don't worry, sweetheart. Don't worry.'

'Oh, Ian, I just can't stand the thought . . .' She sighs into her hands.

'I know, dear. I know. But we'll work something out, you'll see. And maybe it'll be different when the baby arrives . . .'

Claire takes her hands away from her face and nods thoughtfully at the middle distance. 'I'm talking about breakfast,' she says.

2

'BIT OUT OF ORDER'

Saturday evening

'You know what's going to happen now.' Ian nods towards Alastair, who's bobbing up and down behind a crowd standing three deep at the bar of the Pig and Whistle.

'What?'

'Herds of wildebeest will migrate across the Serengeti, wide-eyed children will become wizened pensioners, entire civilisations will rise and fall, and Eck still won't have been served.' Ian drains the very last of his lager and slumps. 'Might as well get comfortable. We're in this for the long haul.'

Graham shifts in his seat. Not much chance of him getting comfortable, unless he could give himself a jab of anaesthetic. His head is aching, his left arm is badly bruised, his back is just sore all over and he seems to have wrenched something in his neck. So here he is, sitting like Whistler's mother. And whenever he wants to look to either side, he has to swivel like a fucking robot. Anyfuckingway, never mind all that. This is his chance. 'Ian, there's something I've got to ask, all right?'

'Ask away.'

'Who do you know with a first name starts with J?'

'I don't understand.'

'Perfectly fucking simple question.'

'Okay, well, in that case, Jenny.'

'Don't get fucking smart here.'

'Serious, man. And I thought that you thought that J was Jenny. In Rob's diary.'

'Nah. Turns out that the person she's seeing is called J something as well.'

'Not Rob, then?'

'No, not fucking Rob. It's someone who knows someone I know and his initial is J. All right? So who could it be from your pals?'

Ian frowns at his empty pint glass. 'To be honest, I don't know anyone else called J. Wait . . . No.'

'What? Who?'

Ian grimaces. 'No, sorry, Graham. I mean, I know a Jean-Pierre in Paris, and there are two Juans I used to pal about with in Madrid, but I've only been back here a few months so it's not as if I have this great social life full of Joes and Jacks and Jebediahs, you know what I'm saying?'

'Have a think, though, eh?'

'. . . Look, Graham, you want my advice?'

'No.'

'Forget about this J business. And say you do find out that Jenny is seeing somebody called J something or other, then what? Telling you, man, let it go.'

'Oh, aye. Easy as that.'

'I'm not saying it's easy, Graham, but you have to do it. And after all, it was you that split up with her. And it has been over a couple of years now.'

'So?'

'So, maybe you should stop worrying about what Jenny's up to, start worrying about yourself. Maybe it's time to move on. Fresh fields, pastures new.'

'You've tried this shite before and I'm going to give you the same answer. Just what the fuck would you know about it? Twelve years me and her were together. Twelve fucking years. That's not something you can forget about like that.' Graham finishes the sentence with a contemptuous snap of his fingers, then winces as another current of pain shoots up and down his neck.

'You all right?' asks Ian after long moments of silence.

'Twisted my fucking neck, that's all.'

'Bad one.' Ian taps his fingers against his pint glass. Boy seems stuck for something to say but Graham's fucked if he's going to help him out. Time to move on, eh? There speaks a man who can leave entire countries on a fucking whim. Who walked out on that Spanish bird after about half an hour of marriage. Who expects a Duke of Edinburgh Award for staying with Claire for all of two years.

'So,' says Ian at last. 'How's it going with Audrey?'

'Audrey? All right.'

There's another long silence, then Ian has another go. 'You any idea how Louise fits into all this?'

'How do you mean?'

'Her thinking that she's Rob's girlfriend. And Rob being a bit of a one for the ladies. That.'

Graham shrugs then winces.

'What I was wondering,' says Ian, 'was maybe Rob didn't have all those girls on a paternoster after all.'

What the fuck is he talking about? 'The fuck you talking about?'

'Remember? The paternoster of oiled bimbettes.'

'. . . Oh, aye.'

'Or he did have the paternoster and just lied to Louise.'

'I suppose.'

'But here's the thing, Graham. Rob talked a good game, always banging on about the women he was chasing after and chatting up and shoving out of his bed. But did you ever actually see Rob with any girls?'

'Oh, aye, Ian. All the time. Me, Rob and one of Rob's birds. The perfect set-up for a perfect night out. What am I? His chaperon? Some kind of professional fucking gooseberry?'

'Okay, okay.' More tapping on his glass. 'What do you think to Eck's news about Rob?'

Rob, Rob, Rob, Rob, Rob. Fucking Rob. Aye, he's still really pissed off with Rob, and not just because he has spent far too much time thinking that Rob was cheating on him with Jenny to forgive and forget and not be pissed off with Rob for being exactly the kind of flash fuck who would have had no qualms at all about getting Jenny into his bed. 'I don't have a scooby,' he says, after summing up the will to remember Eck's news about Rob. 'Eck's found out that Rob told Louisa he wasn't allowed in America? So what? Rob was spinning her a line. And Rob didn't tell her about us or us about her. What's the big deal?'

'Yeah, but there's also the thing about Rob being overdrawn.'

Graham shrugs his shoulders and swallows a yell. 'Aye. Bit out of order, though, Eck and Louisa going through the man's financial stuff like that.' No, he's still really pissed off with Rob because he has also spent a lot of time remembering how Rob encouraged him to leave Jenny when things were getting rocky and he was taking a first good look around London and the scene in Shoreditch and the women, all those women . . . Not that Rob said anything. It was just the example he set – the bachelor boy, always out on the town, chatting up dolly birds and screwing around and living the life of Jason King. Back in the real world, though, life without Jenny turned out to be just that.

'Way hay,' Ian says into another silence. 'Here's the wee man now.'

Alastair places the three glasses carefully on the table and sits back down. The other two are looking at him expectantly. He offers them a smile that he's sure comes across as weak and sickly. In fact, his stomach does seem a bit queasy – a symptom of his not-good feeling about how the final bit of his report is going to go down. However. And there are a few items on the agenda before he gets to the crunch. Oh God, though.

Alastair clears his throat. 'Another thing that's odd,' he says, 'is Rob's passport. That it's still there, for a start, so what we're assuming . . .'

'Oh ho,' says Ian. 'We now, is it?'

'Nothing like that, honestly. So what we, Louise and I, are assuming is that Rob's got a new passport and the thing he said in his note about him getting a new name and so on and so forth is real. But what it is about the old passport as well is that there's only a couple of pages that are stamped. And he's had it since ninety-one.'

'Aye, Eck, but you don't get it stamped when you go abroad these days.'

'Only the EU, Graham. And maybe it's slackened off a bit this year but Rob used to have to go all over. The States, Japan – he was always out in Japan. Brazil. Singapore. Mexico. On top of the European trips. But his passport was nearly blank.'

'What did they say at his work?' asks Ian. 'Maybe the bank did the visas or something.'

'I don't think it works like that,' says Alastair. 'But that's another thing. We checked at his office and they don't have any record of Rob.'

'That's ridiculous,' says Ian. 'Where was he working, then? He must have been doing something to pay for the flat and the car and everything.'

Alastair has been puzzling over exactly this question ever since he and Louise went to the NatWest and found themselves back out on the pavement after three minutes. The only answers he can come up with (Rob used the NatWest job as a cover while working for MI5, for a hush-hush arms dealer, for a drug baron) are still ones which he hopes owe far more to hours he's wasted gazing at movies on cable than unsuspectedly honed intuition. 'I just don't know,' he says. 'That's one of the reasons why, and I know this sounds stupid but there didn't seem any other option really, so what we've done, I mean it wasn't my idea originally, it was Louise who really made the running on this, but I must say, I do think it's quite sensible if you think about it, so what we've done, you see, is hire a, well, a private detective.'

'Fucksake.'

'Christ.' Ian gives him a little smile. 'And what's your dick like? What has your dick told you? What have you learned from your dick?'

'Ah, well, you see, he's only just started but we, Louise and I, saw him for an update yesterday and he's already found out something about that chap Maddox, the lawyer. Concentrating on him, you see, because Maddox probably knows more than he lets on, and maybe could even have helped Rob get a new identity, if that's really what Rob's done. Anyroad up, Mr Hilton, that's the detective, he drew a blank with an official approach, a phone call that is, but then he went undercover, you see, and caught up with Maddox in the evening, in the Coach and Horses. He got talking to Maddox, got Maddox talking about Rob, and it turns out that Maddox thinks he knew Rob rather well. Although he didn't even know him as Rob. Maddox kept calling him Mac.'

'Mac?' says Graham. 'Fucksake, that's even worse than Bobby.'

'I know. Mac.' Alastair's shoulders give an involuntary squirm of distaste. 'But from what Mr Hilton gathered, Rob was part of a crowd that went to the Coach and Horses and then often ended up back in Bateman Street. For a smoke. Apparently, Rob was well known among Maddox and his buddies for his high-strength grass.'

'Aye,' says Graham. 'He got that right, at any rate.'

Alastair squeezes his hands between his legs and leans forward. 'But did either of you ever come across Maddox?' he asks, anxiety pitching his voice up an octave. 'Surely we'd have met him, or at least Rob would have mentioned him if he was this big drinking and smoking pal?'

'Boy never said anything to me about any Maddox,' says Graham. Ian just shakes his head.

Alastair gives his hands another squeeze then takes a deep breath. Here goes. 'Another weird thing that came out of the conversation is that it was only recently Maddox realised Rob was in banking. Presumably when Rob asked him for whatever legal help Maddox has given him. Most of the time Maddox has known Rob, though that can't be long, he has thought that Rob was . . .' He's going to have to say it. '. . . some kind of artist.'

'You what?' Graham looks as if someone's just said something very nasty about him. 'What kind of *artist*, exactly?'

'Well, Maddox seemed to think that Rob was . . . of the struggling variety.'

'Oh, aye? And what kind of thing was he supposed to be struggling at?'

'Maddox seemed to think Rob's most recent project was a way-out, experimental thing about his bed or some such.'

'Really? Really? Is that right.' Graham frowns at his pint. 'So did this Maddox say anything else about Rob's artistic career?'

'Er, yes.'

'Aha?'

'What Maddox said is that Rob did give the impression that he made ends meet by . . . doing illustrations and things for magazines . . .'

'Fuck*sake*.'

'. . . and sometimes teaching English as a foreign language . . .'

'Jesus Christ almighty.'

'. . . which, according to Maddox, Rob had first done to get by when he lived in Paris . . .'

'Jesus.'

'. . . in a flat off the rue de la Réunion . . .'

'Christ.'

'. . . with a girl called Claire.'

'Woah.'

And to think that he had been only a bit pissed off because he might not have a trendy flat in Soho to visit any longer. And that there's still this part of him that envies Rob as well, just to screw with his head even more.

Ian nudges open the cubicle door, back-heels it shut, takes out his wallet then the wrap in his wallet. Yes, all right, this is a Saturday, but it's a one-off and bollocks to the rule in the first place. He sorts out a line on his mirror and leans over it, straw at the ready. Hell with it . . .

. . . What it is, what it is, what it is is that Rob needed to boast and clearly thought his own life didn't sound exciting enough, so he nicked the artist bit from Graham and got the rest from him. Naturally enough, for who else could provide such a rich supply of impressive exotica? And, given that he nicked Claire for a mention as well, erotica. And there was him assuming all these years that Rob must have been running up a tally of conquests like a Test match score, Rob never having been keen on anything that might smack of the long term. But maybe not, though. Maybe not, maybe not, maybe not. Backing up the new theory about Rob's empty paternoster.

Ian sniffs. Time to get back. 'Poor guy,' he whispers, smiling as he packs away the gubbins. 'That poor guy.'

3

'OH, SURE, EVERYTHING'S COOL'

Sunday evening

Is he making a mistake here?

No. He's phoned Eck, Col, Hermann, Tim, even Marty, and drawn a complete fucking blank with the lot. The more he's thought about it, the more he's certain it has to be somebody Ian knows. One of his teacher mates, maybe. Or, and this is the favourite theory, one of his unwashed fucking hippie neighbours from Bonnington Square – doubtless the kind who tries to impress women by teaching them how to fucking juggle. Aye, right – soon as he finds out who it is, the boy'll be having his balls to play with, that's for fucking certain.

Graham is hunched over the steering wheel of the decaying Golf as if he's driving through a heavy snowfall, although it's a crisp, clear evening, and he's not driving anywhere because he's parked outside a big, red mansion block in St John's Wood, and he's leaning over the steering wheel so that he can just see the mansion block's main door where, if Claire's right, Ian should be appearing in a few minutes.

Sundays used to be great with Jenny. Lie-in, coffee and croissants in bed, read the papers, a shag maybe, then a bath and out for a walk, or just muck about and watch stuff on the telly. He assumed they were merely normal at the time, but now all those uneventful Sundays with Jenny are pangfully cherishable, highlights that he had no idea were going to be highlights until after they'd happened, highlights he has to replay again and again and again.

Graham has another peer through the windscreen at the mansion block's entrance – nobody there – then tries to relax back in his seat, because his neck is giving him terrible gyp. Nearly a quarter of an hour he's been sitting here in the Golf, waiting for Ian to come out – fifteen minutes that have managed to be both boring and fraught, but very much of a piece with a day that has been, in stark contrast to those remembered Sundays with Jenny, utterly fucking shite. Having started with a panic attack a second after he awoke, today went from worse to worst. The first couple of hours he tried desperately hard to be normal – made himself breakfast (which reminded him of Jenny), bought *Scotland on Sunday* and the *Chronicle* (and left both unread, since reading the Sunday papers would have reminded him of Jenny), went for a walk (which reminded him of Jenny) – but by midday he'd run out of steam, and it was all he could do to sit down in the kitchen and brace himself for what he knew would be a dark afternoon of the soul. Which it certainly was . . . Until he finally managed to get his head out of his hands and his arse into gear and have another go at finding out who this J is.

Ian's answerphone was on, but Graham was determined to leave the flat, so he'd risked the car and driven down to Vauxhall anyway. Then waited outside Ian's place for a full hour until Claire turned up, carrying two bulging Sainsbury's bags and looking none too chuffed. She's all right, Claire, if you like the pointy-nosed, boyish type. No idea what the body's like, though, because every time he's met her she's been wearing a floaty dress or a smocky number, just to add to that chorister look. So he'd given her a couple of minutes, then invited himself in, coming up with the line that he had to see Ian to return fifty quid he owed him. Aye, *that* would be right. She'd been okay about it, a bit distracted, come to think of it, but happy enough to hunt through Ian's battered notebook for him and find the address where he'd be doing his regular freelance teaching stint. The first Graham had heard about any such thing, but he'd kept cool, because you never knew with Ian, and no way was Graham going to be the one who fucked up and alerted Claire to what could be Ian's regular freelance bit on the side. Aye, he'd kept his cool, said he'd have to dash and got the fuck out of Bonnington Square's strange wee hippie ghetto, gunning the Golf up Vauxhall Bridge Road until the engine began to rebel and the speedometer almost touched thirty.

Fucking car. Still, better to be sitting in it than hanging around outside waiting for Ian to . . . That's him now, marching out with a poly bag slung over his shoulder. And heading this way.

Ian still hasn't noticed the car or him inside the car when Graham stops him in his tracks by the simple method of swinging the door out in front of him, making Ian do a sudden Riverdance step to the side.

'What the . . . Jesus, Graham, what the hell are you doing here?'

'Waiting for you, the fuck do you think?' It strikes Graham that he's at a vague disadvantage sitting in the car with Ian looking down at him like this. Trying to ignore the fact that his body obviously doesn't want to do it, Graham clambers out. 'It has to be someone you know,' he says.

'Graham, I've told you . . .'

'J. Somebody you know whose name begins with J.'

'Yeah, you did mention this before, and I've . . .'

'You hoakay here, my frenn?'

There's this dodgy-looking boy come out of the same mansion block and right up to Ian. He must be the freelance assignment although he looks more like an apprentice waiter than someone over here to improve his vocabulary. Trying his best to look hard, though, coming right up, planting himself in front of him.

'Oh, sure, everything's cool,' Ian says. 'This is Graham, he's a friend of mine. Graham, this is Ram . . .'

'Johnny,' the waiter says, and starts to return his stare.

'Johnny, is it? Johnny. Well, very nice to meet you, *Johnny*.'

Ian has three grams of coke on his person and he wouldn't put it past his pupil to have a knife on his. Two very good reasons for him to step between the two of them before this develops into anything. 'Now, Graham,' Ian says, as he makes a move forward, but that's all he has time to say before Graham pushes him back while keeping up his playground staring match.

'You never told me you had a friend called *Johnny*. So how's your sex life, *Johnny*?'

Johnny looks understandably puzzled by the content and tone of the question. He continues to examine Graham's eyes, then he says, with worrying calm, 'Very good.'

'Is *that* right? And what's the name of the lucky lady? It is a lady, I presume.'

'*Qué?*'

This, Ian notes to himself, has to stop now. 'Get a grip, Graham,' he says. 'You're making a . . .'

'Just having a wee conversation here about your friend Johnny's romantic life.'

Graham steps forward. Jesus Christ, the two of them really are squaring up. Before he can have second thoughts, Ian darts behind Graham and puts his arms around him, as if he's executing a Heimlich manoeuvre or an abrupt rear entry. Ian has just enough time to register Johnny starting to smile and, in the background, Johnny's sulky girlfriend shuffling out of the main door – and wearing, Ian notices, clothes – before he feels Graham's elbow thump him below the ribs.

'Huh,' Ian hears himself say as he feels the air rushing out of his lungs, then his feet giving way beneath him. Next thing he knows, he's sitting on the pavement and forgetting to breathe. Ian coughs, splutters, grabs air in his throat with the long, dry gasp of a dying man, and gathers his wits just in time to look up and see Graham suddenly stagger back, clutching his face and yelling incoherently, into the side of the car.

'*Muy bien*,' Johnny says, nodding approval at the silver canister in his right hand. 'You hoakay?' he asks while he helps Ian to his feet.

'Sure, fine,' gasps Ian.

'Your frenn, huh?' Johnny smiles at Graham, who is still leaning back against his car and moaning behind his hands.

'Yeah . . . yeah, my friend.'

'Mad man. Hey. You.' Johnny moves over to Graham and shakes him by the shoulder. Graham replies with a high squawk. 'You wanna know my girl? You wanna know? See.' Johnny beckons the sulky girl towards him, before grabbing her by the elbow and pushing her towards Graham. 'See. My girl. You like her? You wann her? Eh? Eh?'

Graham seems to be too busy swearing and rubbing his eyes to respond at first, but after a few moments he risks a brief squint.

'And now, my frenn, you are nice and say hello, yes? Thees ees Heidi. Heidi, thees ees mad man. Say hello to Heidi, mad man.'

Graham manages another squint. 'Heidi?' he says. 'Heidi?'

Johnny pokes Graham's shoulder. 'I ask you before, mad man. Say hi.'

'Heidi. Hi.'

The sulky girl lights up a cigarette. 'Fook off,' she says.

There's a nature programme on BBC2 until seven, then the news on Channel 4, Spanish football on Sky Sports One . . .

Alastair lets the TV guide fall to the floor. Clunkingly ironic, but the only thing he can think of which might just have a chance of shaking him out of this dark mood would be a phone call to Rob, arrange to meet for a quiet drink in Soho, maybe saunter up to a Pizza Express for a *quattro formaggi*.

How many nights have he and Rob spent exactly like that? Fifty? A hundred?

'A lot,' Alastair announces to the spurned TV guide. 'Specially before Friday Night Club started up again.' But what was Rob up to all those other nights when they didn't meet up? Alastair forces himself off the sofa and begins to pace the room. 'I have no idea,' he has to confess to a Doisneau poster. 'No idea whatsoever.'

So why is that? Is it just because they're blokes, like Louise said? ('So what exactly have you pair of bosom buddies been talking about for thirty years if you don't have the foggiest idea what he's up to?' she'd asked that first afternoon at Rob's flat when she was upset and got a bit snippy. 'Football? Really, *men* . . . There *is* more to life than Range Rovers, you know.' 'Raith,' he'd replied as pointedly as he'd dared, because he'd felt frustrated by her falling back on a stereotype. 'Raith Rovers.')

No, the bloke thing is a lame excuse, because of course there are men who seem able to conduct deep, candidly confessional friendships with other men. Gary, for instance, who was only a year at the subs' desk before he got that cushy job on a glossy travel mag, but who spent so much of that year describing the troubles then breakdown of his marriage that Alastair felt he'd known Gary all his life. Gary, who had to wipe away the tears at one point when they met up last month and discussed how devastating it was for Gary to see little Amber only once a week. Gary, who seems to have a clutch of mates he can rely on and talk to and cry in front of.

So he can't just blame not knowing about parts of Rob's life on being a chap. Nor can he blame it on his own shyness. Nor another potential excuse he's mulled over – one that tried to make something of the way Rob's always had of presenting himself so completely, with a casually debonair assurance, and turn that into a reason for not doubting Rob or quizzing him for further details.

No. Enough with the excuses. It's him, Alastair, who's to blame. Because right from the start, from the moment when Rob came up to him in Torbain Street and wanted to play, he, Alastair, has been so grateful for the fact of the friendship that he hasn't asked or tried for more, not having had the least expectation of getting what he's got. And, it's now pretty obvious, because all the time he's been telling himself that he values Rob, he has never sat down and really thought about Rob. Except maybe when Rob suddenly took up with the hippie crowd at uni, or when Rob upped sticks for London and went his own way for several years, failing to return calls, not relaying new numbers or addresses, while he, Alastair, fretted over and over about what he could have said or done or not said or not done to have caused offence. There. You see? Thinking, really thinking, about his friends is clearly something he does only when things go wrong. Taking everything for granted the rest of the time. Like electricity. Being alive, even.

Now that he does have to think about it again, what he always blithely assumed was a best-pals thing with Rob clearly emerges as amounting to not much more than mucking around together, the adult equivalent of hunting for Jerry soldiers in the woods. Fair enough, Rob was good about it two years back when Alastair got upset a few times after his mother died, but that was Rob being good about it, and, for all their three-decade heritage, that was also Alastair asking a lot of Rob and probably in rather an embarrassing manner. Not that he didn't appreciate it, of course he did. But when Rob wanted to talk about his parents' accident, who did Rob talk to? Louise. Not him.

However. There is this in his defence, that it does seem more natural to open up to a girl. Rob must just be like him and find it easier to talk seriously to women. Who've always seemed to him somehow more . . . *evolved* than men – graceful, white-robed Athenians to his own tribe of bearskinned barbarians.

Typical mummy's boy, he thinks as he enters the kitchen – worshipping women. So much so that, even though he has always admired Rob – marvelling at Rob's success, being amazed at Rob's latest romantic escapade or the size of Rob's Christmas bonus – that doesn't really compare to the complete adoration he has felt for Fiona and Cathy. And he's told them stuff he'd never tell Rob. Look at when he was at school, how he talked to Fiona, not Rob, about his secret ambition to do English at uni. Or, much later, how he blurted it all out only to Cathy about not really being in love with Rhona.

Alastair brings out the little wooden box from its hiding place behind the coffee jar. He pauses before he opens it because he's reminding himself not to rewrite his past here. For all that he's just gone on about his great openness with Fiona and Cathy, he has to remember that there was something else going on with Fiona and Cathy, and he wasn't at all honest and open about that something else with either of them or himself . . .

Alastair shudders. Yes. Sometimes it's only right to have low expectations.

4

'IT'S LIKE JEFFREY ARCHER'

Monday evening

'I live in Warsaw but I am living near the station of Dalston Kingsland.'

'Very good. Miroslav?'

'I live in Bratislava but I am living in Shepherd's Bush.'

'Excellent. Sayuri?'

'I live in Yokohama but I am living in Hendon.'

Of course Hendon. Who'd've thought that London would have a thriving Japanese community and that it would be based in Hendon? Not Ian, that's for sure. And why Hendon? Having studied the map – because he always does in a new city, to avoid looking like a bamboozled tourist – he has come up with a theory about this, which states that the first, intrepid Japanese colonists had to keep going, past Kilburn, Kensal Rise and Brondesbury, past Willesden and Harlesden, beyond Cricklewood and Dollis Hill, to find sanctuary in the first bit of London they could stay in and pronounce.

Two minutes to six. 'Excellent, Sayuri,' says Ian. 'Well done, everybody. We will continue with the present tenses tomorrow. Workbook exercises seven and eight for homework, please. See you all at five tomorrow.'

The eight members of the new intermediate class have just trooped out when Chantal appears in the doorway. She's wearing a bright, white T-shirt, a little pinkish cardigan thing that emphasises her breasts' upsetting promise, and a tight black skirt that stops short of those knees, so cute he could draw a face on them.

'May I come in?' she asks with what could be a coquettish smile.

'Of course,' says Ian, who has already scraped back his chair and sprinted round to the front of his desk. He props himself up against it, his hands behind him, in an attempt to look cool and casual. Chantal, meanwhile, has shut the door behind her and sashayed forward, then does her own leaning-against-the-desk manoeuvre. A nanosecond's glimpse is all Ian needs to check out the sheen of her auburn hair, the elegance of her profiled nose, the well, the everything about her. What a complete and utter babe. A complete and utter . . .

'Thank you for the lesson today,' she says. 'Now I think I understand "like".'

'That's good,' says Ian, despite the fact that his mouth seems to have lost all its saliva and that, behind his back, her fingertips seem to be touching his. If his hand remains absolutely motionless, she might not notice and this moment will continue.

'Now I like to study like,' she says. 'And I like studying it.'

'Good.'

'So I want to say thank you.'

There's a chance he's got this hopelessly wrong, but if he had to bet on it, he'd have to say that the tips of her fingers moved a fraction of a millimetre against his just there. And again. She can't think his hands are a book or part of the desk, surely? Surely? Ian turns slightly towards her. Chantal turns slightly towards him. Her fingers are still touching his. Now he looks her in those big, brown eyes. She returns the look, and, as she holds his gaze, her soft, full lips part. And, no mistake about it, her fingertips are moving, with startling delicacy, across his knuckles.

Oh, Christ, Ian thinks. Oh Jesus Christ almighty. She's still holding his gaze when, somehow or other, their hands suddenly clasp each other and, somehow or other, her eyes get closer and closer to his, and he feels his lips meet hers. They are soft and warm and sumptuous.

The door clicks.

They jump apart and stare at the door as if it has burst into flames.

'You did close it, Chantal?'

'Yes. I am certain I . . . It is the wind, perhaps?'

'Yes. Yes, maybe the wind.' What with one thing and another, Ian can feel his heart banging away at his ribcage. If that was somebody at the door and that somebody was Foxsmith, then he could be in a bit of bother. Although it happens all the time, language schools have to keep up the pretence of going through the motions of frowning on teachers getting off with their charges. A nice quartet of phrasal verbs there, Ian finds himself noting. Still, it wasn't as if they were spotted, if indeed they were spotted at all, shagging on his desk. He glances at Chantal. Now that, thinks Ian, is one hell of a thought.

Chaz has assumed the air of an art director who's been around the block a few times, a veteran who can appraise an illustration when he sees one. He performs another close inspection of the businessman standing underneath a light bulb.

Some time later, Chaz delivers his verdict. 'Yeah,' he says. He scratches the side of his orange Lycra top and nods once. 'Cool,' he says. 'Yeah, I'm into the . . . the vibe, yeah?'

Breathing in. And breathing out. 'Good,' says Graham.

Chaz turns to his twelve-year-old assistant. 'Wotchoo think, Tamsin, man?'

Tamsin scratches the back of her T-shirt. 'Yeah,' she says. 'Yeah, it's got that, that . . .'

Chaz examines the drawing again. 'Vibe,' he declares.

'Vibe,' agrees Tamsin.

'Yeah, I'm into the . . . yeah, this is a vibe I can big up to.'

. . . eight, nine, ten. 'Good,' says Graham. He's about to

add that he'll be sending Chaz the invoice but thinks better of it, because that would be an oration which would obviously mark him down as a real fucking has-been . . . And keeping calm, keeping calm. 'See you later,' Graham says, and he tries to shake Chaz's hand – with no success, because Graham's conventional move is confounded by the angled palm of Chaz's soul-brother clasp.

Graham hirples out of the *Business Matters* office, stroking his sorer left eye, trying very hard not to move his neck or goad his back, and feeling as young and with it as a golf commentator. He negotiates a urine-scented flight of stairs and steps out on to Camden High Street.

'Speh some chynge?' immediately drones a slumped urchin.

Just fucking tremendous – accosted by a . . . human being with real problems. And one who is providing another test of the new resolution. The new Graham. 'Sure,' says Graham. He fiddles in his trouser pockets and gingerly lowers a fifty-pence piece on to the urchin's sleeping bag. 'Good luck.'

'Chairs, mite.'

You see. That wasn't so bad, was it?

He is pondering what life must be like for the sort of folk who are always being nice to tramps – expensive, presumably – and picking his way through burger-bar debris when he is approached by a small, old man vibrating inside a greasy pin-stripe suit.

'Thing is, pal,' says this raddled creature to the person standing invisibly behind Graham's left shoulder, 'ah wantay buy a submarine. Could you see your wye fur tae contribyootin a wee . . . contribyooshin? Towards the cost, like?'

The tramp with the allegedly amusing line in patter was one of the old Graham's pet hates. But this is the new Graham, and the new Graham should be thinking at this point that at least the guy is putting a bit of effort into his job. Graham rummages inside his trouser pockets again. He brings out a pound coin. Oh well. He places the coin on the old man's blackened palm, wishes him luck and, having narrowly failed to avoid the outskirts of a remarkably large, coiled, possibly human turd, has to rub the side of his shoe against the edge of the pavement before resuming his trek to the Tube.

Sudden and heavy raindrops are beginning to add their own stains to the pavement's pocks of old gum. As he ups the pace, Graham finds himself wondering just how the citizens of Camden achieve that distinctive Camden look. It must be a co-ordinated effort so that everyone knows when and which dustbins should be emptied on to the streets. Probably through some fucking rota from the fucking council . . . Stop that.

Okay. So.

Keep calm.

Keep calm and be nice.

'Seer. Oh, seer.'

A dishevelled woman, carrying a baby and wearing an unlikely number of dull-patterned skirts, has materialised in front of him. She's thrusting a piece of cardboard at his face. 'Homless form Sarajevo,' claims the scrawl on the cardboard. No, no. That is not on. Graham shakes his head and pain clobbers his neck. Fucking *hell*. When he opens his eyes again, the woman's still standing there. Well, you never know, he thinks, resigning himself to it. She might really be a refugee. And even if she is part of a beggarly mafia, she's clearly not doing too well. He shoves his hand in his pocket and gives her the rest of his change – a few coppers and two 5p coins. The woman mutters what he trusts is a thank-you. The rain is getting heavier.

'Skews may.'

It's a teenage girl standing in the doorway of a trendy hairdresser's. Her own hair is spiky and sort of green. She's also got the regulation torn army fatigues and, to complete the image, she's holding a thin, black dog on a leash of string. 'Goh any cheh hange?' she whines.

Crusties. Another of the old Graham's pet hates. What with

crusties being lazy wankers whose great protest against society is not having a bath. And who obviously have a way of looking at him and seeing some fucking old guy with a sad, orthodox, humdrum life. 'I'm not some fucking *suit*,' he always wants to explain to crusties. After pinning them up against the nearest wall. 'I'm an artist, for fucksake. An *artist*. What do you want? A smock? A fucking *beret*?' But this is the new Graham. He forces himself to offer this one a rueful smile. 'I've run out,' he says.

The crusty girl scratches the dog's ears. Then she looks up and returns his smile. 'I hope you get cancer,' she tells him sweetly.

Fretting over this several hours later in the relative safety of the flat, Graham will conclude that he just wasn't ready for a fight, that this was a blow that simply caught him unawares, like the punch that killed Houdini. As it is, he stands there, gazing forlornly at the still-smiling girl for what feels like minutes, the surprised hurt growing into a sense that he's utterly, abjectly on his own here, abandoned in this endless, endless city teeming with millions upon millions of strangers.

He blinks away tears. Move on, he tells himself. Move away. He heads towards the Tube in a capsule of misery, all but unaware of the rain, the mêlée at the pedestrian crossing, the nudge from behind that forces him to step into a roadside puddle, the sweeping, flailing arms of the two down-and-outs who launch themselves into an infuriated and inept fight near the Tube entrance, the throng at the Tube entrance, and the old biddy sporting a Biggles helmet who veers wildly through the throng, stops abruptly in front of him, jabs at his ankles with her shopping basket's wee wheels, mutters, 'Rude, rude, rude,' and, when he replies with a baffled 'Sorry', hisses, 'Bloody Scotch' and fends him off with a final sharp shove of the basket into his shins.

His automatic pilot guides him towards the ticket machine. He has no change.

He'll try the ticket machine that takes notes.

The ticket machine that takes notes says 'EXACT MONEY ONLY'.

The ticket booth is besieged by a gang of excitable youngsters who might be trying to ask for travelcards in what might be Italian . . .

The escalator is blocked by a group of triangularly obese Americans.

The concourse at the bottom of the escalator is extremely crowded.

The electronic display says that smoking is forbidden but gives no information about the next High Barnet train.

A grey-faced official emerges and warily yells out the news that there has been an incident at Euston so all Northern Line services have been suspended indefinitely.

Jenny, thinks Graham as he stands in the shifting mob, his shoulders slumping as he gives in at last. Jenny. Where are you, Jenny? Maybe if he stands here long enough – a month, six months, a year – Jenny will pass by . . .

Carried along by the outraged scrum, Graham is swept back up the escalator and out into the rain.

Credit to Davina, she's not giving up yet. 'But I do think,' she says, only a slight tremble in her voice, 'that this is a superb review. Extremely well written, very acute, funny, I mean, yes, it is negative, but . . .'

'But nothing,' says the editor. 'Who is this reviewer anyway?'

'John Updike? He's, he's, he's one of America's . . .'

'A Yank, eh? I might have known it.'

Like every one of his co-workers, Alastair is looking at his screen but eavesdropping on the heated literary debate taking place behind him. Making only the slightest clicking on his keyboard, he gently types out a message to Barry – 'any idea wot this is abt?' – and tenderly presses the Send key.

'As far as I can see, Davina, this is a prime example of you and your literary chums ganging up on someone out of sheer snobbishness and jealousy.'

'Really and truly, Jonathan, I don't . . .'

'Davina. I have spoken on this matter. Several times now. So you will put this review in the bin where it belongs and find me a critic our readers will like. A critic our readers will *understand*. A critic our readers might just have *heard* of.'

MESSAGE has flashed up on Alastair's screen. He gives the Receive key a soft push. 'big trauma re review of new j archer,' starts Barry's message. 'god knows how but davina managed to get john updike to do the piece. only trouble is, updike has slagged off j archer s/thing rotten and last nite ed was at his 1st j archer party – shepherd's pie and krug, acc/ding to b/bttle. so ed wants updike rev spiked, nice rev of book by his new best friend in its place, and d threatening to resign. again.'

'But Jonathan,' says Davina with a plaintive, dying fall.

'Spoken.'

'I.'

'Spoken.'

The next thing Alastair knows, the editor has breenged past his desk, dislodging sheaves of layouts in the process, so Alastair is busily gathering these together when his phone rings. 'Subs.'

'Alastair, it's Louise. Is this an okay time to call?'

''Course. Hold on a moment, though . . . Right. There we are. Any news?'

'No. No news. I was having a bit of a relapse, so this is me just phoning up for some TLC.'

'I'll do my best, Louise. What's the matter?'

'Oh, only everything. It's like splitting up with someone. Well, it *is* splitting up with someone, but with an extra little twist to make you feel even worse. I mean, I try to keep up the chirpiness when other people are around, and that does help, like putting on a smile can make you feel there's something to smile about. Sometimes I can even kid myself that I'm coping. But then I get back to that flat and it all hits me. I mean, why am I even in that flat? The work could be a drag and I had a commuting relationship, at least that's what I thought I had, but I did love it in New York. I had this lovely little apartment on MacDougall, right in the heart of the Village . . . But here, I get back to Bateman Street, as late as possible, and I close the door behind me. And I feel like throwing up. Really. I mean, it's a physical thing. Why does nobody warn you about this when you're a child? That it'll be so bad it makes you physically ill? Oh, Alastair, where's Mr Buggles when I need him?'

'Sorry, Louise, Mr?'

'I forgot. That was another musketeer. Silly me. But that's what I am, isn't it? Just plain *silly*.'

'That's about the last adjective I'd use to describe you.'

'I dunno. Dictionaries of the future should illustrate the word "schmuck" with little pictures of me. Yes. A real mugshot. I mean, how could I be taken in by such a pathetic liar? Fair enough, if the man was an international criminal or a master of disguise, then, you know, fine, I was conned by an expert and what can you do? But what really gets to me is that I was quite happily taken in by a twit.'

'Rob isn't a twit, Louise.'

'No? What kind of person pretends to be a great globe-trotter and, according to his passport, never leaves his own postal district? Or who explains that despite being this great globetrotter, he can't come to see me in New York because he's wanted by the FBI? A twit, that's what kind. So how come I didn't suss him out as a twit? Because I must be an even bigger twit.'

'I know what you mean, Louise,' says Alastair, and indeed he does, having spent several nights lying awake until the wee small hours, the pillow itching, the alarm clock ticking louder and louder, the thought running round and round his head that he used to know, deep down, that Rob was at least embellishing the truth when he said his dad had invented a new kind of hovercraft or that Daleks were real and he'd seen one in Lancaster. But when Rob had boasted about having a steamy affair with a sexily boss-eyed CNN reporter or getting off with a woman who had a surgically enhanced bottom in Brazil, then he, Alastair, had believed that this was what had happened. Which has led him to what seems, particularly at three in the morning, the terrifyingly clear conclusion that his own perceptiveness and judgment peaked when he was eight and have been on a downward curve ever since. 'But,' Alastair continues, remembering how his subsequent pep talks to himself have gone, 'it's not us being twits. If someone tells you something, you believe them. Unless the person tells you that they're Elvis or that they've just come back from Jupiter, and then you know they're mad.'

'But Bobby's lies were so rubbish, that's the thing.'

'Yes, but my point is, not really unbelievable rubbish.'

'That's exactly what they were.'

Alastair is trying to think of a way to continue his argument when Davina stomps past, muttering theatrically to herself. Aha. 'It's like Jeffrey Archer,' he says.

'Great. I've been going out with Kirkcaldy's answer to Jeffrey Archer. Not a comfort.'

'Listen, though. Jeffrey Archer's got away with all manner of terrible lies. About going to Oxford, about that prostitute, about that story he copied, anything. The ironic thing is that the crap lying has helped Jeffrey Archer get to the position where he's rich and famous and a target for investigation. But if the lying is done by someone like Rob, and the lies aren't outrageous, then who's to suspect anything's wrong?'

'You've been concocting this over a few joints, haven't you?'

He decides not to let on about his three-in-the-morning frets. 'Well, yes, as it happens.'

'Lucky man. This is a bit cheeky, but I'm going to suggest it anyway.'

'Suggest away.'

'You still on for Wednesday evening?'

'Our confab? Absolutely.'

'Would you mind bringing round a little bit of your grass with you?'

'Delighted.'

'First few days of this I tried drink, then coke with your friend Ian, so now I'd like to give hash a bash.'

'Worth a shot, I'd say.'

'Thanks, Alastair. You're a brick.'

'You too, Louise. See you Wednesday.'

'Another hot date?' says Barry, who popped his head over the top of his terminal as soon as Alastair put down the phone. 'Al, you dog.'

'Just good friends, Barry.'

'Aaaaaah, of course.'

5

'IS THAT A COMPLIMENT?'

Wednesday evening

Of course, this is exactly what he needs. Absolutely superb. Thanks, God.

'Most, ah most, to be, as it were, regretted. Very.' With a final, sorrowful shake of his head, Foxsmith leaves the classroom and Ian staring at the sheet of paper on his desk – a course assessment form handed in by Monique, who has suddenly left the school a week early, stomping off to Heathrow and a plane back to civilisation.

What has he done to upset her? Clearly something bad, going by the stuff she's written in the Remarks bit and the series of vitriolic zeroes she's awarded him. And this after he went to all that trouble reorganising her digs. Jesus.

The only explanation he can come up with is ridiculous – that Monique has clomped off in a huge huff because she got wind of his flirting with Chantal. Which means that Monique did have a crush on him *and* she thought she was in with a chance. Either that or she and Chantal were embroiled in a lesbian love pact. No, not that. Definitely not that. Maybe Chantal told her about the kiss. After all, girls tell girls everything. So Monique throws a wobbly, chucks in the school and runs back home. Making damned sure in the process to put him in the shit by telling Foxsmith that Ian Murray is the worst teacher in the world and the very spawn of Satan. Cheers, Monique. You troll.

When the door clicked. That might have been her, or someone she knows – someone anyway, and spying on them . . .

Well, however it happened, it's happened and the consequences are far from good. Foxsmith is bound to have reams of desperate teachers' CVs lying around his office and, unless he failed to interpret Foxsmith's meaning correctly, that's him now one mistake or one bad report away from being kicked out and replaced. And sent scurrying off to one of the really shitty cowboy schools where he'd be lucky to get five quid an hour doing the present perfect thirty, forty hours a week. She has pissed on his chips (recent action). She has pissed on his chips (in the past and time not specified). She has pissed on his chips (action that started in the past and continues into the present). Yeah. That little witch has pissed on his chips, all right.

Don't panic, Mr Mainwaring, he thinks. This is a blip, no more. He'll be fine, everything will be all right . . .

No it won't.

It's the Fear. Oh Christ. It's been stalking him. And now it's beginning to close in.

He's got looks and he's got brains and he's got fluent French, excellent Spanish, good German . . . And Claire's beautiful and . . .

Ian hugs himself tight. He could have a line, that might work. Or it could just sharpen the dread.

He can't stay here. He has to go. But where? Where can he go? Where will he be safe?

Rob's . . . He can't go to Rob's. Rob's gone. Maybe this is what happened to Rob. He got the Fear and had to run off. If that's it then he's not going to cast any blame on the poor guy because nobody can mess with the Fear. You think you're fine. You think you're in control. Then along comes the Fear . . .

Oh Christ. Oh Christ. Oh Christ.

He's got to get out of here.

A friend of someone he knows and his name starts with J. A friend of someone he knows and his name starts with J.

A friend of someone he knows and . . . Whoever it is, the bastard is screwing Jenny, and for that the bastard will pay. Initial J. Initial J . . .

Stop that. He has a job to finish off. And he is a man of steel. He forces his attention back to the nearly finished drawing on his workbench. The drawing stars an inspired-looking gent in a stripey suit, holding a finger to his chin and standing below an enormous, floating light bulb with a pound sign for a filament. A day's work and it'll mean half a page in the December issue of *Management Monthly* and, more to the point, a cheque for £150. He tries not to compare that figure with the sums on his invoices eight, nine years back when wheelbarrows of cash were being tipped into his lap, morning, noon and night. Aye, well . . . He was about to remind himself that money doesn't grow on trees, but that's exactly what money did in the grand old days of yore, when he took all of thirty minutes to do the new logo of the Oakham Building Society (an oak above a squiggle), thereby achieving his best-ever rate of £6,000 an hour.

The phone rings.

'Hi, Graham, I've got some very good news for you.'

'Audrey. How are you?'

'Oh, the usual, you know. So thing is, I ran into Marty last night at the Cantaloupe and I told him about you having an exhibit and so on and so forth, and he's on for it, really up for it, really keen, all the rest of it.'

'That's excellent, Audrey.' Not that it's easy to tell, but it sounds like Audrey's being normal, so either she doesn't know about his fight with Jason, or she has heard about it and Jason's getting the blame. 'So what did Marty say exactly?'

'Oh, most of it was the usual blah-di-blah-di-blah, but he does want to host your thing in D:Zine's reception.'

'Really? Great. When?'

'Starting next Friday if you can manage it. Could be up for

a while maybe and Marty'll lay on a launch do, party-type thing, get a sponsor for the drinks, blah blah blah.'

'Fucking hell. Thanks, Audrey. Thanks a lot, honestly.'

'Oh, whatever.'

'No, I really appreciate it. I don't know how to repay the favour.'

'Oh, blah blah *blah*. Tell you what, buy me a drink if you want. You doing anything Saturday?'

'Buying you a drink. How about eight at the Cantaloupe?'

'Sure.'

'Maybe we could get a bite to eat as well.'

'Sure, sure, whatever. And, you know, give Marty a call.'

Moments later, Graham is making two entries in his normally barren diary. 'Skibble dibble dip dibble,' he sings to the tune of 'What A Difference A Day Makes' as he turns back to the drawing of the businessman underneath the sterlinged light bulb. 'Skeeble dee dibble deedoo.'

'. . . Oh, blimey, have I been bogarting this?'

'Ta. No, you haven't. Lawks a mercy, it's strong, though. What is it?'

'Home-grown mixed with some stuff I got from Rob. Bobby. Mac . . . Mac, I ask you. Anyway, him. Kind of skunk, I think . . . What were we talking about?'

'Can't remember. Hold on . . . Half the Cabinet being Scottish, Scottish accents on adverts . . . there being ways of telling someone's Protestant or Catholic . . . Yes, what on earth was that all about, Alastair?'

'. . . Ummmm, right. Got it. Well, back home, things like your name or which school you went to are giveaways. Even looks. So, in Scotland, most of the actresses and newsreaders and so on are called things like Annemarie Rafferty or Madeleine Murphy or . . . or Isabella Ravioli, because the good-looking people are Irish or Italian. Hence the ET joke.'

'What ET joke?'

'All right, Louise, I'm going to tell you the ET joke. This is it coming up, all right? The ET joke. Starting now. How do you know ET is a Protestant?'

'Okay. How *do* you know ET is a Protestant?'

'Because he looks like one.'

Louise frowns and takes a deep breath. 'Right. So Mackenzie was fanciable because he was Catholic, is that the kind of thing you're saying?'

'... Rob is Protestant, Louise. Otherwise he'd have gone to different schools. And wouldn't have a name like Mackenzie.'

'... Oh. So why did he tell me he was Catholic?'

'Did he?'

'Yip. Lapsed, but Catholic.'

'Who knows? ... Maybe he thought Catholic was more interesting. Why did he come up with any of his stories? ... Mind you, fair enough, he has cheekbones so he doesn't look terribly Protestant. Me, I'm more typical.'

'... You know, Alastair, I think you might almost qualify as an honorary girl.'

'Is that a compliment?'

'Usually. Not sure in this case because I was referring to ... yes, your less than high self-esteem. Most men I know, they think they're God's gift, but you, you're like one of us, talking yourself down, assuming everyone else is better than you, all that. Here. Take this.'

'Eh thang yaw. That's not low self-esteem, Louise. That's me not being completely crazy.'

'Tish and tosh, Alastair Carr. You're a catch.'

'And that's definitely the grass talking.'

'Possible because I am feeling nice and woozy, but the fact remains. A catch.'

'Don't be daft.'

'Not being. For a start, unlike most men your age, you're not burdened by a wife and two veg. Or fucked up by an ex-wife and two veg. And you're sane, normal, solvent and straight.'

'Yes. Shame about being a bald, ginger runt.'

'Honorary girl, Alastair. You're nice looking, you're in good shape, bald, yes, but at a curious time in the history of men's fashion when it's cool to have no hair. I bet you're a right little heartbreaker on the quiet.'

'Just to show that you're well meaning but completely wrong – exactly the opposite.'

'Uh-huh? What about the women in your office? Or your chum's ex you were talking about? The one you took to your works bash?'

'You mean Jenny? Well, I didn't do her any favours by taking her to that party, I can tell you.'

'Why?'

'Oh, complicated. It was a real shame, though, not just because it worked out badly for her in the end. I was kind of hoping . . .'

'To fuck her?'

'. . . 'Scuse me, Louise. Frog in my throat. No, no, Jenny's way out of my league. No, just that there was a time when we were getting to be quite good friends. And I kind of hoped that we could be again.'

'You don't have any dastardly designs on her? What a man.'

'That's hardly a reason to give me a gold star.'

'Disagree.'

'Blimey, have I been bogarting this?'

'Don't think so. Thanks. Now where were . . . Who can that be? See, that's living in Soho, the one part of London where you don't have the normal London advantage of being spared people popping in on you. I'd better pass this back. Hold on . . .'

'So I was at a loose end and I thought I'd pop in on you. Eck, my man!'

'Hello there, Ian. How're you doing?'

'Oh, you know. Hey, that a jazz cigarette you're smoking?'

'Yes.'

'Okay if I join you kids? But, hey, I wouldn't want to be interrupting anything.'

'Not at all.'

'Find yourself a bit of floor and join Alastair and me in our drug-crazed orgy.'

'*Vraiment formidable*. You have no *idea* how welcome this is.'

6

'I BET IT WAS A GIRL WHO HAD A CRUSH ON YOU'

Thursday evening

'Bog,' Ian explains before heading for the stairs to the basement.

Right, then. This is his chance to have another go with the wee man. He puts on a nice, friendly smile. 'So, Eck, how's it going?'

'Not bad actually, Graham, although I must say that I've been a bit taken aback because according to some of Rob's diaries . . .'

He tunes out as Eck drivels on about his ridiculous investigation, tormenting himself with an image of Jenny's mouth poised over a salami-sized penis, until he forces himself to tune in to Eck again. '. . . for at least five years without any of us knowing.'

'Aye,' he says, nodding sagely, since that seems the kind of thing to do, guessing by Eck's tone. Okay. Now.

Graham's head is going like one of those toy dogs that used to live on the back shelves of cars. It's only a quarter past eight but it's obvious from his reddening face and bellowing voice that Graham must have been raiding his own drinks cabinet before he came out. At first, Alastair had felt rather chuffed that Graham wanted to tweak the routine again and go for a Thursday evening in place of the regular Friday bash, thus giving him, Alastair, the chance, second week running, to have a proper night out rather than one that involves racing over from Canary Wharf to arrive in time for last orders. But now it doesn't seem such a great favour, especially with Rob painfully conspicuous by his absence, Graham drunk, Ian popping up and down to the loos as though his bladder's a walnut, and Alastair beginning to suspect that Graham has some sort of agenda on the go.

'So, then,' says Graham through an ugly, forced grin. 'You heard from Jenny recently?'

'Jenny?' So that's the agenda. Blimey, Graham's looking rough these days. Which only makes him wonder what Jenny saw in Graham in the first place, because, no denying it, he can come across as just a great big galoot. 'Yes,' Alastair says. 'We talked on the phone not so long ago.'

'You seen anything of her?'

'Not for a while.'

'Ever introduce her to any of your pals?'

Well, thinks Alastair, bang goes any pretence of subtlety. 'No,' he says, not, strictly, untruthfully.

'To be a wee bittie more specific,' Graham continues, apparently trying to focus on the ashtray, 'did you ever introduce her to a pal of yours called J something? Like John or Jim. You ever do that, Eck?'

Alastair takes a moment to reassure himself that he won't be lying. 'No, Graham. In fact, I can't think of anyone I'm friendly with whose first name begins with J. Apart from Jenny.'

Graham's glaring at the ashtray now. When he speaks it is with a dangerously clenched tone. 'Taking the pish? Just answer the question, all right?'

'Okay, Graham,' replies Alastair as steadily as he can and hoping that he doesn't sound like a kindergarten teacher. 'No, I have not introduced Jenny to any friend of mine called J something.'

* * *

'Hey,' says Ian. 'I've just passed Graham on the stairs. What's with him?'

'Jenny,' says Alastair. 'One minute he was interrogating me about Jenny seeing some man, the next he was stumbling off. To the loo, I presume.'

'Yeah, he didn't say much to me either,' says Ian, choosing to pass over the detail that the few words Graham did utter on the stairs were that Ian was 'fucking charlied up', which is only partly true, him having chopped out only the merest tiny thread on the cistern, just to keep alert. 'By the way, by the way, by the way,' Ian says, 'that was an excellent little time last night at Louise's. I haven't been so stoned since I last had Rob's skunk. And it was very well timed, I can tell you.'

'Trouble at the school, you said.'

'Yeah, big trouble at the school. A student dissed me in a report and they've landed me in the shit.'

'I bet it was a girl who had a crush on you.'

'A gel? With a cwush on me? With *my* weputation?'

'That's *The Fast Show*, isn't it?'

'Didn't know you were a fan, Eck. Hey, how did you guess it was a girl? Apart from my reputation?'

'Because you used they for one person.'

'I did?'

'You did. One student, you said, but *they've* landed me in it. And people unconsciously use they in the singular when they want to avoid an incriminating he or she.'

'Or or or when people don't know the sex of the person. Like when the telephone voice says that the caller refused to leave *their* number.'

'Because there's no equivalent in English of a neutral pronoun, like *on* in French.'

'Eck, you really are quite the cunning linguist. I didn't know.'

'Well, that's one reason I like subbing, I suppose.'

'Kind of like my job in a way.'

'Yes . . . I hope you don't mind my asking, Ian, but is this they an annoying they or an important they?'

'You really want to know?'

7

'CIAO'

Friday afternoon

'Right, then,' says Barry. 'Who's doing what? Derek?'

'Finishing off Josh.'

'Yvonne?'

'Checking Hugo's recipe for pumpkin soup.'

'Alice? Bloody hell, where's Alice gone?'

'Emergency appointment with her reflexologist,' says Yvonne.

'Oh, bloody hell. Al?'

'Trying to get a headline for the latest instalment of Tamara's Caribbean epic.'

'Any luck so far?'

'Well, I have got "No, she went of her own accord" but I don't know if that's rubbish or any good.'

'The former, I think, but don't bin it yet. Any sign of double oh bloody seven?'

'Bond, James Bond?' says Derek. 'I think he's still busy writing his little piece for Arts.'

'So much for our extra bloody sub. How Bluebottle and all the rest of them bloody expect us to do all the bloody work on the shallow end of this bloody paper with only five, make that four, bloody subs I do not bloody know. Okay, then, team. Bottoms on seats, backs to the wall, noses to the grindstone, and we'll all be out of here by Monday.'

Alastair returns to staring at the list of headline ideas in his notebook. Should he even bother to jot down 'Jamaican funk'? No. What he really wants to do is give her another call. It felt so good, talking to her earlier in the week, after he'd dared himself to phone her up. Alastair reaches forward but then his palm stays on the handrest while he gives himself a pep talk. It was great just having that chat, and, yes, of course she is very fanciable but he's not going to let himself fancy her. He's going to behave himself. Because he is quite content as he is and he's fought long and hard to get to the stage where he is quite content as he is. Because if he starts hankering after her, the result will either be unrequited longing or a traumatising no-thank-you. And because there's a very good chance that they could become really good friends – the very thing he needs. And seeing her could provide an antidote to his glooms about Rob, those three-in-the-morning glooms when he's been lying awake and convincing himself that his own attempts at friendship are obviously rubbish. So he wants to be her friend. Yes? Yes. And he's got a good reason for calling her. Yes? Yes.

'Jenny, hi, it's . . .'

'Alastair. How are you?'

'Bit frantic. Not just at the moment, though.' Ignoring his own instructions about bottoms and seats and noses and grindstones, Barry pops his head above his terminal and gives Alastair a scandalised look – eyebrows raised, eyes boggling, mouth pursed as for whistling. Alastair shakes his head and takes cover behind his computer. 'The thing is, Jenny, I thought I should let you know that I saw Graham last night.'

'Oh? And how was he?'

'Well, mainly very keen to quiz me about the chap you were going out with, see if I knew who it could be.'

'Oh God . . . You didn't tell him, did you?'

''Course not, Jenny. But I thought I'd better warn you that Graham's on the case. However. All he knows is that it's someone whose first name starts with J.'

'Yes, Megan told him that, the stupid girl. That must be

from when I mentioned that the one thing you-know-who and I had in common was that our Christian names started with the same letter. Thank goodness I never said anything else about him. If Megan had known, I'm sure she'd have been delighted to tell Graham I'd become the Mata Hari of the *Sunday Chronicle* . . . You don't think there's any way Graham'll read any of you-know-who's stuff, do you, and realise it's supposed to be me?'

'How would he realise if nobody tells him?'

'You're right, Alastair. Oh God, though. I just feel so terrible about all of this.'

Alastair takes a deep breath. 'Look, Jenny, if you ever want to get it off your, have a chat about it, just say the word.'

'I might take you up on that offer if you really don't mind.'

This is good, Alastair tells himself. This is going well. So this is no time to bottle out. All he has to do is keep going here and he'll be fine. 'Tell you what, Jenny.' He has to clear his throat. Okay. Keep going. 'First free date in your diary, why don't I cook you supper? Or maybe it'd be wiser if we ordered pizza.'

'As I recall you used to be a dab hand in the kitchen, Alastair. Anyway, it's another unwise offer. You should see my diary. Tumbleweed drifting across it.'

'Nonsense.'

'True.'

Maybe it's only because she's belittling herself but he feels the confidence growing inside him. 'I'm going to call your bluff, Jenny. An evening at my place first free date you have.'

'Tomorrow, Sunday, Monday, Tuesday, no, not Tuesday, but . . .'

'See. Tuesday, you're booked . . . Tomorrow, then.'

'You sure you're not having to cancel some five-star gallivanting for my sake?'

'Positive. Eight o'clock be okay with you?'

'Perfect. See you tomorrow, Alastair. And thanks. Really.'
'Least I can do. See you tomorrow, Jenny.'

His mouth twitching into a smile, Alastair puts the phone down, fetches out his diary, almost forgets to notice that there's no FNC marked for tonight, and in tomorrow's entry scores a line through 'Gary and Co., Star of India, 8.30' and below it writes 'Jenny, supper at house, 8'. Which is all it will be. All he wants it to be. And the last thing she needs is some other dolt drooling after her.

Alastair turns back to his computer, calls up the unsubbed version of Josh's latest column, and dares himself to reread as much as he can of one of the offending paragraphs.

The lady in my life is looking so gorgeous that I decide their and then that I must have her. Rising from the chair and adjusting the long black skirt, I lead her away to a quiet nuke where I start to carress her breasts with my hands although she is wearing a blouse and a bra. I fall to my knees in front of her and I keep carressing her breasts with my hands while I press my face against her skirt and I am feeling that I

No thanks to the prose, Alastair is visited by a vivid image of Josh kneeling and trying to bury his face in Jenny's crotch. It is a picture that makes him feel like he's just drunk old milk. However. At least this'll be Josh's final ode to sexual joy, what with him getting chucked the day after this party, immediately after Jenny read his first column about her. And it is rather gratifying to know, from their promising chat on the phone earlier this week, Jenny's version of events on this particular evening – namely, that Josh invited her to a do at his parents' house in Belsize Park, got himself squeaking drunk, dragged her off to the conservatory, tumbled over a pot plant and hugged her knees while declaiming that it was his intention to make love not to her but with her. At which point, Mrs Todd had appeared, asked Jenny if she was all right and sent Josh to bed. 'Without any supper,' Jenny had added. 'Or me.'

Not that Josh has admitted to any such anticlimax in his latest column, which gives the distinct impression that he'd sent the lady in his life soaring high above alpine peaks of carnal bliss. Alastair scrolls down to the end of the text, fails not to register the finale – 'I am sweating. I am spent. I am repleat.' – and closes the file.

'Okeydokey lemonsmokey. Now let's try some phrasal verbs with get. Anyone? Dieter?'

'I am getting into British food.'

'Excellent. Is that true, Dieter?'

'Naturally, no.'

'Okay. Stanislaw?'

'I take a Tube to get to the school.'

'Yes, yes, yes. To get to somewhere. How about, let's see, Chantal? Do you have an example with get, Chantal?'

'I . . . I . . . I get up in the morning?'

'*Excellent*, Chantal. Very, very good indeed. Anyone else? Paolo? Do you have an example with get?'

'*Sí.*'

It's only now, halfway into the lesson, that Ian realises Paolo hasn't been acting the idiot as usual. 'And would you like to tell us what the example is?' Come to think of it, the little tosser's hardly said a word all class.

'*Sí*,' repeats Paolo, who is apparently trying to make some sort of a point by staring at him and not doing any blinking. 'To get off with a girl. To get it on. Means sex,' Paolo explains to the others while maintaining steady eye contact with Ian.

'Wow, that's very impressive,' says Ian brightly, pretending to ignore the fact that Paolo is now making a real show of shoving his books and pens and paper into his doubtlessly expensive leather bag. 'Right, everyone, let's move on to look. Look into, look up to, look . . .'

Paolo scrapes back his chair and stands up. Back to performing his hard man's act, he hoists his bag up on to his shoulder and marches up to Ian, who doesn't budge. They're standing almost nose to nose in front of the silent class. 'I am getting out,' Paolo announces. 'And you will not get away with what you do.'

Ian musters a puzzled smile which does nothing to appease Paolo, who turns to the rest of the class, waves goodbye like a child to a passing train, gives them a '*Ciao*' and marches out, making sure to slam the door behind him.

Is that better? Graham takes a step back and looks long and hard at the slightly rejigged arrangement. Yes, he decides. That's closer to the informal effect he was after. Certainly feels better this way, and what else does he have to go on apart from the way it feels? Answer: fuck all.

He reaches for the can of McEwan's, finishes it off with a couple of gulps, crumples it in half and lets it fall to the floor. Will all this have the same effect in D:Zine's reception? Well, that's the fucking question . . .

Maybe he could fit in one more drawing on the left?

Probably not. In fact, he's fairly sure it's just about done. What he'll do, though, he'll treat himself to another can and have a think about it. Then a quiet Friday night in, the FNC having apparently died a death, and he'll be all set for Audrey tomorrow.

8

'I HADN'T EXPECTED CHAMPAGNE'

Saturday night

Here's Ian, sitting in a pub in Vauxhall, drinking lager and marvelling at the fact that it'll be closing time in half an hour. Christ, even Scotland's figured out that letting people drink beyond eleven doesn't mean night-long brawling on vomit-splattered streets. Yeah, well, what do you expect? Welcome to England, where the time is 1897.

Not entirely true, he has to concede, and this pub's clientèle offers an awkward reminder of London's often startling hipness. This place is crammed with cool-looking twentysomethings all set to give it large in what Ian has gathered are Vauxhall's surprisingly jumping clubs – the all-niter for gay bikers just over the road, the joint near the MI6 building that's supposed to be at the cutting edge of trance, the fetishy place underneath the arches . . .

'Excuse me. Is someone using this?' A guy whose lime-green T-shirt says 'Aceeed' is pointing at the little wooden stool next to him.

'Go ahead,' Ian says, and he swirls lager round his glass to look busily unconcerned as the Aceeed guy drags the stool over to a group of lean, laughing boys and lean, up-for-it girls who all seem keen to display their flat tummies and jewelled tummy buttons. So that'll be him being the old geezer in the corner, then, the one on his own, nursing his lager and his memories of the Blitz.

Well, it could be worse. Because right now, at this very moment, he could be up in Crouch End, listening to the green blethers of Ben and Ruth. Which is exactly what Claire'll be doing and what he'd be doing too had they not had their worst-ever row earlier this evening. Soundtrack to his life right now – the repeated crash of doors being slammed in his face. By petulant youngsters, and through no fault of his that he can see, unless he's to blame for Chantal having a crush on him rather than that little Italian tosser, or it's suddenly a huff-making offence to dare to mention the slight drawback about going to Ben and Ruth's for a tofu bake or a beansprout soufflé – the distinct possibility that Ben and Ruth might be there.

Thank the living Christ that he didn't tell Claire about being fired yesterday. Mood she's in, she'd've executed him. Fucking Paolo, though. Little tosser. Defeated in a game of lust, he goes for revenge by telling Foxsmith that Mr Murray is crap at teaching modal verbs but excellent at supplying his students with charlie. 'Ah, Ian, ah, one has no, that is, not to blacken the school's as it were, ah, but no option remaining but to, ah, given the um, less than, ah, so all for the best if, ah, yes.'

And that was it. Goodbye London Oxford School of English, goodbye view of the Krazee Kost-Kutter Klothes Kompany, goodbye 240 notes a week, hello cowboy joint in Soho, eight hours a day, three days a week, six quid an hour, starting nine o'clock sharp Tuesday. Utter, utter crap, and the worst of it is that he has to count himself lucky to get even that. Cheers, Paolo. So that's what he gets for giving – giving, mind you – the little tosser a couple of lines. What do you call an Italian boy with a grudge? A little Eyetie tosser, that's what . . .

'Time's up,' calls the barman.

Ian finishes his lager. Crap flat, crap job, crap city, zero money, girlfriend pregnant and in a permanent strop. Yeah, time does feel like it's up.

'Anyway.' Jenny props her elbows on the table and gives him a smile.

'I didn't realise,' Alastair says. 'I suppose I'd always assumed that it was Graham and Jenny and that was that. You know, as you do with couples. I mean, you'd been together since just after student days . . .'

'Yes. I suppose I was like that as well. Not taking it for granted exactly, because that was never an option, the way he was carrying on, but not being able to see past it. To think that there could be life outside that relationship.'

Alastair purses his lips, trying for a solemn expression although an unworthy part of him is delighted. Because this is the kind of conversation he's been wanting to have with her. And because it shows they're getting on. No other reason. 'Absolutely,' he says, attempting now to look empathetic, although being in a relationship and not being able to think about life outside it is something he last felt not very pressingly and nearly a decade ago.

'So I think that I have to accept some of the blame too.'

'That's ridiculous. That's like the police saying someone chinned them in the fist. Come on, Jenny. How on earth could it be any fault of yours?'

'Okay. I know that I didn't force Graham to be an emotional – what's the right word? – twerp'll do. Although of course I did think that for a long time. No, I just mean that I had to be stupid to put up with it for so long. Putting up with it for five minutes would have been bad enough but . . . I'm sorry, Alastair. Here I go again. What I should be doing is saying thank you for dinner.'

'Don't thank me, thank Delia.'

Alastair is wondering if he might add a little line of patter here. Delia be praised, perhaps, or hallowed be Delia's name, but then Jenny gives him a breathtaking smile and says, 'My compliments to both of you.' Probably just as well. 'Any news about your friend Rob?'

Keep it simple, stupid, Alastair reminds himself, because this is exactly the sort of situation when he can find himself blethering rubbish, lots and lots of it. 'Not really,' he says. 'We've hired a detective to find out what's going on and we've got another appointment, a third appointment in fact, to see him on Monday afternoon so . . . Well, we'll see.' Alastair coughs. 'Sorry the food was nothing very fancy.'

'Alastair, it was a triumph. And I get quite enough of mango risotto and seared humming-bird during the week.'

'How *is* work?'

'Completely ideal if you want to spend half your life setting up overhead projectors or explaining to some executive how to open the minibar. No, I'm still enjoying it really. Though I could do with less dashing around now that I'm getting middle aged.'

Alastair smiles and shakes his head in what he hopes is a rueful way. But maybe he got that slightly wrong too. It probably came across as patronising. Why can't his face behave itself? He caught a glimpse of his reflection in the kitchen window when he went through to serve up the salmon and this pouch-cheeked daftie glanced back at him, a silly grin stuck to his face like a false moustache. So that was what he looked like when he was having a great time. An epsilon-minus nincompoop.

Whereas Jenny . . . well, Jenny is looking terrific. Dangerously so.

Alastair tops up her glass. As he does so, he reminds himself of all the points that make it rather a good idea for him not to notice the down on her forearm or, let's be honest about this, the way her chest pulls at her jersey.

- Jenny is Celtic to his Lochgelly Albert. Hanker after Jenny? Hmm, good idea. While he's at it, he could start lusting after Emmanuelle Béart as well. Who looks a bit like Jenny in a way – similar shape of face, and something about the mouth as well. Though Emmanuelle Béart's lips are much fuller, of course. Some might say too full. Anyway.

- Jenny is Graham's ex, so falling for her would be like marrying a cousin – not exactly illegal but still somehow dodgy.
- Jenny is in recovery, first from Graham and then from the *Chronicle* business, as Alastair now wants to call it, since it seems something like obscene to put Jenny and Josh Todd together in a phrase.
- Also. He has learned from past mistakes and he's not going to blow it this time. He's not going to fall for her, he's not going to make a pathetic, doomed play for her, he's not going to do anything that'll end up with her upset and him humiliated. Especially because
- he's got the chance here of having this amazing and, yes, lovely woman as a friend. Someone he can have a great chat with. Muck about with. Go out with. Well, not go out like that go out, obviously, that's the point, but go to places with. Which, to be openly selfish about it, is something he's going to need in his life, if it really is going to be Robless . . .

But she *is* lovely.

'Mm,' says Jenny, inspecting her glass. 'And this is a real treat. I hadn't expected champagne.'

Neither had Alastair, but when he'd taken her coat and seen how she looked in her black jumper and black trousers, her nut-brown hair pinned back with a little tortoiseshell comb, second thing he'd done, if you count as one the managing to control his stomach's sudden tightness and his knees' threat to buckle, had been to sprint into the kitchen, rummage frantically in the fridge and unearth a bottle of Moët. On the grounds that giving the vision sitting on his, Alastair's, candy-striped sofa a slug of the just-uncorked Chardonnay would have been like offering Audrey Hepburn a bite off a Curly Wurly.

Next item on the agenda had been to excuse himself, do another sprint, up to the bedroom this time and on tiptoe. Halfway up the stairs until it dawned that the glee on his face together with his high-stepping dance would do just fine in a very bad impression of Tom sneaking up on Jerry. Then a quick-change act to replace the dark blue polo shirt and black jeans – the kind of outfit which he'd thought would be appropriate for an evening of pally morale-boosting but which he now suspected made him look like he'd just done a stint in the garden – for his best white Ted Baker and a pair of Armani trousers. Another sneaky prance down the stairs and for the next hour it had been the pair of them perched at either end of the sofa, her looking terrific and him trying to sit cross-legged as uninelegantly as he could without the pins and needles in his right calf becoming too unbearable, and feeling that this was a cocktail party he'd thrown for some unthinkable reason and Jenny had been the only one compassionate enough to turn up.

'But what about you, Alastair?' Jenny asks. 'Are you seeing anyone at the moment?' She takes another sip of champagne, for all the world as if she's genuinely curious, though she might as well be asking if he's played for Scotland recently.

'No,' he manages to reply, with what he hopes could resemble a straight, serious expression. 'No, I'm not seeing anyone at the moment.'

'I should take you along to my book club,' she says. 'Ten women, two married, one gay, the rest manless and on the Häagen-Dazs. Five minutes in and you'd be having to fight the girls off with a stick.'

This can only be intended as a nice tease, since the alternative explanation is that Jenny has suddenly turned into the kind of person who delights in asking if your dog is still dead, but even so. Alastair clears his throat, then smiles at the table while he tries to think of something to say. Something that will provide a smooth segue to another subject. Any other subject. Something funny, by preference. Definitely something light and witty. 'Well,' he hears himself saying, 'I hope I wouldn't have to resort to a stick.' Oh, *brilliant*, he yells inside his head. You blithering *idiot*.

She leans down to give him yet another peck. But then he feels her tongue poke at his lips so he opens his mouth for politeness' sake. A loose strand of preposterous purple hair flops on to his cheek. His penis is a chipolata, slumped forlornly on his itchily moist pubic hair. Her tongue twitches around inside his mouth, like something he's eating that's suddenly come alive.

'Mm,' she says after she's finished her kiss. 'I need a drink.' She leans back until she's upright and resting a considerable part of her weight, comfortably for her presumably, on his balls. I'll get us a glass of water.'

'Good idea,' says Graham as she – thank fuck – gets off him and out of the bed, although he could do with something stronger. A bottle, for example, of tequila. She jiggles over to the door, where she unhooks her dressing gown. He hadn't expected that orange peel at the top of her thighs. And her skin smells strange – kind of like almonds. Not like Jenny. Jenny had a scent like vanilla.

It's as if somebody flicked a switch in his head the moment he finished coming. Up till then, just the kind of evening he would have asked for. Couple of drinks and a shared snack of chunky chips at the Cantaloupe, just him and her and her being encouragingly positive when he told her about the installation. So that was good. And it had been such a long, long time since he'd done anything like this, he'd been going mental with anticipation. And everything had been fine. More than fine. Excellent, really. Exactly the kind of date he thought he'd be having every week after he and Jenny broke up. So next thing they were snogging like teenagers in the Cantaloupe, then hopping in a taxi back to her flat in Stoke Newington. And now this. What the fuck has happened here? Well, long as she doesn't go all snuggly-wuggly when she gets back . . .

She reappears at the doorway of her bedroom. She rehooks the dressing gown and jiggles back towards him carrying a full glass of water. Graham reaches out for it, but she brings the glass up to his mouth and carefully tips it forward. Prone, he can manage only a sip before water pours back out of his mouth. She places the glass on the floor then lies down beside him. She throws an arm round his neck just where it's sorest. Graham grimaces. 'Mm,' she says into the side of his chest. She presses his neck. This time he can't prevent himself taking a sharp intake of breath. That is fucking *sore*.

9

'HE STILL DOESN'T KNOW, DOES HE?'

Monday afternoon

'. . . how to deal with lawyers like that in the Flying Squad, I can tell you.' Mr Hilton opens the slim manila folder marked 'Mr R. Mackenzie' and pats it flat on his desk. 'Nevertheless,' he says decisively. 'Two lines of enquiry have born fruit. The first concerns your friend's career. Perhaps I was mistaken but you did say that Mr Mackenzie worked as a banker?'

'That's right,' says Louise.

'In the City,' Alastair explains.

'In so far as the bank was situated more or less in London, yes, Mr Carr. Your friend was employed, as you thought, by the NatWest Bank. But, to clarify matters if I may, first of all at a NatWest in Leytonstone, and then, until he was made redundant earlier this year, at a branch in Theydon Bois.'

So that's how you pronounce it, Alastair finds himself thinking in the middle of his bewilderment.

Louise gives Mr Hilton a disbelieving look. 'What on earth was he doing in banks out there?'

'In each location, Mizz Turner, Mr Mackenzie was a member of the customer services team.'

'. . . You mean he was a cashier?'

'Precisely, Mizz Turner. In fact, Mr Mackenzie remained in this post and at a grade-nine salary level for his entire term of employment with NatWest. In its way, quite an achievement. But then your friend was no high-flier at his previous employer, the Bank, my apologies, the *Royal* Bank of Scotland, was he?'

'No,' says Alastair. 'But this was the early eighties. Rob and I were about the only people we knew who had any kind of job at all. And nobody gets going when they're young, unless they're a pop star or something. So Rob was doing all right, even during that stint at the Newington branch. In Edinburgh,' he adds for Louise's benefit. 'But he got fed up. That's why he came down here in eighty-five and joined the NatWest. In the City.'

'And what exactly did Mr Mackenzie claim he did in . . .' Mr Hilton holds up a pair of index and middle fingers. They pat the air twice. '. . . the City?'

'Corporate investment,' say Alastair and Louise in chorus.

Mr Hilton replies with a sorrowful smile, as though they've just come up with a particularly unconvincing alibi.

Alastair takes a deep breath because he's decided that he really has to set things straight. 'Look,' he says. 'I'm sorry, Mr Hilton, but I think you've made a mistake. Perhaps you've got the wrong records. Maybe there are two Robert Mackenzies at the NatWest. Or more. I mean, it'd hardly be surprising, it's not that unusual a name. No, the Robert Mackenzie we want works, or worked, in banking. Not *a* bank. Banking. In the City. In corporate investment.'

Mr Hilton leans back in his chair and gives Alastair an is-that-so? nod.

Alastair squeezes his hands between his knees and frowns. 'All right. Let's say for the sake of argument that Rob did work as a cashier. How do you explain his car or his flat, for instance? I don't know what a NatWest cashier earns but it's not going to be enough to buy an MG and an apartment slap bang in the middle of Soho.' Alastair shrugs helplessly. 'You must have got the wrong man.'

Mr Hilton clasps his hands behind his head. 'Might I ask, did he talk about his work, your friend?'

Alastair and Louise exchange a glance. 'Not in any detail,

if that's what you mean,' says Louise. 'But that only proves Bobby wasn't one to bang on about work.'

'Indeed. But if you'll bear with me for a moment, I'd be willing to put a small wager on my guess that neither of you ever actually visited Mr Mackenzie at his place of employment.'

Alastair looks at Louise. She shakes her head. 'Well,' says Alastair, 'it does seem that neither of us did . . . But that's hardly unusual. A corporate investment department isn't the kind of place you call in on, is it? I mean, it's a busy office.'

'I imagine so. But now I'm going to take another little punt here and suggest that Mr Mackenzie was probably very anxious about not being phoned at work either. Perhaps he said something about personal calls being forbidden?'

Louise is looking thoughtful. 'No,' she says. 'He didn't give me a work number. I'd call him on his mobile or at his flat. And we used e-mail a lot when I was in New York.'

'To conclude, then,' says Mr Hilton, 'the only evidence either of you had for your friend's career as an investment banker were a few signs of his apparent wealth. So when you, sir, said how did I explain his car and his apartment, for instance.' Mr Hilton's fingers pat out another pair of inverted commas. 'That was in fact the start and the end of the list.'

'Hold on,' says Alastair, who's busy assessing the thought that maybe his far-fetched, TV-movie-inspired notions may not have been too far fetched after all. 'Are you saying that Rob pretended to have a job in the City as a cover for something else? Drugs or crime or spying, something like that?'

'I favour a simpler explanation, Mr Carr. It seems to me that Mr Mackenzie's alleged job in the City was a cover for his actual job as a cashier in Theydon Bois. An odd commute, I'll give him that.'

Alastair has a picture of his brain fizzing and sparking like a wet socket. 'But if Rob worked as a clerk in a bank, how do you explain the money?'

'Very easily, Mr Carr. His inheritance.'

'No, I'm sorry,' says Alastair with a smile of tolerant disbelief, 'but you really have got this completely wrong. Rob's parents were not exactly landed gentry. His dad was a foreman in a linoleum factory.'

'If I may.' Mr Hilton lifts a sheet of paper from the manila folder and gives it a brief appraisal. 'Let me take you back to the summer of 1985 when Mr George Mackenzie of Torbain Street, Kirkcaldy, suddenly retires from his employ at a kitchen-flooring manufacturer. The same week that Mrs Joan Mackenzie receives a cheque for two hundred thousand pounds.'

'Two hun . . .?'

'The couple seem to have kept this good news quiet, as such lucky people often do, and quite sensibly so in my book, but they do celebrate their good fortune by taking a month's holiday in Yugoslavia as was. Two days into their dream vacation, they take a coach ride to Trieste, the coach driver fails to negotiate a hairpin bend, the coach plummets into a ravine, killing everyone on board.'

'You're right about the coach thing,' says Alastair.

Louise seems too stunned to say anything.

'Your friend loses both parents in the tragedy but as their only child he does inherit the sum of two hundred and four thousand pounds and twelve pence. Two months later, he leaves his job in Edinburgh and moves to London.'

Alastair tries to catch Louise's eye but she's still staring into space. 'So how come Rob's parents had all that money?' he asks.

'Premium bonds, sir.'

'*Premium* bonds? That's where Rob's money came from? His mum had a win on the premium bonds?'

'Initially, yes. It seems that Mr Mackenzie Junior then set out to be a freelance capitalist. His initial dabblings in the stock market were . . .' Mr Hilton waggles a dubious hand.

'But he did happen to do rather well in the property market for several years, buying, renting out and then selling flats in Highbury . . .'

'That's right,' Alastair interrupts. 'He had a place near the Arsenal ground.'

'. . . Kentish Town, Archway and Brixton.'

'Blimey. Really?'

'With the profits from which he purchased outright the Bateman Street property in 1990.'

Alastair looks at Louise, but she's still too busy staring in front of her. She looks even more shocked by this than he is. He shakes his head as if to clear it. 'Then what was he doing as a bank teller if he was this big-time property mogul?'

Mr Hilton holds up a warning index finger. 'Not quite big-time, Mr Carr. Certainly not big-time enough to be full-time, if you follow me. And however modest his salary – eight thousand pounds a year when he returned to work in eighty-nine – it did provide a steady income at a time when your friend's various fiscal ventures were of a nature that he might as well have taken a suitcase of notes and thrown it in the Thames.' Mr Hilton opens the manila folder again and reads from another sheet of paper. 'Eighty-six, he invested heavily in a Kenyan ostrich farm which was declared bankrupt six months later. Early eighty-seven, he came a real cropper with an ill-fated venture into the futures market. Later the same year, he had another try at the stock market and came a real cropper on Black Monday. And so it goes on. Until last year, when he switched most of his remaining capital into Far East stock and . . .' Mr Hilton gives them an encouraging nod.

Louise still seems incapable of making any response. 'Came a real cropper?' suggests Alastair obligingly.

'When the Korean economy went into freefall barely a week later. Precisely. If you don't mind my saying, it's just as well for NatWest's corporate investment arm that your friend didn't work there, because he did have an extraordinary talent for losing money. So much so that he had to remortgage his flat. In fact, from the documentation I've seen so far, Mr Mackenzie had bankrupted himself.'

There follows a silence which Alastair ends with a dry cough. 'You mentioned that there were two fruitful lines of enquiry. Can I ask about the other one?'

'Indeed you can, Mr Carr. It concerns Mr Mackenzie's present whereabouts.'

Alastair feels his heart suddenly banging at his ribs. 'You know where Rob is?'

'Indeed I do.' Mr Hilton consults the manila folder. 'He's going by the name of . . .'

'Stop,' commands Louise. 'Don't say any more. Or say what you have to say to Alastair. I don't want to hear it. I'm going outside. Call me in when you've done.'

She's right, thinks Alastair. He holds his hand in front of her to stop her getting up. 'No need,' he tells her, then he turns to Mr Hilton. 'From what you know do you think he's okay? I mean, are debt-collectors going to break his knee-caps? Or the police, are they after him? Is he in any danger?'

'Neither line of enquiry gives any indication of that, sir.'

Alastair stands up. 'Then that's all I want to know too. Thank you for all your hard work, Mr Hilton.'

'Much appreciated, Mr Carr, though in all fairness it was very straightforward, routine work. When I think of some of the cases we had on the Flying Squad . . . Yes. Well. I'll bid you goodbye, then. If you could settle the bill with Mizz Maguire in reception.'

Alastair offers his hand to help Louise up. 'You're right,' he tells her. 'We'll leave him alone.'

Louise is staring at the manila folder as though it's just called her by name. Alastair puts an arm around her and leads her out of the office. You're coping, he says to himself, and you're doing jolly well. But then he shuts the door to Mr

Hilton's office behind him and, all of a sudden, it seems like he's just smoked one of Rob's specials. In an unthinking daze, he monitors his signature being written on a bill's dotted line, then the approach of a flight of stairs, then the opening of a pair of glass doors.

He pushes open the doors, to be roared at by the traffic. He feels a tug on his arm. Louise is pointing at a nearby coffee bar. They walk towards it and in. Louise orders two double espressos. Following her example, as if she's guiding him through a complicated ceremony, he places his coffee on a long counter and perches on a high stool. Then he realises that she's just asked if he's all right. Come *on*, he shouts inside his head. Get a *grip*. He brings Louise into focus and takes a deep breath. 'Fine,' he says. 'I'm fine.'

Louise lights a cigarette and smokes in silence. They both gaze off into space. Alastair is trying to rewrite Rob's life, to discard the established version of Rob as a whoop-de-do ladykiller, high-flier, go-getter, and put in its place a Rob who was . . . ordinary. Who had an ordinary job. Who didn't have a big salary or a lavish expense account. Who didn't travel the world. Who may not have spent most evenings of his life wining and dining and chatting up girls at the latest in places. He tries to imagine Rob taking the Tube out east each morning, spending his days counting out other people's money, squandering the money that fate had given him, a fortune, really, especially to a bank clerk in 1985 . . .

Why, though? Why did he feel he had to lie all the time? Why couldn't he just have told the truth? What would he, Alastair, have done if he'd known that Rob was a cashier with an accidental nest egg? Spurned him? Hardly. Though that's probably missing the point . . . But it does mean, however it's looked at, that the trajectory of Rob's life has been quite different from the one he's always assumed it to be, the straight line arrowing ever upward, from school to university to financial apprentice to lavishly rewarded City mover and groover. In fact, the trajectory seems to have been a long slide downhill for Rob from what could now be seen as his peak, when he was sixteen, seventeen, at the centre of everything, liked by everyone and looking foward to a life of adventures . . . Maybe that was one reason Rob was so keen to establish the FNC second time around, because it evoked his glory days . . . Another thing – how easy it was for Rob to take off like that, how it took over a week for anyone to notice that he'd gone . . . And how would it be different for him, Alastair, if he wanted to disappear? There'd be his father to consider, of course, and before all this happened, he'd have cited Rob too, but, as Mr Hilton would say, that's the start and the end of the list.

Louise takes a quick puff of her cigarette. 'Did you have any idea about any of this?'

Alastair rouses himself. 'None.'

Louise shakes her head. 'You lot. You're just middle-aged teenagers, aren't you? I mean, for goodness' sake, the Friday bloody Night Club . . .' She sucks at her cigarette, spits out smoke. 'Funny. This seems worse than anything even I've come up with . . . You know what I think?'

'Um . . . no.'

'We both know that he was keen on his spliff. So many blim burns on his shirts and his dressing gown it was like he'd been shot by a twelve-bore. I mean, I just used to think that the dope thing was one aspect of his rich and multifarious, whizz-bang life. But now . . . now I think that was the only aspect there was. I think Robert Mackenzie was nothing more than a pathetic stonehead.'

'I don't . . .'

'Something I noticed when I was wandering round and round his flat the other day. Or actually something I noticed wasn't there. The only things missing that I can see. His little box was empty.'

'Not with you, Louise.'

'His dope box. The one with the fancy carvings. Nothing in it. So those were his two indispensable items of luggage. His bag of skunk and his king-size Rizlas.' Louise takes another brief puff of her cigarette. 'All that time I spent in New York worrying if I could trust him, wondering which club he'd be going to that evening, which restaurant with which scheming, gold-digging bitch. You've seen his diary. About as empty as his passport, hardly anything in it apart from his good chum Jeremy and you and the musketeers. There was me worrying myself sick about what he was up to and what he was up to was coming home after a day's slog at a bank in the burbs and rolling a big, fat one. To spend the rest of the night rolling more big fat ones, chain-munching Hob-nobs and dreaming up rubbish. How for me he'd be this rich City boy with a sob story about . . . and about how he'd be this rich, all-singing, all-dancing, party-time bachelor to you lot. An impoverished, avant-garde *artiste* to his great chums we never knew existed in the Coach and Horses.' Louise smiles at her cigarette and gives a short, joyless laugh. 'And there was me thinking I couldn't have been more stupid.'

'What do you mean?'

'When I'd been assuming all along that Bobby upped and went because of me.'

'But he did, Louise.'

'Right. He was broke. Beyond broke. His high-flying job was a sham. His whole life was a pretence. He was due to be rumbled. It was nothing to *do* with me.'

'Come on, that's just not true.'

'Okay, but only because my return meant that it was going to get harder and harder for him to keep everyone in their different boxes. Keep those different fantasy worlds apart. But I wasn't even his downfall. I think his downfall was the fashionable flat in the middle of Soho. Any other part of London he might still have got away with it. But Soho, people pop in on you.'

'Maybe that was why he was always asking us to phone him first. I always . . .' Thought that this was in case he'd be interrupted in mid-seduction, is the rest of the sentence, but Alastair decides not to say it out loud.

Louise looks off into the distance and smiles. 'Honestly, what a pathetic little scheming dopehead liar.'

'Come on, Louise,' says Alastair, although he's started to wonder just how many of the things Rob told him were made up. The CNN reporter, for example. The Brazilian girl with the bottom. The three-in-a-bed adventure with the sisters from Milan. Maybe he never even played strip poker with Kirsty Barclay.

Louise stabs her cigarette out on the saucer. 'You don't see it, do you, Alastair? Just how rubbish he was. And just how thoroughly he took the piss.'

'No, I . . .'

'I thought I was his girlfriend, you thought you were his best friend. But you know what we really were? We were members of his audience. For two of the different parts he liked to play. If we'd mattered to him, he wouldn't have lied to us, would he? And he'd still be here, wouldn't he? But he could leave us behind like he left everything else behind. Apart from his precious grass.'

It's understandable, Alastair reminds himself. She's bound to be wound up and bitter. Not that he can say such a thing, but how could she not be? 'I'm sure there's more to it than that.'

'He *used* us, Alastair. And you know why? One, because he was a sad, self-centred prick and two, because we could be used. The pair of us were only too willing to believe any old rubbish he came up with. Me because I was so worried about the relationship that the last thing I was going to do was demand to see his P60. You because you're . . . you. And I was conveniently stowed away in New York, while you were always there for him. When it suited him.'

Can that be right? Possibly, Alastair concedes to himself. Sort of. A bit . . . It could fit in with a few episodes in the past. Starting with the way that Rob did seem to drop him when they both went to big school and Rob began to hang around with the hard men. Until Rob hoved back into view in fifth year, and perhaps it could be argued it wasn't coincidence that by then he, Alastair, was not only in the school football team but was also pally with the Bill-Fiona-Steve set whom Rob was keen to co-opt into what would become the Friday Night Club. There was also the time when Rob drifted off at uni. And, granted, Rob certainly showed that he was no returner of phone calls or postcards after he moved to London, so that the two of them hardly ever saw each other until he followed Rob south four years later . . . Rob's enthusiasm for the second version of the Friday Night Club, wasn't that a bit suspect, given that these group nights out suddenly seemed to replace their one-to-ones and on what is for him, Alastair, the worst night of the week? Even Rob's last communication – those two ten-pound notes – maybe that wasn't Rob being decent and doing the right thing by a friend but Rob just squaring an account, dusting his hands and thinking that was that, discarding his friends like he left behind his furniture and his toothbrush . . .

Alastair gives his head a quick, impatient shake. This is just him feeling sorry for himself. 'I don't think so, Louise. I think maybe it's a bit different for me. You see, Rob and I have been friends for nearly thirty years.'

'Please don't give me that.'

'But it's true.'

'So you're saying that he could exploit a newcomer like me but not his best buddy and old pal Alastair Carr.'

'No, but . . .'

'His great chum who shares this enormous *heritage*, this *bond* that's so strong from knowing so much *stuff* about each other, like, oh, let's think of an example – yes, that his parents died in an accident umpteen years ago.'

A very good case in point, Alastair notes to himself. 'No,' he says, then he coughs. 'I'm not saying that.'

'Uh-huh?' Louise leans towards him. 'Okay, I didn't know about his parents' accident. Because his story to me was that his mother had been struggling with the infirmities of old age.'

Alastair shakes his head sadly.

'Until she died early last year.'

Alastair gives his head another shake and sips his coffee.

'Of Alzheimer's.'

The cup is stuck to his lower lip. Black and sticky and surprisingly hot liquid dribbles down his chin.

'A very moving account he gave of it. And I have to admit that it proved very effective as a seduction tactic.'

Alastair manages to replace his cup on its saucer and wipes his mouth. 'Fucking hell.'

'Quite . . . Something else that occurs to me. The way he kept puffing himself up, first of all by boasting and telling me what turns out to be a pack of lies, and then by putting me down. How he was the one with the glitzy lifestyle and the terrific salary, how I was so lucky to be going out with him. But in real life I was the one with the job and the big pay packet and the office with a view of Central Park.'

Alastair dabs at his chin and the dark spots on his chest. He'll have to buy a new shirt on the way in to work . . . He's in such a daze that there's a moment when he has to remind himself what he's doing here with this woman he doesn't really know. Come on now, he tells himself. Snap out of it and think through what's happening here.

So. Louise is obviously looking for solidarity and he'll give her as much as he can. But he's got to stick to his guns and not do it at the expense of rewriting his own emotional history. This malarkey may have shown that his friendship with Rob wasn't quite what he used to think it was, but it'd be going much too far to blame Rob for things he just didn't do. Okay, so Rob might have boasted a bit but he never put him, Alastair, down. 'I couldn't say, Louise.'

'I can't believe you're still sticking up for him.'

Alastair smiles wanly. 'It's bound to be different, though, isn't it? A relationship and a friendship.'

She shakes her head. 'You mean he was always this great, positive force in your life?'

'. . . Yes. Of course.'

'Oh, come on, Alastair. Haven't you ever noticed that you've been better off when he wasn't around?'

'I haven't, no.'

'Really? What about your relationships?'

'What about them?'

'Something that struck me after our heart-to-heart the other night. Every relationship you talked about. The girls you went out with your final year at college, the same final year at college when he wasn't around because he'd taken up with a new set. Rhoda or whatever her name is, when you were still in Edinburgh but after he'd upped sticks for London. Far as I can tell, Alastair, your love life has happened only when he hasn't been around.'

She's still looking for him to enlist and he really does want to offer her some support here. And joining in by blaming Rob for all the world's evils might help quell the hurt that's still growing inside him at the idea that Rob actually stole his own bereavement for a chat-up line. And he really does want to offer her some support. On the other hand . . . well, on the other hand, she is talking nonsense. As off the mark as the convolutedly fanciful analyses people come up with when they've been converted to therapy. 'That's coincidence, Louise. And me being not exactly a ladies' man.'

'Maybe. And maybe it's coincidence that he also latched on to you when you split up with Rhoda, Rhona, whatever, lured you down here and got you started smoking grass the moment you arrived. I mean, what better way to keep you docile? And happy enough to dodge around at home on your own? At his beck and call, always ready to be impressed by the latest story to make him look great and you feel small?'

This is worse than therapy. This is astrology. 'No, Louise,' says Alastair. He is surprised by the firmness in his voice.

'Uh-huh. So you're telling me that he never held you back? Never put you down?'

'Rob was my friend, Louise. No.'

'You sure about that? . . . Eck?' She looks at him with a grim smile. 'Because what I'm sure about is that he held *me* back, he put *me* down all the time, and my life is going to be a lot, *lot* better now that I don't have to deal with that devious, pernicious, cowardly, selfish, lying, stonehead *bastard*.' She lets out a high, strangled yelp, hides her face in her hands and starts to sob.

'Oh, Louise,' murmurs Alastair. He reaches over and strokes her hair. 'Oh, Louise.'

'But, you know, like I say, I *was* kind of like, yeah, I'm expecting him to call.'

'Audrey, I really am sorry. And like I've said, I was going to call you today. I mean, it's only Monday.'

'Yeah, yeah, boy time, of course, I forgot. Boy time. It's a classic men are from Mars, you know what I mean?'

No is the answer to that one, but Graham gives her a non-committal 'uh' instead.

'You know, and it *is* specially kind of, like, weird, even with boy time, the Mars–Venus thing and the blah blah blah, not to call when, you know, you were, like, goodbye, and it's, like, four o'clock in the morning. Yeah? I mean, you know.'

He had his way, the phone would be in smithereens right now. This can't go on for much longer, surely? He checks his watch. Five-thirty. So that's her been yapping away for over an hour now. Fucking price he has to pay, though. Hefty price, mind, time-wise – about ten minutes' yap for every minute's shag. He should have called yesterday and avoided all this shite. Just as well he's only got a couple of tweaks, if that, to do for the exhibition and zero on the illustration front, bar a crappy little commission to do an Earth covered in a spider's web for *Computing Now* with a Friday deadline. 'Look, Audrey,' he says, 'I'm sorry, right? Like I've said a hundred times already, I couldn't sleep. I'm sorry.'

'Yeah, right, yeah, I know, but, you know, four o'clock in the morning and then no phone call Sunday, no phone call today, I'm, like, what's going on? You know?'

Here they go again. How many times, how many fucking *times*, do they have to go round this short loop? 'Yes, I am sorry, Audrey, but it's just . . .' What? What can he say here that he hasn't already said? Maybe he could tell her the truth. Audrey, while you were sleeping, whistling through the crust in your nostrils and stinking of marzipan, I stared into the darkness, gagging for a drink, even of water, and thought not about you but about Jenny, and wondered if Jenny'd been doing what I'd just done and, if so, who with. End of story. '. . . It's just that things are complicated at the moment, Audrey,' says Graham. 'What with the exhibition and everything . . . Look, I'd better go. I've got to get this work done before the courier arrives . . . Audrey? . . . Audrey? You still there?'

'. . . Yeah.' This tiny, pathetic voice.

'I've got to go, okay? . . . All right? . . . Okay?'

'. . . Is that it, then?'

'I've got to go, Audrey. Honestly . . . I've got to go . . . Okay, so, 'bye. I'll talk to you soon, all right?'

'. . .'

'I've got to go now, Audrey. Sorry, but I've really got to go. 'Bye, then . . . 'Bye.'

Graham bangs down the phone. 'Jesus,' he says. 'Jesus fucking *Christ* on a fucking *bicycle*.'

They're about to turn the corner into Bonnington Square when

Ian remembers that the flat'll be in a mess. But that's good, because it'll back up the impression he may have given her that he lives on his own. Ian lets go of Chantal's hand and rubs his nose, not because the nose is its usual troublesome self – in fact the nose has been feeling good today, not running, not itchy, not too blocked, not anything really, despite a couple of nice little lunch-time lines – no, not because the nose was giving him the usual bother but because it gives him a reason to let go of her hand. You never know – someone might be looking out of a window at exactly the wrong moment, and that someone might be someone Claire has got talking to at some point or other, for some reason or other. No, you never know. And one thing Ian's learned over the years, when it comes to situations like this, you cannot be too careful.

They've reached the main door. Nothing to see here, he thinks. Just him with a friend, that's all – couple of pals popping in for an afternoon coffee or an afternoon spliff. All very innocent. He shuts the door and takes Chantal's hand again to lead her up the flight of stairs.

He's fiddling with the keys when she taps him on the shoulder and beckons him forward to kiss her again. His mouth melts into hers again. He's holding her shoulders but – he can't help it – his hands roam down to her hips then cup her dinky bottom. He gives her one of his best moves – the one where he concentrates on a corner of the mouth, a surefire winner. His wilful fingers begin to spread over the soft-denimmed bottom and are about to start clutching.

He forces himself to hold back. All the time in the world for that once they're inside – or, more accurately, all the time in the world until, say, seven o'clock, because Claire's due back at eight after a day up in Stanmore with her folks. Still, that gives him a good three hours with Chantal. Who, on top of everything else, told him over lunch that she was gym champion of her lycée. Her eyebrows lifting a fraction as she said that, to let him know. His groin fizzing at images of how she might hoik her long, pliable legs. Not too easy to eat a mozzarella-and-tomato ciabatta after that. In fact, he'd given up on food, swigged his Badoit instead, then taken himself off to the loos of the trendy little café in Greek Street for an adjustment of the boxers and another quick line.

Now he ushers her into the main room, where he checks for any telltale signs of Claire – none, really, apart from her pink-edged trainers, but they're hiding over in the far corner – and then he's with Chantal on the sofa and kissing the corner of her mouth again.

'*Un moment*,' he says when he eventually summons up the willpower to disengage his lips from hers. '*Un moment. Reste ici.*' Ian limps through to the bathroom, where he runs a tap and flushes the loo – like he could use it in his state: maybe just, if he had ten minutes to spare and could place the bowl halfway up the bathroom wall – while he sets about hiding the stuff that's unmistakably Claire's, shoving her potions and lotions and salady-sounding pots into the bathroom cabinet. Then it's through to the bedroom, where he stashes some *Cosmo*s and a nightie under the bed.

That's all he has to do. It's so easy. But that's only in keeping with this assignation, which has gone like a wet dream – from the moment Chantal agreed that they should meet to the moment when she told him she'd be leaving at the end of the week and went all meaningful on him. Allowing him to up the romance, in reassuring French, by stroking her hand and murmuring, '*Alors, nous avons seulement ce moment.*' Corny, but it worked, as corn has a surprising way of doing with women, in his experience. Although he has a theory that that's maybe just because he doesn't have to try too hard. Or, in this case, at all.

But that's what he means – everything's been so easy. Which only goes to show that this was somehow meant to happen. And in any case, where's the harm? This is a one-off, she'll be back in Toulouse by the end of the week, and as long as Claire doesn't find out – and how on earth would she find out? – then this'll be a treat, nothing more than that, like having a final, pick-me-up toot at the end of a party. Plus, come on, what red-blooded man could pass up the chance of an afternoon sesh with a quality French babe gymnast? Not Ian Murray, that's for sure.

He's returned to the main room, where she's waiting for him on the sofa. He sits down beside her, puts an arm around her shoulder and pulls her towards him, ready to start the kissing build-up all over again, because he's bound to have lost a bit of momentum here. She, however, thinks otherwise, judging by the way her free hand has come to rest on his trousers' pleasingly prominent bulge.

'I like kissing you,' she murmurs into his ear.

'And I adore kissing you,' he murmurs back, choosing English now that things are getting serious – the safe option in such circumstances, even for someone as fluent in French as he is. He gives her his best crinkly-eyed smile. 'Let's go to bed,' he says, taking control now.

He stands up, pulls her upright, leads her through to the bedroom. He back-heels the door shut behind them, leans forward to nuzzle her ear as a token distraction, and peels off her jacket. Next to go is the pink cardigan, which he slips off her shoulders and down her svelte, tanned arms. She takes a step back. She tilts her head. She smiles. She holds his gaze as she crosses her hands and begins to pull up her T-shirt. Very, very slowly. Revealing inch after inch of perfect, brown flesh. Eventually, the first glimpse of a lacy white bra. This, he thinks, is about as agonisingly gorgeous as it gets. And this is only the start. He stands there, transfixed. More lace now, the suggestion of rosy nipples underneath the lace, the white of her string-thin bra straps, the smooth, lighter brown skin of her underarms as she ducks into the T-shirt and yanks it over her head and her thick auburn hair.

Only now does he take a step forward and pull her towards him. Then it's time to kiss again, while his left hand buries itself in her hair and his right sidles round her back to find the bra clasp. Girl her age, she probably won't be expecting the sheer smoothery of this, he thinks, as he nibbles her full lower lip and prepares to undo her bra one handed. She's making little straining noises in her throat. His fingers are easing out the clasp and . . .

And there's a noise at the front door. Which cannot be. That cannot be happening. But it is. It is happening. Someone is opening the front door.

'. . . them tomorrow instead.' Claire. It's Claire. 'I don't know what I'd do without them at the moment, I really don't.'

Ian and Chantal stare at each other, their hands by their sides now, but the pair of them rooted to the spot. Chantal's mouth opens in a silent 'What?', or it could be '*Quoi?*'

'Oh, absolutely.' That's Briony. Her unmistakable whine. Fucking, fucking Briony. 'Maybe we could do an afternoon film or something. Have you got a *Time Out*?'

'On the table, I think. Or maybe in the bedroom.'

Briony walks in on them and yelps. A moment later, Claire appears behind her. She doesn't say anything at first, just takes in the scene. He blurts out something about it not being what she thinks, that he can explain everything. How? Saying what? This girl from the school was feeling faint so he took her home, loosened her clothing and was about to call the doctor . . . Claire replies with a sneer then sprays the room with an Uzi. He can see it all.

And that'll be it. No more Claire.

No more Claire. For all his vague envy of Rob's walk-off, for all his occasional little daydreams where he finds himself by himself somehow, in a bar in Le Marais or a flat with a rooftop view of the *sixième*, he has never really thought about what no more Claire would actually mean. Only now, as he stands there in the bedroom, listening to Claire and Briony next door, looking at but not really seeing a plainly terrified Chantal, sickly saliva trickling down his throat, does the reality dawn on him. Claire. No more Claire. What'll he do? Where'll he go? How'll he cope? What'll be the point of anything if there's no more Claire? And the baby? Christ, the baby. His baby.

'Here it is.' Claire. Still in the main room. She must have found the *Time Out*, thank Christ. 'Any suggestions?'

'*Women on the Verge of a Nervous Breakdown*, that might be appropriate.'

'Yeah, right.' Claire again. 'Or *Clueless*. Something something.'

'He still doesn't know, does he?'

'Oh, he doesn't know anything about anything.'

'But you haven't told him, have you, Claire?'

Is he the he they're talking about? And told what? What hasn't she told him?

'Because I haven't decided for certain. Something something Stanmore.'

'But, Claire, you've said yourself that it's hopeless. Bad enough being totally poor and living in this . . . this *tip*, but he's never there for you, he's the opposite of supportive, he's making zero effort, he doesn't help you, he's horrible to all your friends, his first reaction to the baby was to ask about an abortion, and he hasn't got much better since, from what you've said yourself. And he seems to have no *idea* what you're going through.'

'Something something something.' Claire, muttering.

'I know. And at his age.' Briony's voice coming over loud and clear, Briony having a foghorn where human beings have tonsils. 'And do you want a cocaine addict as father of your child? I don't *think* so.'

'I know.'

'Look, Claire, you'll be much better off with your parents,

even if it's for a little while, and if he still doesn't see any sense, then you've empowered yourself, you've made the first move.'

'I know. You're right. I just don't feel very empowered, that's all.'

'No, you feel ill. Look, Claire, it's not only yourself that you have to think about now. And you can't keep on fainting in supermarkets. On your own.'

'I know, Briony . . . Oh, Christ, let's just get out of here, shall we?'

Ian risks breathing for the first time in what feels like years. Chantal hasn't so much as blinked. Petrified, he finds himself thinking. She's petrified.

'We could go up to Leicester Square and take pot luck, what do you think?' Claire, near the front door.

Yes, Ian pleads inside his head. Yes. Leicester Square. Right now. Do not pass go.

'Wait a minute, please, Briony.' Claire again. A slight rummaging sound, then a chink, of keys maybe, or coins. 'I'd better take my specs. Now where? . . . Ah. I know. Bedroom.'

10

'WHAT DO YOU RECKON?'

Wednesday evening

'No, really,' says Graham. 'I'm delighted.'

Fionnula, Marty's new and controversially female assistant, nods keenly. 'Good,' she says. 'It's . . . exciting work,' she adds. She's quite sexy, Graham has decided, even though she's on the plumpish side, could do with sending herself to the dry-cleaner's and has five silver rings dangling from her left ear.

'Yo, Graham. Sup.' It's Marty, looking as svelte and as somehow untrustworthy as ever. Today he's wearing a pair of baggy beige breeks with enormous pockets on the sides, and a blue fleece, zipped up so that Marty can tuck his chin into the collar and nuzzle it for something to do when he's not speaking. He untucks his chin again. 'Early doors, I know, but, still, good few people here. And the work's looking . . . good.' Now it's Marty's turn to nod. 'Good.'

'Good turnout from the press as well,' Fionnula tells Marty.

'Who?' asks Graham.

'*Blueprint* and *Design Week* said they might come. Guy from the *Ditch* has just arrived and, best till last, the *Sunday Chronicle*'s here.'

'The *Chronicle*?' asks Graham. 'Where?'

'Over by the desk. Chatting to that man with the stubble.'

Graham squints around a group of standard-issue trendy freeloaders. It's Eck and Ian. 'You mean the wee baldie bloke?'

'Guy in the black Armani, yeah.'

Graham flinches. 'Naw, that's a mate of mine. Works at the *Chronicle*, like, but that's it.' *Fuck* it. Typical Eck. Trust him to turn up early. And spend all of a minute gazing at the installation, smiling half heartedly and stammering the blandest praise before launching into a long, wandering monologue, with a lot of sorrowful head-shaking, about what he'd discovered about Rob. Apart from the pools win, nothing Graham hadn't really known – after all, he has become so used to thinking of Rob as the man who betrayed him, lied through his teeth and used and abused the FNC for his own nefarious ends, that it couldn't come as any great surprise to be told that Rob had done all of those things, if not quite in the way that he had once thought. But Eck had said his piece like he was reporting a death in the family, happily mistaking Graham not giving much of a shite for grim acceptance of this supposedly terrible bombshell. Then Eck had fallen into conversation with Fionnula, that being an obvious thing for the pair of them to do at a time when the only other people in the room were Marty and himself, and Marty and himself had both become occupied at the table of freebie drink. What did Eck expect, though, turning up at quarter past for a 6.30 kick-off? Mind you, the place is still only half full, but that's good going for a quarter past seven. Isn't it? Come on, 'course it fucking is. And reactions so far have all been good. Well, they would be, wouldn't they? But they have. All been good, that is. The reactions so far.

By fuck, he could go another beer.

'Six quid an hour?' asks Alastair.

'Six quid an hour,' says Ian.

'Blimey.' It occurs to Alastair that Ian would earn more cleaning people's houses, but it also occurs to him that it might be a bit tactless to point this out, so he makes do with what he hopes is a sympathetic-looking headshake.

'I'd probably earn more asking people if they want fries with that.'

Alastair directs a dry cough into his fist. He's had a thought. 'This is only a vague idea, Ian, okay?'

'Okay.'

'Just a suggestion, I mean, nothing more.'

'With you so far, my man.'

'Well, you know how you know about grammar?'

'Uh-huh.'

'And you can spell.'

'Ye-es.'

'And you worked on that magazine in Paris?'

'Well, I don't think that doing little things for a hippie English news-sheet . . .'

'And you can work a computer?'

'Sort of. Depends.'

'Never mind, Ian, I mean, that's easy enough to pick up, and I could give you the rest of the basics, like how you do a delete sign or what thirty-six point means . . .' Alastair stops himself. He's getting carried away here, because it seems such a brilliant idea. Yes, but then there must be something obviously wrong with it. It's probably of no interest to Ian anyway. And possibly very presumptuous of him to be thinking of this at all.

'You're talking about subbing, right?'

'Well, yes, but it's only a . . .'

'But I'm not trained as a journalist.'

'Nobody's trained as a journalist these days, Ian. Even subs. Once you've got the basics and you know how the language works, then subbing's one of those jobs which you can only learn by doing it. And there are jobs going for subs. I know of at least two chief subs on magazines who need staff. One of them, Gary, he's quite a good friend, so I could put a word in for you if you want. There's even a job going at the *Chronicle*, although Barry'd probably be looking for someone with experience. But the *Indie*, say, you might get shifts there, they'd take anyone. God, sorry, Ian, I didn't mean . . .'

'No, that's fine.'

At least Ian looks vaguely intrigued rather than outraged. Although he's also noticeably subdued, and 'subdued' isn't one of the words he associates with Ian. Even so, Alastair judges it time to change the subject. 'So what do you think?' he says, nodding towards Graham's exhibition. This occupies the far corner of the reception area and consists of one work or piece or installation or whatever the right noun is. One part of it is on the floor, a white but slightly stained and rather crumpled-up duvet, on which are scattered a weird variety of objects – here an empty bottle of whisky, there a paint-brush, and everywhere scrunched-up sheets of paper which occasionally reveal little squiggles, and which, according to Fionnula with the earrings, are meant to be opened up by members of the audience who'll then see that each sheet of paper contains a pen-and-ink self-portrait. So far, the scrunched-up pieces of paper have remained pristinely scrunched, but Alastair reminds himself that this is an opening party attended by a lot of arty types who'd doubtless think it very unhip to engage with Graham's whatever-you-call-it. Anyway, the objects on the ground are far less striking, to his eyes at any rate, than the second part of the whatsitsname, which takes place above, on one of the white walls. And this second part consists of seven rows of photographs, twelve in each row, which curve in a rainbow over the duvet. And which, more to the point, at least as far as he is concerned, are all the one colour snapshot of Jenny, kneeling pertly on a tartan picnic rug in a field somewhere sunny, smiling up at the camera and, because she's wearing only a bikini bottom, displaying surprisingly large breasts with surprisingly big, pink nipples. He wonders if Jenny knows about any of this. If she doesn't, and he can't see how she could, and if she had she'd surely have mentioned it, how will she feel about her latest starring role? Not best pleased, reckons Alastair. Not best pleased.

When he arrived – as early as he possibly could to tell Graham about Rob, and because the couple of times he's dared hold anything like a party he's spent the first couple of hours panicking about people not turning up – he'd taken a good long look at the thingummy while Graham was engrossed in chat with the thin chap with the weaselly face who keeps on ducking into his fleece. Once he'd got over the initial shock of seeing eighty-four reproductions of Jenny and Jenny's bare chest, he had done his best to be mature and objective and assess the whole thing – and completely failed. Hard enough to figure out anything from the world of contemporary art, a world which seems as trendily remote as fashion – both being worlds, as far as he can see, run by a handful of people in the know telling people not in the know that apparently silly things are actually very important and exciting, although few people in their right minds could surely want to put those things on their walls, just as you'd never even think about wearing a hat made from shrubbery – but completely impossible when it features eighty-four reproductions of Jenny and Jenny's bare chest.

He can't even judge whether this whole do is going well or not. There's maybe fifty people here, but is that normal, good or bad? And there's still only a few of them paying any kind of attention to the actual exhibit – is *that* normal, good or bad? Alastair looks over at Graham, who's currently shaking someone's hand and laughing heartily, but all he can decode for certain is that Graham has already had quite a few drinks.

Alastair takes another sip of his Japanese lager while Ian, who really does seem quite under the weather, takes another look across at Graham's thingummyjig. 'Really, Ian,' says Alastair. 'What do you think?'

* * *

'I think we get the hell out of here, Alastair.'

'Are you feeling all right?'

'Fresh air would be good. But mainly I think we should just get the hell out of here. Come on. Follow me.'

Ian sidles through the small throng towards Graham, mouths 'See you later' at him because Graham's ensconced with a couple of people, sticks up a thumb just as Graham turns back to his conversation, reaches the door and then the cool of the early-evening air.

'Phew,' says Ian.

'Phew indeed,' says Alastair.

'You fancy a wander? Maybe a drink if we stumble across a not crap pub? If there is such a thing around here.'

They set off down a narrow street featuring warehousey-looking buildings with hoist things coming out of some upper-storey windows, and leading God knows where.

'You didn't think much of it, did you, Ian?'

The pair of them come to a halt and gaze up at the gable of a derelict building. Ian sighs. 'No. No, I didn't think much of it . . . Oh, who knows, it might be brilliant, and he might get rave reviews and what we've just seen might be the start of a new and spectacular career for Graham as an installation artist of great and trendy genius.'

'But?'

'. . . But I wouldn't bet on it.'

Alastair puffs out his cheeks and raises his eyebrows. 'Well,' he says eventually, 'do you suppose Graham's happy with it?'

Ian shrugs his shoulders. 'I think Graham doesn't have a clue. Not that that singles him out.'

They move off slowly down the street. 'This could be bollocks, of course,' Ian says after they've sauntered another couple of yards. 'But I remember reading somewhere that there are now more people in Europe working as artists than there were people alive in Renaissance Italy. Pub over there that doesn't look too appalling. Fancy a pint, Alastair?'

11

'LITTLE HICCUP ON THE LUNCH FRONT'

Thursday afternoon

'Waldemar?'

'. . . The woman is buying cloazez.'

'Good.' He has to have another quick check of the class diagram on his desk. Then he looks up again at the dozen people crammed into this tiny room with crumbling walls and a sink at the whitewashed window. More or less what he'd expected, in fact, from a place calling itself the International Oxford English School. In Lisle Street. Above a minicab office. 'Miroslav?'

'Thee boy. Eez eating. Thee ice gream.'

'Very good.' Damn, he's forgotten the next name. And it's far too warm in here. Only another fifty-three minutes until his lunch break. He takes another peek at his diagram. 'Boris?'

'Barees.'

'Barees.'

'The man is playing the golf.'

'Good.' Oh, bugger it. He glances back down at his class diagram. 'Natsuko?'

'*Sumimasen*. You say Natsko.'

'. . . Right . . . Natsko.'

'the sun-kissed slopes of the Andalusian sierras, where earthy peasant cuisine and the'

Alastair is trying to concentrate on Hugo's piece about tomatoes. Not an easy task, and one that's made even harder when he sees the editor lumbering this way, accompanied by a chubby-faced and bespectacled young man who looks like he would be much happier swanning about a campus or minding a second-hand bookshop than picking his way through the shallow end's shambles of workstations. The pair of them weave towards and then into Bluebottle's office. There's something familiar looking about that young man. Something about the glasses, maybe . . .

Josh Todd. Blimey, it's Josh!

He goes to Alt Screen and hurriedly taps out a message to Barry. 'wot josh here for? and why with ed? and why ed down here? wot going on?' Alastair presses Send.

'delightful news, al,' starts the reply, 'ed and b/bottle taking josh to lunch to discuss recent brilliance of josh's columns.'

Alastair studies the message then sticks his head round the side of his terminal. 'Barry?' he whispers. 'Are you being serious?'

'Oh yes,' Barry whispers back, then he ducks his head back down and starts hammering away at his keyboard.

Soon Alastair's screen flashes MESSAGE. 'just to make you even happier, al, i shd add that b/bottle planning to invite 007 to lunch as well so b/bottle can push 007 forward as new bright young theatre critic for arts section which is wot 007 wants to do, and as far as b/bottle concerned, wot 007 wants 007 gets.'

Alastair is wondering if there's anything he can type in reply to this terrible news when his phone goes off. One long ring – an internal call.

'Hello?' says Alastair.

'Alastair Carr? Front-desk security here. We have a Graham Anderson in reception to see you.'

What? Graham? Here? 'Ah, yes, okay, I'll come and collect him.' Graham? Here? What? Alastair scrapes back his chair. And Josh Todd in the office at the same time? Oh God. Could Graham have got wind of Josh? Oh God. 'Back in a minute, Barry.'

'Be quick. Lunch-time soon.'

Okay. This is the plan. Keep calm, act nice and normal, spin Eck the line, take him to the nearest pub, if there is a nearest pub in Canary Wharf, sandwich, couple of drinks, and take a more subtle approach. Because the more he's thought about it, and he's thought about it only all the time, the more he's convinced that it's got to be someone she's met through Eck. Because Jenny and Eck have kept in some sort of touch, unlike Jenny and Col or Jenny and Ian. And because he can't come up with any other feasible explanation. So get Eck talking about his pals, people at his work, then suss out anyone Eck mentions who has an initial J. Because he's got to find out. And if he wasn't trying to find this out, Christ alone knows what he'd be doing with himself. No, he's got to find out.

There's Eck now. Looking like he feels – i.e., like someone's died on him but he's doing his best to soldier on.

'Hi, Graham,' he says, still with this air of smiley desperation. 'Congratulations again on the exhibition.'

Shows how much the wee man knows. Graham shrugs, as though modestly. 'Aye, well . . .'

'So,' Eck says into the gap, 'what brings you to this neck of the woods?'

'Afternoon appointment,' Graham replies. 'With the art director of the colour supplement,' he adds, gesturing to the portfolio he's lugged all the way from Finchley to back up the spiel. 'So I was wondering if you wanted a cheese roll and a couple of pints somewhere near by.'

He couldn't have been more laid back and pleasant but Eck gives him an anxious stare. 'Yes, well, that'd be nice, Graham, but . . . but, you see . . . the thing is, we usually all just pop over to the canteen.'

'Nae bother, Eck. Canteen it is, then.'

'. . . Sure, sure. Um, I'll have to get you a pass.'

Like a pass is a fucking jar of plutonium. 'Fine.'

Eck proceeds to fuck around for a few minutes, in a particularly Eckian fashion, with the security bloke, who seems exactly the sort of bloke a security bloke would be securing an office against. Eventually, the security bloke beckons him over to sign his name and collect a plastic-covered sign that announces VISITOR. Graham clips it on to the breast pocket of his leather jacket, an action which makes him feel, for some unfathomable reason, a bit of an arse.

Eck does one of his wee coughs. 'If you don't mind, then,' he says, 'we'll just head straight to the canteen.'

'Right you are,' says Graham, then he notices that Eck is staring at him in horror. Must be because there's a gang of suits coming towards him and he's blocking the way. He moves to his left, but only slightly because he's fucked if Eck's going to have him bowing and scraping to a bunch of suits. Having themselves on that their lives have some fucking purpose and picking up a big cheque at the end of every month. Fucking suits. Although, to be accurate about it, the two younger blokes of the four aren't wearing suits and one of the other two is jacketless. Aye, but they're still salarymen, that's the fucking point. The suit who's actually wearing a suit has given the Eckster a brief nod. The other three just ignore the wee man.

'See you later, Richard,' Eck says to the suit's back. Richard. Can't be him, then. But whoever he is, he's obviously got the knack of soothing Eck, who's switched from something like panic to something like normal.

'So, Eck, you not going to show me around?' Graham asks, now that the wee man's got rid of his fear grin, and because maybe a quick tour might give him the chance to ask Eck about people he mucks about with here.

'Um, well, yes. If you want. A good time to do it, actually, because it'll be quite quiet.'

Right. He'll have to do it slightly different, then, if nobody's around . . . He'll think of something. 'Who're that lot?' Graham asks, on the grounds that he might as well, although anyone would think it's a devilish trick question going by Eck's sudden fretting.

'Oh, um, well, that was Richard Marshall, who edits the Lifestyle section. And the chap in the shirtsleeves was . . . the editor. And the thing is, you see . . .' And that's Eck gone off on one again, as they set off towards a pair of double doors, stammering drivel about calling an editor an editor. Or some fucking thing.

Graham tunes out as he takes in his surroundings – typical newspaper office, or at any rate very like the ones he used to visit when colour supplements really were commissioning him, except none of them had a view of France. They head off through a right old mess of desks and computers and garbage and towards the only people left in the office, a clutch of nerds in the far corner. Then something happens which he really was not expecting. One of the nerds suddenly puts a foot on his chair, throws his arms wide and bursts into song. 'Hi ho,' he bellows, 'hi ho.'

Big bloke beside him takes it up, miming that he's got a mike. 'It's off to lunch we go.'

The female's turn. 'With a spade and bucket,' she sings. Then she and the two blokes turn towards *him* and point. What the *fuck*? Ah, she's pointing to Eck.

'And that girl from Nantucket,' Eck sings back as they approach the karaoke crowd. The other three give Eck a brief round of applause, then all four of them do the 'Hi ho' bit again. What in the name of *arse* are they like?

'The subs,' explains Eck with a what-can-you-do? smile. 'I'll introduce you. Maybe we could all go to the canteen together. Does that sound okay?'

No it does fucking not is what he's thinking as he returns the smile and nods, but then he remembers why he's come and the nodding turns sincere.

Before he does the introductions, Eck goes into all this detail about them both being members of the fucking Friday Night Club. As if all the . . . well. Boy's an embarrassment.

No Js, as it turns out. So no fucking point to this after all.

'So,' the bald one says heartily, 'you'll have to give us the gen on Al here. The inside info on the famous FNC. Al's secret life.' Cunt gives him a wink.

'Aye,' he replies. 'Ha ha. Right enough.'

A bit of faffing around and then they're all heading back the way he's just come. They're about ten yards from the double doors when these swing open. A large man strides towards them. It's the big bloke in the shirtsleeves, one of the editors Eck was going on about. And he's followed by those three others. The big bloke in the shirtsleeves is muttering to himself and looking grim. The other three are looking a bit sheepish. The big shirtsleeves bloke stops and turns round. 'For God's sakes, Richard,' he says. 'I mean, for God's sakes, why didn't you *say* something? Wait here.' He strides past, leaving the other three lingering there like farts in a trance.

That Richard raises his eyebrows as they approach. 'Little hiccup on the lunch front, Barry,' he says softly. 'Editor forgot his jacket.'

'Aaaaaaaaaaaaaaaah,' says this Barry meaningfully, drawing it out for so long that he's about growling by the end of it. And that it's now no longer the thing for the two groups to pass each other. 'So where are you off to for lunch?' the Barry bloke continues.

'MPW.'

'Very nice.'

'I'm certainly working up an appetite for it.' More of the eyebrow raising.

Since it seems to be the thing here to exchange significant looks rather than actual words, there follows a long and awkward silence. Which gives him the chance to check out this younger pair, although it's only as he offers his hand to the one nearer him that he remembers that neither of them had paid Eck any attention when they passed by before, so this has to be a complete waste of fucking time. 'Graham Anderson,' he says nonetheless, having to raise his voice to make himself heard over a sudden outburst of coughing from the wee man.

'Oh,' says the one nearer him, clearly taken aback by this new-fangled fucking procedure of introducing yourself by shaking someone's hand and telling him your name. 'James Bond.'

At first Graham is too busy controlling the adrenalin which has surged through him at the thought that this arsehole's taking the pish. But after he's steadied himself, he realises first that maybe somehow the arsehole isn't taking the pish, and second that if he really is called James Bond then he's a J.

'Right, then,' announces Eck very loudly. 'We'd better leave you to it, Richard.' Eck taking a step forward now. And the fear grin has returned.

Graham ignores Eck's attempt to get them all moving and offers another handshake to the second younger one, buying a bit of time to figure out what's going on with the James Bond arsehole.

'Graham Anderson,' he repeats.

'Josh Todd.'

Another J. And that name sounds familiar. 'Ah,' he says, pleasantly, like, keeping up the charm, 'you're the one that writes those articles in Style.'

'Lifestyle, yes.'

'I should have recognised you from your picture,' he says, while frantically searching his brain for a way of quizzing this pair of Js further.

Eck's grabbed his arm. 'Really, Graham. The canteen.' Eck's giving him this pleading look. The boy's all over the shop. Now why would Eck be in such a state?

He shakes off Eck's hand and stays his ground. 'I don't suppose,' he says, sensing his mouth twitch as he tells it to adopt a smile, 'that either of you know Jenny? Jenny Newman?'

'Yes, of course. Jenny Newman. Ho, Jenny *Newman*.'

It's the other one of the editors, the big one, who has arrived at his side and is clumsily shrugging on his jacket. Graham turns to face him. 'Jenny Newman?' he says, the Newman coming out in a falsetto. 'You know Jenny Newman?'

'Yes, yes, yes,' the editor bloke says in a booming voice. 'Marvellous. Phwoar. Always had a thing for Jenny Newman.'

Eck's tugging at his arm again. 'I'm, I'm, I'm sure,' he stammers, 'that the editor is . . .'

'Graham,' says Graham, smiling and holding out his hand. 'Graham Anderson.'

'How remiss of me,' the Richard man says. 'This is the editor of the *Sunday Chronicle*. Jonathan Witherington.'

'Jonathan, eh?' Graham says through his teeth.

So this is the man who has been fucking Jenny. *His* Jenny. He lets go of the cunt's hand and feels his own hand curl into a fist so tight that his entire forearm is like an iron bar. 'Is that fucking right?'

'Graham!' he hears Eck shout.

As if that's going to stop him.

12

'YOU REALLY THINK I SHOULD?'

Saturday night

'Go for it, man. Seriously.'

'You really think so, Ian?'

'Definitely. Look at today's result, even. The force is with you.'

'I suppose . . . You really think I should?'

'Absolutely. Hey, Alastair, we've been over this a hundred times.'

'I'm sorry, I know. And I really appreciate all the . . .'

'Hey, least I could do. Just go for it, all right? And by the time I see you you'll be completely sorted. Honest.'

'Oh God.'

'See you tomorrow, Alastair. Good luck.'

'Thank you, Ian. I'll need it.'

'Not at all. See you tomorrow. 'Bye.' Ian puts the phone down and gives it a thoughtful look. Does Alastair have any chance? Maybe. She was daft enough to get off with Graham all those years ago, wasn't she? And he's told Alastair during his pep talks how to do it – play it safe, give her his own best chat-up line, the one that strikes an endearingly diffident note and, in the unlikely event of failure, provides room for a dignified retreat. Oh, Alastair can do it. Or, remembering that this is Alastair he's talking about, maybe not . . . He'll find out when he sees him tomorrow.

'Course, it will be odd spending a Sunday evening at Alastair's house instead of Johnny's flat, but not going to Johnny's flat is something he's going to have to get used to.

And he's looking forward to the sesh with Alastair – if it's anything like the impromptu lesson they had after Graham's exhibition, it should be good fun. No, fair play to Alastair, because the Carr crash course, as Claire has christened it and as they all now call it, looks like it could already have paid off – as long as he doesn't screw up his second interview at *European Traveller* magazine. Now who would have thought that he'd get such a break and that it'd be courtesy of Alastair? Not so long ago, he'd have said Rob was the only break-giving kind of guy he knew – before Rob turned out to be such a galling disappointment.

The thought of Rob's sham life threatens to become depressing, so he distracts himself with the daydream he has been constructing, one where he's working in the surprisingly cool, almost glamorous office he had a brief look at yesterday when he met up with Gary, the chief sub who knows Alastair. He sees himself at a desk, one with a computer, a mug of pens maybe, and a telephone, studying a page proof as it's called, scoring out a mistake and, with a certain suave confidence, making one of those curvy delete marks in the margin. Then glancing out of the window at the planes gliding above and the bustle of Carnaby Street below. He'd never have thought it possible, but he really wants to work in an office, or at any rate that office, with its trendy furniture and its laid-back buzz.

Not to mention the salary – twenty grand a year, near as damn it, plus any fee he'd pick up if he gets the chance to do an article, and as Gary himself said, Ian does have four languages and an insider's knowledge of various countries, so it wouldn't be beyond the realms of possibility that he could soon be enjoying the occasional freebie to Rome or Barcelona or . . . Time permitting, mind you, because he'd only go if Claire was okay about it . . . Or, and here's a thought, if he could wangle a joint trip. Then take the baby as well. Write an article about what Rome's like with a toddler, where's good for kids in Paris . . . God, it's going to be great – if he gets the job. If he gets the job. Looking like a good if, though.

Ian checks his watch. Quarter to eight. 'Claire,' he calls out. 'We'd better be going soon.' A night out with Ruth and Phil, Ruth's new boyfriend, Phil having stepped in as soon as Ben announced that his father had pulled a few strings and got him into the MBA course at Harvard so that would be Ben off, then. As the man himself would say, bizarre. Or, come to think of it, maybe not so bizarre after all. Oh, tonight will be okay – at worst, another evening ticked off without the charlie. Not that going without charlie has been at all bad. He's had a sense of loss, occasionally, but about as much as the sense of loss he feels at the passing of the FNC (i.e., not much). Definitely nothing like as bad as it was giving up ciggies. 'Claire,' he calls again.

'Through here,' she calls back. From the bathroom, by the sound of it.

Ian goes through and finds her still wrapped in her blue towel, standing in front of the washbasin and examining the mirror.

'This is terrible,' she says. 'Even my face is getting fatter. Look.' She turns and puffs out her cheeks. 'I mean, I *am* Oliver Hardy.' She blows a raspberry and her cheeks deflate.

'Claire, even Françoise Hardy looked crap compared to you.'

'Singer, right? Nice-looking singer or enormous soprano kind of singer?'

'Very nice looking.' He takes in the sight of her smiling back at him, turning that towel into a designer frock. To think that if she hadn't rummaged around in her bag one more time, if she hadn't found her specs . . . And if he hadn't been given the chance to realise how much he wants this child . . . Or if he still didn't know how crap he'd been, how ill and lonely and scared she'd been . . . Well, none of it bears thinking about. As it is, she's responded brilliantly to the new, improved him, her initial come-off-it wariness soon giving way to amazed relief then eager affection. Just like it used to be. Better even. 'But not half as nice looking as you.'

'I bet you say that to all your girls,' she says, and Ian keeps up his smile. She prods at the towel where it covers her stomach. 'Getting as big as a bus,' she says.

'Nonsense. You're lovely. I love you.'

She replies with a smile, then untucks the towel's fold above her breasts. The towel drops to her feet. 'Oops,' she says. 'It's come undone.' She steps over the towel and comes closer and closer until she's almost standing on his shoes. She circles her arms around his waist. He strokes her soft, warm, just-out-of-the bath skin and nuzzles her wet hair with his chin.

'Claire,' he says, 'we'd better be going soon.'

'Really?' she mumbles back into his chest. 'The thing is . . .'

'Aha?'

'I'm feeling a bit peaky.'

'Are you, love? But according to the book, the queasy spells should be over by now . . . Anything I can do?'

She gazes up at him, putting on the look of doe-eyed innocence that always creates havoc in his boxers. 'Well, yes, Doctor, I think there might be something.'

'Um, yeah, but what about . . . ?'

'I hope you don't mind, but I phoned Ruth and cancelled. While you were at Sainsbury's. Because I've been feeling like this all day.' She goes on tiptoes and caresses his stubble with her mouth. 'Kind of tingly,' she whispers. 'Hot.' Her mouth moves to his ear. 'Bothered.'

'Goodness,' Ian manages to say. 'Sounds serious.'

'Yes,' she breathes into his ear. 'So I thought maybe I should lie down for a while. In bed. All nice from the bath. No clothes on . . . What do you think, Doctor?'

Claire turns in his arms so that they're facing the mirror together. She sways her bottom gently, slowly, to and fro. His hands move down to stroke the firm little bulge of her tummy. 'Of course,' she says, raising her eyebrows at their reflections, 'you go out if you want. Saturday night, after all.'

'I don't know,' says Ian, shaking his head and pursing his lips. 'Girl in your condition, you shouldn't be left alone.'

'Maybe after the lie-down,' says Claire, 'I might feel better. Then we could have a party on our own, couldn't we? The two of us.'

He strokes her tummy. 'Three,' he says, because it's too good a line to waste. 'The three of us.'

Graham is standing in the crammed hallway. The flat's really too small for a do like this, but he wasn't to know that so many people would come – not only the old studio crowd but a huge squad of arty hangers-on who've emigrated from Shoreditch for the occasion. 'Where'll I put this?' asks Col, holding up a bottle of champagne. 'Through there,' says Graham, nodding towards the kitchen and a large black bin full of ice and bobbing bottles. Someone pats him on the back. It's Marty. 'I rather think,' he says, 'that Saatchi's going to up his offer.' 'Mr Megabucks,' says someone else who's sidled up behind him. Graham turns round. It's Chaz, who seizes his hand and shakes it.

The doorbell rings. Graham glances over and smiles, because he knows that'll be Jenny behind the frosted glass. 'I'll get it,' he shouts, as he squirms past some of Marty's anonymous pals. Keep calm, he tells himself, then he opens the door.

'Not prudent,' says Gordon Brown, who takes a step forward and inspects him with slack-jawed disdain. 'Not. At all. Prudent.'

Graham jolts awake. He stares along the surface of the kitchen table, taking in the whorls of the pine, then the silence of the flat, and then the soreness of his back and his neck. Very slowly, he lifts his head off the table, and sits back in his chair. He blinks a couple of times. Then he reaches for the bottle of Johnnie Walker Black Label and fills the tumbler again.

'Fuck,' says Graham.

Ian's told him how to do it and if anyone knows how to do it then it has to be Ian. Yes, of course, he has qualms – that's only natural because it's a nerve-racking business. But all he has to do is follow Ian's instructions and he'll be fine. And if Louise is anything like right, then even Rob no longer being around is a good omen. Not forgetting also the point that he's got nowhere by not having a go, so if he does have a go and fails then he'll be no worse off. So he's got nothing to lose. Has he? No. Well, then.

His resolve quivers again as soon as Jenny walks into the kitchen. 'I thought so,' she says, holding up the cover of *Northern Exposure*.

Alastair nearly drops the bottle of champagne he's trying to open. 'Is it all right? I can easy put something else on.' As Ian said, it's a Saturday night. A hot date. The second Saturday night she'll have been here. So, as Ian says, that means she's keen . . . But would she be wearing that long black dress, would she have pinned her hair up again with the tortoise-shell comb, if she really were after something non-platonic? That long black dress, that tortoiseshell comb, very becoming though they both are, aren't they the kind of thing she'd wear in the expectation not of being pounced on but of being treated in a friendly, civilised manner? And doesn't everything about what it was like the time she was here before, and now this first ten minutes of her being here again, indicate that pouncing on her might be a very wrong thing to do? Or not? Oh God. Oh dear. Oh God. But if he does it Ian's way, he won't come across as a moustache-twirling lech, so even if she does turn him down it won't necessarily be a catastrophe. Will it?

'No. I like it.' She studies the CD cover and gives it a couple of twirls. 'Any word of Graham?'

Far from having had any word of Graham, Alastair has spent much of the last two days trying very hard not to think about Graham as he's psyched himself up for this evening. But now he can't stop his memory presenting a sudden still of Graham about to punch the editor, and James Bond, who arrived in what turned out to be a brown belt's blur, at Graham's side, gripping his arms and standing hip to hip, holding Graham there for this paused image as if to begin some salsa shimmying, before flipping him over, with speed and skill that would have impressed his namesake. 'Not since Thursday. I haven't known whether to call him or not.'

'Well,' says Jenny with a rueful look, 'a little light bruising isn't usually fatal.'

Alastair tries very hard to think of something else to say and fails.

'Any more news of Rob?' asks Jenny just before the pause gets awkward.

'No. No more news of Rob.' He's never been a world champion at small talk but now it seems as impossible as figure skating. And if he can't handle this, then how on earth is he going to cope with giving her the chat-up line? Even if he can not think about Graham or, more accurately, Graham's attempt to duff up the editor, and that's a big if, can he really follow Ian's advice? Trace a finger down her cheek and say, 'Jenny, I wonder if you'd mind if I made a pass at you?' Ian might be able to bring that off, but when Alastair has practised it in front of the mirror – 'Jenny. I wonder if you would mind if I made a pass at you?' – he's seen only a gawky eejit failing to be smarmy. He tries to concentrate on thumbing the cork out of the bottle and prays that Jenny will say more words very soon.

'Oh yes,' she says. 'Something else I've been meaning to ask you. Why did your editor say he knew me?'

The champagne, he wonders with a jolt of panic. Isn't that a bit over the top? A sign that he's trying far too hard? Or not? Oh God. He clears his throat. 'The editor's not very good with names, you see. We haven't found out yet who it was that he confused you with. Barry at work's started a book on it.' He manages to stop before he starts to witter about Nanette Newman being the evens favourite but him going for Jenny Agutter at two to one. That's a good sign, the not wittering, because that shows he's got his nerves under control. All he has to do now is thumb this cork up without breaking a window or seeing half the contents disappear in an explosion of foam.

Alastair eases the cork out with a restrained pop and, with a steady, dry hand, fills two champagne flutes with white froth. Okay, he thinks. He's in control. He's going to do it. Which means, he acknowledges with surprising calm, that this is one of those rare moments in life when you know that, one way or the other, life is about to change.

He tops up the champagne. When should he do it, though? Is now too early? Shouldn't he wait until much later, at least until after the meal? But who knows what kind of tizz he'll be in by that time. Why not now? While he's feeling confident. Yes.

Jenny. I wonder if you'd mind if I made a pass at you.

Now.

'Jenny?' He offers her a flute with an almost steady hand.

She smiles. 'Yes?'

'Jenny, I wonder if you would mind . . .' He breaks off to clear his throat. And as he does so he realises that he is being completely ridiculous. What does he think he is doing? Who does he think he is?

She's still giving him a heart-rendingly fond smile as she waits for the rest of the question. Yes, fond. Not yearning or lustful. Fond.

'. . . chives in your salad,' says Alastair, his voice falling to a whisper.

'Chives would be good.'

'Right you are,' he mumbles. 'Back in a tick.' He finds himself doing a poor impersonation of someone picking up a pair of scissors, walking across a kitchen, opening a back door and heading towards a herb garden.

He's reached the chives. He hunkers down as if to examine them. How idiotic can he be? Once bitten, twice bitten, thrice bitten – brilliant. Hasn't he learned anything? And not only from the Fiona and Cathy disasters, but also from Rob?

Alastair gazes at the snipped chives he's holding. Each one a short straw, he thinks, but then he orders himself not to be so self-pitying. He's old enough now to accept what he and his life are like, not to make Rob's mistake and kid himself on that he's something he's not, that his life can be something it won't.

As he sits on his heels and stares at the chives, he tries to acquire a new resolve – to behave himself and be mature about this. This time there will be no embarrassing, humiliating fiasco. He will recover the situation. With luck, she will be his friend. And he'll be happy with that.

'Alastair?'

He looks up to see Jenny standing at the kitchen window. It's a sight that provides him with another terrible moment of clarity. He really has fallen for Jenny, completely fallen for her, and he is not going to cope with that just as he didn't cope with falling for Fiona and Cathy. And even if he does cope with it, what would that coping amount to? Him pretending to be untroubledly chummy with a woman he secretly adores, claiming to himself that it's perfectly fine as she tells him about some date she's gone on, some man she's in love with . . .

Well, he reflects ruefully, at least he's become more efficient with age, having managed to condense the whole process – self-delusion to unrequited longing to abject misery – from a couple of years down to a couple of dates. Oh, well done, him.

'You all right, Alastair?' Jenny has come out of the kitchen and is coming towards him.

'Yes,' he says. 'Thank you.' He straightens up and has to rock back on his heels to keep his balance.

'Careful,' says Jenny. Her hands clasp his shoulders to steady him. So that's what her touch feels like, he thinks.

'Alastair?'

Her hands are still on his shoulders. 'Yes?'

'Aren't you going to kiss me, Alastair?'